Bound by Providence

Bound by Providence

*An unforeseen happening links four women
and influences their destiny*

CAROL ALFORD

Gratuity
Direct Number: 2134389957
(888) 290-0987
9350 Wilshire Blvd, Suite 203,
Beverly Hills, CA 90212

Published by Gratuity: 10/21/2024

ISBN: 978-1-965386-14-9(sc)
ISBN: 978-1-965386-15-6(e)

CONTENTS

This book is lovingly dedicated
to my precious daughter,

CHRISTIN LYNN MURRAY.
(1962-2019)

I cherish her kind nature, spunk, and bravery.

ACKNOWLEDGEMENTS

I greatly appreciate my writer's group, Broad Horizons. The members inspire me, and I thank them for their encouragement, advice, and wisdom in reading and critiquing my work. The comradery, sharing, and laughter are added pluses.

CHAPTER 1

Columbia

"We're hit where it hurts. Hang on. We're going down." Ben Jameson's bellow reflected the horrific jolt of the Cessna 51. Vast branches with heavy foliage smashed against the pilot's window, smearing muddy green on the glass. Miraculously the window held as the belly of the plane torpedoed atop the jungle canopy. The surviving right wing strained each time it whacked against another treetop.

Jameson's mind whirled. Keep the nose up. Slow this baby. Don't panic.

He had kept the plane from nose-diving following the debilitating strike. They could have survived the hits from the machine guns, but not the missile that exploded about mid wing on the left side.

Miguel Vasquez hunched forward as if to protect himself from debris that any second might crash through the front window panels. Ignoring their ominous situation, Miguel screamed over and over into the mouthpiece. First in Spanish and then in English he called out for help, begged for someone to answer.

Gavin Humphreys had been hit by those first shots. He felt the searing of his flesh and probably would have heard the splitting bone just below his left knee had it not been for the roaring of the turbines and the exploding left wing. The plane continued its skid along the treetops as Gavin watched the denim of his pant leg change from blue to red. Still belted in his seat, in rapid-fire action he ripped off his shirt scattering the buttons.

Randy Rabinowitz, his partner across the aisle, puzzled as he saw Humphreys grip his shirt with his teeth and rip two strips from the back. Rabinowitz yelled above the engine's howl, "What's going on?" He saw Gavin point toward his bleeding leg. "My God, man. Let me help."

Like a boat banging against choppy waves, each wham thwarted Gavin's attempts to wrap his leg. Gavin waved Randy off. "Stay belted."

The plane jolted and shook as the reverse turbine took hold. Pilot Jameson held firm against the vibrations of the steering mechanism. Then the Cessna shuddered its last, its fuselage dangling nose down. It plunged a dozen feet, stalled briefly then inched downward in a jerking dive until it wedged between giant tree limbs, the right wing caught in a tangle of jungle growth.

Once the shifting and trembling ended, Humphreys refocused on his bloody leg. Randy released his seat buckle, jerked his T-shirt off and kneeled beside his friend, bracing himself to keep from sliding toward the nose of the plane. "We can use this too. Stretch your leg out. We need to get it tight."

Woozy from loss of blood, Gavin did as he was told. Relief washed through him as he felt the pressure against his wound, then he closed his eyes.

In front, pilot Jameson braced himself against the gravity pulling him toward the cockpit window. Eyes darting between one gauge and another, he turned toward Vasquez, "Getting anything? Anything at all?"

Miguel twisted the radio dials and began again. Minutes later, he responded, "Nada, nothing. No crackle, no pop. Those first shots got us where it hurts. No more mouthpiece, Señor."

Five years later
Monica

MONICA COULDN'T STAY IN BED one more minute. She needed to start her day. Managing to maneuver herself and her broken leg out of bed, the determined woman made her way to the top of the stairs. However, she couldn't shake the feeling of being shackled in the jaws of a bear trap, dragging a heavy chain loosened from its stake.

Sprawled on the top riser of the stairway that curved to a spacious foyer, she eased her bottom down one stair, then onto the next and the next. The injured leg that had been pinned and stapled, bumped ahead of her in its fiberglass casing. Monica decided that descending on her rump was safer than any attempt to balance on the lush carpeted steps with those "sticks" she was supposed to use for walking the next six weeks.

By the third step the phone began to sound. It continued its incessant ring until it drilled her nerves like a dentist's tool. Peter had set the answering machine to pick up on the eighth ring and someone used all eight rings. Well it could keep on. She couldn't move any faster.

It irked Monica that Peter had left her alone her first day home from the hospital. He couldn't take one solitary day from work. Too many clients needed him at his investment business. Besides he said, she was tough. Just once she wanted to be first in line. How had she gotten into this life mode—serving Peter's every whim? Dutiful was all she knew how to be. It had been the same with Gavin, her first husband, before he left seeking adventure and fortune in some forsaken locale. Not knowing what happened to him haunted her.

Comparing life with Peter and Gavin was like comparing jalapeños and salt. With Peter it was jalapeños—cocktail parties, wheeling and dealing, knowing important people, entertaining, country-clubbing. His charm, hot, energetic, and magnetic, seasoned the atmosphere.

Gavin Humphreys the mechanic had dreamed of having his own business. The salt-of-the-earth type he made a name for himself with one job and another until this mammoth opportunity. "Monica, it's the chance of a lifetime. They can't do it without me. And I'll be able to get us that house we want."

She had argued, "But Colombia is so far away. And dangerous. You'll be gone too long." In the end he had convinced her. That had been five years and four months ago.

Monica pondered the oppositeness of her two husbands. While success had eluded Gavin, his knowledge of and ability with engines, pulleys, batteries, bolts, screws and metal parts held no boundary. Each tool was cleaned and shined after use. The toolbox that was old when Gavin's father used it, didn't show its age because of Gavin's care. Even his black lace-up boots maintained their well-preserved appearance from routine polishing.

Peter's shrewdness included investing in the right markets and helping others do the same. Success came easily. Neatness and organization did not. He littered their bedroom with towels, socks and shirts despite Monica's request that he use the laundry chute. Expensive clothes draped his tall frame in a rumpled miss-match and though one might think his disheveled hairstyle was on purpose, it was not. The effect was boyish appeal, which Monica embraced. However, she found his lack of common sense and the ineptness that had caused her accident irritating and downright unacceptable.

The memory sickened her. Peter had borrowed a flatbed wagon to haul stone to build his waterfall and fishpond in the backyard, the ones he promised he would finish. The wagon hitch did not fit the ball on the SUV, so Peter rigged something he vowed would work. It might have if he had not jack-knifed the whole thing. In frustration he gunned the SUV ahead, wrenching the hitch and leaving the twisted wagon in gravity's grip on the steep hill. Unfortunately, it headed right for Monica.

Her leap from danger was insufficient. When the wagon ended its run-away, her leg was pinned between it and the wall that barricaded them from their neighbor's. Miraculously her memory of the agonizing fifteen minutes it took to get her extricated was foggy. She recalled vividly, however, the ambulance ride and Peter's incessant gab.

"Hang in here Babe. Be there soon. We'll get you the best care.

Don't worry." He addressed the EMT who kept Monica's leg stabilized. "She's some tough woman, you know. Bet you never saw one this brave. No hysterics. What a beauty she is. Isn't that right?"

That was a crock. Ruddy, freckled skin and a long thin nose did not signify beauty, though she had a decent build and healthy wavy hair. Had he been trying to make her feel better about the accident? It was the closest thing to an apology that she remembered.

Landing on the final step at the foyer she glared at the crutches she had shoved. Three feet away the supports had landed in a perfect V, as if signaling a victory for them. *Even you guys are against me. Damn, damn, damn.* Providence had lent her another blow.

"Aaahhk." Her voice resounded against the walls as she rolled onto the floor. On her side Monica inched herself along, pushing with her uninjured leg until she reached the sticks with which she knew she must make peace. Feeling as awkward as a maimed ostrich, she twisted and pulled. Finally, her body in position, she gripped the crutches, jammed their rubber ends against the glistening oak floor, then hauled herself upright.

The grandfather clock chimed the melody she usually ignored. Not today. Each ensuing gong stabbed one more jagged piece of discontent. The echo of the ninth followed her into the kitchen. Answer me, answer me, answer, answer me the flashing phone demanded. Too annoyed to listen to the message, Monica seized a hand towel from the drawer. Monogrammed MM in a shade of coffee on ecru, it had been a wedding gift from her mother when she became Monica Monahan. She tossed it over the blinking beast, relieved to smother the irritation, and hobbled to the refrigerator.

Stale pizza, a carton of smelly Chinese take-out and two pieces of shriveled chicken peered at her from inside. Nothing was properly covered. She cupped her hand over her mouth and nose to stifle the gagging action crawling up her throat. She fought the teetering queasiness that threatened to land her in a heap on the coolness of the fawn tile.

Peter Jonathon Monahan. How could you? She grabbed one item then another and flung them on the nearby counter. A rusty lettuce salad with its plastic lid popped open, a half-eaten sub sandwich and a chunk of cheese—too dried out even for a rat—were added to the pile. Things are going to change around here. Who cares about monogrammed towels? Golf at the club? Fawn tile? Perfect hors d' oeuvres? Wine with salmon? The disposal did its vicious pulverization. Monica relished the jarring reverberation.

Then the phone began its ringing. Again.

Conchita

MORE THAN FIVE YEARS WE struggle without you Miguel. Who knows what would have happened if you had lived? Could I protect the niños from your anger? Mamá would say 'Your place is with your husband.'

Conchita fumbled with the shiny new key and tried again to turn the lock. She heard the bar slide against the metal jam and turned the doorknob. Just the sound made her heart do an extra thump. Moving day. A brand-new home. She couldn't believe it.

Greg would lead the pack of movers. Conchita Vasquez was proud to know such a fine man. Without him and the treasure of Habitat for Humanity volunteers, she and the kids would have been doomed to live in the cramped rental trailer on the east side of town, maybe forever. Her neighbors were good people, but Conchita worried about the increasing petty crime and vagrancy. No more. So different from the four walls we had when Mamá and Papá worked in the fields. Mamá. What to do about Mamá.

Since the death of Conchita's father ten years ago, Señora Padilla maintained her matriarch status with a staunchness that bordered on obstinacy. She refused to move from the old neighborhood where gang members congregated. She refused to use the little bit of English she had learned. She criticized everything and everyone—her daughters-in law, the way her grandchildren were disciplined, the way they dressed, how money was spent, the neighbor with the dog. The matriarch expected the whole family to come when she wanted, and that included dinner most Sundays. It usually ended chaotically in her small house with eighteen people crowded on chairs, sofas and beds holding plastic plates of food.

In quick clipped Spanish Señora Padilla had shouted disapprovals at Conchita. "You only want to put on airs. Why do you need this fancy diploma? And this new house you want. Selfishness. Some people want more than they deserve. You are that person. You put a stain on your family, on your lost husband."

From the moment she was born, Conchita had possessed a face that caused others to take a second look. It wasn't that she was so beautiful. It was the sunbeam she radiated. Even when times were the roughest—when she was on welfare, taking nurses' training at night, house-building every free hour, making the best for her three children, and her insides were twisted and broken—the sunbeam endured, that is, except when her mother unleashed her angry tongue and piercing eyes. Today Conchita did not need the angry tongue and piercing eyes. Maybe the Señora would not come.

Conchita had seen her mother's rebuke toward Greg. "You cannot be friends with a man. Don't be ignorant. Yes, he helps you now, and then you know what he wants."

Her mother was the ignorant one. There was no mistrusting Greg. Conchita liked his smile. On the verge every moment, and then it emerged. The same whether he talked of her new Habitat home, the sunny day or his wife who had died. Gregory Hope was much like his name Conchita thought, full of hopefulness. Fifteen years caring for an ailing wife might have felt like sinking in quicksand. Not with Greg. Speaking of his wife he had said, "She needed hope and something special each day. I think it was so." He looked upward and added, "I'm sure she's in heaven now. Only place she could be. Was a fine lady, that one."

In Conchita's mind, he was the fine one. When his father was struggling with Parkinson's disease, Greg sold his mountain home and property and bought a fifth-wheel RV. Who else would plant himself in an RV beside his father's place on the edge of town? Who else would encourage and advise when all the paperwork needed to be done for the Habitat application? Who else spent double hours on her house while keeping up his full-time job at the tire shop?

THE ACTIVITY OF THE DAY swallowed the hours as the volunteers trudged in and out, setting beds, tables, chairs, and appliances in place. Several women and two elderly men carted boxes plastered with angular print—bathroom, Jack-room, pantry, Pamela-room, Jenny-room, and these were deposited in the appropriate places.

Moving from place to place, one woman slid a box cutter along the clear, sticky tape and others began to remove the contents until an interruption stomped in. The woman who disrupted the afternoon was short with a bun twisted at the back of her head. She flapped her apron as if to shoo flies from the room. Her bark issued commands understood by all, despite the difference in language.

Conchita graciously thanked each volunteer for the help and tried to explain her mother's intruding domination. No one would know whether her tears were those of happiness and gratefulness or frustration and embarrassment. When the boxes were emptied, Conchita and the Señora set about putting everything in order.

Why can't she ask me where I want to put the pots and pans, the shampoo, the towels? "No Mamá. Aqui por favor." To this the Señora spit a diatribe of commands and putdowns. Once Conchita let her mother have her way, the two worked side by side quickly and efficiently and by early afternoon every towel, plate and dustpan had found its place. At Conchita's suggestion that it was time to rest, her mother plopped herself in a lawn chair on the tiny porch and sat fanning herself with her apron.

Conchita found Greg in the laundry area just off the kitchen working over the washer and dryer. "I just put the washing machine through a quick cycle, and everything works. I left the hot and cold valves open. These are new hoses and they should last a good while. But if you are away for a few days, I suggest you close both valves. Any questions about the operation?"

"I don't think so. I've never had my own automatic machines before.

Thank you, thank you. I appreciate this so much, but it cost you too much money."

"Conchita, they cost little, just needed a little repair. Pleased you can use them. Now how about a tour?"

Conchita Vasquez virtually danced from room to room. Greg followed, smiling as she opened each closet, each drawer. Jack's room was all boy. Two ball bats leaned into the corner. On the wooden one hung a new catcher's glove. A lilt in her voice she said, "You know Jack has oiled and rubbed that glove every day since you bought it. It's his favorite possession. No?"

Greg's shrug said 'it is nothing'. "I've never seen such a scrappy catcher, Conchita. You're raising a real athlete…a fine kid. Course he has a fine mother." Greg stepped toward the chest of drawers and looked long at a framed photo. The man, dressed in a Rockies baseball uniform, was in a pitcher's stretch. "Suppose the athlete part came from his dad."

Conchita sighed and took her time to speak. "Miguel just made it to the major leagues…then the automobile accident. He never was the same after that. Yes, Jack is pretty good. His father would be proud, but last time he saw him, Jack was not quite three." Or maybe jealous, she thought. Conchita turned a smile toward this gentle man, thinking how she liked his frequent use of the word fine. "And this is a good room for a fine eight-year-old," Conchita added.

The largest bedroom held two brand new beds placed exactly as the twins had instructed—under the windows to the north. Jenny's spread was crocheted in vivid purples, while Pamela had chosen lavender and cream. Conchita had been surprised when the Señora allowed her granddaughters to choose their own yarn, and the coverlets reflected the nature of the two four-year-olds—different as diamonds and pearls.

Conchita's dance ended in her bedroom where the bedside clock stared back. It was time to pick up the kids from school. Greg offered to get them. His hazy brown eyes with the hovering lashes searched hers, waiting for her answer. How this man continued to grow on her.

"You already took the whole day off. You've done too much." She wagged a pointed finger at him and stepped toward the doorway. Greg stood there shifting his weight. "Thank you again," she said and stretched up on her toes and reached her arms around his neck. "You deserve a fine hug."

"And you also." His arms wound round her solid frame, and for a moment her cheek pressed against his chest while he nestled his face in her tousled, dark hair. "You are some gritty gal. Be proud."

"Conchita! Conchita!" They both heard the angry tongue coming down the hallway. The words that followed stung like the pelting particles of a sandstorm. Greg knew some Spanish and Conchita hoped he had not understood the crude names her mother spewed at them.

***

CONCHITA'S EYES BORED THROUGH THE car's windshield. Her fingers squeezed the steering wheel. "Mamá how could you?" She dared not look at her mamá. She drove too fast, but with intense concentration.

"My daughter, if you do not listen to your mamá, trouble will bite you. You are very foolish, the way you behave. Those names I called you are not false. They are the truth. You will see."

With jaws clamped, both fumed. When Conchita jolted to a stop at her mother's house, a swirl of black dust billowed around the car. It fit her mood and Conchita continued to glare ahead. Then she felt the slam of the car door.

When she arrived at her children's school Conchita's irritation melted into a smile. There they were. Waiting. She had been fortunate to get the twins into the pre-kindergarten class, so they could attend the same school.

The threesome raced to the blue Saturn, the car she and Miguel bought when he started in the minor leagues, the one that had become a fixer-upper after Miguel's accident. Jenny claimed the front seat. Jack and Pamela were too eager to protest that she always got the front.

"Can we order pizza and celebrate?" Jack begged. He would have eaten it every day, but pizza was for celebration, a change from the beans, rice and tortillas that got them through the slim times.

"Maybe later. We have to clean up the trailer first."

Conchita felt Jenny's stabbing look. "That's not fair. You said we could see our new place after school. You promised."

"Stop the whining. We will, but first we have work to do and that is that."

Inside the trailer stood the lone vacuum cleaner Conchita had left, and a tub of cleansers and cleaning rags. The children set about doing their jobs. Jack ran the vacuum and the twins wiped the finger marks from the cabinets.

At the last flush of the toilet Conchita looked up to see Pamela standing in the doorway. She held a rumpled paper toward her mother. "Is this important?"

"I don't know. What is it? Where'd you get it?"

Jenny shoved her sister aside and yelled. "It was taped to the drawer."

"Let me tell. I found it." Close to tears Pamela handed the paper to her mom.

Jenny pushed closer. "Who's it from? What's it say?"

"Jenny, calm down, stop pushing," Conchita demanded. She examined the scrawled message, then spoke, "It's from Clifford."

Clifford lived next door and Conchita was going to miss the old man. Dauntless and determined, he maintained his status as patriarch in the mobile home park. Despite his frailty, no one disputed Clifford. He didn't smile much, and the banging of his walking stick signaled business, yet no one missed the merriment of his eyes. He'd say, "Dirty cream of wheat, if you don't study yur lessons, you'll be pushing a wheelbarrow of dumbness yur whole life. Now you take these here cookies to your mom and write out yur lesson."

Conchita fingered the note and puzzled at the unexpected message.

Conchita,

After your mover friends left with a load, your phone just rang and rang. I knew I better check it out since it didn't stop. Hope you don't mind.

She said it was real important. Here's the number to call...

Clifford

Mel

THE MEMORY OF MEL'S FATHER had its own special place in her mind. That memory always spewed forth when she prepared for a flight. Nearing the gate today she remembered their last time together. How long would her father's last words harbor in her heart? "What a rare daughter, woman and pilot you have become. Those first moments I held you I had no idea what was ahead for me. You looked me square, steady."

Mel had put her hand up to quiet and push away her father's tenderness. It was too close. But he had gone on. "I want to say it all. Just listen. I don't know if other babies talk to their dads right away, but you had a lot to say and I heard it all. I knew exactly what you meant. 'Hello world, I'm finally here…Hi Dad…I'm your little girl…I'm going home with you…We'll have adventures…You'll see'."

The memory of the resonance, the strength, the character in his voice never left her. No other man had that perfectly modulated bass, the gentle musical rumble, like the lingering sound of a timpani. "You have always been more than I expected, more than I deserved. I never had one moment of disappointment. You'll get that job you're hoping for and we'll celebrate when I get back."

They had held tough. There were no tears. Then she had watched his plane do the final circle and head south. There was one last glistening flicker before he was out of sight. Their last good-bye.

It was more than five years and she still missed him, probably always would. He and the plane disappeared before she was hired by AirChief. Against her mother's wishes, her father taught her how to fly. From the first time in the cockpit, Mel knew she would follow her father into the skies. And today was her first flight as Captain. It had been a bull ride all the way—bucking the man's world as a pilot. Benjamin Jameson would have been in his daughter's corner, but he would have let her fight her own fight just the same, combating unfair remarks and antics designed to make her look foolish and incompetent.

A few women had slept their way to the top, which sickened Mel. Yet what upset her most was dealing with people like Captain Erik King who always sought her out. He tried to make small talk and tease her. When she looked away, he made some remark.

"Don't you ever thaw out?" His laugh came from deep down. His eyes smoldered. "You don't even know you're a babe, do you?"

Her response was always the same. With the palms of her hands she would extend a powerful push and walk away, saying nothing. How many times she wanted to crush him, wipe that grin from his face. He was not alone with what she considered badgering. Other pilots either treated her as though she didn't measure up or seemed to register surprise when she did her job with ultimate expertise.

Ben Jameson would have said, "You're a professional. So, what if you meet a jerk. They can't get to you if you don't let them. Your mother and I gave you wings early on. You used them then, you will now."

She had won the admiration of those who mattered, but not without a price. Once her co-workers found that she could be tough and stand up to them without malice, the harassment declined. They would say that Mel Jameson was one of the most competent, professional and respected pilots they had worked with, but that she was arrogant, aloof and difficult to get close to. People paused to admire the imposing, tall woman, her dark eyes, prominent cheekbones, illustrious ebony hair—cropped short. However they rarely spoke to her. She often told herself that in this business, respect was far more important than friendship and achieving that respect was not a sacrifice.

Providence had its cruelty, however. She had to contend with Erik King as her First Officer during her first flight as Captain. *Dad, how would you handle this? How can I stifle this grinding in my gut and not let it get to me? I'd like to talk with Mom, but she doesn't know my world. She was the cheerleader, the prom queen, the president of her college sorority. Not me.*

Charlotte Jameson called her daughter Marilyn. Always had. "I wish you'd get off this kick…going by Mel. Of course, your father is no help. Can't get him to call you by your given name. Mel is too harsh. Marilyn is well-bred. Like you are." Charlotte repeated that speech numerous times and finally gave it up about the time Mel completed high school.

Mel smiled thinking about her mother and her busy club and

volunteer schedule. In the beginning she worried about her mother's independence and loneliness after her father was gone. But she needn't have. Charlotte took a part time job with a local philanthropy, joined a knitting club and another bridge club. Through the years she added one thing, then another and seemed to thrive with a whirlwind schedule. Charlotte knew the most interesting people with the most interesting stories and when the two met for lunch or breakfast, Mel heard about them all.

There would be more storytelling when Mel returned from Chicago. Charlotte and three friends were off to Beaver Meadows Resort, where there were trail rides, evening cookouts and morning breakfast hikes— most probably led by some handsome cowboy. Charlotte would return tomorrow and most certainly would have some interesting tales.

Mel wheeled her overnight case into the cabin and stashed it in the compartment. She traveled light for her overnight to Chicago. A glance at her watch told her she had an extra ten minutes. Oh, the cell phone. *Don't think I shut it off for takeoff.* Mel dug into her flight bag and curled her fingers around the black instrument.

She'd missed a call and had a message. What a distraction. Her focus should be on dealing with Erik King. Should she listen to it?

Racine

"Oh, go away, Spunky." With fingers encircled by a rainbow of sparkles Racine batted at the fuzzy ball licking at her ear. Spunky nipped at the bands that jangled at her mistress' wrists. She had failed to remove them before finally laying her head on the downy pillow just after one a.m.

Racine Rabinowitz snuggled beneath her downy quilt and shook a finger at her loyal pooch. "It's too early to get up!" Spunky ducked his head in contrition at the harshness of Racine's words and snuggled into her neck. He was buried by the carmine colored coils that tousled themselves around an agreeable face, flickering with mischief-bearing eyes of Caribbean blue.

"You rascal. You know how to melt a woman's heart, don't you?"

The little Shitzu lifted his head and peered through his own shag and a strand of Racine's blazing hair draped over one eye. Just for an instant his eyes closed and then searched hers piteously. A muted cry escaped from the back of his throat. At that Racine erupted into glorious laughter, filling the room like a thousand fluttering sparrows.

Spunky sprang from his spot and scampered around the spacious bed, yipping all the way. Around and around he went while his mistress continued her jollity. At once he stopped, stood on his back feet, pawed the air and cocked his head to one side.

Racine propped herself on one elbow and shot a fierce look toward her pet, then jabbed a finger, its nail lacquered in bronze, his direction. "OK Spunk. I give. Yep, time to get a move on."

The pooch dived into the soft fluff of a lambskin stretched out on the floor beside the bed and pranced off toward the kitchen, his tail wagging in a saucy attitude. Swinging her legs over the side of her bed she wriggled her toes into the lambskin and reached for the thickly bound book that functioned as a journal and organizational digest. It could tell her what she ate on August fourth, two years ago and what was on the menu for the dinner party she planned for Alexandra's birthday party last year. One of her best friends had turned fifty and this year it was Racine's turn. It revealed the budding relationship between Chad, her new bartender, the late-night talks, the growing sizzle each felt in recent weeks.

It was no accident that Racine's Pub was one of the best bars and restaurants in town. Nearly fifteen years now, Racine Rabinowitz had endured the grind it took to run and expand her own business. From the beginning she counted on Carlotta to help run the pub. The two had waitressed together before the restaurant came up for sale. They made quite a pair—Carlotta, the flashy Latin and Racy, the redhead. Neither forgot a face nor a voice and together they filled the place with color and laughter. That is, until Carlotta's heart attack. Women like Carlotta didn't have heart attacks, didn't have to go on life support. That's what Racine thought. She was wrong.

Chad had been a godsend. A godsend that he landed in town looking for work the day after Carlotta's attack. A godsend that he had been a bartender in an exclusive resort around Miami and had taken a year off to travel. He needed some travel money before he went on. He could take the job. While Racine sat at Carlotta's bedside, Chad had all the pieces of running the business in place.

He had great financial sense and suggested new ideas that increased the revenue of the popular pub. Men and women alike enjoyed the Aussie and his humor. It surprised most people that someone who looked so strong and tough had such a proper and polite way of speaking. But what grabbed Racine was Chad's genuine caring when Carlotta began rehab, when Racine was a mess with worry, when she told him about losing her twenty-two-year-old son five years ago. Wherever he was needed, there he was. She had vowed long ago, before her only son was born, that there would be no more men in her life. For twenty-eight years she had lived that vow. Then Chad, who was eight years her junior, had come into her life.

The whole scene of the previous night came back to her. She scooched back onto the bed and propped herself against the pillows, leaning against the padded headboard. Spunky raced back into the room and stopped dead with a look that said, 'Just what's going on? Aren't you coming to the kitchen? I need my breakfast.' His yip was sharp. Two more followed.

"Just lay down and be quiet." This time her finger pointing was wicked, and her voice shot prickles. Spunky obeyed. Two somber eyes shifted in confusion toward his mistress. Otherwise the pooch lay motionless.

Racine pulled her knees toward her chest and wrapped her arms around them. Her chin found a resting place there. "Sorry little Spunk." Her words were velvet-like. "I may have made a mammoth fool of myself." As always, the little dog listened with attentiveness.

"This hard-looking woman marches into my office last night. There she is perched on my desk taking over the whole office. She says she needs some information about the employee who calls himself Chad Chambers. I remember about the phone call Chad received last week when a caller says she's conducting a survey for the Chamber of Commerce—about local businesses. Well Spunk, Chad gets suspicious after the name, birthplace and occupation questions and hangs up. I'm wondering if there is some connection and she waves some newspaper in my face and says to take a look."

Spunky's tail swished as if to say, 'Go on, I'm listening.'

"It has a fuzzy picture of some guy on the ski slopes. The headline says Man Swindles Woman. This man who calls himself Cameron and has an accent, the article says, cons rich widows, then disappears and so do her jewels. This hard-looker thinks it's Chad. Says she got a tip from somebody who saw Chad at the restaurant. Is sure he's the same guy." Racine sighed and slapped her hand hard against her knee. "What if I've been taken in by some gigolo? Am I that easily bamboozled, little guy?"

Spunky cocked his head, seeming to wait for her to continue. "Chad says it's not him. He's never been to Aspen where this took place. What should I believe?"

Racine fingered the fat journal beside her. Her son gave her one like it nearly six years ago. "Now you write everything down till I return," he commanded. But Randy Rabinowitz never returned. She filled the first one and the second and now this one was nearly full. Oh, the years gone. Silence filled the room as Racine patted a spot at her side. Two leaps and Spunky was on the bed nestling beside her. The crimson haired woman found the blank page and began to write.

Is Chad the Swindler or is this a case of mistaken identity?

> Get copy of newspaper article
> Call Gabe on the police force
> Call references on Chad's application
> Talk to…

A piercing sound from the phone beside her caused her to jump. "Oh, who can that be this time of the morning?" Mechanically, she lifted the hand piece.

CHAPTER 2

Monica

Irritated by the phone call, Monica held the receiver to her ear waiting for the response to her less than friendly hello.

The voice that Monica heard rasped like a metal file scraping against a wood block that its carver prepared. It was definitely female, however. "Hello. Is this Monica Monahan, formerly Monica Humphreys?"

Monica's voice was curt. "Yes, who is this?"

"My name is Nicola. You don't know me. I have information about your husband." The rasp was more of a whisper this time.

The rubber pads of Monica's crutches cut into her armpits as she slumped her full weight on them. "What information?" *Peter would never play around on me. What does this woman want?*

"It's Gavin. I believe he's alive."

"What kind of hoax is this?" Monica collapsed into the oak desk chair. *Gavin alive? He's been gone nearly five and a half years. Can't be.*

"This isn't a hoax. I have letters he wrote to you."

"He wrote me? Where is he?"

"We were taken prisoner in the jungles of Columbia."

"Prisoners in Columbia?"

It was a groaned sigh that Monica heard before the caller went on. "Captives, prisoners, hostages—all of that."

"What about the others?"

"Don't know much. They were alive after the plane crash, but your husband was in bad shape. He was brought to the camp where we were held."

"When did you see him last?"

"About two months ago he was taken away. We'd been in the same camp till then. I promised I would find you if I was ever released."

Questions raced through Monica's mind. She fired them to her caller one after another and listened to a portion of the incredible, unbelievable story.

Placing the receiver in its cradle, she grabbed the telephone directory. *Hope I can reach the others. Don't know if they're still in town.*

Before the men left for Colombia, Monica, Mel, Conchita and Racine had known little about each other. That changed following the men's disappearance. For two full years they nearly lived and breathed in unison, searching, investigating and consoling. When their efforts and contacts led to a mountain of zeroes, the men were declared dead, and the women finally gave in to the idea that they would never know what happened. The last time they were together was on Conchita's twins second birthday. *How could we have drifted away from each other like this?*

Gavin Humphreys had named the trip to Columbia The Expedition. Though it was actually a business venture, the idea of calling it The Expedition caught on. Larry McCrae needed someone to build the rigging and drilling equipment at an emerald mine he had acquired during one of his explorations in Columbia. Gavin's mechanic experience and his ability to build and repair most anything was well known, and he had had some mining experience. Everyone knew pilot Ben Jameson. He had flown CEO's and political powers wherever they wanted to go for years. It was said that he could land a Lear jet on a postcard. Jameson was in. McCrae's team would hire some locals and work the mine for a few months to determine how lucrative the enterprise could be before McCrae invested more money into the venture.

McCrae assumed that people would go along with him and they usually did. "Emeralds have always held a fascination for me. I want to see that baby in operation, Gavin. I can gamble a few bucks, but I can't do it without you. You're the kingpin. Two more hands should complete the team. If it looks promising after a few months, I'll have Jameson meet me in Bogota and fly me to the mine. I'll be setting up some markets in the meantime."

Sammy was Gavin's first choice when it came to another hand for the expedition. The team needed someone who was fluent in Spanish, besides Sammy was a real solid guy and the two had been friends since high school football. But Gavin understood. No way was Sammy going to miss the birth of his firstborn. Besides, the possibility of being away from his job for three months was pretty iffy.

Sammy's brother, Miguel seemed to be the next best choice. He was definitely available for such an expedition. Gavin and Sammy had watched the young Vasquez as his baseball career took off. They saw every home game played by the minor league team in Colorado Springs.

Miguel's break came, and the Colorado Rockies called him up. <u>Hometown Pitcher Scores Second Win</u> read the Greeley paper. It could have been the beginning of a great career if it wasn't for Miguel's hot head. Sadly, he got into a road rage thing and ended up dangling through the front car window. The pitching arm attached to his slashed shoulder would never be the same. Perhaps The Expedition would settle Vasquez down and put an end to the bar hopping and brawling.

When McCrae picked up Randy Rabinowitz, the crew was set. Racine Rabinowitz and Larry McCrae went way back. Despite their friendship, convincing Racine that this was an opportunity of a lifetime for her son was a real fight. McCrae won out because Randy, just out of college, had not yet found a job and desperately wanted to go.

Gavin had liked Randy immediately. The only way he resembled his mother was the blazing curly hair. Then again, he had her kindness and heart. His manner said 'I won't be saying much, but I see a lot, I know a lot and I stand tall'.

The mine was located in a remote region nearly one hundred miles from phone service. The women understood that it would be a few weeks before word reached them of their safe arrival, and the waiting had been agonizing. When the weeks turned to a month, panic and hopelessness set in. Mel was the one to instigate the investigation.

"I have Dad's flight plan. I'll investigate the airports where they made stops and radio communication along the way." It took weeks to gather all of the information, some very complete and some quite sketchy.

"Their final contact was three hours from their destination. It's all we have to go on. I'm flying down. I hope to get a search plane."

"I don't know if it's worth it," Racine had said. "That's a lot of territory to cover. We've alerted everyone we can think of."

"No one is out looking. They keep saying, 'We'll keep our eyes open.' Big deal. I'm going," Mel said.

Conchita, her belly beginning to swell with the twins she carried, questioned, "Can you lose your job over this? You're still on the bottom rung. Right?"

"It's just a job, Conchita. Finding our men is more important."

Conchita, Racine and Monica came to learn that it wasn't just a job. Flying was Mel's life and being the second woman pilot to be hired by AirChief was the culmination of years of study, practice, and sacrifice.

She had not lost her job, however ten days flying over tangled jungle produced no clues. McCrae had kicked in a bundle, but Mel refused to divulge the true costs of her search and she was left without a car, television, and sound system. She had sold them to help pay for the search. It was eighteen months before she was able to replace the items.

Now it was Monica's turn to set things in motion. First the contacts. Nicola hadn't given up on her search and she was able to find Monica, despite the name change. It shouldn't be too hard. Amazingly Monica's quest was easy. All three women were listed as she had known them, and she penned each phone number on her notepad.

Was it the sense of urgency that caused her fingers to tingle? She poked the numbers listed beside C. Vasquez and was relieved to hear the ring. Her foot prickled with numbness. Watching her blue painted toenails splay as she wriggled her foot caused a fleeting feeling of childishness and she smiled. Monica let the phone ring. No answering machine to pick it up, she decided. Like Nicola she intended to be persistent. Monica counted, nineteen, twenty…

"Hello."

Wrong number? Sounds like some old man.

"Hello." The voice was insistent, as well.

"I am trying to reach Conchita Vasquez. It's very important. Do I have the wrong number?"

She did not have the wrong number. Clifford—he called himself—said, "I'll tell her to call this number today." Monica knew Conchita would get the message.

One down, or sort of. Monica pulled herself from the desk chair, balanced on one foot and put her crutches in motion. *Boy do I need a pain pill. Thought I'd be over this sharp ache.* She gulped enough water to swish down half a dozen more than the three she took, and leaned on the counter, her eyes closed. A sickly breath swooshed across her lips. Get to it. Waiting isn't going to make it easier.

There wasn't much of a wait when she dialed Mel's phone number. Her answering machine picked up on the second ring. The message was concise. "Please use my cell number…., Mel."

Oh dear, just keep dialing. Why was she dreading these calls? Mel's cell phone number brought about another command. In relief Monica responded, "Mel, it's Monica um…was Humphreys. Got a shocking phone call this morning. Maybe our men are alive. Call me today at…"

She reached Racine on the first try. Racine's whoops might have been heard by the whole neighborhood and Spunky yipped along with her. Monica warned that Nicola's story might carry false hope. She knew little about Ben, Randy, and Miguel, but they all had survived when the plane went down and had been taken captive by rebel guerrillas. Waiting for Nicola to arrive in Greeley was going to be like wandering in a blinding snowstorm. Yes, Racine would come to Monica's to meet with Nicola.

They made small talk and Racine said, "By the way I saw Mel last week. She and her mother had lunch at the restaurant."

"How's she doing? Still flying?"

"Seems just the same. No husband. She's doing well with AirChief. Just made captain."

"Racine, I have another call coming in. Better take it. See you when we meet with Nicola."

Monica disconnected the call with Racine and reconnected. The voice on the other end sounded familiar as it said, "Monica. It's Mel. Just got your message. Of course, I'm stunned."

Monica gave a brief bit of what she knew and added, "I don't know what to think either. A missionary named Nicola was held captive with Gavin. She escaped several weeks back and arrived in Dallas a few days ago. She's flying in to Denver the day after tomorrow. She'll be at my house about 3:00. Can you be there?"

"I have an overnight to Chicago, but I'll be back tomorrow."

"Just talked to Racine. Haven't talked to Conchita yet. She's moving, but her neighbor said he'd contact her. I'll just have to wait on that. Have a good flight."

The waiting game again. Part of her life out of her control. She wondered what to do next. Eat something dumbo—before this wooziness dumps you on the floor. She found the juice container in the refrigerator empty. *Peter, can't you even make orange juice? Or remove an empty jug?*

Peter. What would she say to Peter?

Mel

MEL SURPRISED HERSELF. THE NEWS about her father honed her focus rather than disorienting it. Not a hint of nervousness hovered. When Erik King settled in his chair, she read his cockiness as 'we'll see how you do girl.'

Mel completed her instrument check accurately and efficiently. King nodded his affirmation and for the first time Mel thought she caught a flash of admiration.

"All appears to be ready for take off, Captain Jameson."

She had rehearsed again and again the words she wanted to say to put Erik King in his place and let him know she was not to be walked on. She had pondered over the timing—before the take off, during the flight, once they landed. The words remained unspoken.

If she was surprised at herself, she was flabbergasted by Erik King. His manner remained direct and professional. Cruising at 30,000 feet King removed his earphones and massaged his neck. "Captain, I never met your father, but you seem to have no trouble filling his shoes."

"You've heard of my father?" Mel listened for the sarcasm she expected. There was none.

"Sure. His reputation made the circles. I remember when he and his plane were lost somewhere over Columbia."

Mel's eyes settled on the man beside her. When she said nothing, he continued. "Not knowing what happened must have been…Well, I can't even imagine.

Captain Jameson looked into the foreverness in front of them. "They crashed." Her voice sounded hazy in her ears. "And all of them survived. They may still be alive."

"How did I miss that news? I had no idea."

"Neither did I. Not until a half hour ago."

Erik pushed his mouthpiece aside. "What?"

Opening up to anyone, much less Erik King, was the last thing Mel expected of herself. She was surprised how much King knew about her father. He understood the devastation she had felt. She learned that Erik's mother lost her five-year battle with breast cancer after a double mastectomy and a regime of treatment. His father died in some military fray. He had flown helicopters over Laos. Erik was seven at the time.

To the question Mel posed, "Why not a Mrs. King?" he replied, "Mom needed me."

Nearing their approach to Chicago, they turned all business. Erik drew the subject to a close with his question, "You'll know more about the crash, the location, in a couple days? Right?"

"I hope so."

"Then what? Back to Columbia?"

"Perhaps. And just when I made the next rung." She nodded toward the controls. "Oh, timing. Right?"

"Right."

Racine

RARELY, THE HEAD COOK ARRIVED before Racine. Despite the shaking news, piled atop the hard-looker's warning about Chad, today was no different. The thing that was different was Chad's early arrival.

Racine took his hand and gave it a squeeze as they walked through the door together. Her smile was genuine, but tight.

Chad looked concerned as he said, "Racine, I didn't sleep much last night, worrying about that woman and her accusations. You know I am not the man in the newspaper. I have never been to Aspen."

"I believe you. I know that tipsters can be wrong." She thought of the list in her journal and the last words she had penned after the phone call. The list was on hold for now. "Follow me, my friend I have a story you won't believe." They entered her office and Racine closed the door.

Chad listened, intrigued by what he heard. "This Nicola says that Ben Jameson, Miguel Vasquez and my Randy were taken as political hostages and slave laborers, moved to another camp. The rebels planned to ransom them…for money to buy weapons and ammunition, apparently. They were heavily chained and probably moved from place to place in that confounded jungle."

"What about Monica's husband?"

"Gavin was hurt and stayed in the same camp with the missionary. Don't know the details, yet."

"What a story. All this time. What happened about the ransom? That was a long time ago."

"Not sure exactly. Some fighting and chaos among the guerrillas, I gather, and the ransom didn't happen." Racine sighed. Every day I regret that I let Randy go to Columbia. Every day I imagine what kind of man he would be."

"You know what kind of man you raised." The Aussie's tone was tender.

"Maybe I'll have a chance to see his face again…and that quiet smile." Racine stared into the picture on the wall, the one where Randy stood in his cap and gown. "The other thing is…I robbed him of his father. I robbed his father, too."

Chad's eyes questioned, but he was silent.

"You see, I never told him who his father was. Never told his father, though I'm sure he guessed. About the time Randy finished high school, eighty thousand dollars were deposited in my account. The bank said it was an anonymous gift. It paid for his education. And when the insurance company fought paying the survivors when the men were declared dead, another fifty thousand arrived. I didn't want the money, just my son."

"Will you tell Randy's father about this phone call?"

"I already have. The others don't know, but he'll be there when we meet with Nicola."

Conchita

CONCHITA WIPED THE SWEAT FROM her brow and looked around the trailer kitchen. Cleaning all done, she thought, and I better call that number Clifford wrote down. *Hope they haven't turned off the phone.* There was a dial tone and she hurried through the numbers.

"Conchita, I knew the old gentleman would get a hold of you. Are you sitting down?"

A flush rushed through Conchita' as she leaned her back against the wall and slid to floor. "Yes, Monica, I'm sitting." And then Conchita listened.

The children watched their mother's face grow somber, saw her eyes blink in couplets. "Mamá, what's the matter?" Conchita hushed Jenny with a wave and continued to listen. She shook her head side to side, while her breathing slowed and lost its intensity. Finally, she said, "Yes I'll be there." The clunk of the receiver echoed in the empty room.

Jack looked worried. "Mamá tell us."

What should she tell them? Jack had been close to three when his father left on The Expedition. Conchita had not known she was carrying his twins. Through the years she said little to her children about their father. Miguel had been distant with little Jack, and Conchita could not say, "Your father played and talked to you and lifted you on his

shoulders as he galloped around the room. You were his special hijito."
She did say, "Your papa was a good pitcher and we were all proud when
he played with Rockies, but when he had the accident, he could not
play. He and three men went to South America for a very important
job. They never returned. We don't know what happened."

The children rarely spoke of him or asked questions. However last
week Pamela said something that Conchita barely paid attention to.
It played in her mind now. "Mamá, Papá came to see me in my sleep.
He was a real person, not a picture. He will be here soon. He told me."

The truth. Her offspring would hear the truth. "Sit down, my little
ones. I have something to tell you." With her children surrounding her
Conchita explained what she knew. She told them that her father never
made it to the emerald mine.

"Some rebels saw your papa's plane flying over their rebel camp
and shot at the plane. This caused the plane to dive into the trees. One
wing was twisted off as the plane slid through the jungle. They tried to
get the radio to work. They needed to get help for Señor Humphreys.
He had some bad injuries and could not walk. But the rebels came and
took them away. They locked them up in a jungle camp."

Jack's eyes opened wide. "But Papá was alive? And he was not hurt?"

"That's what the lady said."

"I bet Papá tried to fight the rebels. Uncle Sammy says Papá was
strong as a bull."

"I don't know, my son. Truth and hope. We must remember both.
Soon I will learn more truth and we will keep our hope." Conchita
looked into Pamela's face. "I hope you will see your papá some day. In
real life, not only in a dream."

"Mamá it was not a dream, he was real. He is coming."

"Time will tell, mi hijita. Time will tell."

CHAPTER 3

Racine

Stretched out on her sofa Racine closed her eyes against the glow of the nearby lamp. Nicola, the missionary. What story would she bring? How Racine longed to see her dear son again. Was it possible? She'd have to wait for the answer.

At the tender age of nineteen Racine's guilt had continued to sting for several months. A daughter doesn't walk out on the dad who raised her by himself for ten years. Well, she hadn't really walked out. She had ventured out to make her own life.

Rubin Rabinowitz was a good man. His stern, grumpy nature was probably a cover since the Rabinowitz men were expected to be able to handle anything that life threw their way. He had too.

He managed when after eleven years of marriage Racine's mother abandoned him and their only daughter. He managed during drought years when his crops near Akron, on the eastern plains of Colorado, failed. He managed after he lost three fingers when a wire, caught in the power-take-off of the John Deer tractor, ripped them off.

And he managed without Racine, the independent and full-of-life daughter who cajoled her father time and time again. "Pop if you'll lop off old Charlie's head today, I'll stew him up with noodles for supper.

That cuss of a rooster has been causing too much trouble in the hen house and it's time to get rid of him; Pop can I take the truck down to Matilda's? She's been in bed all week and can use this soup and cherry pie; But Papa, I can't help but dance when the music is on. Besides it's good exercise."

Neither Rubin nor his daughter forgot the morning Racine left. Rubin refused to look at her. He stared at his right shoe, grinding it into the graveled driveway as he growled, "Be gone gal. I can do just fine alone. In fact I'm better off without you and your fancy ideas; wantin' to go out on your own when you have all you need here; wantin' to get a job, when you earn enough money with your chickens and eggs; wantin' to buy new clothes when the ones you sewed up on your Grandma's machine are just fine. Be gone gal."

She didn't care about fancy things, just wanted to be grown up, support herself. His sharp words echoed in her mind, then slid across her heart leaving pricks of pain. The feisty red head wanted to fling up a defense, wanted to explain. Instead, she tightened her lips against the bone parched tongue waiting to form the words, turned and walked away, then drove west.

The idea that Greeley was a farming community as well as a college town appealed to Racine. Thus, Greeley was as far away from the Akron area that she got. She marveled at the spreading trees shading the street where she found a tiny upstairs apartment—such a contrast to the eastern Colorado plains. She smiled about the extra bonus; she could see at least three ranges of those magnificent Rocky Mountains when she looked to the west from her window.

There was no way for the new Greeley resident to imagine how her first job interview would shape her future. Racine barely said ten words before the jolly man with the well-used apron covering a rounded belly bellowed, "You're hired. I can spot a good worker a mile off. Talk to Gracie, she'll get you set up."

Howard and his wife, Gracie owned and ran Gracie's Grill and Tavern. Had for nearly twenty years. It was the place to go for friendly service and reasonable food. Racine, her effervescent nature and stunning looks, spawned an even more loyal crowd. Tips were generous and

Racine's good money management meant a growing saving's account. Thus, she no longer needed to make all of her own clothes. She took a few night classes in business and toyed with the idea of going to college fulltime, but her busy social life and work schedule filled the days and nights. She finally ditched the idea.

Racine became good friends with another waitress, Carlotta, and the two contemplated getting an apartment together. Perhaps a complex that had a Jacuzzi, a pool, a clubhouse. But Racine held back. She decided she preferred privacy to extra amenities. The sense of independence and accomplishment began to melt the guilt of leaving her father alone on the farm.

Weekly phone calls often resulted in her doing all the talking, until a pleasant shock greeted her when her dad called one Sunday evening. "Racine, I don't know how to tell you this. You know how after Matilda lost her husband…you know she was pretty much under the weather for some time and you kept her refrigerator filled with soup and such?"

"Yes, Pop. What's the matter? Is she sick again?"

"No, no, no. She's just fine. Now, that is. But I got to takin' soup over and we got to talking. And, well, you know…we have a lot in common."

"That's great Pop. I always wished you had some friends. You always work too hard."

"I just wanted you to know…we got married yesterday."

Racine, who never lacked for words, could not speak.

"Are you there? Racine did I lose you?"

Finally finding her tongue, she said, "Papa if I would've known you'd do so well without me, I wouldn't have worried so much. Wow. What a great surprise."

"It's good. She's a good woman."

"You're a great man, Pop. I'm thrilled for both of you."

Bless Matilda's generous heart. She brought out the best in Rubin Rabinowitz. Racine had never seen her dad so happy. The couple came to see Racine's apartment, which Rubin had refused to do. For the first time Racine saw the wry humor her father had buried for so many years. Seeing his renewed life relieved her guilt.

With fondness Racine remembered the early years waitressing at Gracie's Grill and Tavern. She, the racy redhead, and Carlotta, the Latin siren often double dated, but mostly hung out with a lively group of friends also in their early twenties. No one was too serious about finding a spouse. There was too much living to do. This was certainly true of Racine. She made great friends with many of the regulars, and she could dish out the banter as well as take it. Larry McCrae was one of those regulars, always on Friday night.

Wavy dark hair and a bushy mustache, a western shirt and Levis, boots shined to a spitting polish, and a burnished buckle at his waist decked out his lofty frame. The vision turned many heads. Racine knew he was married. No one knew much about Chantel, but it was said that she was on the delicate side. McCrae came in alone, made his way from table to table in the bar, patting one and then another on the back, sharing a drink or two, and then ordered the fireburger—a hamburger with jalapeños, cheese, tomatoes, onions—and a pile of fries.

Every Friday, except the last one of the month, he was out of there by 8:00. Though Racine sometimes served him a bourbon and seven, most of the time he swished down Pepsis. Those fourth Fridays, he and three friends used the back corner table in the bar to play a dice game until 11:30 when the bar and grill closed. If Racine happened to have the early shift and clock out at 8:30, they often asked her to join them. On occasion she did well and took home a pile of quarters. Those quarters added to her tip jar. When it was full, she deposited her stash into a special saving's account. How it would be used, she wasn't yet sure.

One snowy fourth Friday of February Gracie's was quiet and deserted. McCrae waited for his buddies to show up for the usual game of dice. No one came. "Racy, when are you clocking out? Want to roll the dice? Looks like I've been stood up."

"Hey, why not?" Racine turned her wrist to check the time. "Shift's over in ten clicks."

Racine was ahead by a couple of dollars when Carlotta stopped by the table. "Larry, sorry to scoot you out of here, but Gracie says we're closing early. It's drifting pretty fast. We might not get home if we wait much longer."

Racine blinked surprise. "It's drifting? I better get going."

Once Racine kicked off her black pumps and slipped into brown leather loafers, she pulled on her tan trench coat and headed toward the back door. Surprised to see Larry McCrae holding the door ajar, she waved him off.

"Hey, I'm fine, you don't need to take time for me," she said.

"Let's be sure you can get out. Where's your car?"

Racine pointed off to the left. "Can't quite see it, but it's blue, in the back corner."

"Well follow me," McCrae said. He stomped the snow creating a path for Racine and headed toward the back corner.

"Is this it?" he said as he stopped beside what appeared to be a giant mound of whipped cream. Two-foot drifts swirled around the mound, tempting the beholder to dip a finger in for an irresistible lick. "Delicious looking, isn't it?"

Racine pulled her trench coat tighter around her and shook her head. "Can't believe it."

"Don't think we can get that buggy out of here tonight. I'll take you home. My truck's on the other side."

Even with McCrae's 4-wheel drive it took several tries, rocking back and forth to get out of the parking lot. When they reached the street, he gunned the truck. It went fish-tailing toward the end of the block, then skidded sideways through the intersection. Racine's words came out with her deep buttery laugh. "McCrae, your show-off driving is going to get you in trouble. That was a fantastic skid, though."

"Hey kid, you ain't seen nothing yet!" They were off. The few drivers who safely crawled along most probably cussed the black truck that zipped around them, billowing the white stuff into a white-out. Racine's cackle and interspersed whoops did nothing but encourage Larry McCrae. "Watch this," he said as they spun a 360.

"Aha, you can't scare me!" she said in a haughty, daring voice. Larry reached his huge hand across the front seat and vice-gripped her leg just above her knee. Her reflexive jerk and squeal sent McCrae into a laugh.

"It's not funny. You can't do that. I'll go through the roof."

"I guess I found your sensitive spot." He reached again to grip her knee and she batted his hand away.

"McCrae, you're a fiend. And I thought you were a gentleman."

Nearing Racine's apartment the couple came upon two women trudging toward them. McCrae leaned out the window. "Do you need some help?" They did.

"We got stuck back that way," the pint-sized woman said, pointing behind her.

The tall one countered, "You mean you got stuck and I'm out here shivering with you in this freezing cold."

"You could have stayed in the car with Helen and Janie," the short one retorted.

McCrae cut in, "Get in ladies. I have a shovel."

Racine squished up against Larry as the two women crammed in beside her. She smelled the spiciness of his shaving cream, a smell that she would always remember fondly.

McCrae parked beside the stuck car and hopped from his truck. "Let me help you ladies to the car. You can keep warm while I dig you out." He turned to Racine, "Stay in the truck while I dig them out."

No one told Racine Rabinowitz what to do. She grabbed the window brush and scraper that Larry had used to clear the truck windows, jumped from the truck, and trudged toward the snow-covered car.

McCrae worked to free the car from the snow drift, scooping one shovelful, then another. Seeing Racing, he stopped short. "I thought I said to stay in the truck. You'll freeze your feet in those shoes. Your hands too. I can't believe you don't carry gloves in this weather."

"Well it wasn't snowing when I came to work," she shot out indignantly, "And I can tell you one thing. I'm no wimp and I can surely scrape off these windows."

Ten minutes later McCrae and Racine waved the women on their way. Five more and the truck eased to a stop in front of Racine's apartment—no skidding this time. Racine obeyed McCrae's command, "Come on, let's get you inside and warmed up."

Stepping into the cozy living room, McCrae continued to bark orders. "Get out of that wet coat. Didn't your mother teach you to wear something heavier in winter?"

"No, she didn't! She left Dad and me when I was nine. Besides, I didn't expect to be out in a blizzard tonight." She threw off the sodden coat and stared him down.

McCrae's tone softened "Here, use this." He pulled a quilt from the back of her sofa and wrapped her in it. When he lifted her mummied body their eyes locked, his brown ones squinting tenderness, and her green ones sparkling amusement.

He placed her on the sofa, her back pressed against the arm. The silent moment stretched like gooey caramel. She liked the comfort of being cocooned in the quilt her grandmother had made for her when she was twelve. Racine often wished to know the history of the various fabrics Grandma had used for each bonneted girl. She remembered only two—one from her mother's apron and a dress she herself had worn when she started school. Sometimes she wanted to feel tied to her past. Others she wanted to run from her motherless upbringing.

McCrae sat on the other end of the sofa and lifted her feet across his lap, removed her brown loafers and dropped them to the floor. "They're icebergs you know." He rubbed her feet and calves briskly, but methodically. "Feeling better?"

Racine fluffed her lustrous hair scattering droplets that had collected from the melting snow and tucked a strand behind her ear. She grinned at McCrae and said, "I guess I was colder than I thought. The tingles and prickles are beginning to leave." She felt his fingers skillfully work from one pressure point to another on the sole of each foot. "Wow! Does that feel terrific. You know what you are doing."

"A little." His look was tentative. "You said your mom left when you were nine. I didn't know. Bet that's why you're such a tough young lady. What happened to her?"

Racine shook her head. "Nobody knows. Even Grandma died not knowing a thing. Maybe she ran off with a traveling salesman or maybe she got picked up by a hitch-hiker and her bones will be found in some ravine someday." Racine saw McCrae grimace and continued, "I used to imagine her living in Las Vegas as a stripper. She was quite beautiful."

"That's where you got your looks. Huh?"

Racine shrugged. "Not the blazing hair, though. That came from Dad. As a kid I hated it. I was called everything from red to scarlet, from carrot-top to Raggedy Ann."

"Raggedy Ann, huh?"

Two friends, sharing things neither had talked about for some time, forged a closeness they would never completely let go of. Racine's eyes teared as she listened to McCrae speak of his wife. She imagined Chantel, her golden curls softly framing a face filled with wide blue eyes and a broad, quiet smile.

"All she had ever wanted was to be a good wife and mother," McCrae said. "After four years and no children, her sweet expression grew desperate. Then over night she got really sick. Bedridden with pain, she spent her days in a groggy stupor."

Racine learned there had been months of tests and specialists. The diagnosis revealed that Chantel had been stricken with a rare, debilitating type of rheumatoid arthritis which often attacks people in their twenties or early thirties. That had been three years ago, about the time Racine moved to Greeley. McCrae had thrown himself into achieving the goal he had set for himself—to be a millionaire by age thirty. At thirty he was pretty near this target. He had made wise land deals and continued to do so. He would buy anything if it could make life easier for his frail wife.

"She rarely leaves the house, even though we have a van for the wheelchair. I'll never stop loving her, but she's not the same person I married. It's heartbreaking to see her this way, her body tight, her hands and feet wrapped in soft gauze to ease the discomfort." McCrae's voice grew quiet. "I watch her crawl into herself more each day. The massages used to help. Now just touching her brings agony."

"There's no help? No medicine?"

His sigh was deep and long. "They're trying something new this month. We'll see."

In an attempt to alter the mood that their storytelling had created, Racine said, "I'm toasty warm now. But hot chocolate still sounds good. How about you?"

"Sure."

She unwrapped herself from her Grandma's quilt and threw it over McCrae's head.

"You rascal," he scolded. Untangling himself he followed her into the tiny kitchen.

Leaning against the counter he watched her stir the mixture heating on the stove. She had pulled her hair back and secured it with a rubber band. Tendrils escaped at her temples and coiled beside prominent cheekbones. Her hips swayed in rhythm with the stirring and her flared black skirt swished against firm legs. The scooped neck of her white peasant style blouse was high enough to conceal cleavage, but soft enough to reveal plenty of shape.

"Marshmallows?" she asked.

"Sure."

Even high on her tip toes, the stretch for the top shelf was a good one. "Let me get them," he said.

Standing beside her he could still smell the freshness of the outdoors in her hair. He placed the marshmallows on the counter and touched the tip of her nose with his finger. "You are a very special young woman, Racine. Whoever catches you will be very lucky."

She reached herself as tall as she could and kissed his cheek "And you are one hell of a man."

His arms pulled her to his chest. Her hands reached around his neck. The smell of his spiciness and the sound of his thumping heart awakened a deep shudder throughout her body. Then she felt his do the same.

The two never spoke of that time again. But for one night, in the comfort of friendship the two were lovers.

Monica

MONICA THOUGHT HER FIRST DAY home from the hospital had been like something out of a Nightmare on Main Street movie. The disgust about Peter leaving her alone, the struggle with her crutches, the imperfectly kept house, which she had put in order, the shocking call from Nicola, plus her efforts to contact the rest of the women left her confounded. Exhausted, she slouched in a chair in the sitting room, refusing to think about dinner.

To Monica's surprise Peter arrived home earlier than usual, carrying bags of take out which he placed on the counter. Amazed, she watched him set a proper table with stoneware, flatware, and napkins, and thoughtfully spoon the Chinese meal from the paper cartons into attractive serving bowls. He carefully reheated the soup before ladling it so that it was just the right temperature.

Where did this come from Monica wondered? Had Peter read her venomous thoughts during the day? Had he realized that his socks, towels, pants, and shirts would no longer be scattered in the upstairs, that the food carcasses in smelly containers were no longer putrefying the refrigerator? Had he felt guilty that in a daze she had bobbled on her crutches putting the house in order?

He made such an effort with the meal that Monica hated to refuse the food. She forced most of the brothy soup. The rice had begun to clump together and remained in globs in her mouth, no matter her attempts at chewing. She speared chunks of cashew chicken, usually her favorite, and found them more gagging than chewable.

"Sorry Peter, everything is very nice, but nothing tastes as it should. Maybe the medicine." She waved her hand in the same dizzying motion spinning in her head. "I think I'll go back to the couch."

Monica watched Peter from her propped position in the sitting room adjoining the airy grand kitchen. She anticipated questions like, "Where do you keep those thingies with the plastic lids? Shall I keep the soup or not? Where's the stuff for the dishwasher?"

But he seemed intent on doing everything right and without her help. His head popped up and down as he searched in high and low in the kitchen cabinets. In lounging pants, a white T-shirt and with his messy hair, he looked more like a college kid than a high financier. She tried to imagine Gavin in the kitchen, but she couldn't. She closed her eyes, thinking she could pull up his image. She could not.

All afternoon she practiced what to say to Peter. The words had rolled through her head in random order. They were in a jumble still.

Monica heard the dishwasher close and begin its water-running hum. And Peter's shoeless feet padded to her side. He pulled the side chair close. He sat and gently lifted her hand into his.

"OK. Something is on your mind."

She looked away from the face with a crinkled brow before she spoke. "I had a shocking phone call today."

Peter nodded. "And?"

"From someone named Nicola. She told me about being captured by rebels in Columbia after her husband was slaughtered trying to fend them off. They were doing some missionary work."

"Columbia. That's where Gavin and the others were headed. Does this Nicola know something?"

Monica's nod was slight. Her eyes refused to meet Peter's. She swallowed hard and allowed a woosh of air to escape her lips.

Bad news, huh?" His caress of her hand was soothing.

"Yes and no."

CHAPTER 4

Monica

Sleeping pills had become regular inhabitants in Monica's medicine cabinet after Gavin's disappearance. During her two and a half years of single-hood, they were what assured her of awakening ready to face the day's work as a bookkeeper with Galaxy Associates. She liked figures and the way they were perfectly ordered. Her days were perfectly ordered, as well. Up at 5:45. Shower, dress, eat breakfast—toast with a slice of cheese and orange juice. Then a fifteen-minute drive to work, which gave her five minutes to spare.

Monica limited herself to two cups of coffee a day, one during her morning break and one during the afternoon. Monday, Wednesday, and Friday were her workout days. After work she grabbed her gym bag and did her forty-five-minute routine at the health club next door to Galaxy Associates. It was there she eventually relaxed her self-imposed rule, don't mix job and social life.

Peter Monahan was one of the busiest associates with Galaxy. Friendly and sociable, he mingled easily with most of the personnel. However, his efforts to engage Monica in conversation were met with crisp responses meant to dissuade further attempts. Monica envisioned him as outside her niche or maybe he was inside, and she was outside. Regardless, she imagined some luscious young thing on his arm, one who seemed to complement his boyish looks.

On occasion Peter worked out in her corner of the health club and soon the intermittent encounter grew to a regular three-day-a-week deal and Monica began answering his questions, then asking some of her own. Eventually Friday workouts evolved into lengthy dinners.

It was four months before anyone at Galaxy Associates realized the two had become a couple and seven months before Monica introduced Peter to her mother.

Peter chided Monica. "Either you think I'm a kook or your mom is a kook. Who are you ashamed of? It's time your mom met her soon-to-be son-in-law."

In truth, Monica could not believe Peter had chosen her. Surely one morning she would awaken to realize it had all been a dream. What did a guy like Peter—charming, adventuresome, attractive, appealing, though often exasperating with his sloppy disorganization and oblivious attitude—see in the serious, dependable, structured, capable Monica? And without a clever bone in my body she thought.

As Monica imagined, Edith was ecstatic when she met Peter. What mother wouldn't want her daughter to have a successful and good-looking husband?

Through pursed lips her mother said, "And surely you'll have an elegant wedding and wondrously catered wedding dinner. A once in a lifetime event, something to be remembered forever."

"Mother, this is the second time for me. I want a private ceremony, short and sweet."

"Monica, how can you be so selfish? There is no way you can deny Peter a real wedding just because you've been married before, and this is Peter's first. And what about his family? You want to deny them, also?"

The 'you've been married before' aroused her ire. "Mother, you act like I threw Gavin out. And without cause. He left me. Remember. For some wild dream. I'm a widow, Mother, not some divorce." The last declaration was intended to sting.

Edith Goldstone had divorced Monica's father when Monica was in high school and for little reason in Monica's eyes. Her father was tied to his work and Mrs. Goldstone wanted out. Mr. Goldstone put up little resistance and in two years found someone else, which continued to irk Edith.

Her mother had her way concerning the wedding and it had been a lavish affair, ten times more so than her first. Edith was even willing to accept her father's role as escort during the processional and the attendance of his younger wife.

The newlyweds could have fought the unwritten rule that married couples could not be employed together at Galaxy Associates. They didn't, thus Monica became a stay-at-home wife. There was much to do in furnishing and organizing the couple's new home and Monica discovered she was indeed clever and resourceful in finding the best fabrics, best seamstress and best deals for furniture, carpets, appliances and landscaping. Interestingly, the friction between Monica and her mother dissolved once Monica was settled in their new home.

During the three years as Peter's wife she had weaned herself from the sleeping pills and felt proud about it. In the hospital with her broken leg the nurses had given her something each night, but she vowed she would not use anything once she went home, and she hadn't taken a sleeping pill the first night. However, today one thing piled on top of another.

When she told Peter that Gavin could be alive, he didn't seem to know what to say. He finally said, "I guess there is nothing to do until you hear more. Wow. What a bolt from the blue. What can I do babe?"

He wouldn't leave her side and hovered over her until bedtime. It was too much. All she wanted to do was sleep. She gulped a double dose of sleeping pills and Peter helped her get into bed.

He positioned pillows under her slightly bent knee and around her leg. "Hon, will this help to take the pressure off? Let me get some more pillows. Need more covers?"

Monica shook her head and closed her eyes.

Peter sat on the bed and caringly stroked her forehead, then took her hand and massaged her hand with tenderness. "Everything will be OK," he said.

How she wished he would stop and just let her be. By the time he left the room, the pills had done little except send her mind in circles.

Monica was relieved that he didn't push her to talk further about Gavin and the upcoming meeting with Nicola, but she didn't need this hovering. There were times when Monica tried to analyze their marriage relationship and the analysis usually included some elaborate illustration. Once, she worked out a theory entitled: Variations in behavior of husbands toward wives. She labeled a continuum from one end to the other: indifferent – inattentive – attentive – hovering - controlling. She decided that husbands who were indifferent and/or inattentive caused their wives to feel unimportant, unloved and unappreciated. Those women whose husbands were hovering and controlling caused wives to feel inadequate, dependent, smothered, and lowly. Surely the ideal was an attentive husband who helped his wife feel loved, appreciated, and significant.

Most days Peter's behavior lingered around inattentive. Monica believed it was not intentional. Her husband was merely off in his own world and oblivious to the feelings of others. Often, she longed for an attentive husband who appreciated her and her accomplishments. But Peter seemed to bounce between inattentive and hovering. This clawed into her like an angry cat. Couldn't he find the balance of being attentive without hovering and making her feel incapable and defensive? Or was she overreacting and was he actually being attentive even though she felt smothered and controlled?

The thought of being smothered was the last remembered until she saw the clock's red digital numbers blip 8:30. The other side of the bed was empty, but its rumpledness indicated Peter had been at her side during the night.

Peter's at work by now she thought. What can I do to pass the time until tomorrow when Nicola arrives?

Monica jumped when Peter's voice entered the room. "Hey, babe. I see you're awake. Can I bring a breakfast tray up for you?" Peter padded into the room, shirtless and wearing lounging britches. Cute as he looked, Monica couldn't keep the irritation from her voice. There he was hovering.

"I can come down. You're late to work. I can manage myself."

"I'm not going in today. I told them to reschedule my appointments. I'm at your beck and call." He gave her a wink

Well, wouldn't you know it? I really needed him home yesterday, but no. Now, I wish he would just get out of my hair and here he plants himself.

Conchita

CONCHITA PUT THE CAR IN gear and drove toward the children's school. It was amazing, she thought, how things had worked out for her and her children. It wasn't easy being a single, working mother of three. The thought that Miguel could be alive put her mind in a greater whirlwind than usual. *Wonder what lies ahead.*

She loved her job at the center for the elderly, Quail Creek Care Center. During her training, she hoped she would be able to use her nursing skills in Pediatrics. Raising her children had solidified her connection to early childhood and her comfort level with babies. However, when she was placed in a care center for the elderly during her practicum, she felt a great compassion for those folks living out their later years. And once she completed her training, the daytime nursing job at Quail Creek was available.

During the interview, the personnel director nearly hired her on the spot. "Ms. Vasquez," she said as she gathered the papers in front of her, tapped them against the desk to straighten them and placed them in a folder, "I'm bound by certain guidelines to interview two other candidates. But I can safely say that you are a very strong one. Not only are your transcripts and recommendations top-notch, but you seem to have an incredible grasp of the needs of our residents."

Conchita blinked her astonishment, yet her voice came out strong and confident. "Thank you, Ms. Fagan. I've heard that Quail Creek is most highly rated, and I'd be proud to be a part of the staff here."

Ms. Fagan rose and extended a hand toward Conchita. "I'm pleased to meet you and happy that you are interested in our center. You'll hear from me within the week."

Two days later Ms. Fagan offered her the position. The first three months were rigorous and verified what everyone continued to tell her, that it took a certain type of person to endure the suffering, despair and downhill spiraling day after day of the patients. Some patrons were cranky, others like vegetables. However, Conchita found many of them full of wonderful stories and fun, and so appreciative when she made her rounds. She knew that she had what it took.

The day shift worked well for her and the children—8:00 a.m. to 3:00 p.m. Monday through Friday and a night shift every other weekend. It was more convenient than she would have had at the hospital where schedules changed from week to week. She also found the staff to be helpful and friendly. Sadie traded shifts so that Conchita could move into her new home. Deb, the nurse with the afternoon/evening shift insisted on coming in an hour and half early so Conchita could arrive on time for the upcoming meeting on Thursday with the missionary Nicola.

Her mother, The Señora took care of the kids whenever Conchita worked the weekend night shift. Conchita was grateful, though often her mamá made it seem like a burden. The sleepovers were a mix of enjoyable times with games like hiding small treasures around the house or showing the children how to make some sweet treat yet could be confrontational when her mother was critical and bossy. After one such night Jack grilled her about their names.

"Why didn't you give us the names of our heritage? Grandmother says that you're ashamed of being Mexican, that you didn't name us a traditional name. Is that true? She says I should be called Juaquin and the twins should have other names, too."

Conchita sighed before she spoke. "In this country there are many different heritages, German, Italian, French and it's difficult to say that a name is German or Italian or Native American. We have a variety of names here. Besides, I guess I never told you, you're named after a friend of your father's. Jack's a good name, but would you like to have a different one?"

"No," Jack's voice was thoughtful. "I guess it doesn't matter if grandmother approves or not."

Conchita smiled at her young son and turned toward the twins. "Your father wasn't here when you were born, and I wanted you to have names that fit your personalities. You look alike, but you're each unique and special. Pamela sounds solid, but easygoing and Jennifer sounds spunky and outgoing."

Jenny cut in, "Well, I don't like it when the teacher calls me Jennifer. I like Jenny better. Besides, there are two other Jennifers in my room."

Pamela added, "I'm the only Pamela and I don't want any other name. And Mamá don't ever call me Pam. OK?"

Conchita hugged her children. *Well Mamá I have you to thank for stirring up another conversation that we might not have had if you hadn't done your usual meddling.*

The twins attended the all-day pre-kindergarten program and were dismissed at 3:30, the same time as Jack's third grade. She arrived in time to see the children piling out of the building. The drive home was more quiet than usual, and Conchita appreciated the children's lack of chatter. *I suppose they are as uncertain as I am about the missionary's news.*

Turning into the driveway she pressed the control of the garage door opener and watched the door go up. This luxury and the others in their new home made her smile. How blessed she felt. As she and the children crawled from the car, Conchita heard ringing coming from the kitchen. It stunned her for a moment until she remembered the new line had been activated by the phone company while she was at work.

Jack rushed inside. "I'll get it," he shouted.

Jenny complained, "Why does he always get to be the one?" Boys are the favorites. It's not fair."

"You'll have your turn. Both you and Pamela, Now hush."

Jack held the phone to the air and said, "Mom, it's Greg. He's bringing supper so you don't have to cook. He says he won't stay since he knows we want to enjoy our new house as a family. He's bringing fried chicken."

"Let me talk, Jack." Conchita clasped her fingers around the receiver and turned to her son. "Thank you." Speaking into the mouth piece she said, "Hi Greg...Yes, we just walked in...If you're bringing in chicken and the trimmings, you had better help us eat it…Well, one of the nice things about our new home is that we can share it with others. You will stay, won't you?…OK see you about 6:00."

Conchita wondered what to say to Greg about Miguel. She enjoyed the connection they had and dared to imagine their relationship growing. A ringing doorbell interrupted her thoughts. A skinny kid about Jack's height, with a ball and a well-worn glove stood erect on the small porch.

"Hi, I'm Jason. We live down the street. Can Jack come over? Can he bring his bat? It's OK with my mom."

Jack squeezed to his mother's side. "Can I? Can I? Mamá, please say yes. Jason's in my class. I told him about my special bat."

"Well." She had seen this scrawny boy hanging around while she and the building crew carried two by fours, tacked the asphalt shingles in place and lathered paint on the siding. Her house was the fourth one to be built in this new neighborhood. She hoped there would be playmates for her children. The girls had each other, but Jack needed a friend. "Can you wait a few minutes? Jack you need to change your clothes first. Come in Jason."

Jason's demeanor changed when he entered the house. His shoulders slumped, his head lowered while his eyes shifted to scour the room, sparse in furniture, but clean and neat.

Conchita smiled to put him at ease and said, "I'm Conchita Vasquez. These are Jack's sisters, Pamela and Jenny."

Jenny blurted, "Hi Jason. Some people get us mixed up, but you can remember me cause I talk more. Right Mamá?"

Jason fingered his ball glove, looked to the floor and nodded.

Jenny continued, "Guess what! Mamá says next week we can start riding the school bus. Pamela's scared to ride."

"I am not," Pamela argued. "I just don't know where to go. Mamá says we have to walk to another street.

"It's not far. I can show you," Jason said, beginning to stand more upright.

"Thank you, Jason. Now girls, you need to put on your play clothes, too. Then we can all have an after-school snack. Jason you can wait here in the living room."

In the kitchen Conchita sliced their only apple and dabbed a bit of peanut butter on each slice. She smeared more of the peanut butter on half of four tortillas and folded them in the middle and cut them into pie shapes. Placing four small plastic tumblers on the blue painted kitchen table, Conchita sighed as tiredness crawled from her head over her shoulders, arms and legs and finally settled in her feet. Reaching for the milk in the refrigerator she wondered why she felt so sleepy. *Can't let up. We'd better go meet Jason's mom, and sometime I need get some groceries. And tomorrow the missionary comes.*

"Come on kids, your snack is ready."

As they dug into the snacks, Conchita cautioned her children to slow down, that it wasn't healthy to eat so fast. She was proud to see her children offering part of their food to Jason. He began to protest, but when her children insisted, he devoured every last piece.

During the walk to Jason's house, Jason seemed to drag his feet. The twins bounced ahead urging everyone to hurry.

In front of his house Jason stopped. "Can you wait here? I'll see if my mom is awake. Sometimes she sleeps in the afternoon."

The group sat on the curb longer than they expected, talking about the new neighborhood, and wondering about Jason's mother.

"It's OK. You can come up to the house," Jason called to the foursome. He leaned forward against the porch railing, waiting. Climbing the front steps, Conchita noticed a woman peer out of the partially opened door. Her hollowed eyes took up most of the narrow face with their darkness. As she cocked her head, a lock of hair, nondescript in color slipped over one eye. The rest was pulled back tightly. The sleeves of a stale blue robe, chenille, revealed emaciated arms and wrists attached to fingers that look as though they could fluidly pluck at harp strings.

The woman swiped the back of her hand against her brow and pushed the escaping strand to one side. As if in defiance the strand returned to conceal half of her face from the outside world. Her words came out slurry and slippery. "Jason says he and your boy are going to play baseball. I been wanting my boy to have a friend. Jason is a good son. Especially with his father gone so much on the road, trucking."

Conchita stepped forward and reached her hand toward the woman. "I'm Conchita Vasquez and these are my children, Jack, Jenny and Pamela. I guess you know we just moved in. We live in the tannish colored house down the street." When the woman failed to reciprocate with her own extended hand, Conchita gently dropped her arm.

Her children stood tin-man stiff, staring, until the bat Jack was holding slipped and clunked against the porch floorboards. The noise broke the momentary silence and propelled Pamela to react. With a wave of her hand toward Jason's mother she said, "Hi." Jack and Jenny followed suit.

Jason took the cue, saying, "This is my mom, Coral Jenkins. There was a catch in his throat when he continued. "Well, we're going to play now, Mom. You better lay down again."

Mrs. Jenkins eased herself away from the doorway saying, "Good to meet you all. Have fun boys. Don't stay out too long now." Then the door closed.

"Come on kids. Let's let Mrs. Jenkins rest. You can play ball in our backyard. With the empty lot behind us, you'll have a good-sized ball field."

Jack questioned, "Can you play with us too Mamá? We need a pitcher, a batter and a fielder."

"Not today, Jack."

"Can we play?" asked Jenny.

"Sure, why not?" said her mother. You can use up some of that energy chasing balls."

In the back yard a bat cracked against a ball. Conchita heard squeals and laughter—bossing and some defiance. But each time Conchita thought she needed to go out to referee, the cheers began again.

Conchita changed from her nursing garb, made a grocery list and set the table for the fried chicken meal Greg was bringing. Ten minutes. She needed ten minutes to stretch out on her bed.

Sleep enveloped her until she sensed something a far off—recurring, reverberating. She could not shake herself awake. Even when her arm jerked and jerked again, she could make no sense of it.

"Mamá, Mamá." The words came closer and closer as her fog began to clear. She squinted her eyes open toward a fuzzy image.

Pamela's little hands tugged again at her arm. "Mamá Greg is here with the chicken. It's time to eat."

It took a few minutes for her to collect herself, splash cool water over her face and re-braid the thick, dark plait that usually graced her back. Arriving at the doorway of the kitchen she saw Greg and her children, void of the dirt and grime of play—and there was Jason, also freshly cleaned up—seated at the table. Greg had brought in the two lawn chairs from the porch. Seeing Conchita, he rose from the green lawn chair and greeted her.

"You look especially beautiful after a much-needed rest. We're hungry, how about you?"

"It smells good in here and you seem to have the tribe all dirt free and under control. But…"

Jenny cut in. "Isn't it exciting? We have company for dinner. In our new house. Pamela and I put on the napkins and Jack and Jason poured the drinks."

"But…?" Conchita's eyes shifted toward Jason.

"It's all taken care of. Jason's mother says he can eat with us," Greg explained.

At the end of the meal Greg brought out chocolate ice cream and dished a portion for each person.

Licking the last spoonful, Pamela looked up at her mother with a look that said— oh I just remembered. Her words held a tone of authority. "Mamá, did you tell Greg about our Papá, that he is coming home? It's true, he told me."

Greg's look of surprise met Conchita's glance of dread as he said, "My goodness. Is that true? No, I didn't know."

Conchita remained silent, except for the exhale of a deep breath, as she heard Pamela continue. "He came to see me when I was sleeping. He was wearing his baseball uniform, like in the picture in Mamá's room. He said he's coming to see me."

Jenny interrupted, "It must be true cause a lady called Mamá. She said Papá was a prisoner in the jungle in Colombia. He went there to find green rocks. A long time ago."

Annoyed, Pamela said, "They're called emeralds. It was before we were born." With amazing dignity for a child, not quite five, she went on, "The plane was shot down by bad men. But the bad men had a fight and the leader was killed, isn't that right, Mamá?"

A hesitant smile stretched across Conchita's face and she nodded toward her daughter, "Yes, Pamela, it's what Monica told me." She addressed Greg, "This has been a wild few days. First, we move into our new house, and last night we learned about the phone call from a missionary who escaped a Colombian rebel camp. Gavin Humphreys and she were hostages. Apparently, she's not certain where Miguel was taken, but he was alive the last time she saw him. We'll meet with the woman tomorrow.

Conchita pushed herself from the table and carried her ice cream bowl to the sink. "Niños, I think it is time for Jason to go to his house. You may walk with him and then come right back."

Jason, a combination of reluctant and awkwardness, stretched his slender body upright and patted his mid section. "Thanks a lot, Bye."

The children out of earshot, Conchita looked at her dear friend as he began to help her clear the table. She said, "Jason seems like a lost soul, doesn't he? It was thoughtful of you to ask him to stay for supper."

Greg nodded. "Actually, it was Pamela who suggested it. Apparently, Jason's mother's too sick to cook. She's quite perceptive, isn't she, that Pamela? And that dream about her father. Ironic isn't it?'

"Yes…I don't know what to think, what to hope for, after all these years. I would be happy if the children could see their Papá. But…"

She inhaled deeply as she filled the sink with soapy water and began to wash the dishware before she found her voice again. "Since the girls have never had their Papá and Jack doesn't remember Miguel very much, I thought they didn't miss him. Maybe I was wrong. I've changed since Miguel left. And I don't know if I can go back to that way of living."

Greg tugged the dish towel from the towel bar. His words were quiet and thoughtful. "What way of living are you talking about?"

"Miguel was…Oh how can I describe him? He could be impatient, harsh, arrogant. What he said was law. In high school I was shy, and he was exciting and outgoing. Despite the fights he got into, he was popular. I was attracted to his good looks, and his possessiveness made me feel like somebody.

"After we married, he became more and more jealous. If I spoke to someone at the store or in the neighborhood, he yelled, called me names, and forbid me from leaving the house for days. There were times that I had bruises where he grabbed my arm and I got slapped hard in the face when I did something like…invite a girlfriend over for the afternoon without his approval or try to talk to him about his temper."

Conchita searched for words. "Alcohol made it worse. Once I tried out some new make-up that he said made me look cheap. He grabbed me by the hair and held my head over the kitchen sink while he used the dish soap and dishrag to wash it off."

Conchita thought of that day, Miguel's body pinning her against the cabinet, her head bumping the faucet as he twisted her one way and another. Water and soap splattering the surroundings, her spewing tears that fused with the soapiness of the rag, fiercely burning her eyes. And all the while Miguel spouting, "No woman of mine makes herself up like a whore. In the bedroom you're my whore and no one else's. Remember that, Conchita."

She squeezed the dishcloth and watched the soapy water squirt between her fingers. "I shouldn't be saying all of this."

"There's nothing wrong with talking to a friend," Greg said. "It's good to get it off your chest. I'm so sorry you went through all of that. It must have been awful."

"Things weren't always bad. Sometimes he'd bring me a stuffed animal, maybe a rose. He'd act like I was somebody special and for a few days I had high hopes." She couldn't stop looking into the soapy suds of the sink. "But it wasn't until he left on the expedition that reality fully hit me. It was like I'd been in prison, afraid that I would say or do the wrong thing. I'd been numb most of the time. Now I was free."

Her words spilled out as if she was unable to stop them. "I was sad, hurt, regretful. I didn't want to feel those feelings. It took me a long time to crawl out of my shell. But alone with a young son, and pregnant with the twins, I had to be strong, confident and find a way to support us."

It was then she looked up into Greg's face. "And when I met you, a man of strength, thoughtfulness and compassion, I…well, I wished that I could have had that in my marriage."

Greg set the plate he had dried on the table and put his arm around Conchita's shoulder. "I hope things work out the way you want and in the way that is best for you and your children. You deserve the best in life."

Conchita closed her eyes feeling the warmth of Greg's body beside her. The comfort of his arm, and the comfort of his words overwhelmed her. Then as if he was ashamed of this modest display of intimacy, as quick as a leaping cat, Greg pulled away. Conchita straightened, feeling her own embarrassment, and turned to look into the weariness in his eyes.

"Mr. Gregory Hope, you are always full of hope. Thank you," she said.

Jack

CONCHITA MADE ARRANGEMENTS FOR A friend to pick up the children from school, since students were released early for a staff meeting. She needed to leave work early to meet with the missionary.

Clair stopped in front of the children's grandmother's house and bid them goodbye. As the children carried their school packs up the sidewalk Jack put his hand out to stop his sisters. His voice held caution. "Remember what Mamá said. Don't tell Abuela about Papá. She wants to talk to the missionary first. Remember." He held his finger in a shushing manner to his lips.

"I won't tell." Jenny announced.

"Me either," her sister chimed. "Never."

At the Señora's, eight-year-old Jack took his grandmother's bossiness in stride during the afternoon, and during the playing of hide the button. The twins shrugged as Señora Padilla criticized their mother. Usually their grandmother mellowed as the hours went by. She relaxed and often teased the children. They waited for that to happen.

Today she spouted off in her rapid-fire Spanish. "Your mother makes many mistakes. She had to have this new house. It will cost her too much money. And that man, what is his name? Señor Hope—she makes a fool of herself with him." She shook her finger at Jack and continued, "She never speaks our language. What does she think? That she is better? Soon you will forget and will not understand your grandmother."

Although the children spoke Spanish, Conchita used it less and less in their home. She wanted them to be proficient in English at school, did not want them to be behind the other children, but they always spoke Spanish when they were in the Señora's home.

Jenny looked up from the picture she was coloring in the coloring book. "But Grandmother, I won't forget. And guess what. My teacher says I must be very smart because I can speak two languages. Do you want me to teach you to talk in English? Then you can be smart, too."

The Señora threw her arms in the air. "I'm not stupid, child. But you have your mother's arrogance. I never want to learn this language, English. I know everything I need to know."

"Not everything," Jenny insisted." I know something you don't know."

"What is that?"

"I can't tell. It's a secret."

Jack put his finger to his mouth to shush his sister.

Seeing the gesture spurred the grandmother on. "You can't keep a secret from me arrogant little one. Tell me."

Pamela cut in, "Jenny, you can't tell. Mamá said."

"See, your mama has no respect for me. Otherwise she would not keep secrets."

Jack looked straight into his grandmother's eyes. "Grandmother sometimes your tongue is very wicked."

CHAPTER 5

Mel

Rain clouds hovered, threatening to dump their buckets on April's greening. Yesterday had been gray as well, and Mel wished it would go ahead and rain. Maybe the sun would sneak through and a rainbow would arch in the eastern sky to lighten the heaviness she felt. She longed for the usual brilliance of Colorado's sky.

Chicago had been dreary. On the return flight both she and Erik King were subdued, nothing like the trip to the windy city when the pair yielded their pasts to each other. It was as though wounds had been opened and now lay raw and vulnerable and neither could risk the closeness they had felt.

Driving to Monica's house where the meeting with Nicola would take place, Mel wanted to feel excitement and anticipation, yet all she could feel was dread. This morning's conversation with her mother had been bizarre. Charlotte Jameson talked of nothing but her week at the mountain resort.

"Wednesday we had a trail ride. Six hours. Those new boots I purchased were just the ticket. Most everyone else had running shoes.

You'd have been proud of your mother's form, heels down, a good sit in the saddle." Charlotte peered toward her daughter before she rattled on. "The only one who didn't need to grab the saddle horn going up or going down the steep trail. Actually, Arthur was the one who commended me on my riding ability."

"You didn't get saddle sore, after such a long ride?"

"Not much. Wish you could have been there. Amazing. The view, the sounds, the air. We rode through patches of snow. Splashed through the trickling streams. And up in the high country we stopped for lunch at a fantastic lake. What a view. So deep it looked inky blue, with snow-caps all around us. Then Arthur and I hiked halfway around the lake."

"Who's this Arthur, Mom? One of the handsome young cowboys?"

"No. He's a surgeon. Semi-retired. Lost his wife six months ago. Lung cancer. Says she never could give up the cigarettes. Imagine that—a smoker married to a surgeon. Decided that a mountain getaway was what he needed. We hit it off. He likes to dance, something your dad would never do."

As far as Mel knew her mother had not had so much as a coffee date with a man since her father went missing. Charlotte had told her daughter, "I don't need a man in my life to be fulfilled. Marriage to someone else doesn't appeal to me."

Now, every other sentence had Arthur slipped into it, just when Mel wanted to tell her mother about Nicola's news. "I'm glad you had such a good time, Mom."

"You could use something like that, too, Marilyn. The fresh air is invigorating and cleansing."

"What makes you think I need some invigoration and cleansing?" *What I really want, is to tell you is that your husband is probably alive.*

"Renewal is always good, you know. And letting go of the past. Both Arthur and I did a lot of that during this week. I don't want to preach, but it's time you let go, and accepted the loss of your dad, as well."

Mel fired, "That is one thing I am not about to do, particularly since I have news that Dad is alive." *Well it's a strong possibility and I'll let her think it's a sure thing.*

"Your dad's alive? Ridiculous. Nearly five years, not a word, not a clue. You want me to feel guilty about meeting Arthur, don't you?"

"This isn't some guilt trip. It's true. I have had news about Dad." Mel sighed. "The timing is just too weird, isn't it?"

Mel explained what she knew and about today's up-coming meeting with Nicola. She was glad that her mother didn't ask to go along.

Mel didn't like her mother's blasé attitude about the news and the sharp way she spoke. "This has got to be some scam. I know I don't believe your father is coming back, and you shouldn't get your hopes up, after all this time."

Charlotte's words and tone of voice occupied Mel's thoughts as she searched for house numbers and eased her car around the corner. *Leave it be Mel…Nice neighborhood Monica lives in. Twenty-four twenty should be in the next block, on the right side.*

Racine

RACINE PARKED HER CAR BEHIND the lone vehicle situated in front of the two-story brick. Her coppered hair tied back with a bright green bow, she stepped out onto the black-top. A breeze caught her caftan, a kaleidoscopic of color, and revealed her still shapely legs. Wicked high heels, always Racine's trademark, fit her spirited attitude. She had a closet-full, all unique. Snakeskin, alligator, patent, satin, multitudes of colors and patterns. One of the young busboys in the restaurant shouted out one day, "Racine those shoes are wicked." It stuck and Racine became known for her wicked shoes.

A tall man leaned against the other car. Waiting. His chocolate colored bomber jacket remained unzipped, displaying the gray blue of his collared shirt. A well-trimmed moustache twitched in amusement as he spoke. "Racine Rabinowitz, what a sight for a suffering soul. You have a way of sunnying up gray days."

Racine waved and walked toward a man with salt and pepper hair. "McCrae. You don't look too suffering to me. Dapper as ever and look at these new wheels. Bet this baby is loaded." Racine stroked gloss of the SUV door panel, such a deep green, it appeared nearly black.

"Yeah. The land business has gone well." Larry McCrae's smile faded. "Sure would have liked to get that emerald mine going, too. But loosing the men was torture. My fault they were gone, and I couldn't try it again." McCrae paused. "And Randy…"

Racine shook her head. "Shh, shh. Not now."

McCrae's steel blue eyes glared into her clouded caribbean ones. "Racy, when are we going to talk about it?" His baritone softened, yet Racine detected the aloof intimidation that most probably cinched many business dealings.

Ignoring his question, the restaurateur wheeled around. "We best go inside."

Conchita

THE WHEELS OF CONCHITA'S SATURN spun on the pavement as she whizzed out of the parking lot at Quail Creek Care Center. Conchita did not want to be late for the meeting at Monica's house where she hoped to find out more about Miguel and what had happened to the crew in Columbia.

The last four days had been chaotic and perplexing. She wasn't sure what she felt. Pride for her new Habitat home and all the toil and sacrifice it had required? Appreciation for all her friends like Clifford in the old neighborhood and Greg who had cheered her on during nursing school and lent a hand whenever there was a need? Compassion for the new patient that was admitted this past week and the debilitating MS that wracked her body at the young age of 42? Hope, uncertainty, and tumultuousness concerning the news about the possibility that Miguel is alive? Sorrow at the death of her treasured friend and patient, Esther Kerns, as she had caressed her hand only four hours earlier? Whew! All of that and more.

The "more" included wondering whether the kids could handle being with The Señora while she was meeting with Nicola and how to broach the subject of Miguel with her mother when the time came.

CHAPTER 6

Nicola

The moment Nicola entered the foyer with its polished tiled floor, Monica stepped back from the door. She balanced against the crutches she was learning to depend on, released her hand from the rubberized grip of the crutch and extended her right hand.

"Welcome, Nicola. Please come in." Monica quieted the deep sigh that yearned to escape her. "I've been a jitters anticipating your visit. Thanks for coming."

Nicola met Monica's hand with hers. Both held their grip not wanting to sever the connection. The guest wore a long-sleeved, silver-gray turtleneck knit top and charcoal colored corduroy slacks. They did not mask the narrowness of her tall frame, and Monica found herself looking up into a face revealing eyes the color of heather at the end of the season, and cheekbones, spare of flesh in their prominence. Void of makeup Nicola had a fresh-scrubbed youthfulness that seemed at odds with her plentiful hair, the hue of pewter. A band held it in a clump so that it draped in one gentle curve over her left collarbone. One strap of a black backpack looped over the same shoulder.

The gravelly coarseness of Nicola's voice echoed in the entryway. "I knew it was important to talk with you face to face. This is not something that I could do over the phone. I hope I'm not too early. Getting the rental at the airport and driving to Greeley took less time than I expected."

The two women exchanged smiles and reluctantly released the clasp of their hands. Monica waved Nicola into the living room to the right of the foyer. "I'm glad to have a few minutes before the others arrive. Please help yourself to a beverage, sandwiches and cookies. It's going to be a 'help yourself' afternoon since I'm not very good at carrying things yet."

An oak butler's table stood laden with hot and cold beverages accompanied by brightly colored mugs and squatty, smoky glasses. Crowded nearby were plates in the same bright colors. Trays of miniature buns stuffed with slivered ham and cheese, and sugar cookies completed the spread.

"Just water, thank you." Nicola slipped the backpack to the floor, then walked to the butler cart and poured water for herself before settling in a leather chair near Monica. "What happened to your leg?"

Monica saw the warmth and compassion in the woman's face, not beautiful, but affable. She explained about the accident during the project to build Peter's fishpond and waterfall, and how she had been hospitalized for several days after her leg had been operated on and pinned in place. The thoughtfulness that Peter had shown yesterday, plus his help in getting refreshments ready for the meeting had dampened her irritation with the ineptness that caused the accident. His actions had muted her exasperation about the unfinished project. No doubt it would remain unfinished a year from now. Monica made no mention of these details but did say the recovery would take six or more weeks and her pain and discomfort seemed to be diminishing.

When the doorbell rang, Nicola rose from her chair. "Please stay seated. If it's alright with you I will answer it."

"I hate feeling like an invalid. But yes, thank you." Racine, Mel and Larry McCrae came in together and after mutual introductions, the group moved into the living room.

Larry McCrae," Monica blurted. "So, here's the guy who sent our guys to…" She stopped, but everyone had detected the blame in her tone.

Racine cut in, "Monica, Mel, I'm sorry I didn't talk to you about McCrae coming today. I knew he would want to know as much as possible about our men." She looked directly at Monica, "And we agreed long ago, it wasn't McCrae's fault, whatever happened to them."

McCrae spoke, "It's OK. I can take the blame." His voice was steady and pleasant. "It was my project even though I hoped all of your men could be a part of it. If the men are still alive, I'll do all I can to find them and bring them home. Isn't that why we're all here?"

Monica forced a smile, "Of course. I'm sure Conchita will be here soon. Won't you have some refreshments while we wait?"

Mel and Racine graciously refused and found a place to sit in the seating group that could hold eight people close to each other. McCrae walked to the food table and popped a cookie into his mouth. "Tasty. Thanks," he said to Monica.

The doorbell rang once more. Monica twisted to grab her crutches propped behind her.

"Let me get it. I'm up," McCrae said.

Monica nodded, but did not smile. *This is my house and McCrae waltzes in and takes over. Wish Racine had not called him. I'm the one who Nicola called…I got us together…Golly neds what is my problem, feeling like this? McCrae's connections should help us. Don't know why I'm so edgy.* "Nicola, more water or something else before we get started?"

"No, I'm fine," she said. The tall woman pulled some scraps of paper from her backpack but seemed to have second thoughts and returned them just as Conchita entered the room.

"Hi all, a little breezy outside," Conchita's voice exposed her nervousness. She made the rounds, hugged and greeted each one of her friends, then paused in front of Nicola extending both hands to grasp Nicola's. "I'm Conchita. Miguel was…is my husband," she stuttered.

Once Larry and Conchita were seated, a silence and eeriness took over the room, as if their pulsing heartbeats could be heard. Nicola slid her hand down from her chin to the turtleneck of her knit top, and gently massaged the area of her voice box. She seemed to struggle to get out the words.

"I'm lucky to be alive, but I will always live with this annoying and grating voice, because my throat was slashed by one of the rebels. It's not quite as difficult for me to speak as it sounds. I can't speak loudly, however, and often the whole voice goes. But don't pity me, it could have been worse."

Nicola shifted her body, slipped one shoe off and tucked the foot under the crook of the knee of her other leg. "Before I explain all that I know, I want to say that everyone survived the crash. The first time I saw your men was the day after they were shot down. Your men were brought to the camp where my husband I were held captive."

Racine interjected, "Gavin was hurt. Is that right?"

"No one went completely unscathed, but Gavin was the worst. As I told Monica when I called her, he was hit in the leg with shrapnel when the guerrillas fired on the plane. He lost a lot of blood and it left a deep wound. He still has some metal imbedded in his femur. It could have been disastrous if the whole bone had shattered."

Monica shuddered and grimaced but said nothing while Nicola went on. "I'm a nurse and though we had very little in the way of supplies, I was able to dress the wound and nurse him through the healing. He lost a good bit of flesh and some muscle from the hit which left an indentation in his thigh. And he'll always have a limp. He was tough and later when I got this, he saved my life."

Nicola pulled a portion of her turtleneck down to expose the scar stretching across her neck like a rib of purple yarn. She tilted her head back staring at the ceiling, blowing a sigh from her lips.

A murmur went up from the group and each expressed their sympathy. Once the moment had passed Mel leaned toward Nicola to ask, "So you saw my father, the pilot, when the guerrillas brought the men into the camp? Did he seem injured?"

"Not seriously, that I know of. I was focusing on Gavin, and the other three were housed up the hill from me. Unfortunately, Randy, your father and Miguel were taken to another camp a few days later and I didn't get to talk to them. In fact we were threatened every time we tried to have a conversation. Your father had a couple of good gashes and the cloth wrapped around his head looked pretty bloody, but he seemed to be in decent shape."

Addressing Racine, Nicola said, "Randy had used his shirt to stop Gavin's bleeding, so he was without a shirt when I first saw him. Ben and Randy were half carrying, half dragging Gavin when they came into the camp. They were ordered to take him inside a cabin that held some beds for sick or injured men. I sat in front of the cabin at the time, chained to a post in a way that allowed me to move only a few feet each direction. Pirulu, the pint-sized boy who lugged ammunition for the fighters needed my help. I had wrapped his wounded. His brother was one of the rebels. Sadly, Pirulu was being groomed to follow in his brother's footsteps. Many of the rebels were quite young, you know."

Racine pressed her fist against her lips, as if to control the emotion emerging from her chest and shook her head. Still focusing on Racine, Nicola continued. "You have a brave son. Despite being prodded by a machine gun, he tried to come to my rescue. He yelled, 'I demand that you release this woman. She should be treated with respect and honor.' Despite the language difference, they knew what he meant. He took the butt of the gun in the back for that. I begged him to do what they ordered him to do, and he was rousted up the hill away from me."

Conchita reached over to grasp Racine's hand in comfort, then asked about Miguel.

Nicola looked into Conchita's face. It appeared so open, so fresh, so innocent. Yet a flash of her dark eyes exposed the hardship, the hurt that lingered there. The rasp of Nicola's voice softened as she spoke, "Something happened to his shoulder. Coming into the camp he held his arm across his chest. He seemed to be in a lot of pain, yet he said nothing."

"Probably the same shoulder he injured in the car accident. That meant the end of his baseball career," Conchita said.

"Gavin mentioned Miguel had played baseball and said Miguel was bitter about his career being cut short. I'm not sure why the rebels picked on him. They taunted him in Spanish and Miguel just glared back. Maybe they knew he understood the language. They kept badgering him. He looked them down with such hatred and with an 'I'll get you attitude'."

Conchita turned away for a moment. Finally, she said, "That surprises me a little. Usually Miguel's anger explodes. He can't control it. I guess when someone's waving a machine gun around, you learn fast to keep quiet." The silence echoed before Conchita spoke again.

"Do you know what happened to Miguel, Mr. Jameson and Randy after they were taken away?"

"The young boy, Pirulu said they were taken to a camp several day's walk from us. He grew to be our friend and helped us when he could. But I don't know much."

McCrae watched the women and wondered what thoughts roamed in their heads. They had been shaken when the men dropped out of sight. They had kept hope and were brave as their lives had to go on without their men. They were different people, now. If the men were alive, if they would someday return, how could old lives and new lives be put together? McCrae knew that prisoners of war often came back all screwed up. And what about Randy, the son he was never able to acknowledge? He would be 26 now. So much of his youth lost.

He finally spoke, "These camps. Pretty dismal huh?"

"Yes," Nicola answered. "They're hidden in the depth of dark jungles and rain forests for a purpose. We were even hidden from the sun. There are dangerous insects and animals, crazy sounds. Rains come often. Trails are muddy, slippery, and difficult to walk on. Many camps have no buildings, only makeshift tents."

Feeling restless, Mel rose, stretched, and walked to the butler's table. She poured coffee into a yellow mug and asked, "Monica, can I get you something?"

"Yes, ah…coffee, please. Black."

It seemed a good time to take a break from the unfolding story. Nicola excused herself to use the bathroom, while everyone else, even Monica with her crutches huddled around the food and beverages making small talk—How were Conchita's kids, and her nursing job? How about Racine's restaurant? What was Mel's latest flight? What about the McCrae's new shopping mall project? How did Monica get the broken leg?

Seated again they were ready for Nicola to continue. Monica set the stage for the rest of the afternoon with, "There's so much to hear. Can you start at the beginning—about how you got captured and ended up with our men?"

"I can do that. My husband Rick and I met in the single's group of our church and married in our early thirties. Though I was a nurse and he a teacher, we both wanted to feel more useful in life, so a year later we left the U.S. to become missionaries. Our church sponsored us as we headed into the jungles of Colombia in the north central section around the Magdalena River Valley. We knew that this area often harbored militia groups associated with FARC, the Revolutionary Armed Forces of Colombia and the smaller, but no less dangerous National Liberation Army, known as ELN. But we wanted to help the farmers of the mountainous hillsides and share the word of the Lord.

"The campesinos or small farmers were struggling. For generations they had grown the same crops—coffee and the foods to feed their families. All they wanted was to live in peace and raise their children in their own traditions. But as conditions changed, they weren't able to make ends meet."

Fascinated by Nicola's expressive lips, the unusual precision of her words and the passion with which she told her story, Mel found herself staring at the silver-haired woman. She wanted to help her when her voice faded in its hoarseness from time to time. Her question might give her voice a moment to rest. "I thought coffee was a good way for Colombian farmers to make a good living. We always see those ads on TV of the farmers high in the Colombian mountains showing their coffee beans."

Nicola sipped from her glass and replaced it in the coaster beside her. She nodded, "You might think so. In fact, for generations Colombia's leading export was coffee, but overproduction in Viet Nam and India drove down the price for these farmers. To feed their families, many of the campesinos resorted to the production of illicit crops, such as coca for cocaine and poppies for heroin. The guerrillas got involved in trafficking these drugs to finance their war against the Colombian government. In an attempt to eradicate these plants, with the 'war on drugs', mostly sponsored by the U.S., I might add, the fields became the target of aerial fumigation. Many families, even those who did not raise illegal crops, had to leave their land because of the dangerous poisons being sprayed."

"McCrae," Racine interjected, "Was there this kind of trouble near the emerald mine?"

"The mine's in a different part of Colombia, Racine," McCrae answered. "The mining area where the men were headed is way south, not in the same mountainous jungle. In fact, the mine is East of Bogotá. I would never send Randy into something dangerous. You know that." A knowing glance flashed between McCrae and Racine. "Getting to Bogotá involved flying over the mountains, however."

Wanting to hear more of the story Monica queried, "Nicola, what exactly did you do with these, what do you call them—campesinos?"

"We tried to help them live in peace and work their land enough to survive. My husband was a fantastic mediator. Rick forged a great relationship with the campesinos and had an uncanny ability to work with the guerrilla leaders and the paramilitary groups that were basically pro-government. We made wonderful friends and worked with several villages in a thirty square mile region.

"Rick's negotiations resulted in our community being quite peaceful during the three years we were there. The farmers definitely increased their productivity. Many of the campesinos were able to start growing patches of coffee with maize or corn between the rows. This gave them two crops to harvest and a better chance at making a living. We felt accepted and believed that we were making a positive impact, that is, until a leftist rebel named Pablo Uribe broke away from FARC and stared an off-shoot group.

Nicola paused and took in the serious faces of those around her. "I really didn't intend to get into Colombian politics today. It is quite involved."

"I think we need to get the whole picture," Larry McCrae said as he rose, walked to the food table, and dropped ice cubes into the squatty tumbler. Pouring tea and taking one of the buns layered with meat and cheese, he asked, "Can I bring anybody anything?" All heads shook to indicate no. "Please continue Nicola," he said apologetically.

"For years, a man called Castaño has led the United Self-defense Forces of Colombia (AUC). Years ago, he seized control of hundreds of small private armies recruited by Colombia's drug lords. These vigilantes—industrialists and owners of the big cattle ranches and emerald mines—were little better than death squads. Castaño consolidated these armies in his AUC, with the mission to exterminate the country's leftist rebels who have made war on the Colombian government for dozens of years.

"Even though Castaño and his men are basically a pro-government outfit it is hard to tell them from the rebels because Castaño's men don't fret too much over human rights. He's killed many campesinos claiming they were guerrilla spies. The AUC also has ties to the region's drug dealers, though Castaño claims he's working toward a narco-free Colombia.

"Anyway, when Castaño learned to hit the rebels where it hurts, in their drug profits, Pablo Uribe got mad, especially after Castaño's group executed his brother.

"With much of the group's drug money dried up, Uribe needed gun money.

Apparently, he had weapons waiting to be shipped in if he could get enough money. Then some of Uribe's men got trigger happy when Mel's father flew near Uribe's largest base camp…"

Nicola coughed and took more water before she continued, "And when the men survived, Uribe thought he had hostages to trade for weapon money."

Monica thought back of the months of agony, of not knowing, the months of no news and asked, "But if that was the case why didn't they try to negotiate for the money? Why didn't we hear anything?"

"A lot of internal fighting occurred, and all hell broke loose, causing chaos in the leadership. But before I explain that whole thing I need to back up—before we were captured."

"As I said, Rick and I were thrilled with the progress the campesinos were making. We were accepted by the villagers we worked with. Travel between the villages was without incident. I credit Rick with leading two guerrillas to the gospel and to the Lord. That's a long story in itself. The two men laid down their weapons, refused to fight and settled in one of our villages. I imagine Uribe was irate about that.

"Anyway, Uribe's men became more hostile in the months before we were taken hostage. We had received warnings that guerrillas might be targeting missionaries from North America. Those of us in remote jungles faced threats of violence and extortion. We heard some missions in other areas had been closed. Increasingly we became more cautious as we traveled from one village church to another. Uribe's men grew more bold and began blocking the roads, refusing to let us pass. Twice they demanded money. We gave them what we had, which was very little."

Nicola explained that with drug money in short supply, targeting religious leaders as hostages seemed appealing. A beautiful Sunday morning Nicola and her husband made their way up the hill toward one of the little churches. Inside they began the usual singing, sharing of blessings the parishioners had experienced during the week and the reading of the scriptures. At once, at least 15 guerrillas dressed in camouflage fatigues, with weapons in hand, stormed the little church.

"You would not think there was a shortage of guns with what they carried," said Nicola. "It was bedlam. The rebels yelled insults, ordered everyone, except Rick and me to get down. Parents gathered their children and covered them with their bodies. Mothers shushed their whimpering little ones. I watched as an arrogant rebel, barely over five feet tall, aimed a machine gun at Rick and stomped toward him barking orders for him to get outside immediately. By that time, I was shaking, but Rick stood his ground and stared back at the angry guerrilla."

All faces intent on Nicola, no one spoke as she sipped more water, then went on. "Rick was surprisingly calm. When he told the rebels we had nothing they wanted and asked them to leave so we could continue our worship, the little man repeated the order to get outside and get moving up the hill. Rick said, 'No quiero ir,' I don't want to go. Then the rebel leveled his machine gun at Rick's head and yelled again. But my husband said, 'No voy', I'm not going. I didn't know what to do. If I said anything it could make matters worse."

Nicola told how things escalated. The short-statured rebel lowered the machine gun and pulled out a 9mm pistol. Anger flew from his eyes as he stepped directly in front of the 6-foot 4 missionary. He chambered a round, rocked up on his toes to give himself a better reach and pointed the gun between Rick's eyes. Yelling profanities and threats, he raised the barrel just enough so that the shot blasted through the roof, just missing Rick's head. The loud crack sent Nicola's ears ringing and Rick screamed out, telling the rebels he would go with them, but only after everyone was allowed to leave.

Rick signaled Nicola to go with the others, but at the door a guerrilla jabbed a machine gun into her stomach. "Before Rick and I were herded up the winding path," she said, "we were forced to watch as the puny, sneering rebel, that I learned to know as Rocco, set fire to our little church."

The listeners learned that Nicola and her husband spent two weeks being marched deep into the remote jungles of the Columbian wilderness. They carried their own packs of sparse food that ran out in a few days, and the mats which they rolled out each night on the bare ground. Huddling together at night did little to make sleeping comfortable or successful. Many days she wondered if she could take another step. Insects gnawed at her unprotected arms. Welts grew each day. Often Rick patted mud over them to relieve the sting and itch. Zig-zagging trails either went straight up or straight down, threatening both Rick's and Nicola's endurance. Trudging through drenching rain, they were often forced to drop to their hands and knees in order to avoid sliding down the slimy terrain.

Nicola cringed in horror as Rocco's men demanded food from the campesinos they encountered along a way, using the butt of their guns to carry out their demands. This kept the rebels reasonably fed, yet Nicola and her husband were permitted only small amounts of food. It was as though Rocco wanted the pair to stay alive, but only barely. When they staggered into Uribe's base camp, they were hungry, exhausted, and nearly delirious.

"Our God-send," said Nicola, "was Pirulu, the young kid who carried ammunition and was being groomed for rebel forces. He brought us food and water. Finally, we had a bath of sorts. I learned from Pirulu that Uribe had left camp and would return in a few days. It was a man named Chuy who ordered the food and water. Pirulu claimed Chuy was angered about missionaries being taken hostage. He said Chuy and Rocco had had a fiery argument when we arrived at camp.

"I can only speculate about Chuy's background," said Nicola, "and why he seemed to be protective of those of us in the ministry. Chuy is a nickname for Jesús and perhaps he had some family background relating to the church. I don't know. Apparently Chuy had been gathering his own group of followers and there was increasing friction between Uribe and Chuy."

"We had two days to get some better food in our stomachs and rest before we were put to work. I was glad to use my nursing skills and to get my mind off of our situation. As I nursed the young rebels—their injuries, cuts and illnesses—I didn't consider them as bad or evil. They hurt and winced as I sutured cuts or cleansed a wound without the benefit of painkillers. Without their guns, they seemed almost vulnerable."

"So, you had some freedom while you worked on the rebels?" asked Mel.

"Not really. I was always chained or guarded."

"What about your husband?" Racine wanted to know.

"Rick worked on a kind of barracks that was being built. He used a make-shift sawmill to cut boards then began nailing them, to enclose the frame that had been constructed. I talked to Rick in snatches because we were kept apart. He told me, though the workmanship left much to be desired, the men he worked with seemed impressed with what he was able to accomplish. Mostly they wanted the project finished so they could get back to warring. Though he was heavily guarded, Rick was allowed to move about freely. Maybe if he had been chained as I was, he would still be alive."

"Why is that?" Monica asked, almost in a whisper.

"When the fighting started, he tried to come to me." Nicola's eyelids, heavy with lashes, closed and her gasp quivered.

Stark silence sliced the air before she recomposed and went on. "Let me back up a bit. Remember I said there had been brewing tension between Chuy and Uribe. Apparently Chuy thought they should rejoin FARC which Uribe had broken away from. Chuy believed it would strengthen their organization. There was jealousy between the two and they didn't agree on various issues, particularly the treatment of missionaries, as I said before.

"It was our seventh day in camp. Your men were herded in, with Uribe behind them. Rocco, the little guy that aimed his gun between

Rick's eyes, acted so pompous about bringing in 'los misioneros'. Uribe was pretty keyed up to think that they now had six American hostages. He was certain the U.S. would pay big bucks."

"Uribe's cabin was right across from mine. I could see the comings and goings. The first two days after your guys arrived, I spent a good deal of time working on Gavin's leg. I boiled a lot of water at the outside kitchen, if you could call it that. I needed everything to be well sterilized. We had a hammock where Gavin dozed nearby. He was fighting infection and was pretty groggy much of the time." Nicola reached to touch Monica who sat beside her. "It was tough, Monica, kind of touch and go."

Monica's face clouded and she nodded.

"Anyway, I treated Gavin as I watched Uribe's cabin. Chuy seemed to be cast aside while Rocco and Uribe plotted. I heard some of Rocco's comments to Uribe's followers and began to see how bloodthirsty he was, even more so than Uribe. Though Pirulu brought us food everyday, usually beans and rice, he remained closed mouthed about what was happening. He was polite and wanted to know about the bandages and medicines, sparse as they were, but I couldn't get him to talk about Uribe, Chuy or Rocco. Perhaps if I had, we could have been ready for the all-out war that ensued. I don't know."

Nicola explained that the camp was sparsely equipped, except for the artillery and ammunition ever ready to intercept opposing forces. It functioned as a lookout and base camp but lacked the satellite and computer equipment necessary to carry out high scale guerrilla activities. Communicating to make contacts and negotiations occurred at the high scale camps. There was such a camp a few days trek away.

"I thought that's where your men were going," said Nicola, "since Uribe ordered his rebels to get ready to march them into the jungle. He ordered Rick and I to stay. Rick was putting up barracks for new recruits. I needed to give Gavin medical care if he could be a live hostage."

Nicola's words picked up speed as she told of the fateful day. "It was early morning—a gloomy one. I was still stretched out on my cot inside my cabin. Actually, it was more of a crude, windowless lean-to made of rough planks. The floor too. I heard the usually stomping around as the rebels headed to the cook tent where they ate. I had rigged up some sort of crutch using a forked branch. That way Gavin could get himself up to go outside when he needed to empty his bladder. He had to stay in sight of the guard posted at the door which annoyed him. I heard Gavin's thumping limp as he left his lean-to beside mine.

"Pirulu had brought me a sack of clothes the day before. He said Chuy had gotten them for me. They were somewhat better than the 'military issue type' pants and shirt I was given when we arrived at the camp. The sack even held a heavy nightshirt for sleeping, and I had put it on the night before. For the first time in ages I felt somewhat comfortable and didn't want to get up."

Nicola heard shouts to get moving. Something was different about the morning. She jumped from the cot, still in the nightshirt, and opened the door just enough to see what was happening. Tied together with thick ropes that kept them no father apart than five or six feet, Ben, Randy and Miguel stood ready to move on command. Nicola desperately wanted to yell out some words of encouragement. She wanted to beg the rebels to allow them to stay in the camp. She hoped together they could protect each other and eventually plan an escape.

Anguish tore through her as she watched a rebel viciously prod each man with his rifle butt, yelling obscenities as the prisoners headed toward the winding trail that left the campground. A handful of armed rebels followed.

Uribe and a half dozen guerrillas stood laughing and making jokes. They talked of a rendezvous with other renegade rebels who wanted to join Uribe's cause. This rowdy group settled bulky packs on their backs, positioned their pieces of artillery and plodded off in the opposite direction. Nicola's guard growled telling her to close her door.

Inside the smoky darkness, she felt for the cot and sat. Minutes later, a scuffle and harsh, muffled words assaulted her ears. *Gavin. He's not returned, there's something wrong.* She grabbed her clothes just as the door tore open. A shadow, black against the back lit door came toward her. Even in the dimness Nicola saw the flashing evil eyes of the puny Rocco. His laugh cackled against her eardrums. "Uribe left. Now you are mine." Rocco grabbed a fistful of Nicola's ponytail and yanked her toward the open doorway. She tried to pull away, all the while telling him he didn't want to do this, he should let her go. The little man sneered, "You have no power over me, you giant freak. Do what I say."

In the open air, she saw the guard was gone. Pirulu watched the scene from the corner of the building across the walkway that separated each lean-to. The look on the wiry kid's face was somber and dark. Then he disappeared. Though the unfinished building was out of her vision, Nicola heard pounding and sawing. She knew that Rick and some of the rebels were already at work. She said to Rocco as he attached the iron band with its chain to her ankle, "Surely you have a good mother, a sister. You would want to protect them. You would not want something bad to happen to them. I am no different than they are."

Rocco punched a fist into her stomach, "You bitch. You are nothing. You know nothing of my family." Then he removed the other end of the chain from the post she was usually attached to. He looped the chain around her neck like a giant necklace. "Now we go, bitch." He motioned toward the back of the cabin.

Helplessness overcame her whole being. She obeyed. Sucking in heavily to get back her breath, she began to move. Rocco had not seen Chuy arrive, and when he turned, he faced Chuy's enraged eyes. Chuy leveled a rifle at Rocco and shrieked for Rocco to let the missionary go. What the little man lacked in size he possessed in speed and strength. In one lightning move Rocco crushed Nicola to him, a knife ready to slice into her neck.

Pandemonium erupted. A dozen rebels came from one direction, an equal number from another. Some defended Chuy, while other supported Rocco. Shouts echoed the jungle. "Let her go." "Kill Chuy." "Let's take the wench." "Get away, everyone."

One man wrestled another to the ground. Pushing and shoving increased the anger and irritation as rebels took sides. A rifle shot toward the jungle canopy meant to quiet the group. It served only to escalate the havoc. As Nicola felt Rocco's grip loosen, she did her best to twist away. "No, whore. You die," screamed Rocco as he slid the knife across her throat.

"As I slipped from Rocco's hold," Nicola said, her voice unhurried and deliberate, "Chuy fired and I saw the little snake fall."

"Coiled on the ground I pressed my hand to my bleeding throat. The front of the nightshirt hiding my nakedness had already turned crimson. I had no idea at that time how fortunate I was that the chain was wrapped around my neck. It kept the knife from going deep. As the fighting continued, I lay motionless. I had to live I told myself. Since Chuy had come to my aid I hoped he would be spared. But no. Things might have been different if he had."

The group in Monica's living room sat looking spellbound, yet depleted. Eyes shifted from one to another and no one spoke until Racine said, "And Rick?"

There was bitterness in Nicola's words. "He tried to come to me. He had no weapon, nothing. Yet they riddled his body with their machine guns."

She shed no tears, but gripped one hand in the other, looking directly at Monica. "When Rocco sent the guard away, no one remembered about Gavin. He ducked behind a shed when the massacre began. When it was over, that's when Gavin came to help me."

In her mind's eye Monica saw the horror of Monica's story and was overwhelmed with a sensation of deep sorrow. Hot tears spilled down her cheeks and plopped into her lap. An image of Gavin flashed before her, his hands bloodied as he cared for the wound on Nicola's neck, his bandaged leg dragging as he struggled to maneuver Nicola into the cabin. For some time now, the rugged features Gavin possessed—the dark bushy hair and eyebrows, the wide nose and square jaw—had dimmed in Monica's mind. She could describe them but could no longer conjure up the face with those deep-set steely eyes and the pock marks scattered on his cheeks. In her imagination, she saw a man full of grit and determination, but could not envision his eyes or hear his voice.

Monica made no attempt to dry her tears and they continued to grow a darkening area on her light blue sweatpants, one of the few pieces of clothing she could pull over her cast. Her voice caught as she spoke, "Unbelievable. You both had to be so brave…Where is he now?"

Nicola shook her head. Her eyes seemed lost in the past, her scratchy voice distant. Finally, she started again. "I don't know. We were together for about four years. But they took him from the camp seven months ago. After the massacre, only a handful of rebels were left at the camp. There was no leadership, and everything was in limbo. It was like they were waiting for orders which never came. They expected Uribe to walk back into the camp, but he never did. Gavin and I believed he had been killed, but the others refused to believe that. The surviving guerrillas were drunk half the time and though we were shackled we were left to fend for ourselves, at least in the beginning. For a while we had a pretty good storehouse of food, or course beans, rice and canned goods.

"In the early months we fought to keep alive. We depleted the meager stash of medical supplies. Gavin was skillful in using the compresses and ointments on my neck and my wound finally healed and I began using my voice again. It will never get any better than this," she said, touching her neck.

"Gavin had a rough time. He took longer to heal and got an infection. He spent several days wracked with high fever and delirious. It's a miracle he pulled through."

"Did you ever see the kid, Pirulu again?" Conchita asked.

"Oh yes, he was a lifesaver. He came at least every couple of weeks. He snuck in during the evening when we were chained and the guard was taking a break. Every time he came, he brought something—food, clean rags, a bar of soap. He was careful to hide from the rebels and we never betrayed his secret appearances. Perhaps because his brother died in the massacre, he decided not to become a guerrilla and found a campesino to feed him in exchange for work. The last time he came, a year or so back, he had on some decent clothes. He brought us a liter of coke. Can you believe that? Warm as it was, Gavin and I thought it was a treat." Nicola smiled, then said, "He left before we really got to talk to him."

The silver-headed woman reached into her backpack and pulled out a fistful of papers tied up with string. Reaching toward Monica she said, "These are for you. Gavin used pages from a small notebook to write to you. For some reason he believed I would make it out someday, even if he didn't. So, I kept the scraps of paper and promised to give them to you if I made it back."

Monica took the packet from Nicola. She dabbed away the tears, then tore at the string around the packet. Smeared and hazy, Gavin's scrawled script in blue ink stared up at her. The room was still as she scanned the first page, reading to herself.

Dear Monica

It is a miracle I am alive. But I don't know how long. I hope someday that I can come home, but things don't look too promising right now. I miss you. I am sorry to leave you alone. Don't morn me. Remember the good times. Go on with your life, live fully. Hope this pen holds out. Was still in my pocket after we crashed.

It's my link to you—the pen you gave me for my birthday.

If you get this its because I brought it back with me, or Nicola took it to you and by now you know much of our ordeal. Was the third day of our trip. Entered Colombian air space on way toward emerald mine. Shot down by Guerrillas in heavy jungle. My leg was damaged by shrapnel...

For the first time in years Monica could hear Gavin's voice, see his face. She wanted to keep on reading, but she put the sheaf of papers aside casting her eyes toward each of her guests. She wanted to turn back the clock. She wanted to throw herself across her bed and wail. But she couldn't do any of these things. Oh, the injustices of life.

CHAPTER 7

Racine

Larry McCrae and Racine were the last to leave Monica's house. The rhythmic click of Racine's wicked high heels on the sidewalk intensified the bubble of silence surrounding them. Flashing her a reassuring smile, McCrae broke that bubble. But the pinched brow and tight jaw reflected his unease. When the pair reached McCrae's SUV, they paused. McCrae placed a comforting hand on Racine's shoulder.

His voice resounded warmly, yet firmly. "You can rest assured we'll get on this tomorrow. Nicola said she wanted us to know before she talked to the officials. I can understand her aversion to being hounded, but I don't see any way to keep this information under wraps. It'll hit the news right away." He pulled his hand away and shoved it into his pocket. "We may be badgered, too. Regardless, I plan to get going right away to find the men and bring them home."

A gusty whirlwind twirled around the pair, temporarily stalling the conversation. Racine involuntarily snatched at the hem of her colorful caftan. Her attempt to focus on the sidewalk beneath her feet resulted in a teary blur. "Is it too much to hope that my son is still alive?" Her breathing halted before she went on. "Nicola has no idea where they took Ben, Randy and Miguel, or if they're still alive. What can we believe?"

"We have to believe. Racine, we have to believe that he's alive," McCrae asserted.

"If the guerrillas planned to use prisoners as ransom for gun money or whatever, why hasn't the government heard anything? Why haven't we heard anything?"

"With these lunatic guerrillas," McCrae said, "it's impossible to know. From what Nicola says, for years the group was in such chaos, they weren't functioning. Maybe the new leadership didn't get off the ground and they're still in chaos." McCrae spoke with the vehemence of an attorney driving a point home to a jury. "Whatever the situation, we have to believe that our son is alive."

Racine's head shot up. Staring into McCrae's clouded face she witnessed his own eyes brimming and threatening to spill. Her heart ached not only for herself, but for him, as well. The saliva collecting at the back of her throat had difficulty going down. The "our son" words jammed like a kick in the stomach. She shook her head intent on stopping the direction of the conversation.

"No, I'm not going to be quiet this time." He grasped her left hand and held on when she tried to pull away. "We have to talk about Randy," he said, each word sharp as a hammer pinging against a shiny nail. "I know I'm his father." The pinging softened as he said, "I know you didn't intend for me to find out. In the beginning I refused to think about the possibility—didn't realize you had a kid for a while. When I found out, I knew he was mine."

Racine shook away from his grip and planted both hands on her hips. Her expression oozed both defiance and depletion. "Oh, McCrae, why now? Let it be. It was my fault, not yours."

"Wait a minute! You can't say that. Please Racine, let's talk, but not out here. The wind's picking up. At least let's sit in the car."

Racine accepted the open passenger door and climbed onto the dark leather seat. Once her door was closed, she twisted sideways, pressing her back against it and curled her left leg under her. Despite the car's smell of newness, the smell of McCrae, masculine with a splash of spice drifted around her. She allowed herself a slight smile.

Once in the car McCrae's eyes searched Racine's and he said, "You can't take the blame for that night. If anything, it was up to me to resist temptation. I was the married one. I still don't know why I didn't. I've been in other tempting situations with sensuous women hanging all over me." He shrugged and went on, "I never succumbed, not before that night and not after."

Shoulders squared, he looked forward, avoiding her face, "I do know that it was one of the most memorable nights I ever had."

"For me too," Racine admitted, "and amazingly I never felt an ounce of guilt, nor did I dwell on that night. I mean, I didn't relive each moment and hunger after more." She raised a hand to touch her forehead. "I tucked that spectacular memory away. I knew it would go no further, that your love and responsibility for your wife would not be diminished…That you were a good man."

He sighed behind his words and said, "I've tried to be. It was a crazy night. The snow that piled and piled. You in those skinny shoes with no boots and feet like icicles. Your laughing squeals, daring me to skid in 360's."

"I dared no such thing. You were a reckless son-of-a-gun. We did laugh a lot, though didn't we?"

"Yeah. Racy, you know, I don't remember having such fun and such laughter again after that night."

The seriousness of the conversation lightened as Racine responded. "Of course the darned ole blizzard and your show-off diving didn't set the stage for a somber evening." She shot him a look. "You haven't called me Racy since then and you just did."

"I did? I guess remembering back got me to feeling like old times. You're right, after that night you seemed like a woman and not the kid I thought you were. I couldn't call you Racy after that."

"Lots of people at the restaurant call me Racy, but not because they think I'm a kid," Racine mused. "I can't believe you thought of me as such a young thing back then. I was 22." Racine pondered before going on. "You were already 30, so mature and worldly. Such a dedicated husband, caring for and sacrificing for an invalid wife who desperately wanted to have children. I felt sorry for you and admired you."

With sarcasm McCrae said, "Yeah, so dedicated that I stepped outside of my marriage that night." He turned to look into Racine's face, sadness in his eyes, and continued, "I was touched by your life story. I kept asking myself how could a mother leave such a beautiful and fun-loving daughter as you? It's not an excuse, but…" He shrugged.

Racine smiled, then reached across the seat and placed her hand on the leather arm of McCrae's jacket. It was supple, smooth, and strong, much like her image of the man beside her. "I suppose the craziness of the blizzard, the bantering back and forth…the connection and compassion between us that night led us to the bedroom." Racine paused. "I'm not sorry. It was a gift. You comforted me, listened to me, and shared a bit of yourself. It touched me. Making love, I felt whole and desired. And…you gave me a wonderful son."

"And you did a good job as his mother. Racine, I can't tell you how many times I wanted to let him know I knew, wanted to be a proper father, make things right. But I held back and tried to respect your wishes."

"I suppose the anonymous funds for Randy's college were a definite acknowledgement. You were the only one who could have given them, but I couldn't quite admit it to myself. And I said nothing to Randy… Thank you. They were a great help." Racine pressed her fist against her mouth and blew into it before she added, "I'm sorry I kept your identity hidden. All those years. It wasn't fair to either of you."

"Why didn't you want me to know? McCrae's tone was pensive.

"Lots of reasons. I couldn't let my foolishness disrupt you and your wife. I couldn't rub salt into the wound of a suffering woman who could not bare her husband a son. I didn't want to ruin our friendship, such as it was…And of course those stubborn Rabinowitz genes were not about to look for help, for the financial support you would have felt obligated to contribute." Racine tilted her chin upwards. A piece of me said 'he's my son and I won't share him with anyone'. Besides if my father could be a single parent, so could his daughter."

Racine removed her hand from McCrae's arm and asked, "Tell me, how is Chantcl?"

"Well, as you know she was a trial case for some experimental drugs about 23 years ago and now those drugs are being used routinely on similar cases. They were quite successful and though Chantel never regained her old self, her vitality and strength, she was able to get out of the wheelchair and live a more normal life—that is until the last year." His jaw tightened and he went on. "It's been rough, lots of pain and she's unable to walk now. She's fragile. In fact, I have periodic nursing care for her at home. There's no way I will put her in a facility."

"I'm so sorry to hear that, McCrae. I had no idea. Just when all this other comes up. Let me know what I can do. Chad, my assistant has been a godsend. He dropped in my lap after Carlotta's heart attack. I can get away for short periods if you need me to make contacts with some officials. Just tell me what you think we should do. I can make lots of phone calls, for sure."

"We'll see. How is Carlotta anyway? Never saw two people like you two who make such perfect partners."

"She's doing better, but the heart attack left some heart damage and the balloon procedure didn't seem to work. She's scheduled for by-pass surgery next week. I'm not allowing her to come back to work for a while. She pushes herself too hard at the restaurant."

"Please give her my regards when you talk to her…Oh, I better take this call."

McCrae fished his phone out of his pocket, punched the on button and answered. Racine saw his mouth tighten as his eyes darted in every direction and heard him say that he would be right there.

"Sorry, we can't finish this conversation Racine." This time his voice sounded brusque and hurried. "Something serious has happened at home."

Monica

Six o'clock. It had been a heart tugging afternoon with all of them listening to Nicola. Her mind raced with the thoughts of Gavin and his ordeal, of Peter who had been at her side this morning, empathetic and helpful. Where was her life going? What did the future hold? If she eventually had to choose, how could she?

Monica looked hard and long from her upstairs bedroom toward the far-off mountains. A melon sun eased toward them as it blasted out beneath the dense ceiling of cobalt and gray clouds that hovered from Greeley all the way west. The Colorado Rockies provided a backdrop for magnificent sunsets and tonight's would be haunting with its many contrasts. Monica glimpsed the brilliance of Caribbean blue growing in the open sky beneath the ominous darkness. The sun's luminosity began transformation. Fringes of scalloped clouds glowed pink, then an iridescent orange blush saturated the remaining day light.

The total effect reflected her melancholy mood, dark and menacing vying against the morphing glow, not unlike the churning inside of her. She was numb when Nicola was talked out and everyone left. The group seemed subdued and let down at the news that Nicola and Gavin had been separated after four years of captivity, that Gavin had apparently been taken to a camp where other captives were held. She had no idea if the other captives included Ben Jameson, Randy Rabinowitz and Miguel Vasquez.

Nicola had explained about the disorganization and lack of leadership after the massacre. Once they were both healed, Gavin and Nicola became the slaves of the camp, preparing food, sweeping cabins, cutting wood, hauling water and washing clothes and bedding. Often, they were relieved of the burdensome chains, but always they were heavily guarded.

Eight months before Nicola escaped a definite reorganization began when six newly trained rebels marched into the camp. They set up a training program and brought in twenty new recruits. Two of the six claimed to be officers and spoke with authority. They wielded enough power to bring order and purpose, and to bring the focus back on FARC in an attempt to bring down the Colombian government and the paramilitary groups. New drug money poured in and the new officers were intent on getting the eighteen rebels who had gotten soft during the preceding years hardened and disciplined.

One of the rebels that Nicola knew as Joaquin argued against being a part of FARC, demanding that they continue with the offshoot organization that Uribe had initiated. The officer with the deep scar extending from his left cheekbone to his jaw laughed and bellowed that Uribe became a ghost not long after he left the camp those years ago. He said no FARC member would let a traitor live. Then scar-face shot Joaquin dead.

Monica couldn't let the images of the stories of the afternoon roam through her mind another minute. Even the harrowing escape that Nicola made from her captors. She must drive them from her mind before they overtook her.

The glow of the evening subsided as the sun slipped behind a far mountain. Monica turned from the window and hobbled toward her bed. Gavin's notes nestled in a plastic grocery bag looped around her wrist. She plopped on the bed. Releasing the crutches, they crashed to the floor. *Heck.*

Digging into the bag, her hand gripped the packet of notes Nicola had given her. Shuffling through the papers she tried to focus on Gavin's words, but they blurred before her. When her grasp loosened, the papers scattered to the floor. *Oh double heck. Just stay there. What do I care?*

Monica pulled her body onto the bed, rolled to her side, pulled her knees up as far as she could with the awkward cast. As she lay still and quiet, tears squeezed from her closed lids, wetting the silky quilt. Breaths came in short whispers and she floated into a pink haze.

Conchita

AFTER LEAVING MONICA'S HOUSE CONCHITA drove toward her mother's home. What should she say to her mother? So far, she had said nothing about Miguel and the others who had been taken captive in Colombia. All the Señora knew was that nearly five years ago Miguel left with three others on an expedition relating to mining emeralds. When contact was lost, and no amount of searching brought any hope for their return, everyone assumed that their plane had crashed somewhere in the dense jungle, that they were dead.

She was certain the children would say nothing to their grandmother, even though they'd been with her all afternoon. Today had been a rush for Conchita, working until the last minute before hurrying to Monica's house to meet with the missionary named Nicola.

Conchita was impressed with the tall, almost regal woman and her thick head of pewter-colored hair. Conchita wondered if her own hair would some day resemble a similar silvery shade. The Señora's had changed almost over night three years ago. Before then it had retained its deep ebony color and she had worn it braided in one long plait and pinned in a tightly coiled knot at the back of her head. A striking woman, she carried herself with, what some would describe as, a proud arrogance. Now the Señora wore her hair in a coiled bun at the nape of her neck. Usually a few stray gray locks escaped to frame and soften the face that tallied a new crease each day. She could still be called striking, Conchita thought, if she softened her look and offered a smile. Yet real smiles had to come within and there seemed too few of those in her mother.

Before Conchita broached the subject of the men's hostage situation with her mother, she hoped to know more. All she really knew is they had been alive after the plane was shot down. She was amazed to hear Nicola's story, and glad for her escape. Yet, Conchita went away feeling more let down than encouraged. Nicola had no definite knowledge that Miguel, Ben or Randy ever made it to another camp after they were herded away during the early days following their capture. If they did, had they been tortured or beaten? Conchita had accepted the mental image of the men dying instantly in a plane crash in the Colombian jungle several years ago.

Now, visualizing them crawling through the dangerous jungle, being prodded by guns, wrapped in chains at night and being whipped or beaten when they didn't move fast enough, turned her stomach. Miguel wouldn't stand for such treatment. If he resisted or fought back, she guessed the rebels wouldn't hesitate to…Oh, she didn't want to think of his body riddled with bullets as Nicola's husband had been. She wasn't sure if she could be as brave as Nicola, if she could have survived those years in captivity. And her escape…Her kids would like to hear that story. Yes, Conchita decided that tonight she would tell her mother everything she knew, and the kids, too.

When she arrived at her mother's small, but functional house, it was approaching dusk. Suppertime was near, so Conchita expected to see the table set just so, her mother stirring something at the kitchen stove. She opened the door reluctantly.

Instead a giant pizza box lay open on the coffee table. The four missing pieces were being gobbled up by her three children huddled around the coffee table and her mother seated in her sewing chair at the end of the sofa.

"Mamá, you're here," Jack called out. "We're eating pizza."

"I see," said Conchita, casting her eye toward her mother.

"Well, I decided I should try it before I die," said the Señora, avoiding eye contact with her daughter.

"We have a lot," Pamela chimed. "You can have some, too."

"I'll get you a plate." Jenny said, jumping to her feet.

"You surprise me Mamá, Conchita said to the Señora. Pizza? And in the living room? Yes, I'd love some, too."

"It's not so bad, my daughter. I think I'll have another piece," her mother admitted. "Jack told me that sometimes my tongue is wicked. The grandmother's eyes shifted quickly toward her grandson. "See, it is not always wicked. This time it said, 'tell me, how do you order this pizza that you like so well'?"

Conchita grinned at her son, and everyone, including the Señora, laughed. The evening ended up being a most pleasant one, one which left Conchita feeling more optimistic. The Señora remained speechless as Conchita relayed Nicola's story in a way that was understandable to her children. Then came the account of Nicola's escape.

Jenny and Pamela snuggled beside their mother on the couch. Jack sat at her feet. All eyes focused on Conchita as she told the story of Nicola's escape.

Conchita's eyes grew more animated as the escape story began. "After the new leaders came into the camp and began giving orders, Señor Humphreys was taken away. Then Nicola was alone with the rebels. They were very mean to her, more than they had been in the past. When she wasn't working for the rebels, cooking, washing clothes or carrying water from the river, she often read her Bible. She read out loud hoping that the rebels would hear and learn about the Lord, that they would turn away from being rebels. However, it made them mad and one day they grabbed the Bible away and tore it apart, page by page and burned it. They spit on her and told her women missionaries were like pigs. She felt very alone and scared. Nicola knew she had to find a way to escape"

"What did she do?" Jack's eyes widened.

"She spent a few weeks getting ready for her escape. At night in the dark she tore one of her shirts into pieces. Using the suturing needle and suturing line that was kept in the medical kit she fashioned sacks that could be tucked in a kind of backpack she also made."

"What did she want the sacks for?" Pamela wanted to know.

"Nicola knew she would be on the run for a while and wanted to take as much food as she could with her. She planned to find some food in the jungle—like roots, some fruits and even some kinds of worms and grubs."

"Yuck, I'd starve before I ate worms," Jack said as he turned up his nose.

"Not me, 1 could do it. 1 ate a worm once," Jenny said proudly. "Did the missionary lady eat worms?"

"I guess she did when she was hiding in the jungle. She got some food from the storehouse, rice and dried meat and hid it away for the trip. Nicola found a large piece of plastic to protect her from the rain and folded it up small enough to fit in one of the sacks. She collected matches from the storehouse so that she could build little fires to heat water and cook the rice and cornmeal. Sometimes the rebels had canned foods and Nicola was able to sneak an empty can to her cabin so that she could use it as a cooking pot. She even found a plastic coke bottle and filled it with water. She hid everything in the stack of her clothing that she kept on the floor of her cabin. Fortunately, the rebels didn't seem interested in the stack."

The Señora appeared fascinated by the unfolding story and leaned forward in her chair to say, "The missionary, she was very brave and very smart, no?"

"Yes, she was, Mamá. For many nights she stayed awake planning the best way to make her escape." Well into the evening Conchita related the harrowing story Nicola had told of her daring escape.

Nicola

AFTER GAVIN WAS WHISKED AWAY from the camp, emptiness overwhelmed Nicola. She and Gavin had come to depend on each other, had comforted each other and brought hope to each other. With the increased activity in the camp, Nicola believed dangerous times were ahead. She knew the time was at hand to make her escape, and it had to be soon, before they marched her on to who knew where.

Fortunately, the guards had relaxed their routine of chaining her during the day, though there was always a guard nearby. Faid and Saul took turns as night guard. With the cabin door closed Nicola couldn't see them, but Faid was the one she could hear. His relentless off-key whistling had irritated her and kept her from a good night's sleep many nights. Furthermore, between the bouts of whistling Faid smoked one cigarette after another. Invariably the wafting smoke seeped between the planks of the poorly built walls and around the ill-fitting door, adding to her annoyance. She was also aware of Faid's catnaps, catnaps accompanied by incessant snoring.

Surely Faid's catnaps would work in favor of her escape. Each night he stood guard Nicola listened for his sputtering snore. Counting the seconds, one-thousand one, one-thousand two she determined Faid was likely to have five catnaps a night, averaging two minutes and seventeen seconds each. On occasion the snoring continued for five minutes, but those times came just before dawn. To make her emerging escape plan work, Nicola needed at least two hours to make her way into the jungle before her absence was discovered. If a search party caught her, there would be no mercy. Much of the dense jungle made travel impossible without the use of trails. In the dark of night, she hoped to head west using some of the well traveled paths that were kept fairly open. Otherwise she ran the risk of walking in circles and losing her bearings as she wound her way around one mountain descending into a valley then up and over another peak.

With all her supplies stashed Nicola began her night vigils. She believed luck was in her favor when she learned Saul took sick and Faid was ordered to guard three nights straight. Surely Faid would not be able to stay awake three nights running.

Nicola lay fully clothed on her barren cot beneath a heavy blanket. Usually she slept on her side, covering her exposed ear to keep it warm. Tonight, she lay on her back, both ears open to the cool air, listening with great concentration. There was stillness. Was Faid asleep? She didn't hear snoring and could not be sure. Then she detected the smell of his cigarette. No, he was awake. As the hours dragged, creaks, screeches of the night, sounds of scattering insects and other varmints, usually oblivious to her consciousness, pummeled her eardrums with a nerve-wracking racket. But the entire night remained devoid of the sputtering of Faid's snore and left Nicola dismayed.

The following night found the moon dipping in and out between wispy clouds, projecting enough glow to keep the night from being boot black. Again, intent on her vigil, Nicola waited and listened. Faid's off-key whistle ceased the first hour of his watch. Nicola blocked the night sounds and seemed conscious only of her own heart's thumping. Surely it was nearing midnight. Still no snoring. The rest of the world seemed immensely far away and the empty hole in her widened. She fought the gnawing panic that God had failed her, or even worse that there was no God.

Paralyzed by the forbidden thoughts, she lay unaware of the passing time. Did anything really matter? If she died this very night who would care, who would know? No one. Not even Gavin. Numbing sensations crawled from her feet to her thighs. She clasped her hands together in preparation for prayer, but no prayer would come. Her existence felt like nothingness.

The nothingness continued toward what seemed like eternity, until involuntarily her toes and calf muscles contracted, and her body convulsed. A flush of warmth tingled through her being. Familiar features glowed behind her closed eyes, first soft and hazy, then in the clarity of a face warmed by the rays of early morning sun. Nicola whispered to the darkness, "Oh Rick."

Her husband's memory flooded her thoughts. She and Rick in the first lean-to they used as a church. Rick, cradling the campesino, Pablo, when his wife died leaving him to raise six young children alone, she and Rick helping to rebuild a family's hut that had washed down the mountainside the year the rains flooded the area, Rick singing Amazing Grace as they trekked between villages.

Nicola blinked her eyes in the darkness. She felt her own smile broaden across her face. Softly she hummed the song that had meant so much to Rick. When she came to its end—We've no less days to sing God's praise than when we first begun—a great peace swelled through her.

You were such a brave beacon for me. It has been a beautiful life. My sorrow is that you did not get to live the rest of your dream, our dream. We shared our faith. However, you were always the more fervent one. You never doubted, never wavered as I did. At least if you did, I didn't know it…Well, here I am. Oddly I feel you close to me and now I'm not wavering. The Lord has provided your spirit as comfort.

Nicola breathed deeply. Then she heard it. Faid snored good and strong. Easing herself from beneath the blanket, she made the cot look as if she were still there. Raising her hands toward the heavens she paused and whispered, "Thank you Lord."

She attached the pouches she had devised for her escape—stashed with food, a water bottle, matches and a tin can for heating over a fire—to her belt loops. Making no sound she approached the door, and with careful deliberation pulled it open, then stepped outside.

A patch of moonlight filtered between the open spot in the canopy of skyward-reaching trees. It washed over the snoring guard with his AK 47 propped by his side. Gravel crunched beneath her feet. Nicola sucked in a breath. She held it. Faid continued his rattling snore. Three more steps. She rounded the corner and stood behind her hut. Nicola blew out a long breath and sucked her lungs full of the humid air. She no longer heard Faid's snore but dared not look back. Turning right, she headed into the jungle.

Unfaltering, her stride was long and even. She heard the rustle of the surrounding fauna as breezes whooshed past. The squawk of a bird that haunted the night with its eerie cry. As she reached the trail that would take her away from the camp, something scurried between her feet and dashed into the thick undergrowth. It took all she could muster to keep from crying out. She quieted the pounding that arose in her chest, said a silent prayer and headed down the winding path.

Slippery from the recent rains, the path grew steep and rocky. Roots snagged at Nicola's boots, threatening to bring her to her knees. Darkness swallowed her. She gripped the giant stalks that bordered the trail, hand over hand, in order to keep going. *OK, don't lose the trail. Keep pushing onward.*

Sharp grasses sliced across her cheeks, and she tasted her own blood as it oozed to the corners of her mouth. Time after time the legs of some insect wriggled over her, producing shivering tingles. *Take that.* She smacked at the crawling and creeping creatures. Losing balance landed her on a fours in the squish of mucky undergrowth. *Damn.*

The pungent smell of rotting plants, of burgeoning fungi and moss assaulted her nostrils. She pushed her body upright, squeezed her fists and felt the muck squirt between her fingers. *Come on Nicola, you never let the jungle get to you before.* Rubbing the goo from her hands with a leafy bush, she marched on.

A growing sense of steadiness infused her legs and for what might have been fifteen minutes Nicola gained ground and momentum. Then something came at her crashing through the underbrush to her left. Something large. Would it attack her? Should she stop or keep going? Standing motionless, barely breathing, she grabbed a ropy vine for stability. The snapping and smashing of branches and stalks slowed, then picked up speed. When the noise echoed past her and grew distant, she pressed her hand against the wide scar at her neck—*I'm alive. I've survived*—and trudged ahead.

For a while she counted her steps, partly to pass the time, but also to mark how much farther from camp she had walked. When she reached 9,000, she stopped counting. *Time to celebrate.* She reached into her pouch for food.

Sensing the oncoming morn, the jungle creatures came alive. She heard the sound of the animals in the canopy above. She'd heard it all before, but this time the yells and screeches of the monkeys, marmosets and macaws seemed bent on frightening and mocking her. Things fell through the tangled vegetation, bounding off one branch and another. One football-sized seed pod smashed a bush not three feet away. She wanted to yell out to the crawling jungle. "Hey, have a little mercy. I'm an animal surviving like you guys. I'm not here to harm or bother you. Don't hassle me."

Nicola kept her voice to herself, fearful someone could hear her and take her prisoner again. Torture before killing her in frenzied anger. Then it struck her. *I'm free. The first time in 5 years* free. She knew it in her head yet couldn't yet feel it.

Within the hour, the sun would send its rays over the jungle canopy. The anti-government guerrillas would awaken. Faid would find her cabin empty and alert his fellow rebels. Would he be punished for allowing her to escape? Maybe they had more important things to worry about. Maybe they would shrug it off. No, they would figure that she had headed toward lower altitude and in this direction. They would come—and seek revenge.

Nicola picked up the pace with the coming light of day. She could see her way more clearly. *Who uses this path anyway? Friend or foe?* Once the sun lighted the surroundings, she intended to push her way into the bush and eat another tortilla, a little of the dried meat and drink a few gulps of water, while watching for foot traffic in hopes of assessing the peril she faced.

Off she trail she found the going much more difficult than she anticipated. The jungle canopy had thinned allowing a bevy of plant life to overtake the jungle floor. The twisted undergrowth and ropy vines tugged at the cuffs of her camouflage pants, twined around her boots and snared her every movement. *Just where is a trusty machete when you need it?* No more than five yards from the pathway she realized if she went further, she might lose her way.

For several minutes she fought with the menacing jungle growth, stomping, pulling and twisting to make a place to sit. Finally squatting against a giant fern-like plant, she pulled the plastic soda jug from her makeshift backpack and swigged the water. It felt good to sit, yet the flight/fight mode of her pumping heart yearned to get going.

Removing her food from the homemade bags, Nicola forced a few bites. *Keep chewing. It'll go down, even though it tastes like cardboard.* Taking another swig of water, she pondered whether to get back on the trail. Her answer came in the form of voices drifting toward her. Her ears told her they were men. If she had remained on the footpath, she would have come face to face with them. The verbal exchange stopped, but their footsteps drew closer. Were these people friend or enemy? Leaning forward she pulled at the undergrowth, hoping to glimpse those making their way along the route, but it was impossible.

A yell cut through the jungle. Nicola's body jerked, then froze as a succession of harsh words stabbed through her. A second voice bellowed in return. She understood the Spanish diatribe of profanity. Nicola translated the immediate comeback that followed. One more and you die, pig. The angry discourse ended with the echo of a single gunshot.

The surrounding growth had a way of rending gunfire deafening. Nicola's mind replayed the memory of being herded and prodded through the jungle when she and Rick were first taken captive, of the menacing blasts fired against the jungle canopy as a threat to keep them moving and in line. Was she witnessing a similar situation? Was the man who yelled out profanities a captive? Were there others? Were rebel forces taking prisoners to the camp she just left? She couldn't risk trying to find out. *Sit tight. Be safe. Be smart.* Walling out all feelings she allowed numbness to overcome her.

Focusing on the sounds surrounding her, the stirring of the tall grasses, the sounds of flying and scampering creatures, she listened for human sounds. When none had come for some time Nicola pulled herself from her frozen state, then rolled her head and shoulders to ease the stiffness that had set in. Pushing herself through the tangle, she reached the trail and set a quick pace, keeping her senses alert.

A heavy mist descended and turned into drenching rain. She grabbed the square of plastic tarp she had stashed in her pack, wrapped it around her shoulders and knotted it at her neck. Beneath the makeshift raincoat perspiration soaked into her clothing giving her a sticky, itchy sensation, and she shuddered. Salty droplets rolled into her eyes, blurring her vision. She attempted to swipe them away. *Can't feel sorry for myself,* she thought as she tromped on, stumbling and sliding along the muddy path, traversing gushes of rainwater as it tried to find a way down the mountain.

Trudging on, it was early evening before she realized the rain had stopped. *Mother always said you put one foot in front of the other and pretty soon you're there. How many hours have I been doing that? Fifteen or sixteen? Time to stop.* Her feet burned with the intensity of the stings of a hundred fire ants. She couldn't decide if she was hot or cold with the sogginess that permeated every piece of clothing, until a gigantic shiver shook her.

In a hidden clearing away from the trail the tall woman set about devising a cushiony spot to sleep for the night. Once a bounty of leaves and evergreen branches were nestled together, she collected the driest items she could find, arranging them for the fire.

Finally, parking herself on a fallen log, she tugged the rubber boots off her feet. Even through the darkness of her socks Nicola saw the coagulated blood. The women of the villages had taught her how to make a poultice of leaves from a creeping plant that covered much of the jungle floor. She gathered several handfuls and pounded them with a rock until they oozed a gooey green. Wincing, she removed each sock and hung it over a vine to air. She patted the goo to the raw and bloody areas of her feet, wrapped some long wide leaves around the healing gunk and slipped her feet back into her boots.

Nicola allowed herself a short rest after completing the campsite preparations. The iciness of the approaching night awakened her, and she arose and lighted the campfire. It helped to warm her while she heated water for her "stew". The stew ended up being chopped roots, grubs she gathered from beneath the nearby rocks, greens similar to dandelions, a little cornmeal and rice. It was hot and nourishing, despite its unusual flavor, and she forced herself to eat it all. When the embers flickered away, she curled up on her cushiony spot and covered herself with the plastic tarp and branches, waiting for sleep to come.

When morning arrived, Nicola couldn't say that she had had a restful sleep. It had been too cool for that. Yet, she needed to move on.

Afraid of what she would find, she removed the poultice to check the injured areas of her feet. She looked toward the sky. *Wow. Looks lots better.* Shaking as much of the dried blood as she could from the aired socks, she saw a magnificent Colombian Boa Constrictor slither over the log she sat on the night before.

Mesmerized by the ease with which it moved as it made its way past her, the woman sat as still as the owl she had once seen in the backyard of her growing-up home. She studied the saddle like patterns of pale gray on a background of rich chocolate along its back, then eyed the dark brown diamond shapes that decorated the creamy pale sides of the boa. The designs entranced her and verified the wonder of nature. *A good omen.* A message from her husband. They had both loved the boas of the jungle. One they had called Jeremiah. They saw it often as it hunted and lived near their jungle habitat. Tearing herself from the bittersweet memories she readied herself for departure from this place. Thankful for the protection it had provided she chewed on bits of food and sipped from her nearly depleted water container. She'd need more drinking water soon.

An hour into her second day's walk she had not heard or seen another human. Suddenly the giant trees and undergrowth thinned out and she could see the path and where it led more vividly. Sprawling before her was a deep valley. And up the other side was another mountain. She had to decide which way to go once she descended the mountain. Almost at a run she watchfully placed each foot to avoid slipping on the winding footpath. Halfway down the valley she paused to look. A whorl of smoke ascended from below. To her right she saw another, then another. *People live here. They're starting their morning activities. Oh, God may they be friendly.*

Conchita

WHEN CONCHITA PAUSED IN THE relaying of the missionary's escape story, Jack, Pamela, Jenny and the Señora's, eyes danced in wonder. Jack questioned with the exuberance of someone who had just hit the winning home run of the world series, "They were friendly, weren't they? Tell us Mamá, did someone on the mountain help Nicola come back to tell us about Papá?"

Conchita grinned, "Yes, my son. Nicola said it was the hand of God that brought her to the young boy, Pirulu. He was the boy Nicola first met when she was taken captive. He carried the ammunition for the rebels and was being trained to be a rebel. He brought her food and clothing during the first years of captivity. After the massacre, he decided he didn't want to be a rebel and ran off. He had no parents, but a campesino family took him in and he worked for them. Isn't that nice?" Heads nodded in agreement and Conchita continued. "Sometimes he secretly went back to take soap and special supplies to the missionary lady."

"Can you believe it? When Nicola came down the mountain Pirulu met her on the footpath and took her to the hut where he lived?"

The Señora put her hand up to halt Conchita's telling. "What is it Mamá?"

Without hesitation, the Señora nodded a finger toward the listeners and said, "The hand of God works in the way of mystery. I tell you my children. It is no accident, this boy with no parents. He came for a big purpose. There is purpose in everything."

The Señora's head cocked in an aura of authority and no one moved for a moment. Then a glow of a smile washed over her face as her voiced softened, "It is true, you know."

At that moment Conchita wanted to cheer for her mother. Mamá definitely has a soft side, she thought. Instead Conchita rose and walked to her mother's chair, sat on the arm beside her and hugged her mother to her. "You are so wise my little mamá."

The Señora waved an arm of protest, "Well, for the moment. Now my daughter you must finish your telling."

"You are right," Conchita said looking into her mother's face, "Because of Pirulu, Nicola was protected. A few days after she arrived in the village the rebels came looking for her. Pirulu and Nicola hid in a cave until they were gone."

"What kind of cave? Were there bats?" Jenny wanted to know.

"I don't know little one, but they were safe, and Nicola stayed in the village for a week or two as a nurse helping some of the sick people."

Pamela questioned, "But how did she get out of the mountains?"

Pirulu took her to a larger village. They had buses and she took the bus to a city. The church people there paid for her plane ticket and she flew back to our country."

Pamela stood and with same air of authority Conchita had seen in her mother, declared, "Now that the missionary lady is here, Papá will come. I told you. Remember?"

"Will he? Will he?" Jenny asked.

"I don't know my children. We will see." Conchita smiled, yet behind her soft eyes, clouds of uncertainty began to emerge.

CHAPTER 8

Mel

The afternoon with Nicola had been an emotional one. Unlocking the door to her apartment Mel was surprised to hear the phone ring. Quickly stepping inside, she engaged the dead bolt and deposited her keys on the hook concealed inside the coat closet. When she lifted the receiver, her mother's voice assaulted her, "Marilyn, where have you been? I've been calling for at least two hours."

Mother, you know that I was at Monica's this afternoon meeting with the missionary, Nicola. I told you about it. Remember?"

"Of course I remember. Surely the meeting did not take this long. I've been waiting for a report. Is you father?…Well, is he?"

"I don't know. Nicola saw him when he and the others were first brought to the camp where she and her husband were being held captive. We know he survived the plane crash. At that time, he was in reasonable health."

"Good grief Marilynn, that was years ago, and you expect me to believe they've been alive all these years with no word," her mother interrupted.

Mel shook her head with disgust and went on. "Nicola was with Gavin, until recently. If he was alive certainly the others could be. Because Gavin's leg was shattered, he stayed in the camp where Nicola helped him recover. The others were taken somewhere else. There was never any news about them being killed, so she believes they could be alive."

"Well it sounds like this was a wild goose chase and you don't know anything more after talking to this woman," Charlotte Jameson continued in an accusatory tone. "Arthur says that if a woman could escape, surely the men could have escaped as well, if they were alive, that is."

Mel's voice sounded spent. "You know nothing of what we learned this afternoon. My gut tells me that Dad is alive and that the guerrillas have regrouped, and we'll hear soon about ransom demands."

"Is that what the missionary told you?"

"Not exactly. She did say that in the last few months new leaders and several newly trained rebels were brought into the camp where she was. These rebels brought renewed energy and excitement for their cause. It was then that Gavin was taken to be with other hostages, and I think those hostages include my father."

"I'm afraid that your thinking will only bring more disappointment." Her mother paused, then continued, "Arthur is picking me up in thirty minutes. We are trying that new restaurant near the shopping center. Why don't you join us?"

Determined not to meet this new boy friend and irked by her mother's disinterest in seeking out the truth about Ben Jameson, Mel fired, "I'm sure that Arthur would not enjoy hearing about this situation. No thank you. I'll pass. I wouldn't want to upset your plans. You go and have a nice meal with your new beau."

There was a click of her tongue and a sigh before Charlotte responded, "Well, I'll come by after dinner and we can talk, you can tell me everything. I should be there by 8:30 or so."

Mel could think of nothing she wanted less than spend the late evening telling her mother the details of the afternoon and answering her mother's probing questions.

Mel knew she should be hungry. She had not eaten since breakfast and barely nibbled on the sandwiches Monica had provided. But her appetite had bottomed out and she was not about to cook something and force it down. What did sound good was a heaping bowl of chocolate mocha ice cream.

She pushed the buttons on her CD player and heard the turn table position itself for the first CD. Though she enjoyed all types of music, tonight her mood called for movie favorites. She and her father had rented the movie Out of Africa and she had been hooked by the beauty of the scenery and the heart tugging story. The Out of Africa soundtrack always grabbed her with its haunting, lonely and longing melodic themes. They transported her to a faraway place, echoing her own longing, for what she was not quite sure. Tonight that faraway place seized her, even as each spoonful of ice cream caressed her palate and made its effort to comfort her.

As the evening began to close, the walls of her apartment made a few creaking sounds with the setting of the sun and the cooling of the day. The eerie drums resounded their bum, bum, bum behind the violins of the sound track. The music seemed an odd background for the scraping of Mel's spoon on the bottom of her bowl as she spooned the final meltings into her mouth. Ice cream had always been her comfort food, her dad's too. Long before she drank her first cup of coffee, she was hooked on mocha, her father's favorite. How many times had they plotted strategies and weighed decisions over a heaping bowl of ice cream or a double dip spilling the sides of a cone?

Her mother did not agree with all the sugar and cream used to make ice cream, and scolded Ben Jameson for spoiling his daughter and wrecking her appetite for nutritious food. The indulgence didn't seem to add an ounce of fat to Mel's body. She burned it all off running cross country and playing tennis in high school. Her mother couldn't understand how a person could put herself through such grueling physical workouts. Mel had no trouble pushing herself to better her times or her scores. Winning or beating another runner or tennis player was nice but was not her main goal. Bettering herself, striving to improve propelled her, and of course gaining her father's approval.

Her father made every effort to see all of her events. He scheduled most of his flights with CEO's and government officials around Mel's schedule. On occasion there were conflicts that he could not get around and then he always called her in the evening after an event for a report. She heard the pride in his voice even though his words were few, "I knew you could do it, you always give it everything you've got."

Her senior year she placed fifth in the Colorado prep finals running cross county and geared up for tennis season. Her goal was to make it to state in tennis, as well, and she did. The competition was particularly strong that year and she proudly achieved third place in singles. Disappointment hit hard when she and her partner lost to the top seeded doubles team in the championship. Over ice cream she and her father talked about the loss.

The conversation etched itself vividly in her mind. Ben Jameson's voice resonated its sonorous bass, "It's painful to feel such disappointment after training so hard, isn't it? I know that you and Kris counted on that championship."

"I wanted to do well in singles, but mostly I wanted the doubles championship. We're better players. We shouldn't have been the losers. We've beaten them before during regular season," Mel scorned.

Her father looked at her through the warmth of his eyes. "Well, Mel, that's life. On any given day, when there's competition, there will be a winner and a loser for that event. If you played tomorrow you might have captured the championship," Ben told his daughter. "Luck, an extra bit of adrenalin. Who knows what the difference is between one day and the next? But let's talk about winning and winners. You can be a winner and never win a game, you can win in life and never take home a trophy." Mel's father paused to dip his spoon into his ice cream.

"Yeah, Dad, I know it's your attitude, how you play the game…Just do your best. Besides fifteen years down the road, today won't matter one iota." Mel stirred her melting treat and watched it drip from her spoon.

"That's not true." Her father's voice was vehement. "Every experience you've had is tucked in your memory and those memories you've been making all these years built the integrity and strength you possess."

Mel stared into the soupy mixture, seeing only a blur. "What integrity? What strength?"

Ben took the bowl from her hands, placed in on the end table and seated himself on the couch beside her. He slid his arm around her shoulders and pulled her head to lean against his. "Well, Miss Independence, the integrity and strength that grew from every milestone you met. At two, you were already a runner, albeit with skinned elbows and knees. At four you were determined to learn to ride your bike. Only once did you hit the tree…when you pedaled and forgot to steer. Never again. At twelve you took over the neighbor boy's paper route when he was undergoing chemo for leukemia. You hated getting up early every morning and you really hated collecting the payments."

"How did you know? I never complained."

"Fathers notice things about their daughters."

The memories stung. Brought back to the present Mel sighed. *Oh, Dad, how much we've missed. Where are you? Will you ever come home? If you do will they have killed your spirit?*

Mel settled into her cushiony couch. Lying on her side, her head against the pillow, she pulled her knees toward her chin. She let the mournful Out of Africa music wash over her, consume her. The words "music of good bye" wrenched her. She did not hold back the tears. The last she heard before sleep overcame her was the haunting flute capturing the main theme.

⁂

IN HER HAZE THE RINGING phone besieged her. Even if she wanted to, she couldn't seem to pull herself out of her sleep. Finally, the answering machine picked up and she roused enough to hear her mother's voice, more gentle this time.

Marilyn, Marilyn, are you there? Sorry our dinner took a little longer than I thought. It's getting late and I've decided to come over in the morning, dear. Sleep tight."

Mel twisted her watch so that she could read the time. Almost nine. She pulled the afghan from the back of the couch and cuddled it around her and closed her eyes again. Tonight, sleep was her escape.

Mel rested fitfully. A kaleidoscope of activity flew through her dreams. A man who might have been her father jumped into a lake, then he was in a boat. It capsized and Mel saw the long haired and bearded man pull his emaciated body atop the sinking vessel. Mel floated into the air, maneuvering like a sky diver splayed in a free fall and made her way over the sinking vessel, hovering above. But there was nothing left of the man or the boat. She continued to fly, her body soaring over the cushions of air.

Above the trees and into the neighborhood of her growing-up years she flew. People below her worked in gardens, mowed lawns, jogged on a path or removed groceries from a van. Why aren't you all flying she thought? It's so peaceful up here. Why am I the only one who can fly? It's not hard. You just catch an air cushion and keep your balance, and swoop here and there. She continued to soar this way and that, knowing she had to come down sometime. Making one more pass over the neighborhood, she lifted herself over the power lines, then slid closer and closer to a landing spot. When her feet touched solid ground, she lamented the end of her flight and wondered when she would fly again.

The shrillness of the phone's ringing disturbed her dream. She jumped to a sitting position, shook off the fogginess and grasped the receiver. Her hello came out much like a croak.

"Hey Mel, it's Erik. I hope I didn't call too late. I…well you've been on my mind…and the meeting with the missionary. How'd it go?"

Disbelief sent a shockwave through her. A phone call from a man? Men rarely called her. She had a way of blasting out the message Not interested, not available. And though she and Erik had had a pleasant interchange on the way to Chicago yesterday, the return trip had been all business between Captain Erik King and her.

"Went fine, I guess. Nicola is a pretty brave woman. Strong too, I'd say. She went through a lot during the years of captivity and finally things went her way when she was able to escape.

Did she bring good news about your father?"

"Yes and no. She has no first-hand knowledge of his whereabouts and his situation, but before she escaped, she thought something big was about to happen. Maybe there'll be some negotiations to release hostages. Whether my father is one of them, who knows?"

Mel explained more of what Nicola had told them. Erik listened intently and asked questions for clarification. He was easy to talk to, she thought. Then she mentally berated herself for letting her guard down and tried to take the warmth from her voice. She failed and they continued the interchange, genially, despite the subject matter.

Finally," Erik said. "The whole thing's incredible. Sounds like something out of a movie script, rather than everyday life of Americans. What's next?'

Mel shifted the receiver to the other ear before she answered. "Nicola wants to stay out of the limelight. What happened is past and gone. She wants to get on with her life, continue with her missionary work. At this point she doesn't know where, with her husband gone. It probably won't be in Colombia"

"I can understand her feelings, but you can't just drop the whole thing when your father's a prisoner."

Yes, I need to think that way. Dad is a prisoner somewhere. He will come home.

"I think the first step is to contact government officials, give them all we know. And go from there. McCrae financed the expedition and plans to go to the state capital, meet officials, get knowledge about the protocol of such things."

"Sounds like a good place to start…Mel…Mel, turn on our TV, channel 9 news…hurry…"

Mel tossed the receiver aside wondering what the urgency in his words and voice was about. Once the TV power was on it took a few seconds for the picture to come into focus. Rolling across the screen Mel made out the message <u>Breaking News Bulletin-Colombian Rebels Seek Exchange for Hostages-Video Received with Demands</u>. Two masked guerrillas, dressed in camouflage, rifles slung over their shoulders came into view. The news bulletin music continued to blast while the guerrillas shouted their demands in Spanish. Even if Mel understood Spanish the audio of the video was too distorted to make sense of it.

The newscaster's voice punched out the words. "Breaking news just received. Government officials released a video from a group associated with FARC, the Revolutionary Armed Forces of Colombia, demanding liberation of imprisoned rebels in exchange for an undetermined number of hostages, some of whom are believed to be U.S. citizens. No word concerning the identity of the hostages has been received, but our newsroom has revealed that four Colorado residents went missing in December over five years ago. Ben Jameson, a well-known pilot for numerous government officials and high powered CEOs piloted the plane when contact was lost somewhere in Colombian air space. Others traveling with Ben Jameson were Gavin Humphreys, Miguel Vasquez and Randolph Rabinowitz. It is unknown whether there is any connection with these missing men and hostages being held in Colombia. We will keep you informed of any update. Stay tuned…In today's stock market…" Mel clicked off the TV.

All the air went out of her. Involuntary, sluggish movements propelled her back to the couch. She sat hard and air squished from the leather cushion. Her body shivered. At last Mel grasped the dropped receiver. "I heard Erik, I heard. Oh, Erik…"

Racine

SPUNKY'S DOG-SENSE HAD SMELLED THE worry, confusion and uncertainty oozing from his mistress the moment she entered the house. Racine tossed her caftan on the sofa and looked right through Spunky despite his usual routine of tricks.

The ritual began with some yips of greeting and continued through several circles of tail-chasing, a group of hops on his back feet—while his front feet pawed the air, three or four roll-overs, and ended with Spunky back on his hand feet doing a kind of dance, side to side and back to front.

Still waiting for the typical ruffling of his downy coat, the superb catch as he leapt into her arms, and the smothering of coos and kisses, he followed her from room to room. In the bathroom Racine ignored his attentive perch on the peach colored throw rug at her feet. She failed to notice the quizzical cock of his head, but instead braced her hands against the vanity and stared into the well-lighted mirror. Her murmur resounded against the tiled walls.

"Racine, ole gal you look like something the cat dragged in. And you feel like it too. No shower tonight."

She smeared a thick, oily cream over her face, then used a sopping washcloth to remove the layers of tinted foundation, lip stick, blush, mascara and eye shadow. They came off onto the cloth in a rich shade of mud. She rinsed again and again until her face glowed almost crimson in contrast to her emerald eyes. She squeezed a worm of pink moisturizer from the wide, white tube, and with her fingertips, massaged it into every cranny of her face. After her teeth had their thorough brushing, she spat into the sink with such force that some of the cloudy spittle sprayed the mirror. "Oh, well," she said still unaware of the Lhasa Apso's watchful eye.

Spunky trotted along behind as Racine entered her bedroom. He used every bit of spring his legs could muster to jump into the Queen Anne chair beside the lamp table. Again, his posture maintained curious alertness as his head flipped this way and that keeping up with Racine's back and forth movements.

Usually tidy and organized, Racine had a particular routine for dressing and undressing, for putting away her clothes, for organizing which items to place in the laundry. Tonight, her routine was random and disorderly. A shoe kicked off here, jewelry piled over there on her nightstand. Items to be hung up and those to be laundered dropped in mixed bundles on the scattered rugs. Racine pulled a mint green nightgown over her head, smoothed the softness over her tummy and sat on the bed, staring at the floor. It was as if the numbness of the day had numbed her whole being. She didn't want to do anything. She didn't want to think. She didn't want to plan.

Spunky's muted whine went unnoticed as Racine sat frozen in a stare. He could stand it no more. With a soaring leap he left his perch and landed with a thump on the soft throw rug at Racine's feet. He wriggled and twisted, his tail wagging at high speed. He licked Racine's toes. He did his roll over trick again and again. He danced and eyed her coquettishly, his pink tongue hanging happily from a smiling mouth.

The vacant gaze on Racine's face began to transform. A smile eased onto her parted lips. "You little scamp. What do you think you're doing? Won't you let me feel sorry for myself, huh? Well, come on up."

Spunky's leap aimed for Racine's lap. With a little assistance he made it. He settled himself in the crook of her arm and lifted his eyes, peering through his shaggy mop to meet hers. Round as marbles they held a questioning melancholy.

"You worry about me, don't you my funny munkin? Tell you what, you sleep up here tonight. Racine patted the satin covered pillow beside her. That's all it took. Spunky scuttled onto the pillow, stretching out all comfortable and pleased.

Exhausted as she felt, sleep came slowly. What would it be like to have Randy home? Surely he was alive. Spunky had filled a bit of the hole left by the loss of Randy, but as cute and clever as Spunky was, an animal could never replace one's own flesh and blood. She would do anything, promise anything if only Randy was alive and could be found and brought home.

Throughout the hours Racine's trusty friend remained beside her. When she roused during the night because of her restlessness and looked in his direction, she saw the whites of his open eyes peeking through his spiky bangs.

Just before sunup, Racine's sleep came solid and deep, so much so, that when the clock radio signaled wakeup time, it took her several minutes to come awake. As much as she would have liked to sleep a few extra hours, there was much to do, so she'd better get organized. She snatched her journal from the bedside table and propped herself against her lofty pillows. Yesterday's entry had not been finished but would have to wait until she had more time to do justice to the meeting with Nicola, the missionary.

With pen poised on the page Racine scratched the date in the upper right corner of the page and began her list for the day. Remembering McCrae's call on his cell phone and his startling last words Something serious has happened at home, prompted her to list "call McCrae" as number one. As she penned a two and circled it, the phone rang. She stretched to grasp the receiver and the journal slipped from her lap.

"Hello?"

"Racine, its Mel. Sorry to call so early. If I remember, because of late hours of the restaurant you're not an early riser." Not waiting for a response Mel went right on. "Have you heard the news? It was on TV last night and it's on the front page this morning. They're saying that Colombian Rebels are demanding a release of imprisoned rebels in exchange for captives they are holding. They think some are Americans. No names have been released. But it has to include our men."

"Lordy be! No, I hadn't heard. Went to bed early. It was a gut-wrenching day."

"I know what you mean," Mel responded. "Though there is very little concrete information, surely this is connected to Nicola's story."

"It's got to be," Racine agreed. "I wonder if McCrae knows. I'll call him. He'll know what to do."

"I hope so. If Dad and Randy are among the hostages, we can't let them stay one more day in that God forsaken jungle. Four years and ten months is enough. Those crummy militants should get pushed off a cliff. How dare they make hostages of our men."

Racine flipped her covers back and slid her legs off the bed. "How can people be so cruel to other humans? It's damn criminal and immoral. I'm to blame about Randy, though, nobody else."

"You can't say that. You had nothing to do with shooting the plane."

"Mel, he's my son and I shouldn't have let him go. Fantastic opportunity, fantastic experience or no— if I begged him to stay, he would have. I let him miss the prime of his life."

"Racine, life's unpredictable. We never know what's ahead. We couldn't predict the outcome of the expedition. You're not at fault," Mel said emphatically. "Can't help being ticked with my mother, though."

"I don't understand, Mel. What about?"

"All these years…Mom's never been interested in another man. Now she's met this doctor and he's all she can talk about."

"You don't say. How'd she react to Nicola's story?" Racine asked.

"I gave her the basics. She's coming over this morning to hear the details. She's in denial. Thinks they can't be alive. Now with this hostage thing hitting the news…Well, it ought to be an interesting conversation."

"Life's timetable gets screwed up, doesn't it? Ironic that your mom just met someone." Racine offered. "You wonder what she must be feeling, don't you?"

"Oh, la dee da. That's her feeling. At least we can't talk too long; I have a flight out this afternoon."

Racine smiled briefly with a fleeting thought of Charlotte Jameson and her busy life with women's groups and various community activities. She seemed to keep right on going when Ben disappeared, sad, but not visibly shaken. Maybe she was a kind of la dee da woman. "I'd better get a move on. Have a good flight," she said to Mel, "and thank you so much for the call. We will get our guys home, we will."

Hanging up the phone the colorful restaurant owner scooped up her doggie and gave him some good loving. Barefooted and in her nightgown, she padded into the kitchen. Ruffling through the telephone directory, she sought out the Mc's and dialed McCrae. Following the sixth ring a soft voice began. The voice threadlike, included a hint of southern, Racine thought. "Hello, you have reached the residence of Larry and Chantel McCrae. We appreciate your call. Please leave your name and number. Have a delightful day."

During the last part of the message, Racine heard a click, and another woman's voice came on the line. This voice was low and tentative. "Hello, hello."

Racine explained who she was and that she was a long-time friend of Larry McCrae's, then asked where Mr. McCrae could be reached.

The pause on the other line puzzled Racine, but she waited and finally heard a sigh and a response. The woman brutalized Racine's name, but it made no difference as she listened.

"Well, Ms. Rubinowitz, I'm Rosie. I come in on Thursdays to do the housecleaning. I usually don't answer the phone, but I wondered if it might be him callin'. It's just such a tragedy, you know, and I'll do everything I can to help Mr. McCrae. The bedding needs changing, you know. Her whole system let go on it."

What was the woman talking about? Was this the something serious that happened at home? Chantel got sick in bed and needed cleaning up? Where was McCrae? That's it. He had to take her to the hospital.

When Rosie paused, Racine took the opportunity to ask, "Is Mrs. McCrae alright? Is Mr. McCrae with her?"

"Well no, she's not alright. I suppose he's with her. You being a good friend, I can tell you. Guess, while Mr. McCrae was gone yesterday afternoon, the Misses took a bunch of pills."

Racine felt sick to her stomach and leaned her head against her opened palm. Oh, poor McCrae. The solemn voice went on.

"Well, her neighbor was bringin' over an apple pie and when no one answered she let herself in. Found her layin' in the sunroom. Near dead, I guess. Called the ambulance right away."

"Oh, how devastating…she's still in the hospital then?"

"Oh, no. She didn't make it. Guess she's at the undertakers. Least that's where Mr. McCrae is. Be back when arrangements are made, I reckon."

What should she do? Would he want a friend there when he got home? Or would it be intrusive for her to go? Yeah it would be intrusive. McCrae had so much on his plate and surely didn't need this hostage deal in the morning news to add to it. If the two of them hadn't sat in McCrae's car and talked, would he have gotten home in time to save her?

Racine shuddered at the thought. Maybe so.

CHAPTER 9

Monica

Monica's sleep had been restless. Her leg, immovable in the awkward cast made comfort for any period of time impossible. The last time she looked at the clock radio, the numbers 4:30 glowed back at her. Now they glimmered 6:45. At least the last couple of hours had been more restful. Awareness overtook her. She felt Peter nestled against her right side, holding her hand. How long had he been like this? Did his nearness have anything to do with the calming of her troubled sleep?

Monica turned her head to face her husband. She wondered how long he had been looking at her. His eyes held an air of uneasiness, but his smile conveyed warmth. She smiled back and squeezed his hand. "Sorry, I just crashed last night. Didn't feel like talking," Monica said, forcing the hoarseness from her voice in the early morning. "Hope you understand."

Peter's nod said, 'It's O.K'. His shoulders heaved with the intake of a deep breath before he spoke. "Monica, I don't know all that you learned yesterday, but I saw the letters that Gavin wrote to you. I put them on the dresser. He is alive then?"

"Nicola thinks so. She and Gavin were in the same camp until a few months ago. I haven't read the letters, only the first couple of pages. I was sapped from hearing about the kidnapping. Peter." Monica continued, "It was hard to hear what Gavin had to endure and I couldn't take in anymore." Her voice softened as she said, "At this point I don't know what to feel, what to think."

Peter released Monica's hand and planted his elbow on the pillow to prop up his head. Some of the wild spikes of his ask blond hair poked into the air, while others spilled over his forehead. The little-boy disheveled look had not touched Monica so much as at this very moment. She bit into her lip and awkwardly reached her arm across her body to touch the wayward spikes.

"Monica," Peter started, "there was news about the Colombian kidnappers last night on the TV. I saw it before I came up to bed. Didn't want to disturb you, but you should know."

Monica struggled to lift herself to a sitting position. "What…what did it say?" Monica stuttered.

While Peter told her of the news bulletin and the guerrilla's demands Monica felt a flush overcome her. She fanned her face with her hand to diminish the heat and asked, "Do they know who the hostages are?"

"Apparently not. You know how the news is. There's speculation that they include Ben, Gavin, Randy and Miguel, since they've been missing in Colombia all these years. But the Colombians didn't give names nor did they say how many hostages there were."

Talk stilled between them, but unfinished issues hung over them and they kept their eyes focused on each other. Monica though there was a kind of sadness in Peter's eyes. Did he see the uncertainty in hers? Finally, she spoke. "When…if…Gavin comes back, what will happen to us? Will our two years of marriage have been a farce? Nonexistent?"

Peter shook his head but said nothing.

Monica thought back over their marriage. When there were glitches, Peter did not see them or glossed over them. Mostly he was oblivious to her feelings. With Peter everything was always upbeat. He definitely was not a brooding person like she tended to be, and sometimes his good humor irritated her. It irked her that he seemed so satisfied with life and saw no reason to improve or change their relationship. It irked her that he did not see her own dissatisfaction, that he did not see how unappreciated and taken for granted she felt, that he did not search for something deeper with her. Peter was more talkative, was more social, and had more friends than Gavin had, yet with both Gavin and Peter, Monica had the feeling that everything in her life was superficial.

But, in the last few days things had been a little different with Peter. He was more attentive concerning her broken leg. He brought home take-out so she wouldn't have to cook. And when he learned about Nicola and the possibility that Gavin was alive, he seemed to be standing in the wing, waiting to be of whatever help and support he could be.

"What are you thinking? Can you tell me?" Monica finally asked of her husband.

Silence.

"Talk to me. I need you to talk to me."

"I'm trying not to think too much." Peter stared. "Guess I feel that you hold the strings and will determine what happens to us. Like you said, maybe we aren't even married if you're still married to Gavin."

The warmth in his eyes dissolved when he went on. "You've never talked about you and Gavin. I don't know how things were with you two. Never thought about measuring up to him, being compared to him. He was gone, but now I don't know what to expect, who you feel more love and loyalty for."

Monica heard offhanded indifference in his voice and pounded her fist against the coverlet. "Damn, it's not just about love and loyalty."

"Yeah? What's it about?" Peter asked as he leveled a glare at Monica.

"It's also about what's right, what's just, not hurting anybody," Monica burst out.

"So, your first husband's gone through his horrific ordeal. Now it's Monica's duty to make it all up to him and help him live happily ever after, while Peter-come-lately is left in the dust. That won't hurt, will it?"

Peter's tone of bitterness stung, and Monica shot back, "I didn't say that. Why are we fighting, anyway?"

"It was you who kept saying 'talk to me', besides, I didn't know we were fighting. Anytime I say what I think, you think we're fighting."

Peter looked away avoiding Monica's eyes, while Monica stared at the ceiling. One by one, tears trickled down her cheeks. As her nose began to drip she sniffed, then opened her mouth to get a breath. "Just look at me," she said. "I'm a mess."

Peter slipped his arm around her shoulders and hugged her to him. "You're not a mess."

Through her own blur, Monica looked into her husband's eyes. She gasped in another breath while the tears came in the torrent of a storm.

He rocked her with him. "It's been rough, Babe. First a crummy broken leg due to something I did. Then I wasn't at the hospital much, couldn't stay home with you your first day out. You probably think I didn't care. To be honest I just can't bear to be with somebody that's suffering, and of course I had that big deal I had to cinch at work. And now this thing about Gavin."

Monica started, "It's not…"

"Shh," Peter pressed a finger to her lips, then continued, "I also know how independent you are, and I didn't want to make you feel otherwise. You always seem to be able to handle everything. That's one of the things I noticed about you, first off…your confidence and strength."

Between sniffs, Monica blurted, "I'm not all that confident. Sometimes I need you to hold me. I need to know that you love me. I'm not all that good a catch, you know. You could have had any cute chick."

Exasperation flooded Peter's words. "Oh Babe, I never wanted some flakey cute chick. What do you mean you're not all that good a catch? You have character; there's not a lazy bone in you. I appreciate your high values, not to mention your good bod." His voice softened as he said, "I do love you. You know that."

Monica wanted to say back that she loved him, too. Why couldn't she? Was it because Gavin might be in the picture? Was she still irked about the stupid little things that bugged her about Peter and unwilling to let them go? She wasn't sure. Instead she merely nodded her head and faced him with a meek smile.

Peter eased her head onto the pillow and stretched out beside her. He continued to hold her as close as her bulky leg would allow. Finally, Peter's hushed voice said, "Would you like to see what they are saying on the morning news about the hostage situation?"

Monica nodded her head in the affirmative and dabbed at the wetness of her eyes and cheeks with the sleeve of her silky pajamas. Peter grabbed the TV remote from the bedside table and pressed the on button. The seven o'clock news was in progress.

"Now we bring you our mobile unit standing by at the Marks Hotel in downtown Denver," said the news commentator, "where Gail Richards has more information concerning the hostage situation. Gail what can you tell us?"

"Thank you, Steve," said Gail as she came into view outside of the hotel. "We have word that Nicola Kaplin, a Colombian missionary, who was missing for nearly five years, has arrived here in Denver. Nicola, and her husband Rick Kaplin, spent four years under the auspices of World Wide Christian Outreach in the Colombian jungles before their disappearance. World Wide Christian Outreach verified the return of Mrs. Kaplin in their weekly publication, but no one in the agency has returned our calls. We do not have information about her husband, but Mrs. Kaplin spent the night at the hotel and is reported to be in seclusion. We do however have a short clip of her arrival at the hotel last night."

The scene cut to the underground parking garage where cameras captured the form of a female stepping from a taxi. The face of a tall woman with long silver hair draped over her left shoulder stared wide-eyed in near horror from the television screen. A young man in a bright blue windbreaker slipped into the picture at her side. He gripped a microphone and leaned toward her. His voice was smooth like flowing hot caramel.

"Mrs. Kaplin, I'd like to ask you a few questions if I may." The woman flinched and a hand flew to block her face. The man in the blue windbreaker went on. "Is it true that you were held hostage in Colombia by FARC guerrillas?"

The woman stood her full height and stared into the room from the TV screen. "Yes, that is true," said the woman in a hoarseness that was barely audible.

The caramel voice continued, "You've been held all these years then?" When he saw the unhurried nod of the woman he asked, "Can you tell us about your release?"

There was pride in her stance as she answered, "There was no release. I escaped."

"Mrs. Kaplin, you must have been very brave and resourceful. Are you aware that just today a group of Colombian guerrillas released demands for the release of imprisoned rebels in exchange for a handful of FARC hostages?"

The woman appeared to be taking in the question. "No, I have not heard of these demands."

The interviewer continued the questioning. "Were you kept with other American hostages? If so, do you think they could be involved in the exchange if it is carried out?"

"I had contact with four Americans, but I do not know of their whereabouts, whether they're alive, whether they might be part of an exchange." The woman's words were wrapped in weariness. "Please, step away. I need my privacy. I need rest."

Gail Richards returned to the screen and spoke. "We'll keep you posted concerning further developments and hope to talk more fully with Mrs. Kaplin. In the meantime, we also await forthcoming information from the FARC leadership.

Monica sat and scooted herself back against the headboard of the bed. "Confound those news people," she said, her arms flailing the air. "Nicola was afraid of getting hounded when any word of her escape got out. Did you see the look on her face? She's gone through so much. Can't they let her have some peace?"

Peter moved to sit cross-legged beside his wife. "Anything titillating makes the news. Journalists and the public eat it up. Sorry Babe, that's part of our world." He tapped his knuckles against her cast, then added, "I just hope you're not next."

"Me too. I can just see it now, some cameraman following me around the grocery store, me on my crutches trying to hobble away…Actually, I could be quite dangerous with those sticks." Monica laughed for the first time since the accident.

Peter took Monica's hand and kissed each finger. *He's never done that before. How nice. I do need Peter here. I think he senses that. What's ahead? What will happen if Gavin is alive and comes back?*

She gazed into Peter's eyes and couldn't read their message.

Conchita

MONDAY MORNING, ACTUALLY, EVERY SCHOOL morning, found Conchita bustling to get the lunch boxes filled, breakfast on the table and her active children ready for school before she headed off to Quail Creek Care Center. This morning was especially frustrating. Their new Habitat for Humanity home was such a novelty that the twins wanted to play in their new room rather than get ready for school Conchita found Jack rearranging his treasures—his two bats, a ball glove and the picture of his father in a pitching stretch, wearing a Colorado Rockies uniform.

He looked a bit sheepish as his mother entered the room. "Jack, what's got into you? You're still in your pajamas and breakfast is waiting. Jason said the bus arrives at the bus stop in fifteen minutes and it's a block away."

OK, I'll hurry. You do think my father is alive, don't you? That he'll be coming home?"

The coming home part cut into her. This is our home. He doesn't have a home. Then guilt set in and she said to her son, "I just don't know, but we can't think about it now. You can't miss the bus. Now hurry."

It was a miracle when the kids bounded out of the house, jackets and lunch boxes in two, with barely a minute to spare.

Conchita stacked the breakfast dishes in the sink, grabbed her purse and headed toward the Saturn parked in the attached garage.

She noticed that the car's back door had been left ajar. She pulled in fully open to give it a good slam. "Kids," she said. Turning the key in the ignition, she heard the engine sputter and then nothing. It had threatened to die before, but each time she had given it one more try, and it had taken hold. Not this time. The car was more than five years old and the battery had never been replaced. No doubt the dome light had drained what little juice was left.

She rushed into the house and dialed Greg's number. Once Greg answered, Conchita blurted, "Hi Greg, I'm so sorry to bother you, but my battery's down and I can't start my car. Can you help me?"

Yes, of course he would help her and said he would be right there. When he arrived, he suggested it would be faster for him to take her to work in his truck. Getting the car pushed out of the garage, jumper cables attached properly in order to get the car started would take more time. Using a quick route Greg had Conchita to work only two minutes late. In spite of her protests he insisted on towing her car to his garage where he could check the cables for corrosion and test the battery. If she needed a new one, he promised to find a cheap one or a rebuilt one. He would have her car ready to go by the end of her shift. It would be parked it in the Quail Creek lot at the end of her shift so she could pick up her kids on time. And that was that, there would be no protesting on her part.

"You are a lifesaver, Greg Hope," Conchita said as she climbed from the truck. "I'll pay you of course, though it might not be until the end of the week when I get paid. I hope that's OK. I owe you. Will you join us for supper tonight?"

"It's a deal. Now don't you go worrying about costs. You deserved to have a good day." He waved her on, then waited until she went inside before he left Quail Creek.

Sure enough, just as Greg said, the car was in good running order and parked in the lot when Conchita finished her workday. She picked up the car keys at the main desk where Greg had left them and hurried off to get the children. She was grateful for the after-school program for kids whose parents needed some type of day care in the late afternoon.

Unless she had the day off, they always attended it. The children seemed happy to do craft and art activities and work on their reading skills.

Conchita's pride blossomed to see the five-year-old twins reading simple books already. The school even provided mats for sleeping and Conchita knew that often the twins needed a rest after the long day. Her schedule enabled her to pick up the children around 4:30. With the car running well, she was right on time.

At home, Jason sat at the curb waiting for their arrival. Conchita said to herself, "It's the neighborhood boy with the odd mother who never seems to get out of her dirty blue robe." Should she offer him an after-school snack again? He seemed almost malnourished. Not this time, she decided.

Jumping from the car, Jack ran toward his new friend, "Hi, Jason. You wanta play?"

Jason worked his toes in the dirt, not yet sprouting the newly planted seeds and looked up with a shy grin. "Sure."

Conchita emerged from the garage saying, "Jack, you know…"

"Yeah, Mom, I know. I have to change my clothes and help clean up the kitchen first. Then I can play. Can't I Mom?"

"It'll be at least fifteen minutes but yes you can play."

Just before six Greg arrived carting in two bags of groceries. Conchita eyed him in exasperation, "What's all this? I'm cooking. You don't need to bring food."

"Well," Greg said in his country twang, "I don't want to eat you out of house and home. Besides, this is more a housewarming gift."

Greg would bring something practical, Conchita thought. They were alike in that way. They would all enjoy the fresh fruits and vegetables that Conchita could rarely afford. She ooed and awed over the red juicy strawberries, plump oranges, purple grapes, ready to ripen bananas, and crisp apples. She washed the cucumbers, green peppers, romaine lettuce, celery and broccoli, then tucked them in the vegetable crisper thinking that it could not hold one more thing.

As Conchita bustled around the kitchen, Greg sat at the table smiling at her quick movements. "Thanks for all the wonderful goodies," Conchita said, her face radiating its perpetual sunbeam. She danced to him and made a twirl that landed her on his lap. Greg wrapped his arms around her to steady her tipsiness and the pair laughed. "Didn't quite mean to land like that. Guess I tripped on my own two feet," she said, and then wondered if it was an accident.

Greg's arms remained clasped around her, and for a moment she closed her eyes relishing the strength and comfort she felt. Goose bumps crawled over her body and she jumped up, embarrassed by her foolishness.

The moment passed and the couple moved on to polite talk about the car, about work, and about the children being so pokey getting ready for school. Conchita checked the casserole baking in the oven and surmised that it would be ready in ten minutes. The table was set. The tortillas were ready. She headed for the door to call the children to come in and wash up.

Greg caught her arm, gripping it gently. "Before you call the children, sit down for a minute. There's something I want to tell you."

Surprised by the seriousness in his tone, she sat down. "What is it?" she asked.

"I don't suppose you read the paper or watched TV today."

"Sometimes I glance at the paper at work. But not today," Conchita said shaking her head. "Why?"

Greg told her about the guerrillas and the demand for a prisoner and hostage exchange. Conchita looked puzzled, then asked, "Did they say who these hostages are?"

"No," Greg started, "but I have a buddy, well we went to school together and have always kept touch. Anyway, he's high up in the Pentagon, and I got a hold of him today."

"You did?" Conchita was more puzzled. "Guess you've had a busy day. Does he know anything?" Conchita wasn't sure she liked where this was going. What if one of these hostages was Miguel? How was she going to handle it? And here was Greg willing to find out what he could for her.

"They are keeping things fairly hush, hush at the moment. They knew about the guerrilla demands before the news reported it and wanted to check it out and see if it seemed legitimate." Greg's easy drawl quickened as he said, "No names have been verified and everything is pretty classified. I got the feeling that at least some of the hostages were from Ben Jameson's group." His eyes flickered as he continued. "He promised that when there is clearance, he will let me know the situation before it gets reported nationally. I hope you don't mind if I called my friend. I just wanted to help."

Conchita's wide eyes darted with uncertainty. "As I said this morning, you're always my lifesaver. Thank you."

Mel

MEL FOLDED HER UNDERWEAR, A bra, a running outfit, jeans with a shirt, and some lounging clothes, that also served for sleeping, then shoved them into her flight bag. She needed to be at Denver International Airport by 1:45 for the 3:00 flight to Atlanta. The return hop the next morning was scheduled for 10:00. She'd fly with Erik King again. She had been prepared to continue her hateful feelings toward him on the flight to Chicago, but in the air, she had found him warm and charming.

Mel remembered the lump in her throat when Erik told her about losing his father in Laos. He was only four. She could tell that he had great admiration for his mother and had been there for her as she suffered through breast cancer and two mastectomies.

Apparently, she had been valiant in her struggle to survive, only to lose that battle less than a year ago. She remembered his answer to her question, "Why isn't there a Mrs. King?"

"Mom needed me."

Not many men would put their lives on hold to care for a mother, Mel thought. She couldn't believe he called last night to see how the visit with Nicola had gone. The call had taken on another avenue when Erik alerted her about the news bulletin concerning the hostages.

Still, she was wary about him and his motives. She had labeled his previous actions as sexual harassment, when perhaps he had been attracted to her and was being a little flirtatious. A long time ago, Mel had decided that flirting was frivolous and beneath her. She pushed everyone aside when she detected such behavior.

The doorbell jangled, interrupting Mel's thoughts. Before she was able to reach the door, the doorbell played its routine two more times. "Mother, you are so impatient," Mel said out loud, then unlocked the door bolts and drew the door open.

"Are you ready? It's already 8:00 and we need to get off if we're going to have enough time for a good visit over breakfast," Charlotte Jameson said in her mothering tone.

Mel wished she could feel the same admiration for her mother that Erik had felt for his. Then guilt crawled into her mind. *What if mother was gone tomorrow and I could never again see her face, hear her voice? I need to appreciate her more. At least she's alive. I have her. And maybe I will have my father again. Oh, let it be so.*

"Yes, mother. I'm ready. Where are we going?" Mel said trying to give her voice more lightness than she felt.

"To the Egg and I," she replied. "I've got our names on the waiting list.

The restaurant opened for breakfast and lunch only, and people were forever lined up waiting for a table. A couple of women, also waiting for a table eased toward Charlotte, their eyes flashing. The short, round one spurted, "The doctor is quite the gentleman, isn't he? It was nice to meet him at the new restaurant last night. You make a dashing couple." The woman turned toward her companion, not waiting for a response from Charlotte.

The companion peered over the reading glasses perched on her nose and spoke, "Charlotte, surely you know something about the hostage situation in Colombia. It's all over the news. Have you been contacted? Tell us. Is Ben one of them?"

Mel's chest heaved in frustration and she stepped away from her mother, not wanting to be drawn into the conversation. She heard her mother say, "Yes, Arthur is a gem. We have so much in common. Goodness, I know nothing about the hostage situation. The news media is out of control. Who knows what's what?"

"Jameson, party of two," a voice announced. And Charlotte and Mel left the two women wondering.

Seated, they perused the menus and ordered. "Marilyn," her mother said, "you don't believe this hostage situation has anything to do with your father, do you? After all these years it seems highly unlikely that the men are alive and only now the guerrillas want to negotiate an exchange. That would have happened shortly after they were taken hostage. Why wait all this time? These must be different people."

Mel chewed on her lip before she began, "Now that you've met Arthur," Mel said the name with malice, "you don't want my father to come back, do you?"

Appearing startled by the question, Charlotte said, "You're wrong. Arthur has nothing to do with it. I'm trying to be logical and realistic. I would be thrilled to know your father is alive."

Mel shook her head. "I doubt it. Besides, I told you the reason for the delay. The leader was killed and there was inner fighting and turmoil. The sect was in limbo for years. With new leadership, things changed. Nicola saw Gavin alive a few months ago. Why not the others?"

Charlotte impatiently tapped the handle of her spoon on the table. "I just don't want you to get your hopes up and be devastated once again. It was tough on us both back then, not knowing what happened. We lived through it, and I don't want you to have to live through such anguish again."

Mel breathed in a deep and exasperated breath just as the phone on her belt vibrated. "I think I'll take this Mom," she said, glad for the diversion.

Mel's eyes shifted and blinked as she listened to the caller on the other end.

"What is it Marilyn?" Charlotte queried.

Mel dismissed her question with a wave of her hand, then pressed her finger against her lips in a shushing gesture. Finally she said, "How tragic. Only saw her once. That was before the trip. She was beautiful, but frail even then." Mel paused. "Yes, I'd like to go. Particularly for McCrae. You say the memorial is in the morn? Heck, Racine I won't be back. Sorry. Can't go."

Charlotte listened as Mel told her about Larry McCrae's wife, that Chantel had taken enough pills to snuff out her life, that the neighbor had found her in a coma and called McCrae.

"Racine feels pretty bad. She and McCrae stayed after meeting with the missionary and talked. Then McCrae got an emergency call. Maybe if McCrae had been home things might have been different."

Charlotte stared into her lap, saying nothing. The silent moment was interrupted by the server who brought plates of whole wheat toast and omelets, loaded with sautéed vegetables. Assured that the food, coffee and water were to their liking, the server left.

"Why would a person take her own life?" Charlotte asked quietly. "I've never understood it."

"You've never wondered if life was worth living, Mother, wondered if you wanted to go on tomorrow and tomorrow?" Mel posed.

Charlotte looked up stunned by her daughter's question. "No, never. But…you have?"

"There are times," Mel admitted, "when the black cloud of doom seems too heavy, when crawling out from under it can be hard. And when you get out…to what?"

"Huh," Mel's mother started, "it's like your dad. As confident and powerful as he was, he had his gloomy times. But you? I had no idea. I wish you would open your life to more friendships and activities. Maybe a man. You are such a beautiful and intelligent woman. Even finding a running partner would be good."

Mel had to force herself to keep from rolling her eyes as her mother continued, "Anyone would get depressed focusing only on flying or running. Everyone needs several baskets in life and shouldn't put all her eggs in only one."

Charlotte pushed a piece of omelet around her plate, then speared it and put it into her mouth. Swallowing, she asked warily, "You would never take your own life, Marilyn…would you?"

"Of course not." Oh, why had she confided in her mother? "I just wanted to make a point. If your life is miserable, your health is deteriorating and there is nothing to look forward to, why would a person want to go on?" Mel pointed her fork toward her mother. "Everyone, except you with your la dee da life, has down times. No doubt Mrs. McCrae was in a hopeless place, both physically and emotionally. Ending her life was the only way to stop the pain."

"I guess we are at a place that we must agree that we disagree. Isn't that so?" Charlotte asked with a wink that was meant to lighten the moment.

"I guess I understand despair. Yes, we must agree that we disagree." said Mel. *And just about every other issue, my lack of friends, an interesting social life, a man in my life.*

During the next hour they avoided talking about Chantel's suicide, the hostages in Colombia or the possibility that their men were alive. Neither was able to finish her food. But Mel tanked up on water and Charlotte drank three cups of coffee, while the conversation focused on the doctor. He had a son who was now single after a gut-wrenching divorce.

"Fortunately, they didn't have children," Charlotte explained. "Apparently the wife wanted to go to New York to pursue a modeling career. Perhaps the two of you can meet. He's an outdoor person, very athletic as you are. You need to get out more with others."

Intending to squelch the possibility of being paired up with the doctor's son, Mel exaggerated the connection with Erik King. "Well, actually, Mother you will be pleased to know that I do have a male friend. In fact, we are flying together today. Now that I have made captain, he has been designated to be my co-captain for a few flights."

"You've been dating each other?" Charlotte seemed surprised. "Why didn't you tell me? What's his name?"

Mel avoided the 'so you've been dating each other' question and answered, "Erik King. I've known him for a while."

"I'd love to meet Captain King. We'll have to set it up soon."

"Sure, Mom," said Mel, wondering how she was going to dodge her mother's request to organize a dinner get-together with Captain King.

THE FLIGHT TO ATLANTA WAS uneventful. Mel decided to maintain an all business approach to the trip, besides, she didn't feel much like talking. Erik followed suit. He seemed to be taking his cues from Mel and when she didn't mention his call the night before and the subsequent news bulletin about the hostages, he didn't bring it up either.

After landing in Atlanta, she rolled her flight bag onto the concourse and Erik walked at her side, matching her quick stride. His gaze held a flicker of amusement which corresponded to the tone in his voice. "Do you always head out like a house-a-fire with a face full of determination?"

"I guess I do. Especially in airports. Can't you keep up with me?" Mel asked, surprised at her sudden light-hearted approach. Ordinarily she would have taken offense and her comeback would have been politely sarcastic, something like *I'm sorry if you find my pace and focus offensive. Perhaps you can establish your own, Captain King.*

"Actually, I was hoping to have a good run before my evening meal," Mel added.

"There's an open space near the hotel."

"You must be staying at Plaza Royale. It's convenient, and I also enjoy the open space with good running trails," Erik said as he steered around a couple coming toward them carrying and hanging onto five stair-step children.

Mel's pace slowed as she stared at Erik. "You're kidding. You're a runner?"

"Well," he said, "I guess I am more of a jogger, but I do find that it's invigorating. "When Mom was sick, it helped—during her painful suffering, when she wasted away to nothing. That's when I took it up seriously."

Did he say it's invigorating? I guess that is how it feels with me, she thought. "When I'm feeling out of sorts," Mel explained, "a good run gives me a lift. After the craziness of the last few days, I need the invigoration."

Mel should have expected Erik to be staying at the Plaza Royale as it was the number one choice because of location and cost for flight staff who had a turn around in Atlanta.

"Mind if I join you in your run?" Erik asked as they waited for the elevator after checking in at the hotel.

"If you don't keep me waiting. I'm quick. Ten minutes and I'll be ready."

"I bet I can make it…guess I'd better if I want your company. Bet you won't wait for any man," Erik added as he grinned at her. "It may be a disaster on the trail, me trying to keep up."

He wants my company. Oh, oh, just like all men. He wants to get me in bed. Well, Captain King that will be the day.

HER RUNNING CLOTHES SOGGY WITH sweat and her face shimmering with salty droplets, Mel crossed the line they had established as the finish right in step with Erik. "I thought you said you were a jogger. That was a good run. I couldn't pull away from you."

Erik tossed his head offhandedly. "All this time I thought I was jogging. You're good though. What do you think? Was that five miles?"

"At least," Mel said, nodding at her running partner and really assessing him for the first time. His height exceeded Mel's 5'9" by at least four inches, thus she had to look up slightly to search his dark, coffee colored eyes. They were deep set, fringed by thick lashes, and set off by straight bushy brows. They looked out from a rugged face, softened by a slightly crooked grin. Erik was more muscular than lean, and Mel imagined that he had lifted many weights to maintain such fitness. He was definitely good to look at.

She flashed him a friendly smile as he stepped toward her. Erik threaded his fingers through a sopping strand of her hair and caught the globule threatening to splat on her nose. His tone was warm as he said, "Captain Jameson, I think I said once before, you're beautiful and you don't even know it."

Erik had crossed that tender space between them, the space she allowed no one. How dare he. She tried to look at him boldly, to hold her chin high in tough pride. Yet, she couldn't.

Neither spoke as they both turned to walk toward the hotel. Mel was glad for the silence and heard only the soft hum of a tune as Erik strode beside her. She fought the quiver of her lip from time to time. *What's wrong with me? No one threatens my confident exterior. I've always been untouchable. I won't let a thoughtful word, a tender gesture change that.*

Mel expected to have a light sandwich by herself before turning in. Therefore, she said "No," when Erik invited her to dinner. "Other than my uniform, I only have my loungers and jeans, and neither would be acceptable at a nice restaurant."

"Me too, only jeans and a sweater. I know a fine hole-in-the-wall that serves delicious Jamaican food. It's pretty casual. How about it?"

Later the pair settled in a cozy corner of the Jamaica Caribbean Restaurant and she was glad she said yes. The underground restaurant in downtown Atlanta seemed to be a favorite spot. Even with the live group that played reggae, the crowd was not overly lively, and they did not have to yell to hear each other as long as they sat close and leaned into each other.

Mel told Erik of the visit that morning with her mother, about Arthur, the doctor, and that her mother wanted her to meet his son. She didn't mention that she had used Erik's name as she intimated that she had a guy in her life.

"You never know, he might be a gem," said Erik, "though the doctor's son I knew in high school was spoiled rotten and always had to be bailed out of one scrape or another. I think his parents paid dearly to refinish the front of the school building where he sprayed paint all over the brick and pillars."

"Apparently this guy's wife left him for a modeling career in New York. He's probably carrying too much baggage for me. Besides the last thing I need is the responsibility of a relationship." Mel decided that would let him know where she stood. So, what if he thought she was a selfish bitch.

Erik's only response was his crooked grin. Their food arrived and they enjoyed the oxtail special, spiced with a special blend of jerk spices. Even the beer, which she usually did not drink, went down smoothly without a hint of bitterness.

Later, in her hotel room as the hour approached 10:30, Mel pulled a crisp sheet over her body and decided she didn't need the light blanket. The memory of the casual and pleasant evening dissolved. She rolled over and punched the spongy pillow trying to make a nestled spot for her head. She gave up and tossed it across the room. Mel stretched out on her stomach and lay flat with her cheek pressed against the firmness of the bed. I guess he got the message. No attempt at a kiss. No hand holding. Just a warm "good night". Then she thought of the light pressure of his leg against hers at the restaurant. Neither had tried to move. Stinging tears rolled out of her eyes and wetted the sheet beneath her. She couldn't stop them.

CHAPTER 10

Racine

Chantel McCrae's memorial was scheduled for 10:00 a.m. at Peace of Dawn Mortuary. Racine knew the crew at Racine's Tavern could open for the day without her. She had a good staff of workers who were loyal. Racine treated them right and there was little turn over, unlike most of the restaurants and bars in the area. Chad had offered to attend the memorial with her, but she decided that it would be more awkward with the Aussie by her side than it would be to be alone.

It didn't look like any of the others would be attending. None of them had known Chantel, and until recently no one had seen much of McCrae, though they would have been happy to go, if only for his sake. However, Conchita was fairly new to her job at Quail Creek Care Center and didn't want to make it difficult on the staff by being absent. Monica had a doctor's appointment and Mel would not be back from the overnight assignment with the flight to Atlanta.

Racine sent an elaborate spray of peach colored roses, her favorite, and signed everyone's name as she had told them she would. "Please don't send me any money. I just want to do this from all of us, if you don't mind," she said to her friends. Each one had reluctantly conceded and thanked her. Racine toiled over a sympathy message which she planned to send to McCrae's home with a check to be forwarded to a charity of his choice in memory of his wife. She reread the note she penned on the card she had chosen.

Dear McCrae,

I was stunned and saddened to hear of the death of your wife Chantel after years of struggle with her debilitating disease.

I am sorry for your loss and hope you may have healing and peace surrounding her passing. Please call on me if there is any way I can be of help. May the enclosed check be used in recognition of Chantel's memory.

We never know what is around the bend, just as you did not know what direction your life would take when your wife became ill. Nor did you know what would happen to our men as they embarked on the journey to Colombia.

We don't know what is ahead for the son that I denied a father. I hope I will be able to rectify that.

Please do not worry about the events of the past week. Take some time for solace, healing and reflection. Too often you are so involved with others or business that you do not take time for yourself. I hope you can take that time now.

Fondly,
Racine

I guess it will do, she thought. Should she have said the part about Randy, the son she had failed to acknowledge to McCrae? It has to be said. *Oh, I do hope that he is alive, that he is well, that he'll return.* She raised her hands, pleadingly. *Oh, God let him come back. I would trade places. I would live chained in the jungle forever to give him a chance to complete his life. God, please.*

She dabbed the mistiness from her eyes and tucked the card into the blue envelope, addressed it and pressed the stamp in place. She pulled a shirtwaist dress with a flowing skirt over her head, buttoned the buttons and cinched the wide belt. It was the darkest thing she had in her closet, the color of deep russet, which set off the carmine tendrils she tied together at the nape of her neck. No sparkly jewelry today. Small gold hoop earrings and a necklace of three delicate strands of gold links were her only adornment.

At the funeral home, the parking lot was packed. She scoured the rows looking for an empty space. The spot she found at the far end required a lengthy walk, but she found the walk invigorating and counted the steps as her snakeskin heels clicked against the asphalt. By step one-hundred-sixty-three she had reached the front doors. Inside a long line snaked toward the guest book where the attendees quickly dashed off their names before entering the softly lit room filled with rows of pews. Once inside, an usher escorted her to an empty spot two rows behind the family pew where McCrae sat. Muted music filled the room. Racine detected Debussy's Clair de Lune with its halting piano.

McCrae leaned toward his right to speak to a woman with expertly coifed silver hair. He directed her attention to the front of the room where at least a dozen floral arrangements perched in a careful array. The woman nodded then reached across McCrae's lap to gain the attention of another much younger, but similarly dressed woman. The younger woman mouthed, "Yes, mother. They are lovely." Her demeanor and gaze appeared cool and faraway.

Chantel's mother and sister from Boston, Racine thought. Next to the sister sat two boys, probably high school age. The younger in a short-sleeved shirt slumped in a nonchalant pose, looking about the room, while the older, dressed more formally in a sport's jacked, sat stiffly. To their left, a mature version of the jacketed youth shifted impatiently in the pew, then studied the memorial brochure.

The last funeral that Racine had attended was for a rancher who had been a bronc rider and lived an active and colorful life. The whole affair had the feeling of a hoedown with guitarists and fiddlers playing away. It had been a happy celebration of memories and included funny stories and much laughter. What a contrast to this event. In spite of the lovely flowery color, somehow today's setting emitted such somberness and stifling weightiness that hardly a word was uttered, even when friends discovered and greeted each other.

At precisely 10:00 a.m., the sister in her black suit stepped to the podium. She fixed her eyes above the crowd impassively and spoke, "The family of Chantel McCrae wishes to welcome you to this remembrance occasion. My sister was very specific concerning the music and readings for this day." Rebecca Stone continued in her well modulated voice, "But first may I tell you about her. She grew up in the Boston area where our father was a lawyer. She was born with a tender heart and fell in love with music and art. Chantel was forever drawing something." A hint of a smile flashed across the woman's face, then faded as she paused to gather more erectness in her posture and went on. "One day it was a kitten, the next it was a group of flowers or a bevy of clouds. As the first born in the family she was encouraged to attend the University of Colorado where father had earned his law degree. There she began her studies in business, but soon changed to music and studied the harp. At the university she met Larry McCrae and they were married at the end of her sophomore year and moved to Greeley, Colorado where she began to paint. She had a natural talent and her oil paintings gained notoriety. She made plans to open a gallery in their home.

Yet a bitter disappointment of life befell her when she was afflicted with a debilitating rheumatoid arthritis that cut short her artist life. Her husband tells of her valiant fight, her bravery and lack of complaint. In her delicacy, she had strength about her. We honor her today." Rebecca lowered her head, then cleared her throat. "Chantel chose two notable works to be read today. I will read Emily Dickenson's *Because I could Not Stop for Death.*"

> *Because I could not stop for Death*
> *He kindly stopped for me*

The carriage held but just Ourselves
And Immortality

We slowly drove—he knew not haste
And I had put away
My labor and my leisure too,
For His Civility

We passed the School, where Children strove
At Recess—in the Ring
We passed the fields of Grazing Grain
We passed the Setting sun

Or rather—He passed us
The Dews drew quivering and chill
For only Gossamer, my Gown
My Tippet—only Tulle

We paused before a House that seemed
A swelling of the Ground
The Roof was scarcely visible
The Cornice—in the Ground

Since then—'tis Centuries—and yet
Feels shorter than the Day
I first surmised the Horses' Heads
Were toward Eternity

The words of Chantel's sister hung in the air as she returned to her seat where her mother nodded a you-did-well-my-daughter. Rebecca had read well, Racine thought, yet the full emotion of the work had been missing. The memorial brochure indicated that there would be a moment of reflection while a song by Robert Schumann entitled Dreaming played. The effect of its melancholy tone and the poem imparted an ethereal aura and settled heavily on Racine as her eyes focused on the oil painting centered at the front of the room.

At least twenty inches from side to side, the portrait, amply framed in an ornate gold design, portrayed a beautiful woman, delicately boned with soft blond tendrils framing her face. At her neck and shoulders floated a filmy accordion of folds in soft pink and lavender that feathered to nothing against the palest of variegated gold background. Even at this distance the vivid blue-lavender of her eyes and the quiet smile were evident. Peaceful, thought Racine.

Following the time of reflection, the program indicated that Larry McCrae would read a poem by Robert Frost, then an original poem by Chantel herself would be read by someone named Constance Brown. It surprised Racine to see the concluding music was to be The Prince of Denmark's March by Wynton Marsalis. Racine thought it odd that Chantel had chosen a march to conclude the memorial.

McCrae's shoulders straightened as he stood in front for the reading of Frost's poem. Racine thought he seemed uncomfortable and out of his element. The missing men came to mind. It struck her that they had done nothing since they vanished to remember them, no celebration, no gathering—everything suspended and unfinished. In the beginning, they had waited for news, hoped for a thread of information. When the months and years passed, the limbo had continued, yet a part of her lurched forward, trying not to look back. At this moment the stuck-in-time feeling grabbed her once more. The waiting demon reared its ugly head.

If there was no hope for Randy's return, Racine decided she would definitely honor his memory with a fantastic gathering. She thought of the shy little boy she raised, the way he looked up from a down-cast face when he expected a reprimand. He was always a good boy, too good perhaps, wanting to earn everyone's approval. His teachers told her they wished they had a classroom of Randys. What a joy it would be, they said. He was obedient and an eager student as well. He endured the teasing that often accompanies being a freckled red-head. Randy worked hard on the football field, the basketball court and the track field. He was never a star, but always a fine team player. By the time he was in high school, girls constantly called, inviting him to events.

A late bloomer, he declined politely and no doubt disappointed may young gals.

Did my attitude discourage his dating, he wondered? She had tried not to be jealous of any potential girlfriends yet was silently relieved of his disinterest and glad to keep him all to herself. Besides, a girl worthy of such a prize would be hard to find.

During college he dated a little, but again, he seemed unready for anything serious. By graduation he still possessed some of the slender, lankiness of his teens, but she could see the muscular man blooming. He had been so handsome and full of hope the day they left.

In front of her stood Randy's father, the father she had denied him. Did they have the same stance? Yes. She hadn't thought about it before. McCrae's voice sounded a soft rumble as he began to read. He read with such expertness Racine was sure he had read this poem many times, most probably to Chantel. Hearing the strength of his voice, tears welled beneath her closed eye lids. What were his thoughts, she wondered?

Reluctance
By Robert Frost

Out through the fields and the woods
And over the walls I have wended;
I have climbed the hills of view
And looked at the world and descended;
I have come by the highway home
And lo, it is ended.

Racine felt tingles crawl over her head and down her back. Where had the years gone? Surely the highway for Randy and her had not come to an end. He has many hills to climb and so much more to see in the world, she thought. Touched by McCrae's voice and each stanza of the poem, she found herself in her own world. As he continued reading the words hung over her and touched her: *The last lone aster is gone; The heart is still aching to seek; Ah, when to the heart of man, Was it ever less than a treason…(to) bow and accept the end of a love or a season?* Surely there would be many seasons for her. And for Randy.

McCrae's frame blurred before her when she opened her eyes. She was unable to stop the tears but saw the nod as their eyes met. It was as if new air had filled the room, new vigor. He had truly loved Chantel. Racine had never doubted that, and she had heard it in his voice today. She swallowed the catch in her throat as a rather dumpy gray-haired woman made her way to the front.

"I was Chantel's neighbor and friend. It was a privilege to have her read many of her writings to me. This is the last one she read to me. I do hope I can do it justice." Her voice was rich and buttery. She did it justice Racine thought.

The Harpist
By Chantel McCrae

The harpist plucks her strings and the melody floats
I catch the refrain, but it escapes my fingertips
Arpeggios echo their melancholy replica
The resonance lingers a little longer
Yet, it too eludes me and wanes to nothing
Not unlike the fullness and completeness
Just beyond my essence, inaccessible

Nonetheless, moments well up enlivened
Ah yes, her fingers virtually dance on the strings
Hope abounds, a quiet smile, a gentle murmur
Before this musical litany once more departs
Yet, forever the echo dwells in my soul
Though none other can hear my song
Oh, let not the harpist put away her harp

At that moment, the Prince of Denmark's March began. Quiet and somber it eased in to fill the room as Chantel's family quietly began to file out. McCrae stopped to grasp Racine's hand, just as a timpani rumbled gently. "Thank you for being here. It means a great deal to me," he said softly.

Racine blotted the wetness from her nose and raised her eyes to him with a smile. Their gazes lingered and McCrae continued up the isle while a horn made its announcement. The echo of strings filled the room and then the trumpets trilled—one melody, then another. It indeed was a royal sound full of pomp and circumstance. As Racine began her exit, she held her head high in exultation for the woman who had spoken her last with a regal and triumphant march.

Conchita

Conchita rounded the corner near her home and spotted Greg Hope's truck parked in front of her house. She hadn't spoken to him since last night when he told her about the call to his friend at the Pentagon.

Greg sat with the door partially open and one leg cocked against it. Ready to jump out quickly, Conchita surmised. He must have news. Should I allow the children to hear or should I keep them in the dark until I know something? She decided on the latter and sent the children in to change their clothes and do some chores.

Approaching Greg's truck, she pushed an escaping lock of hair away from her face and shoved a hand into the pocket of the printed top she had worn all day at work. Retrieving a mashed tissue, she wiped it across her forehead. Weariness overtook her and she was unsure if she wanted to hear any news at all, good or bad. Her words were quiet ones. "Did you hear anything from your friend at the Pentagon?"

Greg nodded before he spoke. "It's not much, he said, but our government has secured pictures of the hostages. The pictures are not very clear. There are a twenty or so people in each photo."

Conchita's voice lacked its usual buoyancy when she spoke. "On the TV they keep saying there are 49 hostages and five of them are from the U.S. Are there Americans in the pictures?"

"No one knows. A few have been identified as important political hostages from Colombia. One may be a Venezuelan who was captured last year. But don't give up hope Conchita."

Conchita leaned against the open door of the truck. The sun hit her square in the face, and she looked through squinted eyes and tried to smile at her dear friend as he continued. "No names yet. He said it is likely that a family spokesman for each of the missing will be contacted. That would include you. I can be there if you want."

"When will they contact us?"

"Soon, I think."

⁂

'SOON' CAME MORE QUICKLY THAN Conchita imagined. Because of Greg's Pentagon friend it was Conchita who received the initial contact. When she called McCrae to express her sympathy about the loss of his wife and to let him know that family members would be meeting to examine the pictures secured from the rebels, he insisted on coming. As they spoke, McCrae said, "Conchita, these were my men too, and I want to be there every step of the way, no matter what happens. I'm not family, but I'm coming."

Saturday morning two government officials greeted each person who entered the local city council meeting room. A large oval table, chestnut in color, nearly filled the space. Roomy leather swivel chairs provided more than ample seating and the group gathered at one end. As he had promised, Greg accompanied Conchita and sat beside her near the two officials who sat at the head of the table.

McCrae, handsomely dressed in his usual western style, scooted his black cowboy hat down the table toward the empty chairs. He helped Monica into her chair and positioned her crutches nearby before he folded his lanky body onto the chair next to her. Monica leaned toward him and murmured her thanks, then sympathetically spoke about his wife's death. McCrae smiled and nodded.

On the other side of the table Mel and Racine greeted each other and settled into their chairs. In the waiting silence the light hum of air

137

conditioning took over, and the coolness of the room felt unusually damp in the dry Colorado air. Conchita shivered and drew a shawl splashed in reds and golds around her. She disliked air-conditioned places and though there was air conditioning at her place of work, the thermostat was set fairly high. Today everything felt dank in the building.

As the government officials spoke, a smile flickered here and there, but the pair appeared stiff and serious. The hefty man introduced himself as Archibald Lindenmeyer. His voice boomed from an expansive chest that seemed to protrude beneath the dark suit jacket that he wore. His shiny bald head looked as though it had seen many days of sun. The other man, Lieutenant Colonel Jefferson Sipes, stood over six feet tall and wore army fatigues. The air of importance in his stance, and the noticeably prominent cheekbones in his glistening black face, gave him a strikingly good-looking appearance.

"We appreciate being able to use this meeting room," Lindenmeyer stated, "and have set up equipment to show the two pictures we received from the guerrilla group known as the Revolutionary Armed Forces of Colombia. You may have heard them called FARC, their initials in Spanish. We have enhanced the pictures to the best or our ability."

Lindenmeyer pushed his hands into his pockets, pacing before them, yet continued to focus his eyes on one and then another. "You will see three faces that have been circled in yellow. These have been identified by the Colombian government. The woman in the first photo is Brita Vogelstadt, a German-Colombian national who was campaigning for president when she was captured three years ago. A rising political figure in Colombia at that time, there has been a great deal of pressure to secure her release. We believe this may strengthen the opportunity for the exchange."

The photo projected before them included three rows of bedraggled and shoddily dressed captives. Brita Vogelstadt was in the back row on the right and seemed to be staring directly at them. Her face appeared gaunt and as one would expect, her mouth looked grim. Yet if one had known this woman, she seemed identifiable. Another yellow circle surrounded a face in the middle of the front row.

Lindenmeyer stopped his pacing and turned to point to the figure. "This man is a Venezuelan official who was captured two years ago.

There has been much effort to find his location and effect an agreement for his release. Until now, however, no one knew if he was alive or dead. So, we have the Venezuelans who can help put pressure for a release. The question is, are any of these Americans?"

The Lieutenant Colonel's voice was smooth and liquid as he interjected, "Of course FARC is expecting the release of some 400 imprisoned rebels, some of whom are in American prisons, in exchange for these hostages. If there are Americans in the group of hostages, I imagine they believe this gives them more clout concerning the release of the rebels. Of course, we are not certain," Sipes said as he leveled his eyes at each one around the table, "whether we would release those rebels in exchange for Americans." Stepping to the side, the Lieutenant Colonel signaled with a movement of his hand for Lindenmeyer to continue.

"I know you all brought pictures," the voice of the broad-chested man boomed, "which we can take back for digitized examination, but now look carefully to see if any of these could be your men."

Everyone focused on the photo projected on the screen. Several in the photo possessed scruffy, but sparse facial hair. A couple had full, thick bears, and one man sported a particularly long one, extending onto his chest. In the black and white photo, most everyone's hair looked somewhat dark and lengthy.

Conchita's eyes went immediately to the second man from the right in the second row. His face looked to be clean shaven and his dark hair much shorter than the others. She squinted at the slender face, hoping to draw it into better focus. His features appeared sharp. Drawing in a deep breath, she held it for a few second, then let it whoosh out.

"I'm certain," she said in a halting voice, "that is Miguel." She pointed a finger toward the spot, pushed herself from her chair, and forced her feet to move one in front of the other. Standing in front of the screen her short frame cast an eerie shadow, blocking some of the picture. She reached up and ran her fingers gently over the spot where the face was projected. The back of her hand reflected the distorted picture and she stepped to the side of the screen and just looked.

Up close, she thought he looked sad, put proud. "If this is not Miguel, he has an identical twin," Conchita said, her voice no longer halting. Turning toward the Lieutenant Colonel she added, "He looks thin of course, but I have no doubt. At least you have one American, sir."

Conchita's declaration brought vitality to the room. For the next fifteen minutes, they studied the pictures they had brought and scrutinized each face on the screen, first of one photo, then the other. Back and forth they went, talking about the features of each face.

"That one could be Gavin," Monica stated. "It looks a little like the way he furrows his brow. But that one resembles him as well," she added in frustration. "A man can change a lot in nearly five years."

"Especially," Mel cut in, "when they have endured captivity all this time. It may be that Miguel is the only surviving American hostage in this group. I don't see anyone that I think looks like my father… at first I thought, maybe the long bearded one. But now I don't think so." Disappointment wrapped around Mel's words.

Racine, eager to see someone who looked like Randy, paced around the room. She stood at the very back searching out each face. Perhaps if she looked from left, the right, or got right up close. Not one looked like the Randy she remembered. She threw both hands toward the ceiling, shaking her head.

"If only the photo was in color," she blurted. "Surely he still has his reddish hair and vivid blue-green eyes." All was quiet until she pointed toward the man who stood by Brita, the German-Colombian national and said, "Maybe that one. He looks pretty tall. Kind of thin but looks like he could be a strong man. I believe by now Randy would be a strong muscular guy." She jutted her chin at McCrae who had been mostly silent and more brooding that usual, and asked, "What do you think, McCrae?"

He looked back at her with a look that said, 'why are you asking me'? Yet glaring, he responded, "I'm sure he would be a strong, muscular man by now, Racine."

Racine thought about McCrae's stance when he read at Chantel's funeral and how Randy's had been similar. She noted the cock of McCrae's head, then looked back at the screen. Did the tall man beside Brita tilt his head, too? Yes, she thought, but a lot of people do that.

Thirty minutes later, the group left the government officials to gather their things, with the understanding that any news would be relayed once the photos had been analyzed. They had discounted at least eighteen figures that were extremely unlikely matches. However, it seemed certain there was one match. Miguel.

Relieved to leave the air-conditioned building, Conchita drank in the warmth and aridity, unusually so for mid April. Making her way to her car, she felt the muddle of loss, joy, pain, sorrow and uncertainty roll in her heart. She sensed Greg's thoughtful nature as he walked at her side, slowing his gait to match hers. He smiled but remained wordless. What should she tell her children? Even if Miguel was alive when the picture was taken, even if he is still alive, she thought, there is no assurance that he will be coming back. And if he does…Her thoughts ended abruptly when they reached her car.

"Thank you for being with me today. You're always so helpful, always there when I need a friend."

Greg nodded. "You are indeed welcome. I'll always be you friend. Just call anytime if you need me. OK?"

She took comfort in his smile. He was so easy to be with. From the moment they met, she had considered him to be a trusting friend. How long could this friendship last and where would it go? She wanted to wish for Miguel's return, but she didn't want to think about the end of this friendship.

An allusion of sorrowfulness dangled from her voice as she said, "I'm sure the children and I will be fine. I do need to pick them of from my mother's. Good-bye my dear friend."

Minutes later Conchita pulled to a stop in front of her mother's modest home in a section of the town populated by Spanish speakers. Señor Garcia, the portly, elderly gentleman who lived next door rushed out of his yard waving the newspaper in his hand.

"Conchita, how are you?" he asked in Spanish, then continued in English," "The newspaper say…your husband, he is one of the hostages, no? He is famous, no?"

She had asked Greg to bring her a newspaper when he came, and she had read it this morning before the meeting with the government officials. The headline story did not include anything about their meeting, and she wondered how it had been kept secret, even for a day. It did insinuate that the four men were indeed included in the group of Colombian hostages, though no evidence was presented to back it up. The news reporters had done their homework and had written a feature story about each of the missing men. Much of it was a rehash of what was written after the men had gone missing. When a reporter contacted her yesterday hoping for an interview she had declined, so they didn't have any quotes from her.

Since Miguel had risen to major league baseball status before the automobile accident, much was written of his rags to riches baseball career. In fact, his story was the longest and most colorful. Conchita cringed, thinking of the way the writer had described Miguel's cockiness on the mound and with the press. She had been embarrassed by his actions at the time, but the worst was his arrogance, his violence and his 'I own you' attitude at home. It had nearly emptied her bucket of self confidence. Things were different now. She had survived on her own, raised three children, completed nurses training and now she had her own home and a fine job and her bucket of self-confidence was plumb full, or nearly so.

"Oh, hello Señor Garcia, I am fine. Well, I wouldn't say he's famous. We don't know for sure about Miguel, though. I think we will know soon if he is one of the hostages. All we can do is wait." Conchita tried to hide the uncertainty she felt. She didn't wish to stand here on the street explaining to the Señor what had happened this morning. In fact, she hadn't decided what to say to her mother and the children. "It's good to see you. And please give my best to your sister. I need to collect my children from my mother's home."

"Your madre say you have a new house, it's true? You like it?" the Señor continued and came toward her. Conchita closed the car door and started up the sidewalk.

"Yes, it's true and yes, we like it very much." She waved the man off and called out, "Have a nice day."

At that moment, the twins burst from the house. "Mamá, Mamá, you are back," yelled Jenny.

Pamela scooted in front of her sister pleading, "Come, come see what we made."

Relieved by the interruption of the twins who bounced to her side, Conchita bent down to draw them into her embrace. Their faces glowed with the exuberance of a fluffy puppy greeting its owner. Conchita stepped back to admire them. Her own smile widened to its fullest. How beautiful they are, how much they have grown in the last weeks, and I have not noticed. I've been so preoccupied with the house, Nicola's information, this hostage thing. I do hope Miguel comes home to see his daughters and his son. Surely, he will be proud. Yes, she would tell them that she saw their father's picture. She would give them hope, all of them hope.

Inside, the house smelled of pepperoni, oregano, basil, and cheese, yet there was no pizza box. Conchita's body flushed with the joy of a child's Christmas morning and anyone who looked could see the tears dancing in her dark eyes.

Jack stood beside the table sprinkling the last bits of shredded cheese over a freshly made pizza in a shiny new pizza pan. He stood erect, taller than her mind remembered. His shaggy mop of dark hair, a replica of his father's poked here and there giving him a quizzical, yet handsome appearance.

He addressed her proudly, "Grandmother said we should not order pizza this time. We should make it ourselves. So, we made two. Look Mamá."

Conchita spotted a pizza, hot from the oven still steaming on top of the stove. "Now I'll put this one in to cook." Conchita watched her son, his proud set of the jaw and his deftness at maneuvering the large pizza into the hot oven and securing the oven door. With an air of confidence, he asked, "Are you hungry Mamá?"

There would be no beans and tamales today. Her mother had somehow garnered instructions for making pizza and two brand new pans, and she and the children had made pizza. Will miracles ever cease, she wondered? "Yes, Jack your Mamá is very hungry."

Monica

MONICA AND RACINE WERE EACH lost in their own thoughts on the drive home from the meeting with Archibald Lindenmeyer and Lieutenant Colonel Sipes. Monica appreciated the ride since she could not yet operate the car with her broken leg. It would be polite to initiate a friendly conversation, but she did not feel like talking. *Hopefully Racine feels the same.* Seeing the captives' faces looking out at her had been unnerving. It brought unimaginable images to her mind's eye concerning their captivity. Who knew what all they endured? Here she was feeling sorry for herself for being temporarily crippled and uncomfortable. *How can I be so self-centered?*

The rhythmic plock-clop, plock-clop of Monica's gate echoed eerily in Monica's roomy combination kitchen-family room. Otherwise her house was quiet. Peter was in Denver for a one-day conference and would not be back until late.

Clutching the stack of photos, she had gathered before the meeting, Monica maneuvered her body onto the leather recliner, and put the footrest at the highest position. Dr. Perry said to elevate her leg as much as possible and she guessed she better do it. A yawn crept into her throat and gushed itself out of a gaping mouth, then finished in a mournful sigh.

"Oh, Monica, what's going to happen?" she said out loud.

She had selected nearly a dozen photos to take to the meeting. The officials would return the two they kept in a few days. She hadn't really studied the photos before she left. She barely had time to remove them from the album which had been tucked away since she and Peter married two years ago. It wasn't fair to Peter, Monica thought, to have the album staring him in the face every day.

Moving at the speed of cold molasses the weary woman began placing the photos of Gavin back into the album. Why hadn't she studied the eyes more carefully this morning? Despite the fuzziness of the pictures and profusion of facial hair on the figures they examined, she should have been able to recognize the eyes, even if they were fuzzy, that looked back at her. They always had a lazy, soft look and though

Gavin was confident in his work, there was a shyness in the way he looked at you.

In the photo, Gavin leaned against a glossy powder blue 1961 Camaro. His humble smile and velvety eyes looked into the camera. The car was his pride and joy, rescued from a junk yard and refurbished from top to bottom before he and Monica met. After they married, he stored it in the barn where he grew up. His mother still lived in the farmhouse, though the 200 acres of farmland had been sold after Gavin's father died in a tractor accident. Gavin took the Camaro out on the first Sunday of every month for a wash and polish. Sometimes his cousin Jake and he tinkered with it, then took it for a drive. Usually Monica didn't go, not that she really wanted to. It was kind of a man-thing.

When Gavin had been missing a year, Monica accepted that he was dead, and his body would never be recovered from an apparent plane crash in the tangled Colombian jungle. She had no use for the car and had given it to Jake. She hadn't seen Jake in years and had no idea if he still had it.

In the photo next to the Camaro, Gavin and Monica squinted into the sun near an overlook at Yellowstone falls where they spent part of their hurry-up honeymoon. At twenty-two, she had just started a new job as a bank teller and Gavin had recently left the Ford garage to work on diesel engines. Thus, neither could take more than a few days away.

Oh, Gavin, I remember how we enjoyed watching the grizzlies and the wolves in the rescue compound. Such magnificent animals. You thought it was criminal that they were penned up even though they had destroyed some human environments. I argued that is was better than risking a human life. For sure then they would have been put down. Funny what the mind remembers—like you were the one who had the tears when we said our vows.

The wedding had been simple, only a few friends and family, unlike the extravaganza when she married Peter. She and Gavin started out with pocket change and she drew up a strict budget those two years before he left. Though they hadn't specifically talked about having children, she imagined that Gavin, then twenty-eight expected to start a family soon. She hadn't been sure she wanted to be a parent. Mostly she wasn't sure she would be a good one.

She flipped through the album. Actually, it was an unfinished album, maybe twenty pages. Half of the photos were pre-marriage and included family gatherings, picnics, a drag race Gavin took her to, and some boating photos on a local lake. Neither of them was particularly into picture taking and their day to day life didn't have many significant events.

Monica wondered what her life would have been if Gavin had not agreed to go to Colombia. Would they have had children? Would they have bought a house? Yes, she was sure they would have purchased a house, but not like the one she lived in now. Would Gavin have started his own business as he had hoped? She recalled their conversation.

"Talked to Joe Connor today," Gavin said as he pushed his chair away from the supper table, "said he's planning to put his shop on the market inside a year. He wanted me to be the first to know. Wondered if I might be interested."

"In buying his shop, you mean?" Monica's flashing eyes raised to meet his steady ones.

Gavin nodded in affirmative and said, "It's only two bays. But it would be a good starter business and there's room for expansion in the future."

"Gavin Dean Humphreys. And where do you think you'll get the money?" Monica's voice exploded more sharply than she intended. "We don't even have an extra hundred a month to put away for a down payment on a house. You have no idea what it takes to run a business. Have you put a pen to the paper at all? There's insurance, taxes, workman's comp, fees when patrons use credit, not to mention the interest on a business loan."

Gavin looked away and said nothing.

Monica's tone softened. "Hey hon, you are a great mechanic. Everyone I know wants you to do work for them. I know you have dreams and someday the time will be right. But not Joe's Garage. Not now."

He'd never mentioned his dream again and neither had she. Four months later he was off to Colombia to earn an extra chunk of cash that would be the down payment on the house Gavin thought she wanted. In actuality, she'd been willing to wait to own a home.

Turning to the last page of the album, Monica studied the final picture. She and Gavin leaned toward each other, heads nearly touching. Monica had never baked Gavin's favorite, the red velvet cake, because his mother always did when his birthday arrived. Two pieces of red velvet birthday cake sat on the table in front of them. Gavin's lazy gaze suggested more smile that did his lips, while Monica's face appeared a bit pinched. Had she known that it was their last photo together, would her expression have been more pleasant?

Gavin was a good husband and she had loved him. At this moment, however she wondered about her ability to love and give from the depths of her heart. Wasn't that what love should be like? She wasn't sure if she had loved enough. So many memories remained muted. Had she blocked them after Gavin went missing or had she been only half alive before he left. What about her aliveness now? She leaned her head against the head rest and closed her eyes. It felt good to let her mind cloud over.

Bing-bong. Bing-bong.

"Confound it. Who's at the door?" Monica gritted.

The bing-bonging persisted as Monica released the footrest and moved to reach her crutches. The album slammed to the floor. She shoved it aside with the rubbery end of her crutch and made her way to the front door. Through the etched glass design of the entrance Monica detected a blurred figure, definitely female. Once the door was open, the blurred figure came alive.

"Hello, Mrs. Monahan, I'm writing for the Sentinel and would like to get my facts correct. May I step inside and ask you a few questions about the Colombian hostage situation? I understand your first husband, Gavin Humphreys is among the hostages."

Stunned, Monica stepped back and nearly lost her footing. In the split second that her mouth fell slack and silent, the reporter stepped across the threshold.

"Thank you, Mrs. Monahan. This will only take a few minutes," the reporter said through a friendly grin.

"Oh, no you don't" Monica planted her good leg and the opposite crutch, then with bolting speed slammed the end of her other crutch against the door frame—thigh high—pinning the lower flap of the reporter's khaki trench coat. The reporter's smile dropped from her face and her notebook hit the floor at the entryway. "You are not welcome here. I have nothing to say. You will leave my premises, now."

"But Ma'm, we want the public to get the right information," the reporter pleaded, making no attempt to pull her coat free.

Monica withdrew the crutch from the door jam crushing it against the fallen notebook, then with one swift move sent it scooting out the door, off the front porch, and into the bushes. Monica then stepped back enough to aim the rubber end of her crutch at the reporter's waist. The contact was enough to push her off balance.

"Please go."

Retrieving the notebook from the bushes, the reporter shot Monica a look of disdain, which served to fuel Monica's declaration. "Hey, you sticks. We done good," and burst into song, "These sticks are made for walkin' as well as for protectin'."

CHAPTER 11

Monica

Experiencing turmoil and waiting was about all that happened during the next four weeks. The officials returned Gavin's photos. Even with technology hostage identification was iffy. Two photos were identified as possibilities for Gavin, one possibility for Randy and none for Ben. Oddly, one other American, a journalist out of New York City, had been identified. He was one of the clean-shaven ones and had been missing only eight months.

Now Monica used a walking cast which made her daily routine easier. Nevertheless, the days often seemed long and she had the nagging feeling that life was on pause, yet it continued. Today's communication from Lieutenant Colonel Sipes said:

We believe there is good news. The Colombian government is willing to negotiate an exchange of political and other high-profile hostages for an unspecified number of Revolutionary Armed Forces of Colombia (FARC) guerrillas in government prisons. The two sides have yet to agree on terms for starting talks. Four members of the U.S. House of Representatives have offered to take part in the negotiations. We believe their presence could give credence to the talks which FARC has been reluctant to begin, citing concern for the safety of its negotiators. Venezuelan leader, Chavez has also indicated a willingness to enter into setting up negotiation terms to aide in the release of the Venezuelan hostage. Chavez has been respected by FARC members in the past. Once a plan for negotiations is determined, the names of all prisoners should be made known. You will be informed as progress unfolds.

Frustrated, Monica crushed the paper in her fist and threw it into the wastebasket. She filled a pot with water, a sprinkle of salt and a glug of olive oil, then set it on the stove to boil. She had already made Peter's favorite spaghetti sauce using fresh tomatoes and two types of sausage. In recent days she'd been moody, and Peter had tried hard to make conversation and help out with the household chores. Thoughtfully, he had established a new routine. After dinner Peter insisted that she sit down, do some reading and listen to her favorite music while he cleaned up and filled the dishwasher.

It was her turn to do something special for Peter. He didn't ask for any of this life-on-hold situation. She put on his favorite jazz, set the table with their best china, chilled a bottle of wine in the wine bucket, prepared a romaine salad and fixed a basket of garlic bread. Hurrying upstairs she pulled a lightweight mohair sweater in pinks and greens from the drawer and slipped it over her head. Peter had given it to her at Christmas and she pretended to like it, even though her colors were browns and tans. She had worn it only once. She nestled her face against the sleeve, feeling the downiness of the fine yarn and wondered if he would notice what she was wearing. Gimping down the stairs she heard the garage door go up and moved a little faster.

She did her best to be lively at dinner, to be interested in the clients Peter had worked with during the day. She actually found his description of the eighty-five-year old lady and her request to set up a twenty-five-thousand-dollar trust for a pet cemetery amusing and interesting. She said nothing about the communication from Sipes.

As Peter scooped a second helping of spaghetti and sauce he looked up and said, "Wow, babe, you really outdid yourself with the sauce. Just the right bite. Everything is de-lish."

He'd taken a quick shower and put on his loungers as he usually did before dinner. His fresh-scrubbed scent was something she had grown accustomed too, but tonight she realized how much she liked it, and how much his blondish hair, uncombed and disheveled roused her sensuality.

"Thanks," she said light heartedly, "We have strawberry short cake for dessert, with lots of whipped cream."

Tonight, Monica was not going to allow Peter to do the cleanup and they ended up working together. Once the dishes and flatware were in the dishwasher, Peter dived into scrubbing the cooking pots. Monica grabbed a dishtowel and dried the first pot. "Boy are you slow," she kidded as he worked on the next pot. Acting bored she leaned against the counter. He flung bits of snowy suds at her and she retaliated by snapping him with the dishtowel.

With a handful of foam Peter darted toward his wife, eyes simmering with mischief. Monica hobbled backwards, squealing, "Don't you dare."

The momentum of her backward maneuvering sent her to the adjoining family room. She landed awkwardly over the arm of the couch and flat on her back with her legs flailing. Stunned, Peter raced toward Monica spattering globs of soap suds. "Monica, are you all right?"

Giggling and swiping suds from her face and hair she said, "I think so."

Peter leaned over the couch and gathered her in his arms, lifting her to a more comfortable position. "You look kind of cute all ruffled up. And especially alluring in that fluffy sweater."

"You think so?" Monica asked as she pulled Peter toward her. He brushed his lips against hers and she saw the sparkle in his eyes.

"Mmhuh," he uttered, searching her eyes. His lips met hers with urgency. Monica's body arched as she answered his probing kisses. Peter slid his hands beneath the softness of her sweater. One cradled her back and the other cupped her breast. "You feel so good," he whispered into the smoothness of her neck.

It had been a few months since they made love. They had been busy, then there was the accident with the broken leg, the hospital stay and the beginning of the lengthy healing and rehabilitation. Then came

Nicola's story, with the up and down roller coaster of the hostage thing. It was as if passion had been kidnapped by some malicious hijacker. Preoccupied, Monica hadn't even renewed her birth control prescription.

Tonight, the malicious hijacker returned its passion to these two hungering souls. With renewed affection and glow, fervor moved first tenderly, then powerfully. Not rushing they explored and relished each other's bodies. Afterwards, they lay cozied together on the roomy couch under a crocheted afghan. Their clothes remained in disarray on the floor.

Monica smoothed her hand over Peter's muscled chest and looked into his face. "Are you ready for strawberry shortcake?" she asked.

"No thank you, Babe. I've already had my dessert. It was the best ever."

Monica closed her eyes and joyed in the comfort of Peter's arm around her. "It was good." Then she thought of the paper rumpled up in the wastebasket.

Racine

PHONE TO HER EAR, RACINE looked past the disarray on her desk. Her hands flew as fast as her words. Food and drink orders for the restaurant and bar needed to go out today and all she could think about was the latest letter from Colonel Sipes.

"I can't believe that our government is so ignorant about what exactly is going on with the hostages. You'd think they'd have some names by now. Can't you do something McCrae? You know some guys in Washington, don't you?"

"Its hell waiting and wondering, isn't it?" McCrae's voice was mellow and soothing. "I've been on the phone all morning. I have a call in to Representative Louis Parks. He's one of the four who have volunteered to monitor the negotiations between FARC and the Colombian officials."

There was breathiness in Racine's voice when she asked, "Does he know if Randy is one of the hostages?"

"Hold on. All I know is what his aide told me. The guerrillas seem to be holding back on releasing the names as a kind of extortion. Maybe they think the U.S. will exert more pressure about setting up the conditions for the talks?'

"What conditions?" Racine plopped herself onto her swivel chair, then snatched the engraved gold pen from the green mug Randy had made for her in Junior High School. Absently she caressed the lettering. Happy Mother's Day, I love you.

"The rebels have demanded the demilitarization of two municipalities in order to have a safe haven for the negotiations."

Racine blurted, "And the Colombian officials won't agree. Right?"

"You got it. The rebels won't come to the table without one-hundred per cent assurance of their safety."

"So, what's next?"

McCrae didn't answer right away. When he did, his voice held caution. "There's talk of sending in some Special Ops, and once the hostages are located, swooping in for a rescue mission."

"No!" Racine shouted, "They can't. Too dangerous. One slip up and the rebels slit their throats just like they did with Nicola. And our guys would not be so lucky to live through it. There has to be another way," Racine said as she pressed the pen decisively on a pad of paper and wrote Spec.Ops, drew a circle around it and put a slash across the whole thing.

"I'm pulling for negotiation myself. I'm thinking that the four U.S. Reps might be able to appease both sides, stimulate some compromise." Then as an afterthought he added, "And I hope to get clearance to go along."

"McCrae, what do you mean to go along?"

"Just that, go to Colombia and keep abreast of the activity. I can relay any news to you all. And don't try to talk me out of it."

After the phone call Racine sat, elbows on the table, chin resting in her cupped hands, and let the tears roll from her closed eyes. The droplets made a little tap each time they hit the stack of orders waiting to be signed. Her voice quivered as she spoke to the air. "Oh, my son, what you've endured I can only imagine. You have to come home. To really know your father. I'm so sorry. I cheated you. You have to be alive." She tried to bring Randy's face to her mind, but it wouldn't come.

Mel

THANKFUL FOR A FIVE-DAY BREAK after five turn-around flights, Mel wanted to go to the mountains for a little clear-your-head time and she wanted someone to go with her. Hadn't her mom been on her back, wanting her to get a social life and appreciate the beauty of the high country?

Erik and she had talked on the phone a few weeks ago, but their schedules hadn't meshed, and she had to decline his invitation for dinner. Last night she shocked herself when she called him. He sounded pleased when he said, "Yes, I'm up for a mountain drive and hike. How about breakfast before we leave?"

They agreed he would drive, they'd do the breakfast thing, then head to Pennock Pass. Mel hadn't been there since she and her father took a day to see the dramatic unveiling of autumn's aspen doing their golden dance against the darkening pines, making ready for winter. It was the fall before Ben Jameson flew the fated flight to Colombia.

Her father and she had taken her dad's 4-wheel jeep to the summit. A long stretch of winding road tunneled through patch after patch of aspen. Riding beside her dad Mel felt the nearness of the golden coin-shaped leaves quaking on each side of the road. They both commented on the amarillo glow surrounding them and the feeling of warmth that filled them. Leaving the dusty gravel road, the two headed off to explore the logging trails.

They laughed as Ben straddled the deep arroyos made by the summer's melt off, bucking over rocks, stumps and sagebrush. Ben stopped the jeep where the higher elevation and oft-time whipping winds caused the vegetation to become scrubby and twisted. It was a spot where Mel and her father viewed the distant mountain ranges to the north and west. Splotches of the famed aspen groves, the ones that tempted poets and non-poets to take up their pens with an attempt at brilliance in describing the beauty spread before them in both directions. An umbrella of the deepest, endless blue hovered above. A few vultures circled to their left until one dropped and disappeared, most certainly spotting some dead prey, Mel thought.

Her father's voice broke the stillness, "What a glorious day. What a treat to spend it with my daughter. Can't think of anything better. Just look." His broad sweeping hand brought to Mel's mind his grace, as well as his toughness.

She nodded and felt the smile on her face, then pulled her camera from its case. The shutter clicked as she aimed one direction and another. Far down one valley a wisp of smoke worked its way upward from a weathered cabin. She zoomed in to pull it closer. She snapped one of her father gazing far off. He looked robust and handsome. His hair of black and scattered-gray suggested his over-fifty age, as did the creases that etched his brown eyes. Yet youthfulness surrounded him. He stood as erect as a well planted fence post and even in hiking or working clothes, there was orderliness about him.

With her camera she captured the soaring vultures and the great expanse of a third set of ridges disappearing in a distant haze. She spotted a scraggly juniper tree with remarkable character, she thought, and sighted it in from several directions.

"Hey kid," her dad said, "If those turn out, can I have some copies?"

They had turned out and she presented him with five of the best, framed to join the wall of photos in his office. He had sent her a dozen roses in appreciation. Even today there was the same stab of overwhelming poignancy, she felt when they arrived with the note, *Roses for my kid who grew up to be a talented and beautiful woman.* The photos accompanied the conglomerate on his walls: Mel in various activities of growing up, Ben Jameson with high ranking officials he had flown with, sights that he and Charlotte had visited on trips abroad. What had happened to them when her mother sold the house and moved into her condo? Mel was away at flight training at the time and didn't know.

Surely, they were packed away somewhere. Mel didn't think her mother would have gotten rid of them.

The image of her father, the spicy aroma of fall, the heart to heart talk they had about being a female pilot, etched its indelible memory in her mind. What about her father? Could it be that the strong, vigorous man was alive and at this very moment remembering?

The bonging of the doorbell pulled Mel away from her thoughts. She grabbed her backpack bulging with hiking necessities—lunch, beverages—and looped it over one shoulder. She had decided not to take her camera. There didn't seem to be any reason to take a bunch of pictures. Somehow since her dad went missing, when she took pictures they ended up in a heap in the bottom of a drawer.

Releasing the two locks on her door, she pulled it open. Erik's relaxed nonchalance helped to quiet the uncertainty lurking in her head. A baseball cap shaded Erik's eyes and gave them a snapping darkness that hinted at amusement as he blinked a once-over look at Mel—a green cotton bandana tied around her head, chunky hiking boots, khaki walking shorts, a roomy plaid shirt tucked in at the waist with sleeves rolled above her elbows.

"I must say, Miss Jameson, you picked a perfect day for the mountains, Erik said as he grabbed a chunk of fabric from his own shirt, one identical to her blue and tan plaid. "I see you have excellent taste."

"I guess we both shop the sales," Mel quipped.

Rather than have breakfast in Greeley, Erik chose to stop on I-25 at Johnson's Corner. A popular truck stop, it catered to tourists and locals as well, and featured humongous cinnamon rolls, hot out of the oven, oozing with frosting. The home-style cooking sported generous portions, and Mel decided the hike required a high energy start for the day, so she ordered scrambled eggs with home-fries and wheat toast. Erik finished his pancakes and sausage, and both gulped an extra cup of coffee before leaving the plains and heading west for the mountains and Pennock Pass.

Both made attempts to fill the space with small talk. Had she heard anything more about the hostage situation? Had he enjoyed his last flight to Atlanta? They surely needed some rain didn't they? Did his Tracker get good gas mileage? The silent pauses grew longer and more frequent until no one tried to stuff the gaps with inflated words. And both seemed comfortable to enjoy the scenery, spot a hawk, notice a pair of horses racing across a pasture and watch the tumbling stream racing downhill as they snaked uphill.

Over a rise and down a prominence Mel fixed her eyes on one of her favorite scenes, a barn built of hand-hewn logs in the 20's or 30's. It nestled against a hillside and was such a masterpiece that it had stood all these years tall and proud against nature's torture. Mel imagined the loft full of grass hay harvested from the meadow stretching east, a team of horses being led from the gaping doorway fully dressed in their harness gear.

When she was very young, she and her father scouted out the barn. It was a thrill to find a horse collar, a hame that hooked into the horse collar and several wide leather straps her father said were used as reins to control the animals in their work. When she was in high school, their trek through the barn was not so rewarding. The stalls were tumbling down, and no horse gear remained. She still held deep affection for the barn.

Erik pulled the Tracker to a screech, sending red dust and pebbles flying. "Look at that barn. That would make a perfect painting." He held his hands to replicate a picture frame and looked through the opening, tipping it this way and that. "Do you mind? I just gotta have a photo of it. It's perfect. The variations of texture, light and dark, the massiveness of the logs paired with the delicate shafts of swaying grasses. The asymmetric balance as the hill behind it cuts a diagonal."

Without waiting for Mel's response of surprise, he reached into the back seat, grabbed a black case and leaped from the Tracker. Mel shook her head and reached to turn the key and extinguish the engine. She followed Erik and watched his eagerness as he shot one and another.

"I didn't know you were one of those artsy buffs," Mel called.

Erik called back. "There's a lot you don't know about me. If it turns out, you'll see this ole barn on a canvas sometime."

Already Mel found herself smiling more than usual, her typical wariness waning. A psychologist would have a hay-day with her psyche. She had trusted her father implicitly, but other men, no way. Usually the experts maintain that having a positive and trusting relationship with her father led a woman to trust men and be able to develop healthy relationships with them. Perhaps Mel's downfall was that no one could measure up to Ben Jameson.

Nevertheless, as they continued the drive, Mel found herself telling of the times she and her father spent exploring the barn, the closeness they felt on these trips and the last time they made the trip, about the pictures she had taken that day.

"You haven't been back to this area?"

"No." Mel shook her head and felt her tenacity for self control dissolve.

"Kind of tough to open those old memories, I bet."

Behind the darkness of her sunglasses, Mel stared ahead, her lips closed tightly without an utterance.

Erik continued, "You know, I don't have such memories with my father. As a pilot flying helicopters, he was stationed in places that were off limits for Mom and me. When he was home, everything was turned upside down."

"Meaning?" Mel asked, turning toward her companion.

"Well, our routine was changed. And with my father, there was no gray, only black and white and no flexibility, only rigidity. He was a good man, but not one for..." Erik gestured with a flip of his hand and let the sentence hang in the air.

"Not one for what?"

"I don't know." Erik chewed a bit of lip before he went on. "Not one for giving any compliments to Mom or me, certainly no hugs or appreciation. I never got used to the gruffness of his voice, his moodiness. I was only eight when he left for the last time. He thought I was a scrawny, clumsy kid and was determined to make an athlete out of me. We spent his whole month of leave on a barren dirt field learning to master the skills of baseball. Hitting, fielding, running the bases, holding the bat just so, turning the glove at the right angle."

Mel heard the little-boy resentment and hurt in his voice. "I'm sorry."

"Three hours in the hot sun was pretty grueling for an eight-year-old. It might not have been so bad if I had one or two moments of praise."

Erik sighed with a shrug. "That's the way it was. Maybe I was a weenie. I wouldn't let Mom sign me up for little league baseball after that."

"I can't imagine you as a scrawny, clumsy kid." Mel gave him a light fist to the bicep. "You glow of athleticism and agility."

"Oh I do, do I? I guess Mom made sure that I grew up healthy. And eventually I caught up to the strong genes I got from my father."

"Do you look like him?"

"Yeah, mostly, but the personality's definitely more Mom."

Parking beyond the summit of the pass, the pair left Erik's car, hoisted their packs and headed through the brush and twisted juniper. The sun rose higher preparing for its midday reign and only occasionally did they find full shade. The quiet surrounded them, displaced only by the swish of their rhythmic gate.

For the next hour there was an occasional comment about the terrain, the brilliant blue sky, a cloud threatening to send showers, but no real conversation. Erik found several camera opportunities and snapped twenty or more shots. He surreptitiously caught several of Mel, resting on a boulder, crossing a trickle of a stream, pointing out the green patches of aspen which would turn golden in the fall, examining a stand of columbines, the state flower.

Following one particularly demanding climb, Mel took an extra deep breath, feeling her heart's thumping pick up speed. "Lunch time. Don't you think?"

"I was wondering if I was going to have to wrestle you for your pack and a little nourishment," Erik responded, moving to a shaded boulder where he sat down.

They ate without rushing or gulping. Erik complimented her on the food, and they talked of favorite foods, his Mexican and hers Italian. "Yeah, Mom was a great cook," Erik said, "usually good ole down-home food, but she could make or bake anything. She was health conscious, being a hospital dietitian. She worked in a small hospital and was able to organize her hours to pretty much fit my school schedule."

"I guess even when your father was alive, she pretty much operated as a single parent.

"Yup."

"She must have been an amazing woman."

"I couldn't have picked better, if I had a chance," he said with affection. "Say, how's your mother handling the hostage uncertainties?"

Mel tossed her head as she spoke. "Humph. She's still in this la la world of denial. She can't imagine that my father's still alive after all these years and thinks…well, I don't know what she thinks. She's all tangled up with this doctor she's been seeing."

"Have you met him?"

"Oh, yes. I've had to endure two dinners with them in the last weeks. It's surreal. She's intent on pushing this relationship forward. If my husband had been missing for all those years and there was a chance he'd be returning, I'd put this relationship on hold, stop seeing the guy. But not her. She's barreling forward with all sorts of plans for trips, cruises and such."

"What about the doctor? Does he seem to really care for her, treat her well?"

"He's quick for the opening-the-door, pulling-her-chair-out, complimenting-her-hair-style routine. They hold hands like some love-sick teenagers, wink at each other over little jokes. It's sickening. I don't think they're sleeping together. Mom's too old fashioned for that and he's the true gentleman. Well, I don't even want to think about that possibility. When Dad gets home…If he comes back…Well I hope she comes to her senses before that."

Erik mindlessly poked a stick into the bed of evergreen needles at his feet and swirled it round and round until a circle of dirt was exposed. "Life's circle is magical, but as we know, it can be painful," he said raising his eyes to meet Mel's. "So often it doesn't turn out quite as we expect or hope. Your mother has gone through a lot losing her husband, and from what you say, all these years she's been faithful to your father's memory."

"Her women friends have always been enough for her. She's had plenty to keep her active and busy. So now she's flirting with this Prince Charming who will carry her off to his highfalutin country club, parties or whatever."

Erik spoke with thoughtfulness and sincerity. "There's another way to look at it, Mel. My mom was so busy working and raising me all the years after my father's death, she denied herself a personal life. I'm still sad about that. She had many opportunities to have male friends. She had many invites, but she wouldn't accept them. She had many friends who were men, but she had a way of letting them know that was it, they were just friends."

Mel's voice rang sharp as she said, "Erik, she made her own choices. You have no reason to be sorry for her. I am sure she was happy. And proud to raise such a good son."

"You don't know the whole story. Once I was out on my own, flying, traveling, she was lonely. I could tell. She had passed up so many opportunities to have a companion to share her life with. And she had so much to offer in a relationship."

Erik rose and heaved the stick as hard as he could. It whipped the air like a twirling baton and crashed into a bush on the other side of the gorge. "Mel, her time ran out. She waited too long. And for what? Sam, I really liked Sam, tried over the years to get her to go out. Finally, with much prodding she said yes. They'd been friends forever, but seeing them spend more time together, I could tell that they were well suited."

Erik's words came out stronger and faster. "He wanted to take her to Scotland where her family came from. It had always been a dream for her. Then cancer attacked and it never happened. The disease ravaged my beautiful mother. She sacrificed so much...and her time ran out."

He looked toward the sky, breathing deeply, then turned toward Mel. "You don't know how much I wish my mother would have had some happiness with a companion. I wish she were still here and that I could see that happiness. Mel, it wasn't your mother's fault that your father disappeared. It isn't her fault that the timing of this new friendship is awkward. Be happy for her. Be thankful that she's still in your life. You don't want her time to run out. It may be years before your father returns, if he ever does."

The chill that ran through Mel not only paralleled the dark cloud that rolled over head, blocking the sun, and the accompanying cool breeze that suddenly swept through the area, but also the smack of Erik's words that felt like betrayal, like pointing the finger at her, making her attitude seem selfish. *How dare he judge me? How dare he take mother's side, when my father has been suffering who knows what, all these years?*

Then it came. Lightning, stabbing into one peak and then another, then all around them; thunder, like a thousand wrathful demons, rumbling across the valley; rain, bucketing around them and down the coiling path they had climbed. Neither had a chance to speak yet shared the same thought. Let's get off this mountain.

The trek that had taken them over an hour in ascension, took less than thirty minutes in the descent. It was a treacherous one, sliding on slippery slabs of rock, catching hold of branches, worn and twisted by weather, only to discover them clamped in a fist after they broke loose.

Mel slid into Erik already lodged against a bristled bush. The fall had resulted in a wicked looking gash on his arm. Raining torrents diluted the blood on his shirt to the color of watermelon. A bolt of lightening struck close, its blinding flash, its deafening crack. Even sopping wet, Mel felt her hair stand on end.

"You're hurt," she said to Erik.

He shook his head and gripped Mel's arm to lift and steady her. He touched her face where blood trickled from a slash across her left cheek but made no mention of it. It might leave a scar, he thought.

"That was close. Here hang on," Erik took her arm and tried to steady her down the path.

She shook his hand away. "We'll do better on our own. I'm fine. Let's just get going."

Finally reaching the car Mel shuddered in the cold and tried to unthread her arms from her backpack. Erik pulled it off and opened the hatch at the back of the Tracker. He dragged out a blanket, wrapped it around Mel, and pushed her into the passenger seat out of the rain. Settling into the driver's seat he slammed the door and said, "I thought we might have a little campfire. I guess that's out. Does it always rain like this up here?"

Shaking from the cold she said, "Afternoon showers are pretty common, but usually not so violent."

"Just so you're alright." He pulled a tissue from a box on the floor and dabbed at the cut on her cheek.

Mel jerked away, "What are you doing?"

"One of those branches sliced your cheek a little. Sorry."

"It'll heal. It's nothing for you to be sorry about." Mel snuggled further into the blanket and leaned toward the car door away from Erik. "I can take care of myself." She continued to stew about Erik's defense of her mother and was not about to forgive his meddling advice.

By the time they reached the main road, all black top, the rain had stopped, and the sun rays had crept back over the hillsides. There was a sparkle on the greens of the pastures and the trees, a freshness in the air. Yet it was as though the bloom of their relationship had been washed away with the downpour. The trip back to Greeley was mostly silent except for the rhythm and blues music that played on the radio.

When Erik pulled in front of Mel's condo, she tugged at the blanket and found it stuck in two places where blood had dried, at her left knee and shin. Gently pulling the green fuzziness away, a clot loosened and began to ooze. "It looks like I'll have to soak the blanket to get the blood out. I'll take it in with me and work on it."

"Just leave it, I can take care of it," Erik said as he came around the car. Still soaked with the afternoon downpour, his shirt stuck to his skin like strips of wet papier-mâché being formed into a statue over muscled arms and shoulders. He had removed his sopping cap and his sandy colored hair poked here and there.

If Mel had really looked at him, his rugged appearance might have been quite appealing. Instead, she rolled the blanket into a bundle, grabbed her pack, and trudged toward her front door. "No, I insist. I'll get the blanket cleaned up. Thank you for the day. Too bad I picked a day for the record books. Good thing the lightening decided to leave us alone."

"Yeah, it was close wasn't it. Can't I help you? Looks like you have a few scrapes to doctor up," Erik said as he followed her up the sidewalk.

Mel turned to face him. "No worse than you. I think a good soaking in a hot tub is what I need."

"Thanks for sharing a little bit of your heaven. Never did mind a little water. In fact, it was quite a memorable day. I'll call you when I get in from my next flight. Maybe we can find another adventure."

"Yeah, bye." Mel waved her free hand at him and walked on. *Yeah, so memorable I'm not sure I want to share any more of my heaven with you Erik King.*

CHAPTER 12

Conchita

Conchita usually didn't have time to read the newspaper at work and wished it wasn't staring her in the face. *Hostage Negotiations in Limb* blasted the headline. She felt like a ping pong ball being batted around. Nothing was stable when it came to information about the hostages and their release.

She couldn't stop to read the article, since she had been called to the east wing. Bianca Muños was having another spell. Bianca dashed down the hall like a banshee rooster with feathers protruding in disarray. Her frantic cry of Eva, Eva, echoed in the hall. Conchita knew Eva had been her younger sister and had drowned as a child when the family lived in Mexico. Apparently, Bianca blamed herself for Eva's death.

Unlike her usual immaculate grooming and dress, her proper and courteous manner, the woman increasingly displayed confusion and irritation. It broke Conchita's heart to see the uncertainty, the fear in her eyes. What if her own aging mother showed symptoms of slipping into senility? Could Conchita handle it? At least, she thought, I can take care of Mamá. Señora Muños has no family to help out.

Reaching Bianca's side, Conchita found her in a muddled heap at the end of the hall. Spasmodic whimpers puffed from her anguished lips in cadence with her rocking body. Conchita lowered herself to the shiny floor, pressed her back against the wall and pulled Señora Muños close, smoothing her unruly hair and humming a lullaby she had used with her children. Eventually the woman turned to look into Conchita's face. Her eyes darted with fright. Conchita soothed repeatedly, "Esta bien Bianca," and wished Bianca could indeed feel and believe the 'it's OK' message.

Waving an orderly away as he approached ready to lift the woman into a wheelchair, Conchita continued to whisper in her ear. Bianca calmed and stood, gripping Conchita's hand with a firmness Conchita did not expect. Once headed in the direction of her room, the Señora's feet tapped the floor in a quick staccato while her mouth voiced the word Eva over and over. Conchita stayed in Bianca's room until the frantic look in her eyes melted away, the softness in her voice returned, and she seemed firmly planted back in the present. Only then was Conchita able to think about the newspaper article.

She found a newspaper in the break room and traced the words with her finger as she read the article. It told the frustrating story, all except the proposal regarding the Special Operatives. Her throat filled and she tried to swallow away the tingling sensations brought about by the words on which her eyes lingered.

The families of the hostages, missing these five and one-half years, have cause for hope, for celebration. Surely by summer's end, if not before, the hostages will be back on Colorado soil. The only hostage unaccounted for is Randy Rabinowitz. What happened to the young man is pure speculation…

The recent four weeks had been as unsteady as a stack of blocks, precariously placed. First came the release of hostage names, including Ben Jameson, Gavin Humphreys and Miguel Vasquez, but sadly not Randy Rabinowitz. In the beginning the Colombian government agreed to the rebels' demands for demilitarization of specific zones where negotiations would take place. Then the government did an about-face and flatly refused to demilitarize the requested zones. This brought the possibility of negotiations to a halt. Next, Conchita and the others met with Colonel Sipes in a hush-hush meeting to consider deploying Special Operatives for a rescue mission. This was the part that did not make the paper.

It was unanimous. No one, not Mel, Monica, McCrae, nor Conchita favored a rescue mission. All believed that negotiating for hostage and prisoner exchange was the way to go. The safe return of the hostages remained paramount. Apparently, the family of the New York journalist pleaded for negotiation as well. Even Racine who was adamant that Randy was alive and would be released with the others, spoke firmly. "Who knows what can happen," she asked, "if some Special Ops swoop in wearing night goggles? So they rescue one of our guys. What happens to the others? The rebel's retaliation will be vicious."

Colonel Sipes had relayed their concerns about a rescue mission and negotiation plans were in the works. The news article included quotes from Representative Parks and three of his colleagues who were cleared to travel to Colombia. Their role would be to assist in the collaboration toward an agreement for release of the hostages. Now, it was a matter of waiting.

<hr>

AT HOME, THE CHILDREN LINGERED around the dinner table seeking answers to their questions. "Jack, don't you remember Papá?" Jenny asked. "You should. You were born before he went to Colombia."

How much did Jack remember? Probably very little. Most of his memories came from the few pictures she had shown her son. She wondered if Jack remembered some of the drinking and raging.

"Sure. He was a famous baseball player. He played for the Rockies," Jack declared.

"I know that," Jenny said in exasperation. "Everyone knows. And what he looked like. But what was he really like? Did he play with you and tickle you? What was his favorite music?"

Jack shook his head with a shrug of his shoulders. "Yeah Mom, can you tell us? I don't remember. He did carry me on his shoulders. We have that picture."

Gosh, how should I answer that? I don't want the kids to be disappointed, nor do I want them to have unrealistic ideas about their papá. "It was a great thing to be brought up from the minor leagues to play with the Rockies but remember he didn't play long enough to become famous. In fact, he only pitched two games and then he was injured in the car accident."

Pamela cut in. "If the wreck didn't happen, he would've been a star," Her chin jutted out and her eyes flashed. "Somebody made that accident. He should be put in jail."

Conchita could not remember telling the details of the accident and wondered where Pamela got the idea about someone causing it. Probably her mother. Yes, she thought, someone had caused the accident. Miguel.

He had been angered by an elderly couple driving ahead of him. Later Miguel tried to defend himself to Conchita. "The old man really made me mad. It was a through street, the jerk. He slowed to a crawl at every intersection till I nearly rear-ended the guy. Finally, I'd had enough and decided to show him a thing or two."

The 'thing or two' meant that Miguel followed the car for a few blocks repeatedly blasting his horn. The elderly driver got flustered at a crosswalk and nearly hit a pedestrian. Then the old man's car stalled, and he couldn't seem to get it started again. As Miguel's rage grew, he continually roared his engine like a dragster ready to take off. At last the older gentleman warily opened his door and stepped out. He stretched his stooped body as tall as possible and placed a hand up in a gesture of 'stop'.

"It should be against the law for old geezers like that to drive a car," Miguel told Conchita. "They're a menace to society. That asshole wasn't going to hold me up one more second."

Miguel left a line of rubber skidding around the stalled car and fished-tailed for fifty feet. He swerved to miss a car coming at his right and continued to race up the street. In the next block he lost control, slammed into a tree, and pitched through the front window. The paramedics found him dangling, his pitching arm and shoulder damaged.

How much of the 'rest of the story' should the children hear? Finally, she spoke. "The other car had two older people in it, and you know people like that are cautious drivers. But your father didn't have much patience and he wasn't very careful when he passed them and lost control of the car. Fortunately, the older people were not in the accident."

Conchita paused to sigh before continuing. "And about tickling. No, he didn't do that, but when he got home from practice he liked to play and wrestle with you on the floor. That's when he played in the minors." Those were the best times, Conchita thought, still some control issues, but Miguel had been satisfied with life. Once his baseball career was over, the fury and lashing-out escalated.

Jenny broke her thoughts with more questions. "When did you and Papá meet? Is he the same age as you? He's not too old to play baseball, is he? He can still play when he comes back."

Conchita smiled thinking back over the beginning. "Well, your father and I met in high school. I was in 9th grade and he was in 11th. Even then he was the best ball player on the team—as a pitcher and a hitter. My girlfriends and I went to every home game; I couldn't go to the out of town games because I didn't have a ride." Conchita closed her eyes remembering. "I'd yell for the team and he spotted me in the stands."

"I bet he thought you were pretty," Jenny interjected.

"Well, I'm not sure about that, but I yelled a lot…and loud. Then one time after the game we ended up at the water fountain at the same time. We talked a little and soon he started calling me on the phone. By the end of 9th grade, we were going out a lot. When he graduated, he asked me to marry him, but I had promised your grandmother I would finish high school, so we had to wait."

"And Papá went to Colorado Springs to play baseball, right?" Jack asked.

"Well, he played American Legion ball that summer. They never lost a game while your father pitched. Then he tried out for the farm team in the Springs and played for them during my last two years of high school. We were married right after I finished high school. I was 18 and your father was 20."

Conchita looked at her son. "You were born the next year. Your papá was called up to play for the Rockies when you were three."

"Then he had the accident. Right?" Jack asked. Conchita nodded.

Jenny pointed toward her sister. "Where were we when he went to Colombia?"

"Honey, you and Pamela were still in here." Conchita patted her abdomen.

"Oh. That's right. We were born after he left. I think he can still play baseball. He's not too old."

"At 29, he's not too old to play with you kids. But he can't play with the Rockies because of his shoulder injury."

Pamela, who had been listening with the ear of a robin intent on hearing an underground worm, spoke at last, "Why did Papá go to Colombia? Didn't he want to stay and be our father?"

"There are many reasons my precious ones. But mostly your papá needed a job and he went to Columbia to work."

She couldn't tell the children that Miguel used up their savings at the bar, swigging it up and buying for everyone there. He played the stud in public, but on the inside he was a mess. He had no desire to find a job and raged at Conchita when she suggested he look for work. He hated the world and insisted that life cheated him. He believed the Colombian job would bring him fame and riches.

Conchita stammered when she answered her daughter. "He...he didn't know about you and Jenny. But if he had, he would have been proud to be your father."

When the questions and answers were over, the children went to play, while Conchita removed the clothes from the washer and hung them to dry. She tried to picture Miguel here with her and the children. It was *her* house and she couldn't quite put him in it. With all her emotions churning in confusion, she wondered if she could deal with everything needing attention in her life. Concerns piled higher and higher threatening to come crashing.

The school year was nearing its end and she must make decisions about day care. Conchita's mother expected to watch the children each day. That seemed like an ideal situation and was one that had worked when Conchita was in nursing school. Yet the Señora's comments made her think twice.

"I'll pay you to watch the children Mamá," Conchita said, believing she'd find the money somehow, "now that I have a solid job. It could give you a little extra pocket money."

The Señora pointed a crooked finger at her daughter and her voice raised a few decibels. "Conchita, you insult me. I am the grandmother. I am the best one to care for the children. And there will be no pay. It's not their fault that their mother has to work. They belong with family."

Since that discussion, the Señora continued to poke jabs of guilt at her daughter. They didn't come all at once, but were sprinkled throughout, day by day. "I know I can't visit my neighbors when the children are here." "I don't know if you realize how much more work the children cause; I'm not so young as I used to be you know." "I suppose I'll have to turn on those children programs on TV. Well there goes my favorites." "Too bad I'll have to miss my afternoon nap." "Not every mother has a built-in babysitter like you do, Conchita. You must count your lucky blessings."

Then there were the concerns about the young boy down the street. Conchita knew Jason wasn't her responsibility, but he was such a needy kid and there was no improvement with his mother. The recluse rarely fed the child, or if she did it was nothing nutritional and substantial. When school was out there would be no free lunches for him. Conchita and the children always ate a hearty meal in the evening and more times than not they included Jason. Thanks to Greg they often had extras—fresh fruit and vegetables, eggs, ice cream, sometimes a hunk of fresh pork that found itself in many tasty dishes.

Yes, there was Greg. When she had confided in him about the daycare situation, he brought a folder explaining the program for low income families. It was funded by United Way and was housed in a local church. Charges included a sliding scale according to the number of children and the family income. Conchita couldn't decide whether the children would be better off with a sometimes crotchety and opinionated grandmother in a neighborhood where there were no other young children, or in a center that provided numerous activities with other children.

Greg had even offered to watch the children on his day off which was Tuesday. This could give the children and grandmother a break from each other if that was the chosen resolution.

Greg never wavered, his listening ear ever ready, repairing the used washing machine when it wouldn't spin, helping to prepare the soil and spread the seed in the front yard which presently looked like a furry green blanket and soon could be used as a play area. The backyard would take more time and work, but Greg said he could have the space prepared for seed by Monday and that was four days away.

Guilt about Greg nagged at her insides. She could never, would never be able to return his thoughtfulness, his kindness. The something between them which started as a mutual respect and friendship had grown, not unlike a bean seed. Once planted in rich moist soil, the seed expands, sprouts a tender bud, unfolds into a stretching stem, and branches off into heart-shaped leaves and other stalks. The bud soon blooms its fullness to produce the slender and meaty pod, green for harvest. They hadn't yet gotten to the bloom part. Would they have if they had never learned of the hostage situation?

With Miguel's return looming, both she and Greg were careful to be polite and respectful. They kept their eyes away from each other's. She had little control over the situation. Miguel is my husband, she thought. When he comes back, could she still claim Greg as a friend? No. That would not be possible, nor would it be fair to Greg, herself, or the children. Will the children feel the unfairness of losing a friend? Greg played catch and hit fly balls to Jack, played Uno with Jenny and Pamela, and rarely won. He helped the children hide from each other—crouched in the cabinet under the sink, coiled under a pile of pillows on the sofa or behind the one lone suitcase in the closet.

Everyone was comfortable with Greg. The children didn't know their father at all. In fact, perhaps she didn't know him either. Will he be changed, she thought, no longer selfish or self-centered? Will he be tender and responsive to my needs? Will he be proud and appreciate all I've accomplished?

Added to Conchita's balancing act, the director of the center had explained that they needed to add hours for the nursing staff and asked if she could increase her workweek from 36 to 40 hours? This would make things more difficult with the children.

Yet how could she feel sorry for herself and her precariously balancing life? She had her beautiful and healthy children. What delight they brought to her. Whatever the future held, she resolved to be strong, to support them and be a good mother.

Yet, she could not push aside the night they were conceived. Miguel came home half sloshed. He wanted her. She was sickened by his actions and his sour breath. She resisted, she begged, 'not tonight'. In the end he had taken her without tenderness, without love, but with entitlement and violence.

The next day she mechanically soaked the blood from the bedspread feeling broken and alone. She hadn't wanted to admit the reality of the rape to herself, so she pushed it aside, remaining in denial. She had denounced the possibility of a pregnancy, when in actuality at Miguel's good-bye, it had been three months that the new little lives had been budding inside her. Over the years she had finally reconciled herself with the paradox that the twins, such cherished souls, bodies, and minds, had come from darkness.

CHAPTER 13

Racine

Nine o'clock, and am I beat. Cripes a few years ago, I was able to close at midnight and still have energy to work a few more hours before heading home. Now I can hardly make it to ten.

Racine kicked off her gold-strapped slings and plopped herself onto the ivory leather recliner. Until the Aussie Chad hired on at the restaurant/bar as her right-hand Friday, Racine's office was mostly barren, except for a massive desk, swivel chair and filing cabinet.

Chad teased, "Rabinowitz, seeing your office, one would think you must be some colorless spinster who hides out in a backroom by the broom closet and never comes out. You need an office that's not only for work, but peace and comfort in this fast-paced business you and Carlotta built for yourselves." He asserted, "There's room here for more than a sterile desk and chair."

He'd been right, she thought as she massaged the balls of her feet, then hitched the footrest in place. Another chair in the same leather, angled toward the one she reclined in and the pair made a comfortable grouping with their own convenient end-tables built from cherry wood.

Hugged against the opposite wall stood a six-foot unit of shelves and cubicles fashioned from the same cherry. A variety of one-of-a-kind objects, mostly gifts from patrons who traveled around the world reposed in their own special spaces in the unit.

Relaxing these few minutes Racine realized how much she appreciated the comfort and attractiveness of her work area, and the peacefulness she felt here away from the hustle on the other side of the door. She needed peace, especially these last three- and one-half months. Even the African mask in orange, red and black with the wretched twisted nose emanated its own tranquility and caused Racine to smile.

A light knock at the door and a, "Racine, it's Chad," generated a wider grin, and the response, "Come-on in."

"Here's your tea." Chad entered the room balancing a round tray bearing a tall tumbler of ice chunks floating in green tea. "Thought cold would be more refreshing tonight."

"You thought right," Racine said, gesturing for him to place it on the end-table beside her. "I certainly need a refresher-upper."

Racine couldn't give you the exact date when the nightly tea began. To be sure it was recorded in her journal. She did remember the event, however. It was after the wall unit had been built and installed. She and Chad assembled the items Racine had collected over the years. Many had been stashed here and there in the restaurant and some remained there today for patrons to see. Others had been packed away in the storeroom until Racine could decide on an appropriate place for them. After studying and measuring the artifacts, Chad had designed the unit.

The day it was put into place was particularly hectic. Two areas in the restaurant had been blocked off for different parties, a birthday and an anniversary. Even the extra help could barely keep up. At the time Carlotta was still recovering from her heart attack, so Racine and Chad were especially busy.

Exhausted, but giddy from the day's wild schedule, Racine and Chad decided to unpack the saved items and place each one in its special spot. They got the giggles when Chad put on the African mask and chased her around the room saying, "Booga, chooga, mooga. Woman of my heart", over and over again. Well past 2:00 a.m. they sat in the leather chairs and admired the unique wall.

Then Chad excused himself and returned to the office with a bundle wrapped in a worn blue hand towel. "What you got?" Racine asked.

"There are several extra spaces for other objects, and I have one, too. I think it would look nice below the Navaho pottery."

Racine watched patiently as he carefully removed the hand towel, then a piece of soft woolen fabric, the color of butterscotch. She watched him grip the handle of a white tea pot, fat and squatty and raise it for viewing. The design, in shades of blue, displayed flowers, leaves and swirls. The top knob of the lid glistened in solid shiny blue. "How exquisite," Racine said, "It looks like an heirloom. I'll be happy to display it, but it could never be mine."

"Well it does have a story. But I fully intend for you to have it, a gift for an amazing woman."

Chad handed the tea pot to Racine. She held it as if it were a globe of wafer-thin blown glass which could shatter from a breath of air. She lifted it to peer at its bottom. "R.S. Do the initials have special meaning to you?" She already knew that they must and a catch caught in her throat. "What is the story?"

"There were pictures on our mantle when I was growing of me with my great grandmother. I don't exactly remember her, since she died when I was a year old. Ruth Sauer was her name and she was a china painter. We had many pieces of her work, always done in a similar style using variations of blue." Chad stood above Racine telling his story. Racine thought the warmth in the soft glow of his eyes belied the sadness there.

"And you lost all the pieces in the fire," Racine said.

"Yes, the fire that took my father and all of our belongings."

"You haven't talked much about that time. Do you want to now?"

Chad's sigh was slow and pensive before he spoke again. "I was away at college. My first year, studying business. Dad was home alone since Mum had gone to a little burg about thirty kilometers away to be with my cousin when she came home from the hospital. My cousin was having a baby. Mum's sister would arrive in a few days, but Mum was to help out until then." Chad's gaze wandered about the room, then settled on the floor.

"It happened at night while Pop was asleep. They think it was the gas heater. A leak and an explosion. Pop didn't have a chance. He was burned," Chad's voice turned acid, "beyond recognition. I had helped my father install the heater the summer before. Racine, I tightened the fittings..." He couldn't go on.

Racine rose from her chair and placed the special tea pot on her desk. She wrapped her arms around the tall Aussie drawing him close. "It wasn't your fault. No one could blame you. Perhaps the whole unit was faulty." They stood melded together for what could have been minutes and Racine felt one and then another tear moisten the back of her blouse as they rolled from Chad's eyes.

Chad pulled away and held Racine at arm's length. "Sorry. I don't suppose anyone ever blamed me, but I always wondered. And Mom was never the same, after. She died of a broken heart three years later. It happens you know, broken hearts I mean."

Racine lifted her chin and walked to the desk to stroke the tea pot. Yes, she knew of broken hearts. Hadn't she lost the love of her life, her beloved son? When the men went missing and the days ran into months and finally years, how had she gone on? She still had the reputation of being high on life, but something of the spark had died, little by little. "It's a lovely tea pot. And you've kept it all these years," Racine said.

"Ironically, it was one of the only things that survived the fire. After Mom died, I wrapped it up and took it with me. It's been with me during all my wandering and traveling days. Don't know why exactly. Maybe it was meant for you, lovely lady. For sure, I've noticed your affinity to tea, either cold or hot." His face began to return to its healthy, sunny glow.

Racine had agreed to keep the tea pot for safekeeping but insisted that it still belonged to Chad. Chad believed that tea pots were intended to be used and it sat in its place on the shelf, except when Chad used it to make fresh tea for Racine, which happened nearly every day at an apropos time. He seemed to make the correct assessment. Sometimes the tea was iced and sometimes it was hot, but always steeped in the special blue and white pot.

Chad settled the tumbler in the coaster on the cherry wood end table and strode across the room to the wooden wall-case. "Need some cheering up today?"

She smiled at the muscled man and her head made a little nod. Chad lifted the mask from its place and held it in front of him, grumbling in voodoo sounds, "Booga, chooga, mooga," as he danced around the room.

She laughed. "I'll booga, chooga, mooga you if you don't put that back and sit down for a minute. You've had a busy day, too."

"Can't. You have someone waiting for you. It's McCrae. Shall I send him in?"

"Yeah," she nodded.

McCrae always seemed to fill the room that he entered, even more than the taller and more muscular Aussie. There was a commanding and judicious aura that encircled the man. Yet, he seemed to be everyone's friend.

"Nice fellow, the Aussie. Appears to have good business sense. He surely admires you, Racine. You must be glad to have him aboard." McCrae pulled his hands from his pockets and sat in the companion chair next to Racine.

What did she hear in his voice? Mockery? Surely not from McCrae. "He's been a God send," she responded. "Even with Carlotta back several days a week, we need his management. His ideas have helped business. Yeah, I'm glad he's aboard." Racine sighed. "Are you doing OK? Did I tell you how beautiful the service for Chantel was?"

"Yes, you told me. And I'm doing fine. You know us work horses; we keep on going. It's still hard to accept how she died. I think she suffered more than I knew. No more suffering." Racine sensed the topic of Chantel was over.

McCrae leaned toward the colorfully dressed woman adorned with gold strands looped over her chest and looked directly into her eyes. "We go way back, you and I. Racy this has been one of my favorite places to eat and meet with business associates or cronies for a few rolls of the dice. Quite honestly however, coming to Racine's Tavern hasn't been only by habit. I wanted to watch you from a way off and see how you were doing and how things were with our son—the one you didn't want me to claim."

Racine held up a hand to halt his speech. "McCrae, it wasn't that I didn't want you to have a son. As I said once before, I didn't hold you responsible for my unplanned motherhood; I didn't want to intrude in your or your wife's life or cause you to have a questionable reputation. And with my independent nature I didn't want you to feel responsible to support Randy or me in any way." Her words continued to spill out as if they wouldn't be said if she didn't talk fast. "I just thought it was better for everyone, including Randy. And I didn't think ahead or even imagine what I'd tell him when he got older. That has eaten out my heart, since the opportunity for him to know that you're his father evaporated when the men didn't come back. And it wasn't that I didn't think you would be a good father. I've always known you're a good man. Now I'm sorry I did it that way," she said as her fist hit the side table.

"Are you through?" McCrae asked.

"I guess."

"Well, what I've come to say is, I've never told you how much I admire you, respect you and appreciate the way you raised our son. I've seen the respect he shows you, and everyone, as far as that goes. You did a superb job being his mother."

Racine returned his solemn gaze. "Thank you."

McCrae continued, "I admit it was selfish to want him on the Colombian expedition. I wanted him to have a taste of adventure. I wanted him to try his wings. I wanted to be as proud of him as you are. And just maybe, I thought, you would decide he needed to know. I'm devastated about taking him away from you."

Racine's response was a whisper. "I know. It's life. Not your fault. It's sure rough not knowing what happened in the hostage camps, though."

"Those bastards can't get away with this. We'll get the answers. We both need to know. And I intend to learn all that I can."

"I…, I refuse to believe that he's gone," Racine stammered.

McCrae's voice came back at her, clipped, but direct. "I hope you're right, that he's alive. I have clearance to accompany Louis Parks and the other three representatives to Colombia and…

"You are going then?" Racine interrupted with sudden life on her lips.

"It's all arranged. We leave Thursday morning and as I started to say…I intend to get some answers. I believe I can learn more there than what we are getting here about the hostages and why Randy's name is not on the list."

Monica

ON FRIDAY, MONICA RETURNED FROM the doctor's office, grateful to know that her broken leg was healing well. One metal pin had been removed and a dressing covered the stitched incision. The other staples and pins would remain indefinitely. She was relieved to have graduated from the ugly and cumbersome walking boot to a lighter one that gave support yet allowed her to feel less awkward.

Fortunately, she arrived home in time to take the phone call from Nicola. After the news flurry when the press found out about the woman's escape from the guerrilla camp, it seemed like she had dropped from the world. The last she had seen of Nicola was on TV being accosted by a reporter as she arrived at the hotel in Denver. Monica knew how some reporters could be pushy and offensive. Hadn't she nearly shoved one off her front porch with her crutch?

Nicola sounded excited about Gavin's name being on the hostage list and encouraged to know that the government officials had arrived in Colombia to assist in setting up negotiations for a possible exchange between FARC and the Colombian government. She asked, "Have you heard anything more?"

"A little," Monica replied. "You remember Racine, the redhead, Randy's mother?"

"Oh, yes."

"She had a call from Larry McCrae. He's down there with the congressmen. Things started as soon as their feet hit the ground in Bogotá. Some Colombian officials and the congressmen have a meeting set up today via satellite with one of the leaders with FARC. I can't believe that these guerrillas are so sophisticated with satellite and all."

"It wasn't that way in our camp," Nicola said, clearing her throat. She went on in her raspy voice. "It's paradoxical. In the jungles the lifestyle can be very primitive, yet in some of the central hideouts the guerrilla leaders have every kind of technology available. Computers, satellite receivers, satellite cell phones, you name it. Not to mention highly developed weapons."

"Apparently so," Monica responded. "McCrae told Racine that the discussion about setting up a demilitarized zone for negotiations would be entirely by satellite. I don't think he can attend, but at least he should be able to keep us up on the news, if it's not top secret."

Nicola's voice sounded hesitant when she asked, "Still nothing about Racine's son?"

"Not that I know of," Monica responded. "It has been hard on Racine to accept that Randy is not listed, and the rest are. If he's alive, you'd think he'd be on the list."

"I can't figure either. Randy was probably the one who was in the best shape when he, Ben, and Miguel were moved from our compound. Anything could have happened since."

Nicola told Monica that she'd put the idea about finding another mission assignment on hold, at least for the time being. During the last five weeks she visited her mother and brother in North Carolina and spent time with her dead husband's family.

"I'm kind of at loose ends Monica. Back in Denver looking for part-time work and expect to apply for the divinity program at Regis."

"I've known a couple of people who attended Regis. Good program. I bet you'll have no trouble getting accepted."

"I studied at Regis two years before I decided to become a nurse, so I'm pretty confident about getting in. Oh, I was able to visit with Gavin's mother last week. She's so excited about seeing Gavin."

"How nice. I hadn't thought of you meeting with Mrs. Humphreys. She must have been pleased to hear about Gavin's life in the camp firsthand. That was very thoughtful of you,"

"Thank you. Yes, she seemed quite glad for my visit. She's thrilled with the news of his return. I also wanted to reassure her that the last time I saw him he was in pretty good health."

Yes, Monica thought, and his recovery is all because of you. "I'm certain you and Gavin will have a lot to catch up on as well. I wonder if he knows you escaped."

"I wonder too," Nicola murmured. "Yes, I look forward to a very good visit. I hope that happens." The pause over the phone line was wide enough to drive a bus through. Then Nicola continued. "Monica, I need to tell you something. I hope you will not take it the wrong way."

A surge of heat flushed through Monica. Was it dread she felt? Or maybe the adrenalin rush was the type that occurred when danger lurked and one needed additional defense. Monica's attempt to keep her voice steady and controlled didn't materialize when she spoke. "Of course not. What is it?"

"I am sorry that we haven't had a chance to talk, just the two of us. I can't imagine how awkward it must have been to listen to all that happened with Gavin and not know whether he would return, especially when you have another husband."

"You think I should never have remarried, is that it?" Monica defended. "I did wait. Three years. And nothing. We all thought they were dead. What were we to think? Our lives had to go on."

Nicola protested, "Of course you had to go on, just like I had to go on when my husband Rick was killed. That's not what I was getting at. I can barely imagine what it must be like to be in your position, a position you had no real control over. When there was no word, for years, what else could one think, but that Gavin was dead? I guess I am feeling guilty for being the one who first brought you the news."

"Guilty? You? How could you feel guilty? None of this was your fault," Monica said feeling another rush flood her body.

Nicola continued. "I was selfish in a way. When I met with you and the others at your home, I believed I was providing a great service. I did not give it a whit of thought concerning your feelings in your situation. I...I always feel uncomfortable when I cause any distress in another person, and now I presume you are facing one of the most difficult crossroads in your life."

Monica's anger vanished at the woman's kind words and anguish took its place. As she squeezed her eyes tightly closed, droplets oozed through, rolling over her cheekbones. Deep emotion pushed to the surface. She sniffed to stifle the gush of fluids that threatened to flow uncontrollably and was unable to speak. She was glad Monica could not see her at that moment.

"You don't have to say anything, Monica, but let me tell you this. Whatever happens in the next months, it will be the right thing. This I believe with all my heart. Gavin loved you and missed you. He also knew that he might never return, that he had to live each day with what he had, and he knew that you would have to do the same. He's a wonderful man. I think I know him well. He gave his life to the Lord in that miserable camp. Whatever the choice, he will be whole and well in his heart."

Once she and Nicola said their good-byes Monica placed the phone in its cradle. She sat motionless at her desk in the corner of the kitchen. It was here that she jotted menus and grocery lists, paid bills, wrote cards and letters, and checked her email. Not today. She pondered over Nicola's words.

Whatever happens in the next months, it will be the right thing. This I believe with all my heart. Gavin loved you and missed you. He also knew that he might never return, that he had to live each day with what he had, and he knew that you would have to do the same.

The words stung yet comforted her in some small way. How would she know what was right? She closed her eyes and envisioned Gavin's face as she remembered it. His gentle smile. Monica leaned her head back and Peter's face, not Gavin's, came into view. His eyes had a mischievous glint. His smile broad. Uncertainty and confusion clawed at her. She could no longer hold the emotions welling inside. They surged upward and outward. She cupped her hands around her face and allowed the sobs fill the air.

CHAPTER 14

Mel

In the late afternoon, Mel circled for the descent and landing at DIA. She frowned at the coiling billows of black, puffing toward the heavens. They assaulted the wondrous view of the peaks of jagged mountains usually frosted with brilliant snow.

June had hit Colorado hard. It had been unusually hot and dry the whole month. The lush growth from April had transformed into brittleness. If July continued as it began, many heat records would be broken. Two fires raged out of control west of Denver and several mountain homes had burned to the ground. How terribly helpless it must be, she thought, being evacuated from a home in danger, taking what few items one could quickly gather, then waiting afar off for news, wondering if their home was still standing.

Mel hated the lack of control that harbored in her chest. The hostage situation seemed gridlocked, and she could do nothing but wait and hope. The helplessness she felt could in no way compare to that of a fire victim, but she felt it just the same.

It had taken two weeks for Representative Parks' team, the Colombian officials, and the guerrillas to come up with some type of timeline and to set up a demilitarized place to meet. Nothing had happened in the two weeks since. Mechanically Mel droned on through the days, powerless to hurry the process, powerless to get her father home. She was getting impatient.

Guilt waved its flag in her face. *How can I be so selfish? I haven't been thinking of the suffering of the hostages. What must it be like to play the waiting and speculating game, not knowing what the future holds or if they have a future? Do they know about the hostage trade? Do they know about all the efforts being made for their release?*

The drive from DIA to her condo in Greeley was a fog. The hostage situation became a whirlwind of thoughts orbiting her mind. She had some information from Racine via McCrae's daily messages the first two weeks he was in Colombia. McCrae was not allowed to be a part of the negotiations, but Parks had been candid about the meetings. They had been frustrating and unproductive until the fifteenth day when some progress was made.

During the negotiations McCrae hired a guide and spent two days visiting the emerald mine southeast of Bogotá. It had been taken over by the Colombian government since it was now illegal for private persons to own such mines. He made friends with the head man at the site and would tell Racine more later.

McCrae also used his time to contact other Colombian officials and local Colombians who helped him to better understand the guerrillas and their cause. Two men, former guerrillas, had been particularly helpful and he planned to get assistance from them. He assured Racine that she should not worry, that he would be out of contact for a while, but he felt encouraged that he was sure he was on to something. There had been no news for six days. More worrying and wondering.

Mel needed to get the hostages out of her mind. *Oh, no.* Erik's image appeared, just when she thought she had washed it away. Not long after the treacherous thunder and lightning storm had chased them off the mountain, Mel read in the paper about hikers who had been hit by lightning in Rocky Mountain National Park. One had died and the other had severe burns and would take a while to recover. She guessed Erik and she were fortunate to be spared from the hazardous lightning that had flashed all around them. Sliding down the rocky hills during the dumping rain brought only bruises and bloody scrapes which healed quickly. Her bruised ego from Erik's comments about Mel's mother had not healed so quickly.

Neither had called the other in the following weeks. They had not been paired as flight partners, either. It was Erik who finally bit the bullet. The message on the answering machine spilled out, "Hey, I thought we were going on another adventure soon. Don't you think it's about time? Call me, I don't fly out until Thursday."

Still peeved about Erik's defense of her mother and his cautions about being judgmental concerning Charlotte's friendship with Arthur, Mel took her time to return his call. When they finally talked, neither could come up with a new adventure and they settled on Friday night dinner. Returning home for a Friday night alone after a flight often left her feeling let down. Perhaps being with Erik would counter that—if she could get rid of the betrayal bug biting at her. Thus, she both anticipated and dreaded the evening.

THE HAZE OF SMOKE HUDDLED over the distant mountains creating an eerie, but magnificent orange glow of sunset as Mel and Erik settled themselves at the outdoor table. They had chosen The Country Porch, a quaint eatery, because of the home-style cooking. Mel decided she needed to clear the smoky haze of dissension that hung between them. Unlike the lingering smoke that amplified the evening view over the mountain, this cloud of discord drove a wedge between, what had been if she was honest, a growing attraction. Whether Erik felt the wedge or not, or whether it had developed solely out of Mel's underlying resentment toward her mother, she would not feel relaxed until the cloud was obliterated.

Once the waitress had taken their orders, Mel fingered the knife placed on the sage green table linen. Without thought, she tapped the handle against the table as if sending a message by code.

After a bit, Erik leaned forward and clasped her hand, quieting the tap, tap, tap. "Something's bothering you. I have a good listening ear, if you want to talk about it."

Mel nodded and smiled. She wanted to ease her hand away but felt comfort in his tenderness and did not move nor speak.

Erik broke the silence. "From what I read in the news, things aren't moving very fast in Colombia. That must weigh heavily." He hesitated, then went on. "My guess is however, you are still hurt about my comments concerning your mother. I said you should be happy for her happiness. I think I said something about wishing my mother had enjoyed companionship, which she didn't do, because of me." There was another pause. His eyes, soft and gentle fixed on hers. "I was out of line to give my opinion. I'm sorry."

He *had* sensed her resentment. His apology cut through her. All the words she had rehearsed dissolved like salt in water.

There would be no—*Erik you have no right to judge me and how I feel about my mother's relationship with Arthur. Can't you see how disloyal she is to my father, cutting the light fantastic with this doctor and his country-clubbing? Especially when my father will be coming home? Sure, you're sorry that your mom waited to have companionship until it was too late, and the cancer took her. But don't put your guilt on me. I need you to let me handle my life without having some guilt trip put on me. Do you understand? If so, I think we can build on this relationship.*

Mel shook her head and cast her eyes away from his. "You're right. I have not thought about my mother's feelings. I didn't acknowledge her right to go on with her life. It was selfish, but also, I've been afraid. Afraid that my father, whom I've always adored—we've always been close, you know—would be hurt." She found his eyes with hers, saw the compassion there. She blinked, trying to control her emotion. "Thank you for helping me to see that."

Like a pack animal whose pack had been lifted away, she felt free and at peace. For the first time in a long time. The honest and caring conversation she and Erik shared during the evening left her with a comfort she had never felt with a man. Plus, she couldn't remember a more satisfying meal. Either the chef had been particularly skillful in the food preparation or her taste buds were on high alert, or perhaps both. Whatever the reason, every morsel churned deliciously over her tongue.

Before Erik helped Mel into the Tracker, he turned her toward him.

She leaned against the vehicle and sighed. Gazing into Erik's face, she said, "Look at that moon glowing through the smoky haze. It's a cozy night," said Mel.

"It sure is." His lips reached hers, tenderly, then hungrily and she returned the passion.

He inched backwards, grinning and asked, "There's no reason to get you home right away, is there?"

"No, not at all," she said with a flip of her head.

"Then are you up for a drive in the glowing moonlight?"

"I'd love it."

Erik removed the collapsible top from the Tracker and folded it away, then steered toward the foothills. July's evening air breezed through her hair and roused her nostrils. How could she have forgotten the romantic fragrance of summer?

Conchita

THE SEÑORA WON THE CONTROVERSY over the summer care for the children. However, there were compromises. Conchita said, "Mamá if the children stay with you this summer, I intend to pay you, at least for the extra food you will need to buy. Now don't argue with me." Her mother finally agreed. The other compromise was: On Wednesday Jack, Jenny and Pamela would attend a day camp. The children would have an opportunity to be with others their own age, giving the Señora a day to herself without constant activity. And she could keep her weekly grocery shopping schedule.

Grocery ads came out on Wednesday. Conchita's mother was certain that sale items would be gone later in the week and was rigid about shopping on Wednesdays. The next-door neighbor, Señor Garcia drove her, often to three different stores, to get the best bargains since the Señora didn't have a car, nor a driver's license. Señor Garcia is a dear,

Conchita thought. *If it weren't for him, I'd be the one driving Mamá to one store to purchase buy-one-get-one-free dried pinto beans and 10-for-$10 items at another.* Conchita suspected that, though her mother would never admit it, she had a crush on the gentleman and considered the weekly shopping like a date.

Conchita sighed in relief about her work schedule. She was able to keep her hours to 36 a week instead of increasing them to 40. *Someone upstairs was looking out for her,* she thought. This enabled Conchita to pick up her children when the day camp ended at 4:00. Some of the parents didn't get off work until 5:00 and the children had to wait alone. She was grateful hers did not have to stand in the hot afternoon sun. Pamela, always looking out for the other guy, had begged her mother to arrange for Jason to attend the day camp with them. After hearing about the suggestion, Greg offered to pay his fee and announced he would pay for her children as well.

Conchita argued, "You are too kind, but I can't allow it. I'll pay for my own children."

"Now Conchita," he countered, "I want to do it. It gives me a good feeling. Besides, I could never play favorites—pay for Jason and not Jack, Pamela and Jenny. Don't you see?" *How indebted she continued to be to Greg. More so every day. She could never repay him.*

Speculation had it that the hostages would be released before summer's end. That wasn't far away. *When would it happen?* In the dark of night before sleep overcame her, she vowed to cut her contact with Greg. Time and time again she uttered the vow. But in the light of day and when he came by to be sure the seed was doing what it was supposed to in the back yard, or called her on the phone, there was no way in God's green earth that she could tell him she and the children could no longer be his friends. She couldn't do that to the children, or herself for that matter. It would bring such loss and sadness. How would she face it when the time finally came?

Arriving at the day camp, Conchita pushed the idea aside. The children took their time to break away from a group that huddled on the lawn. Each had made new friends and Jack had asked if they could have a party before the day camp ended and invite some of their new friends. Conchita said she would need to have names and phone numbers so she could contact the parents before she said yes.

What are they doing? Can't they see I'm waiting? She honked the horn and Jenny came running. "Wait, Mamá. Jack is writing all the names and phone numbers. For the party. Remember? Jason's helping."

"I hope it won't take too long," Conchita said shaking her head. Like a little man, Jack seemed all business as Conchita watched him, listening, then writing, listening, then writing. Finally, Pamela joined her sister at the car and the twins climbed in.

"They're almost done," Pamela said, "We painted our pottery today. Look." Pamela pulled a pink and purple bowl from a plastic bag. Jenny broke hers."

"It was an accident," Jenny defended. "Our leader helped me fix it but I have to paint it again next week."

"Jenny cried," said Pamela.

"No, I didn't."

"She did," insisted Pamela.

"It doesn't matter," Conchita said, "We all cry sometimes when something sad happens." Would they all be crying soon when they had to say goodbye to their friend? Would they be cheering when Miguel returned? Maybe both.

Once Jason and Jack were settled in the car Jack read the eight names and phone numbers he had carefully scripted on the yellow lined paper. He folded the sheet with the concentration of an accountant entering numbers on a spreadsheet. On the way home the talk was lively—all about the possibility of a party. The twins would help decorate with balloons and streamers. What could they eat? Everyone had their own ideas. They had to play games, or maybe they could play baseball. Even Jason suggested having ice cream cones for dessert.

Conchita let them plot and plan until they reached the driveway. She stopped the car in front of the garage and said, "I can't promise that we will have the party. We have a lot of planning to do. We need to think of our schedule. I'll need to talk to all the children's parents, and they may want to meet our family before we plan such a party. It is not something that can happen over-night. And we might have to cut out some of the names on your list, Jack."

"But you promised." There was hurt in Jack's voice.

"My son, I promised that we would look into having a party. And we will, but I can't promise it'll work out. I sure hope so. We will see. Now all of you please get out and I'll put the car in the garage. Please tell your mother hello for us Jason. Maybe you can come play after supper. We all have chores to do."

Conchita sent the children inside to change their clothes while she set about getting the trash container and recycle containers in order. Pick up day was tomorrow, and she had thrown things haphazardly in the corner of the garage all week. Once the items were organized, she grabbed the sprinkler nozzle. The new lawn was parched from the summer heat. She needed to get the hose set before she went in to get the children started on their chores. In the back yard she fought the sprinkler. Every time she had it in position, the force of the water twisted it another direction. Twice she was showered and stood dripping with disgust when Jack called from the back door. "Mamá, somebody needs to talk to you. He says it's important."

Conchita had hidden her extreme fatigue from the children, but the struggle with the lawn sprinkler dragged her down further. No doubt her sopping appearance fit the stumbling, pokey pace as she loitered on her way toward the house. Everything weighed heavily and now the kids wanted a party. She wanted to do it for their sake, however at this moment her heart was not in it. How could she muster the energy to contact the children's parents and make all the preparations? Thinking of Jack and the way he had so carefully written the names and phone numbers, she didn't want to let him down.

"Mamá, are you coming?" Jack yelled, allowing his impatience to ring through to her.

Conchita's words accompanied a sigh. "I'm coming. What can be so important?" Another thing to heap on my shoulders, she thought. She had already agreed to bring treats for the day camp next Wednesday.

Inside the kitchen Conchita dried her hands and took the telephone receiver from Jack. She gazed into his upturned face with the sparkling dark eyes, so innocent, and filled with wonder. Conchita wanted at that moment to take him into her arms, to assure him that indeed they would have the party. He deserved it. She understood that Jack did not want the party only for his own joy, but for the joy of his friends, to bring them happiness. That was Jack. He would be a humble and gracious host. She wondered how he came to be such a fine boy when she had not always been available as he grew up. Too often, studying and getting their Habitat House built took priority. He was a good brother also, always watching out for his younger sisters.

His questioning eyes stared back at her. "Mamá?"

Conchita nodded and spoke into the mouthpiece. She knew the voice. Colonel Sipes. He talked in the clipped lingo bearing his position in the military. A wooziness hit her as the spilling words sought to win the race spinning in her brain.

She reached for a kitchen chair to pull it near. It tipped and clattered to the floor. Jack leaped, jerked it up and righted it at her side. "What is it Mamá?" Jack's eyes flashed his alarm.

Conchita crumpled onto the chair. Her hunched body rocked as if nodding at the words pelting her mind. As if hypnotized she uttered, "Yes…When?… Where?… I see…"

At last she placed the receiver in its cradle and leaned into her arms splayed onto the kitchen table. Why did the news hit her so hard, give her stomach the nauseous feeling that she could throw up? Shouldn't she be dancing on the table with joy and thanksgiving? Even good news can be overwhelming she thought. Then the sobs she could not control began.

Jack remained silent as he stroked his mother's trembling shoulder, then smoothed the wisps of hair escaping at her temples. The twins breezed into the kitchen, Jenny pushing ahead of her sister and blurted. "Mamá! What is it? Why are you crying?"

Jack raised his head to meet his sisters' eyes. "Mom is crying because our papá is coming back."

Mel

CHARLOTTE'S PLACATING TONE FLOATED ACROSS her living room and assaulted Mel's eardrum. "Of course, I want your father to come home. Of course, I want to see him."

Her mother's tranquil composure infuriated Mel. There she sat leaning into the back of the tapestry covered chair, her leg crossed in front of her, with hands resting in her lap. The nicely manicured nails of one hand tapped against the back of the other. She continued in a soothing voice, "But I can't abide all of the falderol of meeting with the medical community, being hounded by the media and having everyone looking over our shoulders."

Mel sputtered her response with vengeance. "You call it falderol? This isn't silly nonsense. Being held captive, living through all the hellish years and now his release. You don't want to go to San Antonio and meet with him once he's examined and released? What kind of wife are you?"

"Calm down, Marilyn," Charlotte said, leaning forward and straightening her back. "I just thought it would be more comfortable for everyone and especially your father if I waited to see him until he gets to Colorado. It would be private, a nice homecoming."

"It's Arthur, isn't it?" Mel asked, her voice continuing to escalate in volume. "You think my father can accept that you've taken up with another man more easily here than at the Army medical center." Mel jerked herself from the chair opposite her mother's and stomped toward the front door of the condo.

"Marilyn, Marilyn, sit down. This has nothing to do with Arthur. I'm trying to be rational about this whole hostage release. My understanding is the hostages are being taken to the air base in Bogota by helicopter but won't be flown to Brooke Army Medical Center for a day or two. Then no one knows how long they'll be at the hospital. Am I right?"

Mel turned from the door to face her mother, feet planted in a wide stance. "Even if it is several days don't you want to be there? Just knowing we are there will give moral support to Dad and the rest of them."

"It seems logical for me to wait it out here rather than down in San Antonio where all the hubbub will be, not knowing how long things will take. I can't do anything there. Don't you see?" Charlotte smiled as though to ease the tension and continued, "If you want to fly down and hang around until they are released, that's fine. I'd rather wait it out and see what happens."

"I still don't understand you mother. What if my father is deathly ill? What if he needs to stay in the hospital for some time?"

"Aren't you being overly dramatic? The government spokesman says the hostages are in reasonable health. Surely the medical examination is a precautionary measure and the men will be released to return to Colorado soon enough."

"I don't think I'm being overly dramatic," Mel said allowing resignation to color the edges of her words. "If you change your mind, call me."

Walking out of her mother's condo, Mel wondered if she would also be walking out of her mother's life.

Racine

BITTERNESS HAD NEVER RESIDED IN Racine's heart, not even in one little corner. Not when her mother abandoned her and her father, not when her father died, not even when Randy and the others went missing. Deep sorrow and crushing agony had lived there a while whenever strife had imbedded its stinger in her life. Yet each time the healing process created a thick scar where the hurt had been, and Racine forged onward determined to scatter good cheer wherever she went. Her easy smile, generosity, contagious laugh and colorful garments were the trademarks that drew people to her.

However, today bitterness moved in and refused to move out. The unfairness harboring in Racine dug at the scars, transforming the hurt lingering there into caustic resentment. Racine sat at her massive desk in the office that Chad had so expertly designed. Usually it was a pleasant place to work. This morning it seemed overwhelmingly oppressive. She glared at the headline splashed across the daily newspaper and read what she already knew. She had received the call last night with the exciting news—exciting to everyone except her. It wasn't fair.

Hostage Agreement Made–They're Coming Home

A SURPRISING ANNOUNCEMENT CONCERNING COLUMBIAN hostages came today. An agreement has been made concerning a hostage trade between FARC, the Colombian government, and the U.S. Originally FARC demanded release of 400 rebels imprisoned in Colombia and the U.S in exchange for less than two dozen hostages. Those demands and the inability for the Colombian government to agree on FARC's demands for specified demilitarized zones created a stalemate. The five-week stalemate over these issues has been resolved.

Among those arriving by helicopter in Bogotá today are Coloradans Ben Jameson, Miguel Vasquez and Gavin Humphreys. The three went missing over five years ago when they flew to Colombia on an emerald mining business venture. There is no word concerning Randy Rabinowitz who accompanied the three and reportedly had been captured with the others when their plane was shot down by rebels over the Colombian jungles.

New York journalist, Paul Constantine, taken hostage ten months ago, was among the 23 hostages released, as was German-Colombian national, Brita Vogelstadt. She has been heralded as a strong leader who had been campaigning for president of Colombia when captured just over three years ago.

In the final agreement 57 imprisoned rebels, seven from U.S. prisons and fifty from Colombian prisons were involved in the trade, a great reduction from the original demand of 400 rebels. Reportedly one of the hostages, Miguel Vasquez was instrumental in helping to solidify the negotiations. Information concerning the whereabouts of Randy Rabinowitz may come forth when the Coloradans arrive and are debriefed in San Antonio at Brooke Army Medical Center.

The remainder of the article was a haze. Racine could not read it.

Neither could she read the locally written stories of each of the four who had been missing. It was a rehash of what had been published when knowledge of the hostage situation came to play.

How could she celebrate the release of Ben, Miguel and Gavin, when the realization that her precious son was not coming home hit her like a sledgehammer smashing into her chest? And Larry McCrae. It had been weeks since any communication with him. His last phone call had been mysterious, as if he had some good news, but needed to check it out first. He said he would be out of touch for a few days, but not to worry.

Oh McCrae, where are you? Why did you go to Colombia in the first place? Maybe you've been captured too. And maybe you deserve it, taking my son away from me.

A light knock came from the door. It was Chad with his Aussie accent, warm and comforting. "Racine, are you OK? Can I come in?"

"No, go away and leave me alone."

Monica

MONICA'S HEARTBEATS SEEMED ERRATIC AS she hefted the travel case on the bed and mechanically began arranging the items stacked nearby. It wasn't the physicality of what she was doing that caused fluttery heartbeats, it was the tornado of emotions assaulting her from every angle. Managing the flight to San Antonio with the gosh-darned clumsy boot made handling luggage tricky. It was nothing compared to her apprehensions.

Mel, Conchita and she had booked their reservations to San Antonio yesterday and fortunately were able to get the same flight. When Peter had offered to come with her, she hadn't known what to say. She decided it would be best to go alone.

Monica had no idea where her marriage to Peter stood legally, since Gavin was alive and coming home. She was probably a bigamist. That could be worked out, but would she be the one who had to choose? How could she choose when she thought of all Gavin had gone through?

She zipped the packed case, walked to the dresser, and pulled open the top drawer. From beneath her underwear she retrieved the stack of papers Nicola had given her, the ones Gavin had written to her during his captivity. She had started to read them that night, until exhaustion overtook her, and she fell asleep. When she awoke, they had been neatly stacked on the dresser. Had Peter read them? She doubted it. He had not asked about them after she tucked them away in her underwear drawer. Why had she kept their contents secret?

Sitting in the cushiony corner chair of the bedroom, she reread them. The first several pages described the conditions of their capture, the dark and oppressing camp. He had made light of his injury but had expressed admiration for the tall missionary with the pewter colored hair who bravely nursed his wounded leg. Gavin told of the horrific massacre when Nicola's husband was killed. He made little of his part in saving her from bleeding to death from the gash sliced across her throat.

He wrote of the boredom of the rigid daily routine, and his appreciation of Nicola's company. In the beginning the writings were days apart, then they became weeks and finally a month or more. She read the last entry recorded in the sixth month of his captivity. The handwriting was small as Gavin had endeavored to get as much as possible on what was left of the note pad he had carried when they crashed. A few places were smudged, but Monica had been able to guess at the illegible words.

No one but God knows the outcome of this ordeal. I try to keep positive and dream of rescue or escape and rejoining you in the life we knew. I've been in this hell hole over six months. This is the last bit of paper that I have. I wonder if you are angry with me for coming to Colombia. Do you feel abandoned? I hoped the expedition would give us a head start on buying a house. Was I selfish to want that? Will you be able to have a house? I hope so. You are independent and self-sufficient so I imagine it will happen someday. I hope that you know I love you, even though I didn't say it often enough. If I die here and if these notes never reach your eyes I hope you know that. Time changes a person and I don't know if I am the same person you married. For some time the emptiness that overtook me left me hollow, unfeeling. I have Nicola to thank for helping to reclaim a purpose in life. One of the first psalms she taught me was the 23rd Psalm and it has helped me in some of my darkest hours. She shared other pieces of wisdom that gave me hope and strength. I believe we are given this gift of life and no matter what trouble comes barreling at us we are not to waste it.

Gavin's words stopped her. What would Gavin think of her now living in this grand house, much more opulent than the one she and Gavin would have been able to afford? Would he think she was wasting her gift of life? Was she? Had she been too judgmental, unable to appreciate, really appreciate either of her husbands? She read on.

Even if I never leave this place, I will live each day the best I can, smiling when I can see the sun, building the best fire on which to cook our beans and rice, being grateful for every breath I take. I've come to realize even the rebels have a human side. I can't hate them. They seem to be doing what they think is right.

I am sorry if I have caused you pain and sorrow. I wonder where you are today. Most probably at work. Later you might go to the health club. You always want to keep fit. I close my eyes trying to see your freckled face. I wish I had carried a picture of you in my wallet. Maybe I could look at your probing eyes, eyes that searched out every detail so you could fix what needed to be fixed. There is no picture, so all I can do is try to remember.

His being sorry for causing her pain touched her, but imagining Gavin trying to remember her eyes brought tears to hers. What did he mean about her eyes being probing, so she could fix what needed to be fixed? The words stung as did the tears that continued to blur her sight. Did he mean his main memories of her were when she tried to fix all his little faults, when she nagged him? He'd been laid back about neatness, putting things away, changing the grimy clothes he had worn for five days straight. She'd needed to have probing eyes, hadn't she? One couldn't leave everything in a mess. That wasn't the way to live. Was it?

Monica cleared the tears away in order to read Gavin's last words to her. They had been squeezed in around the outside of the note paper and Monica had to rotate the sheet to read the message.

My steady and dear friend Nicola has promised to keep these messages in the little pouch she keeps hidden. I can count on her to get these to you if I don't make it and she does. I send you my best and want you to go on with your life and find its true meaning. Your loving husband, Gavin

Holding Gavin's notes against her chest, her breath stalled deep inside. She couldn't swallow or move until a massive sob exploded from her throat. Then the stalled breath came in short bursts wailing against the walls of the bedroom in a mournful cry that had been welling up for years. She gripped the arm of the chair to steady her convulsing body. The notes slipped to her lap and captured the droplets streaming from her eyes. She quieted the woeful cries, but the sobbing convulsions she could not control.

Beside her the phone rang, but she could do nothing except listen to the repeated sound drilling through her. When it stopped, she heard the answering machine pick up downstairs. Peter's voice echoed up the staircase loud enough for her to hear, "Hey Babe. How are you doing? I'm on my way home to help you pack. I left early and am bringing us a light supper. I doubt if you are very hungry, but you'll need something nutritious in that bod of yours. Love, ya."

CHAPTER 15

Conchita

With news of the hostages return, Conchita, Mel, and Monica were fortunate to book a flight to San Antonio. They were unable to arrange seats next to each other and Conchita was relieved, as she was not in a mood to talk.

Once they were airborne and when the cabin caution light had been turned off, Conchita reclined in the seat of the Airbus Jet and leaned into the headrest. The two hour and ten-minute flight gave Conchita time to think of her children. In their minds, the party they had talked about was a definite go. Jack, the young organizer, not only had the guest list with phone numbers written down, he also had a list of the food to be served and the games to be played. When it became certain that his mother would fly to meet Miguel, the father he had not seen since he was two and one-half, Jack accepted that the party would be postponed.

"We can have the party when Papá is back," Jack had called out. "He can help us. And play the games with us. We can play baseball. It'll be a surprise for my friends."

Through a sigh and a cautious smile, Conchita had responded with what had become a common phrase. "We will see my son. Time will tell. There is so much we don't know and won't know until later."

She couldn't disappoint the children. They would have to have the party. Conchita turned toward the window of the cabin. The Rocky Mountains were fading from view as the plane lifted higher into the blue sky. She wished she felt excitement about taking her first flight in a commercial jet. Most people looked forward to such an event. Somehow the mixed feelings she had about seeing Miguel dampened the excitement.

Her only plane ride had been when Miguel trained in the minor leagues at Colorado Springs. Just before he was called up to the majors, a fan had invited him for a short ride. Jake, the full-bellied owner and pilot of the plane insisted that Miguel bring Conchita. In his loud and boisterous banter Jake refused to accept her decline. "Missy, we need some feminine beauty up there. I promise you I'm a safe pilot. On the ground, I'm the reckless jokester, but in the clouds I'm all serious and on guard. Now come on, yer not goin' to disappoint me are ya?"

Conchita conceded, but had to endure Miguel's taunts until flying day arrived. "You're no daredevil. In that tin box you'll be scared out of your skin. Better take a puke bag." In defiance of his mockeries, she would prove him wrong.

She and Miguel arrived at the airport just after sunrise. There wasn't a cloud to be seen in the crisp April morning. Approaching the private prop plane Conchita questioned the sanity of her decision to leave the ground in what looked like a giant mosquito. Maybe Miguel was right. Crawling up into the cabin, Jake directed her to take the rear seat and buckle up near an odd shaped little window. Miguel sat beside the pilot. Once the prop began spinning, the plane vibrated and rocked furiously, and as Jake engaged the throttle they wheeled onto the short runway.

When they lifted from the ground Conchita tried to ask Jake how high they would be flying, but her voice did not carry over the rattling rumble of the engine. The plane banked to the left and made a couple of circles over the Air Force Academy, then headed south over the city and finally away from it. Conchita's stomach rolled as Jake made the turns and she swallowed hard hoping that the sickish feeling would soon leave her. It did.

Stretching tall she peered out of the window hoping to take in the view. Even with the stretch, the angle of the window prevented her from seeing below her. However, she could look out toward the mountains in the west and see snaking roads among the rolling hills. Cars, resembling the toys Jack had pushed along in the dirt a few years back, glinted in the sun as they drove in both directions like so many busy ants. Nothing appeared as she expected. Some fields, deep brown from the recent tilling, formed checkerboard patterns alongside of a green lawn of winter wheat beginning to sprout and the golden coat of stubble from an earlier harvest, not yet turned under with a plow blade. Most of the terrain looked dead with very little green, except for a golf course nested against the hillside, its serpentine fairways twisting this way and that between rock outcroppings. Further west the snowy mountain caps had barely started the spring melt and seemed to wink at her in the early morning sunlight.

The men in the front kept up a quick banter, using plentiful gestures, pointing here or there and driving home a point in the exchange. It was just as well that she couldn't grasp their conversation, as she never felt particularly comfortable with men-talk. She was satisfied to remain silent and sit back to enjoy the buzzing roar of the "mosquito" plane and look around as much as she could.

It took little more than minutes, she thought, to reach Pueblo where steel manufacturing plants belched steam and smoke. They veered west and headed toward the foothills. Jake turned and yelled to her, "We'll fly over Canon City and the Royal Gorge. That's a deep canyon to see from the air. Then we'll loop back to the Springs." If she hadn't been able to read his lips, she would have missed a big part of the message.

The flight over the gorge gave her stomach another jello-jiggly when they hit an air pocket and dropped eight or ten feet. The bridge that spanned the deep gorge met her eyes and caused several moments of anxiety. We can't crash into the massive cables or giant arms holding the bridge, she thought. Miguel twisted around to stare at his wife.

He laughed and waved a shaking finger at her. "See, flying is not for weenies," he taunted.

The memories faded and her thoughts returned to the present. Conchita nodded to herself. She had proven she was not gutless. She had made it on her own all these years without Miguel. He was right, she wasn't a daredevil, but she was brave. She believed that about herself. There wasn't much she feared. There was a time she had feared Miguel's rage and disapproval. But now—heights, hard work, giving an oral presentation when she was in nurses training, balancing work and parenting—none of this brought fear to her. No fear would inhabit her when Miguel returned.

Mel

FOLLOWING AN UNEVENTFUL FLIGHT, THE plane landed at San Antonio International Airport and its passengers disembarked. Mel, Conchita and Monica boarded an airport van and headed toward the Holiday Inn Hotel and Suites. Two couples shared the ride with the women. Two minutes into the ride Mel learned the men were on business and their wives had come along for shopping and site seeing.

"Are the three of you together?" the wife with the dyed jet-black hair asked Mel.

When Mel nodded yes, the other wife, peered over her dark glasses and questioned in her pronounced Texas drawl, "What brings ya'all to San Antonio?"

Mel glared at the others with a don't-tell-them-anything look, and Monica convincingly said, "Visiting friends…" Then as an afterthought she added, "And we hope to see the area while we're here."

The Texas drawl floated through the van as the second wife continued, "You'll love San Antonio. Course ya'all have to take the River Walk. Can spend the whole day exploring. And don't miss the Main Plaza and Fernando Cathedral, right Glendeen?"

Grateful to have the conversation focused away from them, Mel gladly listened to the list of tourist attractions and shopping spots they must visit. She even accepted the personal card offered by Glendeen, the one with the black dye job.

"You can contact us through the concierge. We'll be happy to guide you," Glendeen said, tilting her head so that her nose insinuated aristocracy.

"Why, thank you," Mel gushed in tones completely out of character, "But our friends have already arranged a packed schedule and I am sure we won't have a minute to spare."

At the hotel, the two groups went their separate ways. Greg had insisted on paying for Conchita's hotel which freed Mel and Monica from any obligation to help save money by rooming with her. Mel was grateful to have her own alone-space and believed the others felt the same. She imagined the questions and awkwardness that would occur between the three women who had been thrown together because of the men in their lives. *Who wants to use the bathroom first? Shall we have a cot brought in for one of us or should two of us share a bed? Which towel do you want to use?*

The most difficult part, however, involved the emotional roller coaster they were on. How will it feel to see the men that had been lost to them all these years, lost without hope? How changed will they be? When Nicola appeared, her story brought uncertainty, but hope. Then the examination of photos. Questioning, are these our men? Now, finally the men were on U.S. soil. Unbelievable.

Since the women had taken the early flight, there was plenty of day left to investigate the progress of the medical exams and the reintegration process the released captives would be experiencing. Contacting her father was the first thing on Mel's mind. In her room she drew open the heavy drapes to let in the light and sat on the bed beside the bag she had dropped upon entering. She grabbed the phone and pushed the button to make an outside call. She fingered the card on which she had written phone numbers for the Brooke Army Medical Center, then pressed each number carefully, not wanting to make a mistake. The person who answered on the other end was unable to give her any help and seemed to be either avoiding her questions about her father and the other two men or was completely unaware of any reintegration process going on at the center. He gave her two more numbers to call and the second one proved fruitful.

She learned that her father, Gavin, Miguel, and the New York journalist had arrived at Brooke Army Medical Center two days earlier. They were still being housed at the hospital, though most of the medical assessments had been completed. The reintegration process was pretty involved and a meeting with her father would need to be cleared through proper channels.

Furious with the uncertain possibility about an afternoon meeting, Mel blurted, "You have no right to keep me from seeing my father. Reintegration process or not, I demand to see him this afternoon."

Sucking in a deep breath she sputtered on. "It's a miracle the hostages are on American soil and you have no authority to keep us apart. How would you feel if it was your father who had been held hostage for five years? Don't you people have a heart?"

Mel interrupted the voice that attempted to say something as she went on, "You'd better have clearance issues resolved when I arrive at 3:30 this afternoon. That's all the time I'll give you. If it doesn't happen, I'll call in the big guns and all the media I can find. Let them drag you through the mud concerning your irresponsible treatment of hostage family members. And Mr. Vasquez and Mr. Humphreys better be ready to receive family as well."

A bead of perspiration settled on her forehead and she swiped it with the back of her hand. She had no idea who the big guns she threatened to call in would be, but perhaps the threat of media would hurry them to clear the hostages for a meeting with loved ones. She'd rip the place apart if she had to. No one could keep her from seeing her father. With the phone calls behind her, she left her room.

The three women planned to meet in the hotel coffee shop for lunch. Avoiding the elevator, Mel took the stairs two at a time, hoping to burn off the fury eating at her. Four floors later she hit the ground floor. Monica and Conchita already had a table, and both watched as Mel marched in, fire still flashing from her eyes.

Mel told Monica and Conchita about the phone calls. This riled her further until she realized others were looking her way. Following a deep breath and a roll of her eyes, she quieted her voice, "Sorry gals. I really don't want everyone to hear what's going on. I hope we can keep as much privacy as possible. Guess I almost blew it. We do need to stand up for ourselves and the men, though."

"Yes, we do," Monica agreed.

When their orders arrived, the three had little success getting their food down. Conchita's eyes shifted side to side as she picked at her salad and nibbled at the toasted garlic bread. Monica placed her hand on Conchita's arm and asked, "Are you OK?

"I think so. A little jittery, I guess. I can't eat any more," Conchita laid the toast across her half-eaten salad and continued, "I think I should call the children and let them know we arrived. Don't know if I should tell them I might see their father this afternoon. I don't want them to get their hopes up. Who knows what Miguel will be like?"

Monica's voice was gentle. "It's impossible to predict, isn't it? The news reports have made him out to be some hero concerning the negotiations. Maybe he's really changed."

The conversation halted, each in her own thoughts.

Mel picked up her glass of iced tea, took a swallow and placed it on the table. "Don't know why I'm so thirsty, but I'm like you Conchita, food doesn't appeal much." She sighed. "I guess we're all a little tense, uncertain of what our meetings will be like. It's less complicated for me. I'm worried about my dad's health, and what's going to happen to my parents' marriage, since Mom seems caught up with dear ole Arthur. Tough for you Conchita and I can't imagine your situation Monica. I wish I knew what to say to make things easier."

"There's nothing to say," Monica said shaking her head. "When Nicola first talked about Gavin being alive and spending those years in camp with her, it all seemed so foreign, so unreal, so far away. I couldn't picture him back in Colorado. I couldn't even fathom that this moment was possible. That was stupid. Now that Gavin is nearby, I feel, well… like those silly green gumby men you pull and stretch every which way. Like half of me is over there at the far window," she said spreading her arm to the right, "and the other half of me is stretched clear across the restaurant. I'm pretty thin in the middle."

Monica lowered her head into her hands as her elbows propped against the table. A shiver shook through her. Conchita pulled herself from her chair and wrapped her arm around the shaking woman. "We're strong. We'll know what to do, we will."

Mel watched the tender scene as the lump in her throat engulfed any words she might utter. This should be a fantastic celebration with released prisoners coming home. Yet more than one situation dampened the thrill. First, Randy was still unaccounted for. Mel could only imagine Racine back in Colorado, her pain, and frame of mind.

Then the little comments Mel heard from Conchita indicated she felt obligated to stand by her husband no matter what. The news media had raised Miguel to near hero status with reports that he somehow aided in the negotiations for the hostage release. Mel knew about Miguel's abusive actions and didn't want Conchita to live with that again, especially when anyone could see Greg was hopelessly in love with Conchita and she was definitely fond of him.

And poor Monica, Mel thought. No wonder she felt stretched to the nth. Mel didn't know another woman who woke up one day to the realization she had two husbands. And some of us have never even had one. *Don't kid yourself. You never wanted one. Until…*

At that moment Erik's face came into her mind. The words he said last night when he stopped by her condo touched her deeply "Mel, I can't wait to meet your father. He has to be one hell of a man to have a daughter like you, beautiful, intelligent and talented."

Mel had put her hand up to halt his words. "I think you have me confused with someone else."

"Let me finish. It's all true, yet it's that hint of mystery that's got me." His eyes twinkled with the dancing light of sparklers on the fourth of July. Then he raised a thumb to the air and said, "Go get him, Mel."

Mel smiled to herself. Yes, she would soon see her father. No matter what, she would stand by him.

CHAPTER 16

Racine

The day at the restaurant crawled with the speed of a giant sea turtle stuck on a sand bar. Rather than mixing with patrons and employees as she usually did, Racine stayed in her office, hoping to avoid the inquiring eyes. Numerous orders, receipts and new menu designs scattered across her desk in atypical disorganization. *What happened to Randy? Why is he still missing?*

Memories overtook her, flooding her mind and sending torrents from her eyes, until splotches of teardrops left several papers wrinkled and smudged. The memories were so real that she could smell baby Randy's scent and visualize his shock of russet hair, poking straight into the air as she dried his rounded body fresh from a bath.

How had she been blessed with such an easy child to raise? From the age of a few months he was dragged from one place to another and learned to sleep through anything. He was such a good little guy, never making a fuss. Smiles and coos delighted his mother and his many different babysitters. Since Racine worked from 4:00 p.m. to 11:30 p.m. nearly every day, she resolved to spend as much daytime as possible with the son she was so proud of. And through the years she did just that. They built castles of blocks, turned page after page reading the adventures of Paul Bunyan, of Mowgli in the Jungle Book, or skipped through parks looking for autumn leaves to make into jumping piles. She managed to get him to soccer practice and cheer him on at most of his games.

The waitress job at Gracie's Grill and Tavern was perfect for her. Howard and Gracie made things as easy as possible and never once made her feel awkward, out of place, or like she had done something foolish. In fact, Howard and Gracie, who never had children of their own, treated Randy like a grandson. Yet, they were no competition when it came to Granpop Rubin.

Remembering her father brought more tears. She still missed the man who had single handedly raised her after her mother abandoned them when Racine was nine. She smiled thinking of Matilda. *Thank you for giving Dad so much love in his later years. And you were a fine grandmother.*

The memory of the months before her father's death lingered. Randy and his granpop both shared April birthdays and they always celebrated at the farm near Akron. In mid April Racine and Randy made the anticipated trip. Upon entering the farmhouse Randy sniffed the air, "I think that's good old fried chicken I smell."

Matilda gave him a welcome hug, then held him away from her, "How's my favorite young man? Nearly twelve years old. Your granpop is waiting in the living room. Been coughing up a storm. Might want to stay your distance."

After all the greetings were made, Matilida put Racine's cheesecake, one of her father's favorites, in the refrigerator and led Racine into the bedroom. "Racine," Matilda started in a hushed voice. "I don't like the way this cold or flu bug is hanging on. He's been like this for days. He can't sleep with all this coughing and gagging. And nothing I buy from the drugstore seems to help."

"You must be exhausted too, trying to doctor him and getting no sleep yourself," Racine said. Matilda shrugged as Racine continued, "And knowing Pop he refuses to see a doctor."

"You know the ole goat," Matilda responded, with a glint in her eye and affection in her voice. "Please do what you can to get him to go. I'm worried."

After the delicious dinner, they brought out the birthday gifts. Granpop presented Randy with the usual card and two crisp twenty-dollar bills. Racine brought her father a hefty bag of nuts he could crack and munch on for a week or two. Frugal as he was, she knew he would make them last as long as possible.

Randy handed his granpop a brightly wrapped package. Ruben lifted four hand-tooled leather coasters from the box and winked at Randy. "Guess you heard Matilda tried to throw out this old doily." He lifted a frayed and well-stained doily from the end table beside him and waved it in the air. "Yup, I think these will protect the table when I have my coffee and read the newspaper. Son, you did a fine job. Thanks."

Witnessing another of her father's coughing spells Racine begged her father to see a doctor. "Racine get off my back," Rubin spouted at his daughter, "I've been doing fine all these years. Hardly ever been sick and don't need no doctor telling me to go to bed and drink plenty of fluids or dumping me full of pills."

"Pop, I know you've been strong as a horse, but since this thing is hanging on, it's a different story. What if you have pneumonia? We want you around for a long time and not with damaged lungs."

With that her father stomped out of the room and another coughing spell hit him hard. Racine's eyes followed her father's exit as she shook her head in frustration. "He won't listen to me either, just gets mad. He's a stubborn old cuss."

Randy looked up and spoke, "You want me to talk to Granpop, Mom?"

"No, I don't want him yelling at you, too."

Disobeying his mother's wishes, Randy left the dinner table and followed his granpop into the hallway and bedroom. There were some words spoken between the two, but neither Matilda, nor Racine could make them out.

In a few minutes Rubin and Randy returned to the dining room. "Sorry I yelled at you." Rubin said to his daughter, "Just know your ole Pop is tough. I'm fine. And will be fine, and that's all there is to it."

However, that was not all there was to it. The next week Rubin was hospitalized with blood clots in his lungs. The medical staff administered blood thinners and thought things were doing better. A few days later his blood count dropped horribly, and he received five units of blood. The doctor said he was bleeding internally but could not determine the source of the bleeding. He became sicker and weaker. When it was apparent the loss of blood had damaged his kidneys and he was in kidney failure, everyone knew the end was near. That is how Racine and Randy came to be at his bedside on April 30th when Rubin took his last breath. He died on Randy's twelfth birthday. Through the years Randy had vacillated between thinking it had been an honor and a heartbreak.

Clarence and Ruth Wooly owned the next farm over, and following Ruben's death they began the process of negotiating to buy the Rabinowitz property. Rubin's will stipulated that Matilda could reside in the house as long as she lived, but the farm, one of the smallest in the area, was to be Racine's. Eastern Colorado was suffering a drought—had been for three years—and farm property value was way down. The few calls Racine made concerning property value led her to believe that the offer was fair enough, but would not make her rich, by any means.

"The timing is excellent," Clarence had maintained when he again made the offer, not yet a month after Rubin's death. "Jimmy and his wife want to come back to the farm. They've been in the Army you know and are ready to get back to civilian life. They'll need a house and yours seems perfect. They'll be wanting a young'n soon, I just know. I'm hoping to cut back a little on working the land and with Jimmy, well, I can do that. And with the extra 150 acres from your spot, I think we can make it."

Racine responded, "Clarence, there's a lot to think about before I sell the property. Matilda, for example."

"Well, I'm sure we can work that out. And neither of us will have to worry about the charges of a realtor, so we can both get a break there. You'll get back to me. Soon. Right?"

Soon came two months later when Matilda died suddenly of the heart disease that had plagued her for years. With Racine's stepmother gone it fell upon her and Randy to dismantle the farmhouse. As Racine walked into the home where she had grown up, a kind of darkness filled her. This was an end of an era, she thought. In a few days she would walk out of here and never return. Randy stepped to her side and tried to add cheer to the room.

"I bet this was a nice place to grow up. With Granpop and all."

It stunned her to realize he was nearly her height. Surely, he had grown two inches in the past couple of months. She nodded to him and took a deep breath.

"Look Mom." He picked up the leather coasters stacked on the side table near his granpop's chair. The soiled doily had been discarded after all and the coasters used, if only for a short time. "This one has a coffee stain on it."

Racine turned away from her son attempting to hide the cloud of grief overcoming her. "Yeah," she said, hoping Randy did not hear the catch in her voice, "We'll keep those. Granpop would like that."

"There's more Mom." Racine regained her composure and turned toward her son. He held a beautifully carved wooden lid of variegated shades of caramel. He had lifted it from an equally exquisite matching bowl. "The nuts," he said. Though he smiled bravely, Racine saw the tears spilling down his cheeks.

She stood watching her son and could no longer control her own tears. Randy replaced the lid and stepped close to his mother. His hug seemed awkward and stiff at first, then it softened and tightened as Racine wrapped her own arms around the son, who seemed much more mature than his years. She felt droplets moisten her shoulder as he said, "It's OK to cry when we feel sad, Mom."

"Yes, son, it's OK to cry when we feel sad."

Two farmers in the vicinity brought their trucks and with the help of three local women, the mother and son sorted through the lifetime stored in the old farmhouse. One truck was used for the throw-aways which ended up in the county dump. There was no way Racine could spend the time organizing a garage sale, thus the other truck was packed, load after load, with items to be donated to the community.

She couldn't be away from work very long since Howard was sick. No one knew what was going on with him, something internal they said. Before she left, Gracie reminded, "Take all the time you need at the farm." But without Howard's help Racine knew Gracie needed her at the grill and tavern.

The truck for community items got crammed with clothes, linens, kitchen stuff, towels, canning jars, blankets and even things like cleaners and toilet paper. Then came the furniture. Most pieces were usable but had little value. They certainly didn't fit in the antique category. At the end of two days, the house bare and void of furnishings, not only echoed a bit, but looked sad and dingy. They kept very few items. Racine's small cache included glassware which had been handed down from her grandmother and great aunt, plus the nut bowl and a footstool her dad made one winter when the snow kept them inside for two whole weeks. She wasn't sure why she wanted the wooden cradle and ornately decorated brass hand mirror. They stood for anguish and bitterness as they had belonged to the woman who had born her yet loved her so little that she abandoned her. Racine couldn't think of her as Mother.

Randy wanted one of Granpop's toolboxes and chose a selection of his best tools, then carefully organized them in the rusty compartments. He also wanted the bedroom set which Racine agreed to. The painted set in Randy's room at home looked like a young kid's, and he was quickly growing out of that stage.

The Woolys, taking the last truck load of furnishings to town, reminded Racine and Randy that supper would be at 6:00. Racine appreciated the offer of food and a place to sleep for the night but knew the subject of the sale of the farm would be a topic of conversation.

She was certain Clarence expected some kind of answer tonight. Leaning her back against a wall of the living room, Racine sat on the floor and pulled a well folded paper from her handbag. As she smoothed the unfolded paper in front of her, Randy came from the kitchen carrying a plastic tumbler of lemonade that one of the ladies had brought. "Thirsty, Mom?" he said as he raised the tumbler to the air.

"No, I'm fine, hon. I do need some advice though."

Randy sat beside her and sipped on the drink while he listened.

"Shall we sell, son?" Racine said smiling at Randy. "The Woolys really want to buy—now. Or should we find a renter for the property and hope for a better price in a few years, when, hopefully the drought passes, and land values go up?"

Randy looked surprised yet pleased at his mother's questions. Together, mother and son poured over the lists Racine had scripted. The first heading read, Sell now to the Woolys. The second, List with a realtor. The third, Find a renter and sell later. There were pros and cons for each heading. An hour later, Racine, impressed with her son's questions and insight said, "Ready to vote?"

"Sure, Mom."

Racine tore two corners from the paper and each secretly wrote a choice. "You read them," Racine suggested.

Randy high fived his mom's hand and announced, "We sell to the Woolys."

With the contracts for the sale of the Rabinowitz farm signed, and a closing date established for the final papers, Racine and Randy headed back to Greeley in early afternoon. The mother and son alternated between periods of solitude and moments of remembering times on the farm. After one period of quiet, Randy was the one to break the silence.

"Mom, you never talk about your mother. I know it was wrong for her to leave you and Granpop, but do you remember anything about her? Do you look anything like her?"

Racine took her time to answer. "I remember she complained about most everything on a farm. Somehow, being a farmer's wife was beneath her. I don't quite understand it, because she grew up on a farm, too. I think she hated chickens more than anything—feeding them, gathering eggs, butchering the fryers, particularly cleaning the henhouse. One day she went on strike and said she wasn't going to touch another chicken. And she didn't. That's when I took over the henhouse. I was eight. I fed the chickens and gathered the eggs and your granpop butchered and cooked up a chicken sometimes on Sunday."

She told how her mother liked to sing, liked the sunshine, hated wind and dust. She tried to focus on the good things, avoiding her own feelings of being treated with indifference and the observation that her mother did not like being around children. Racine sighed before she went on. "I guess she was just unhappy and longed for an exciting life. She was very beautiful and spent hours making pretty clothes and wearing them around the house. No other farmer's wife dressed like that, except maybe for a party. Yes, she was beautiful," Racine's voice sounded wistful, but held vehemence when she said, "but I'm nothing like her, inside or outside."

In Racine's side vision she saw her son turn toward her and sensed his own wistfulness. "Mom, I know it's hard to talk about her, but I appreciate it. It's good to know about our roots, don't you think?"

Racine's heart felt the stab of a thousand needles. She bit her lip hard to ward off the intense ache that mushroomed to a near explosion. She knew Randy longed to know the story of his own father, yet she remained silent. She couldn't tell him.

The memory of what was left of her thirty-fifth year lived with her, but in a haze of inky blue. It was like giant dominos crashing into one and another and another. Racine could not stop them from crushing the people who meant so much to her. One week after the closing on the farm, Howard died of colon cancer.

The tavern closed for three days as everyone mourned Howard's passing. Racine and Carlotta expected to take on extra duties as Gracie found her footing and stepped back to running the business. But, Gracie, the one with all the spunk and fire, the one who was the glue that held the business together, fell into a stupor. She could not walk through the door of Gracie's Grill and Tavern without falling apart. Gracie's words came from a mouth twisted in pain as she cried out to Racine and Carlotta, "My life's over. He was the love of my life. I can't do this. Let's close the doors forever."

They hadn't closed the doors after all. In the end Gracie was glad to see the grill continue but requested that Gracie's Grill and Tavern be renamed. By the time all was settled, the legal work, the change of the name and some remodeling of the building, every penny of her inheritance was spent on *Racine's Pub*. Racine's father would be proud that his daughter had her very own restaurant and bar.

Though everyone rallied around Gracie, nothing seemed to comfort her. Deep sadness permeated her whole being and momentary efforts to be lively and cheerful failed to bring her out of her depression. Eventually she moved to Tuscan to be closer to her sister. That was twelve years ago. Last year Gracie's Christmas card was returned and scrawled across the envelope was the word deceased.

She had to stop all this remembering. Racine attempted to organize the scattered papers by stacking them in piles on her desk. She couldn't take it any longer. Though she didn't know what she would do when she got there, she decided to go home. She certainly wasn't any good at the restaurant and bar. It had been a long time since she stayed until closing at 11:30. These days she left about 6:00 and often prepared a salad at home and snuggled up with Spunky and on occasion watched a little TV. Chad had everything going well and she wasn't needed so much at the pub.

The moment Racine reached the door leading from the garage into the hallway of her house she heard a scurry on the slick tile and three little yips. Spunky stood on his hind legs pawing the air as she opened the door. He jumped toward his mistress, wiggling his whole body, tail wagging with the exuberance of a lottery winner.

Racine dragged her tired body across the threshold and eyed the pooch with a blend of exhaustion and indifference. Spunky's enthusiasm stalled abruptly and he stood rigid, his four feet planted. He peered through eyes, both wary and sorrowful, then followed Racine with the obedience of a scolded child. Racine ignored the little Shitzu and wound her way through the living room and into Randy's bedroom.

He hadn't used the room a great deal. They moved into the condo during Randy's senior year of high school. Attending Colorado State University meant living on campus forty miles away. He came home some weekends and during summers, thus the room was used only for sleeping. No hobbies, no projects, no studying as he had done in the apartment. It was, however, a spacious room with windows on two sides.

Even though Racine had kept the door open the five-plus years he'd been gone, the smell of the room bordered on musty. She walked to the dresser, the one that had been her father's and ran a finger across it. Needs dusting, she thought. On the chest sat the carved wooden bowl with its lid. The nut bowl. To the right rested the stack of leather coasters her son's young fingers had tooled. Racine held one to her nose and sniffed. The smell of leather lingered. Then she spotted the coffee stain. Some things don't change. Others…well. She closed her eyes and dizziness surrounded her. "Well, Pop, your grandson may never return," she said to the air. "How do we deal with that?"

In the living room she plopped herself on the roomy recliner. Spunky quietly slithered up beside her and cozied against her thigh. Involuntarily she fingered the fluff of his hair and leaned back, her eyes closed. She supposed that Monica and the others had seen the hostages by now. Surprisingly, there had been little more said on the TV about the hostages arriving at San Antonio. It was time for the local five o'clock news. Since three of the men were Coloradans, surely the local news would carry something. Should she turn it on? She couldn't feel anymore dejected, regardless of what she heard, she thought.

Pictures flashed on the screen. Surprisingly the first one was of Nicola greeting Monica, Mel and Conchita. A newscaster's voiceover identified each one. Pictures of Mel and Ben Jameson waving over some balcony followed. Racine thought Ben looked fit, yet older and quite gray. Again, there was no interview, only the newscaster's voiceover explaining their identity. The two following balcony shots showed Conchita and Miguel. Miguel stood erect with apparent confidence and held Conchita tucked in tightly at his side. Did Conchita appear bewildered, she wondered? Miguel waved and the couple turned and walked through the door behind them. When Monica and Gavin's picture came into view, Racine noticed they stood apart, each one leaning an arm against the balcony. They turned to each other and nodded. The newscaster explained that every effort to respect the hostage's privacy was being made and the reintegration process would be completed before the released hostages could return to Colorado.

"It is not known," the newscaster said, "whether any of the released hostages know the whereabouts of Randy Rabinowitz."

Racine again closed her eyes and allowed the sounds from the TV to drone on without fully comprehending any of them. When the phone rang, Racine roused from her stupor to the darkness of the closing evening. It took precious moments to find the lamp switch and retrieve the phone from its cradle nearby. Surely this call is important, she thought.

The voice on the phone faded in and out, but she was sure it was McCrae. "It's Racine. Is that you McCrae?"

Static answered back. Then, "Yes, I.....you....hang-up.....better signal..."

What did he mean? Hang-up until he got a better signal? No, she wouldn't. She had to talk to him and ask about Randy. "Can you hear me McCrae?"

She finally surmised that she was coming through pretty clear, even though he was breaking up every couple of words. She kept talking. "It's so good to hear your voice. You're alive. Praise the Lord. I just saw Gavin, Ben and Miguel on TV. You know they made it back don't you? Where's Randy?"

With much frustration Racine said things over and over and eventually was able to piece together several of McCrae's responses before the phone went dead. With the line blank McCrae didn't hear her say, "McCrae, be careful."

Larry McCrae had made his way to a jungle village where there was limited phone service. Yes, he knew the guys would be in the states by now. Randy had not been in the same hostage camp as the others. There was word that an American hostage with reddish hair was on the move with a small band of guerrillas. He and a military commando were tracking them. He thought they were three days behind the combatants

Numb, Racine leaned her head back against the chair. Three days.

CHAPTER 17

Conchita

Miguel and Conchita barely had time to greet each other before they were ushered to the balcony for a media shoot. The whole ordeal of making a show by posing for photos unnerved Conchita. And certainly, there was no privacy. She was grateful that after the shoot, they were immediately whisked off to a private room near the hospital food court for the evening dinner hour. It eased the awkwardness she felt at talking to Miguel, the husband who seemed like a stranger.

Once they selected their food, Miguel led the couple to the far corner out of earshot of the other two pairs. When they were seated, Miguel leaned back in his chair and eyed her carefully.

"Look at you," he said. "Haven't lost any of your good looks. Maybe a few pounds heavier, huh?"

Her thoughts rolled over the hint of a jab. Then she dismissed it. Handsome and assured, there was a suggestion of the charm he had used on her in high school, and memories flooded her. "I suppose so. I'm so glad you're safe Miguel. I'm so sorry you had to endure so much all these years. I can't even imagine."

"You're right. It wasn't easy. Not like you. You were comfortable in the trailer park with Clifford next door to help. Me, I wasn't sure if I'd ever see this day. I guess we all have my ingenuity to thank, but it'll take a while to tell that story."

Yes, there was much to tell from both sides, she thought. Probably neither knew exactly where to begin. She'd need to explain about nursing school, the building of the Habitat house, moving out of the trailer park, her job at Quail Creek Care Center. Most important, however, he needed to know about the twins. Could she tell Miguel about Pamela and Jenny without him suspecting she had known she was pregnant before he left and had chosen not to tell him? If he confronted her about it, she would play dumb.

"I'd like to know the story," Conchita avoided looking at him straight on. "They say you had a lot to do with the hostage release. You must've been very brave."

"Did you expect anything else?" Miguel asked, his tone condescending. "Conchita, I'm no coward. You know that. No one backs me into a corner, no one crosses me. If they do, I come out fighting." He stabbed his fork into a bite of chicken-fried steak, raised it into the air with emphasis, then put it in his mouth.

She remembered that defensive attitude and how it had gotten him into trouble. It had left her trembling inside on numerous times. *Stop it. That's in the past.* She needed to move forward, put it behind her and focus on the future. Her children's father had returned.

She swallowed hard. "Miguel, I have amazing news."

He appeared startled and asked, "What do you mean? Can there be greater news than I am here with you?" He reached across the table and gripped her hand. "I'm alive."

"Of course, that's great news. I'm thankful you were released, that you're alive." How should she tell him? Just blurt it out, she thought. "Not only do you have a fine son, you also have two daughters, twins."

Miguel virtually jumped from his chair. His face reddened. "How could you? You couldn't wait until I was gone to get another man in bed? I went through hell and come home to a whore."

Stunned Conchita yelled out. "No, no. These daughters are yours. They already grew in me before the expedition." She hadn't envisioned this reaction. Her worry that Miguel might be angry if he thought she kept the pregnancy from him was unfounded. With his reaction, she wanted to shout out. *Don't you remember? In your drunkenness you raped me. There was no protection. I pleaded. I cried out. When I knew, how could I accept that the miracle of new life had come from such evilness?*

Miguel's eyes darted toward the others in the room. "Conchita, keep your voice down. Everyone's looking." Then he looked her hard in the eyes. "How can I be sure?"

Tears welled up. Yet, Conchita sat tall and returned his smoldering look. "Pamela and Jenny were born six months after you left. When you see them, you will know. There is no question. If you don't believe me, then we don't have a future."

Miguel tipped back in his chair and appeared to relax. The smirk on his face fused with a hint of a smile. He nodded his head, saying, "Well, what do you know? Looks like you grew a little spunk while I was gone. They said to expect this homecoming to be rocky for both of us. Guess they were right."

During their interchange Conchita spoke modestly about her nursing training, her new house and her job, hoping to avoid any sarcasm concerning what she had been able to do on her own. Of course, she did not mention Greg Hope and his helpfulness. She learned little about Miguel's part in making the hostage release happen. That would come when there was more time.

Miguel talked mostly about the plane being shot down, their capture and the various camps they stayed in the first year of captivity. Though he had seen Nicola those first few days of hostage-life and before they were marched on to another camp, there had been almost no interaction between them. Conchita already knew that, because of Gavin's injury and inability to walk, he remained in the camp with Nicola. Miguel said he had no more contact with Gavin through the years, not until a few months back when thirty or more hostages were brought to one central location.

"Speaking Spanish gave me an in," Miguel said, giving Conchita a look of self-importance. "The guerrillas even counted on me to give orders to the others. If there was extra food, I usually got it, particularly in our last camp."

"So, you were in many different camps? Conchita asked, sincerely interested in his story.

"Yeah. At least seven camps during the years. According to the guerrillas, we moved around for security reasons. We'd pack up everything and use it to construct a new camp in another part of the jungle. We only cut down a few trees since they wanted to keep a dense canopy to conceal the location of the camp. Like slaves, we helped build the new camp. We carried wooden planks through the jungle and threw them out on the muddy ground. They became the walkways between each of the bivouacs where some of the guerrillas slept. We put up the main meeting tent and a primitive kitchen. We built latrines for women and men away from the camp."

"There were women guerrillas in the camps?"

"At least a dozen in the last camp. They worked alongside the men, were issued the usual two uniforms, a pair of rubber boots, machete and AK-47."

Conchita felt sorry for all Miguel had endured. She could only imagine what it was like to be watched over daily by rifle-carrying guerrillas, to have five years of life robbed from you. She listened to the difficulties of the conditions, about the times when food was scarce. Fortunately, the most recent months when the guerrillas were more organized, food was more plentiful.

She listened intently but was relieved when officials entered the dining room and announced the men would be going back to their quarters in fifteen minutes. Unlike Conchita, Miguel ate every morsel of his food. She wondered if the cardboard taste was because of the stressful situation. Tomorrow she would be back at Quail Creek and her patients would pick at their food much as she had done today.

What would she say to her children tonight when she arrived back in Greeley via the shuttle from DIA? Greg would pick them up from the Wednesday day camp and drop them off at her mother's house. He helped out so willingly and without any expectation of gratitude. How would the children accept his absence from their lives?

Mel

THE NUMBER THREE HELD SIGNIFICANCE to the three who waited for the returned hostages to complete the reintegration process at Brooke Army Medical Center. It would be three more days before they were released and flown to Colorado. In the meantime, no more family visits were scheduled. In fact, officials handling the reintegration process recommended the women return home to wait for the arrival of the men. Mel knew her mother would have that 'I told you so attitude' upon learning this information.

"Yes Mom," Mel said into the mouthpiece, "Dad is in fairly good health. We haven't had time to talk much about the whole ordeal. There is so much to say. I'm flying back to Denver this afternoon. In fact, we all are."

Mel told her mother of the frustrations involved in setting up meetings with the men, and the irritation she felt toward the officials.

"The military will fly the men to the air force base in the Springs where we can meet the plane on Saturday. You will meet the plane with me, won't you?"

"Of course, dear. We can take my car. You don't mind driving, do you? I can do the traffic thing through Denver, but I don't like to if I don't have to."

"No, I don't mind driving. I know he'll be glad to see you. I'm wondering where he should stay. At your condo or mine?"

"I imagine, unless he prefers not to, that he'll stay here." Charlotte said, a bit indignantly. "He is my husband, after all. When they all were presumed dead, I didn't re-marry, did I?"

Not yet, Mel thought, but a few more months and it might have been different. "Well, I just thought with Arthur spending so much time there..."

"I'll have to admit, my life has taken a little twist in the last months, but I'm not about to let your father down, regardless of what you think of me." Following a slight pause, Charlotte added with growing sarcasm, "I made the right decision not to go on the worthless trip to San Antonio, only to sit and fume about all the regulations. Sometimes mothers know best."

Mel wished she hadn't shared her frustrations with all the protocol and red tape, her irritation with the military. The trip had been worth it, and she retaliated with a jab of her own. "What's best for you is not necessarily best for me and my father. You have no idea how it felt. Dad right in front of me. Wow! Whew! You wouldn't understand."

Mel heard deep breaths from her mother, and before Charlotte could respond Mel said, "We'll talk when I get home. Good-bye, Mom."

Monica

MONICA THOUGHT SHE WAS PREPARED to greet Peter when he met her at DIA after the trip to Texas. Yet, tears squeezed from her eyes when Peter lifted her from the floor and gave her a bear hug. He settled her with care on the glistening tile floor, yet continued to hold her, swaying gently. His face, roughened by the few days of stubble fashionable among some men, nestled in her hair. "Babe, I missed you. It's been a roller coaster, hasn't it? You know how much I love you."

Monica closed her eyes and held her breath in an attempt at control. So much had been bouncing through her head. So many questions. She had worried that someone might be hurt in all of this. The attempt for self-control proved fruitless and all she could do was nod, again and again. Peter released his embrace. With his thumb he dabbed the wetness on the edge of each eye and looked directly into her clouded face. She gazed back and whispered, "I love you, too. Let's go."

Peter, a driver who enjoyed the thrill of speed, usually pushed the limit, cutting around cars, trucks and vans in less hurry than he. Though Peter was skillful and did not take undue chances, the ancient argument over what Monica labeled as recklessness, never concluded agreeably. Monica braced herself as Peter took the on ramp to the highway, expecting him to stealthily accelerate, swerving in and out, until he was in the fast lane. However, Peter slowed behind a string of vehicles in the right lane as others whizzed by on the left and made no attempt to increase his speed.

Surprised, she leaned back, and lapsed into a more relaxed mood than she had been in for some time. With her nerves calmed, she openly talked about her meeting with Gavin at Brooke Army Medical Center.

"He's a good man, Peter."

Peter nodded. His eyes glued ahead of him, he muttered agreement.

"He's been through a lot. We know that. Changed some, I guess."

"How's that Babe?"

"Gavin never was a man to be ruffled. Even when I felt dissatisfied and treated him indifferently, he…well, I guess he let it roll off his back. Didn't retaliate."

"So you're telling me you were dissatisfied with your marriage to Gavin?" Peter paused before he added, "You never told me."

Monica put her hand on Peter's arm. "I never told you because it wasn't the marriage. It was me. It's always been me and I've never admitted it to myself."

She sighed and removed her hand from Peter's arm. "Somehow, I wanted perfection, whatever that means. When I didn't live up to my own perfection, it seemed obvious to see others as imperfect, to focus on their faults."

Peter looked at his wife with surprise on his face. Then his eyes focused again on the string of cars ahead. "I have a lot of faults too, huh? Drive too fast. I'm messy and don't pick up my things. In too much of a hurry to attend to details, like throwing out dried out leftovers. Don't surprise you with flowers. Don't understand your moods. Am a klutz backing a trailer."

Peter grimaced with the last statement before continuing, "Can't cook worth a darn. Play music too loud. What else?" Monica heard the attempt at lightness in his voice but wasn't fooled by the little boy hurt at the edges.

"Peter, I'm sorry," Monica said unable to hold back the gathering tears. "I've been too critical, unloving, and unappreciative. And like Gavin you didn't make a scene about it."

"Life's too short, don't you think?" Peter shrugged before he went on. "Well, about Gavin. How do you think he's changed?"

"Even with all he's missed…lost, he seems quite content, full of compassion—even for his captors. He always believed in God. Now his faith is unshakable. Wants to be a missionary, I think."

"Interesting. Do you suppose he and Nicola might…?"

"I don't know. He admires her a great deal. I can tell that. We talked about you and me. He knows that after a husband is presumed dead, the wife is considered a widow and is free to marry. He knows my marriage to you is the only legal one. He wants the best for us."

There were no sobs, but Monica's tears seemed endless, as she went on, "I'm not sure if we have a lot more to say to each other, Gavin and me. His mother will meet him in Colorado Springs. He doesn't expect me to be there."

There was a short silence between them until Monica said, "I keep thinking back of the letters he wrote and how he said then he wanted me to go on with my life. I think he's had closure about the life we had. Our visit in San Antonio helped me to put a finality to it as well."

Monica turned on the radio. She fiddled with it until she found a station she thought both would like.

"Let's not hurry home," Peter said slowly, "I think we'll take the scenic route." Monica smiled and attempted to dry her eyes with the hem of her jacket.

Peter left the interstate and after a few miles he turned onto a graveled road. Monica turned toward her husband and said, "Can we stop here for a moment?"

Once the car was parked to the side of the road, Peter reached his arms around his wife and held her. She stroked his roughened face and said, "I like your unshaven look. I think it's very sexy."

"Wow. I don't think you ever said I was sexy before. You better watch it gal."

Monica's eyes held his and neither moved. She kissed his nose, then leaned away, gently shaking her head. "I think it's too late to watch it, Peter."

"I don't understand."

Her voice held a gentleness. "We're having a baby."

CHAPTER 18

McCrae

Santo, a long time Colombian Government Commando and an affiliate of the Security and Democracy Foundation in Bogotá was one of the first men McCrae hounded for information and help upon his arrival in Bogotá. Santo had clout and knowledge, as his connections included Colombia's military intelligence that helped coordinate the hostage exchange. He also spoke good English.

McCrae and Santo sat in Resaurante Los Arbolitos at a heavy wooden table bearing a bright cover in orange, blue and green. A server brought two mugs of foamy beer. McCrae squeezed the juice of a wedge of lime into his. "There has to be a way to get info about the rebel camps. I need to know if they're still holding hostages."

Santo sucked foam from his mug and licked his lips. "Yes, of course. We have double agents. Some take messages from camp to camp, then bring information to us. Tomorrow I meet with one. We call him Aradilla—squirrel. The name fits."

"Can I see him? Talk to him?"

Santo slapped a massive hand on McCrae's shoulder. "Not a chance. But I'll see what he knows."

"I've scheduled a chopper for tomorrow. Want to see the emerald mine."

"You know the government won't let you own the mines, anymore."

"I know, but I want to go anyway. Hope to buy a few stones."

"Take plenty of…" Santo rubbed his thumb against the inside of his fingertips.

McCrae nodded. "I should be back by one or two. I'll call you. Maybe you'll know something."

Returning from the Emerald mine, McCrae handed the cab driver a wad of bills and shut the door. He couldn't believe his eyes. Santo leaned against the wall at McCrae's hotel. *The news has to be good.*

"Can we go up to your place to talk? Santo asked."

The two climbed the painted stairs, scuffed by years of use. McCrae pulled the oversized key from his pocket and unlocked the door. "Only one chair." He gestured for Santo to sit and McCrae took the bed. "Start talking, friend."

"Aradilla took orders to three different camps. He gets around. The last group, about ten guys, is ready to move toward the Apaporis River. Going to a bigger camp already laid out." Santo emphasized each word. "They have an American hostage."

McCrae's eyes widened. "And? What else?"

"The hostage has red hair."

McCrae smacked his thigh. "I knew it. I knew it. I have to find him. Where do I start?"

"I can do it. I trust Pablo and Samuel, both paramilitary. They will help me rescue your Randy."

"Santo, I can't let you take that risk."

"These rebels brought a black hole to my family. I do this in honor of my son."

Santo told McCrae about his son, Gerardo, a military officer who was captured and held hostage by rebel forces, tortured, then hanged. As they talked McCrae imagined Santo's pain, and admired this proud man's determination and desire to someway avenge his son's death. Together, they vowed to find Randy.

Santo's voice boomed. "To our sons." Each man raised a fist into the air, and then bumped them together.

"Salud, mi amigo—health, my friend," said McCrae.

⚉

THE FIRST TWO DAYS INTO the mission, McCrae and Santo—with Samuel, the driver, and Pablo seated in front—traveled by military jeep. McCrae usually kept up his end of the conversation with male associates, but usually the topics revolved around business and local goings-on, rather than items of a personal nature. Yet, with Santo, McCrae found himself sharing his innermost thoughts and feelings about Chantel, her debilitating disease, her inability to have children. His loyalty to her—except for that one time he and Racine had become intimate. And of course, about the son he was unable to claim.

Bumping along Santo asked, "And what of this woman, the mother of your son? You call her Racine. You are both free. Why don't you make a family for your son when you go back? She likes you, no?"

McCrae shook his head and rolled his eyes. "First of all, we don't know if we'll find Randy. Anyway, no one can ever make up for past mistakes. There are no do-overs. Just complications."

"Too complicated to fix?"

"First, Racine chose to keep me from being a part of my son's life. That hurt. I guess she didn't want to embarrass me. She didn't want Chantel to feel bad about not giving me a child. And… Racine was independent and didn't want *anyone* to butt in. Anyway, that's the way it was."

"But you called her in the last village. She's important to you."

McCrae wished he could have had a better connection when he talked to Racine. What more would he have said? For one, he might have told her flat out—no more secrets about being Randy's father. If they found Randy, he'd tell him. *Would Randy be proud or humiliated?*

The Jeep jerked and tipped from side to side as Samuel navigated forest roots and boulders attempting to move forward. "Hold on," Santo yelled. The engine whined to climb a steep rise, and beyond the rise the vehicle plunged scraping against heavy branches on each side.

"Yai, yai," roared Pablo. Then the Jeep jolted to a stop, stuck in a deep hole.

The men sat at an awkward angle, laughing at the situation. The Spanish speakers shouted among themselves and gestured wildly as they attempted to free the Jeep. Samuel gunned the engine. The spinning tires spewed odors of burning rubber. No luck. The men climbed from the vehicle. Pablo pointed to the left where a walking trail cut through the jungle.

"McCrae, my friend, we'll start on foot, while Samuel and Pablo get the Jeep out of the hole, moved and hidden. They'll follow," Santo said.

Santo and McCrae organized their gear and hefted packs onto their backs. Heading into the bush they heard the engine grind as Samuel and Pablo worked to free the Jeep. McCrae's heart pounded with each step along the narrow winding path. Well up the hill his erratic breathing gained a healthy rhythm.

At a level spot the men paused. Santo wiped sweat from his brow. "Mi hijo was a fine man."

"A brave man to be sure. Do you have other sons?"

"No… Only daughters. Three." Santo broke off a branch, stripped it, and then stabbed the walking stick into the ground. "Gerardo wanted to be like me, a military man. Because of me he's dead."

"Oh Santo. Your son honored you with his choices. Be proud of him. Be proud of yourself. You didn't kill him. Evil murderers did."

Santo looked to the ground. "His name never comes to our lips. My Rosio forbids it. Her heart will not heal. She goes on with life, my Rosio, and holds her head high." The bellow in Santo's voice grew soft and tender as he said, "So, my friend, I thank you. I can talk about the son who carried the eyes of my Rosio."

McCrae saw Santo shed tears without shame as he poured out the grief bottled inside. Awed at the privilege of seeing into this tough man's heart, McCrae visualized the special bond between father and son, and a father's remorse. Two fathers bonded in pain and compassion.

Though miles would eventually sever their union, McCrae would never forget Santo.

The pair walked on in silence. McCrae tried without success to think of something other than the rescue attempt. The paramilitaries were trained. They would know what to do. Images and sounds shot through his head—gunfire and a horrible gun battle. He imagined the camp empty, Randy chained and waiting alone, blood oozing from his chest. When he pushed those ideas aside, Racine came to mind. *She must be frantic with worry. Oh God, don't let her worry.*

As if he were a mind reader, Santo said, "Don't worry. We will find your son. Then your woman won't say you broke her heart by sending her son to Colombia. Her heart will be full once more. You like each other. True? I am sure she thinks you are a handsome and successful man."

McCrae laughed at his friend. "Santo, what's going on in that heart of yours? Racine's, cheerful, independent and strong. But…Oh, my friend, I've never thought of a future with her."

"Then why you find the beautiful emeralds for her?" Santo's eyes flashed. "A man gives a special jewel for a reason. To win a heart, no? Then you will be a true father to your son."

"Man. You're something else."

Within the hour Pablo and Samuel thundered up behind McCrae and Santo, taunting, "Vamanos. Vamanos." The foursome picked up the pace. By midafternoon, they trouped into a village that seemed to hang on the side of the mountain and unloaded their packs. Santo talked to some campesinos tending to their coffee plants.

"There is news," said Santo. "Yesterday, they came through here. The Rebels. Demanded food and left. The campesinos think they will set up camp for a few days. Then move south for a big meeting place."

Santo spoke in rapid fire Spanish. Pablo and Samuel nodded, pointed to a trail on the left, and marched off.

Santo turned to McCrae. "You can depend on these men. They move fast and can track a mouse through the jungle." Santo held up a tracking dart with a small orange flag. "To mark our trail. I think they find the camp before dark."

An hour later, having stocked up on extra food and tarps, Santo and

McCrae trudged along the marked trail. The jungle seemed unusually quiet and the sound of each step, scrape against a growing bush or plant, echoed beneath the overhead canopy. McCrae's nostrils flared with each eager breath. Surprised by his physical resilience and endurance, he relished the trek through the meandering undergrowth. Despite the slipperiness of the trail and the intermittent rain which soaked him through, he felt energized. They would find his son and bring him to safety. He and Randy would have a future. The thoughts spurred him on.

Before nightfall Santo and McCrae jumped with surprise to be alerted by the paramilitaries who crouched off the trail protected by a crude tangle of brush and branches. The agents had cased the rebel camp, perhaps 250 yards down the trail and saw the redhead being ordered to set up tents for the night and a campfire for cooking.

The news shook McCrae. The hair on his arms stood as if electrified, and he tasted bile rising into his esophagus. He decided it was not fright, but excitement and anxiety with the knowledge that Randy, in shackles, was probably no more than ten minutes away.

"We'll survey the camp, observe the layout, their routine, decide the right time and method for the rescue," explained Santo. "It will be a long night, lying in wait."

"I'm ready," said McCrae.

Samuel showed them where to stash their gear and which gear to take for the night's vigilance. Utilizing the remaining daylight, the foursome, dressed in camouflage, strode with caution and silence as they made their way toward the guerrilla camp.

The rebels had chosen a secluded area in a gently sloping valley surrounded by prolific flora and giant trees of the rainforest. Once they were close enough to hear the rhythmic hack of an ax splitting wood, Samuel signaled for McCrae to follow him to the right. Santo and Pablo circled the camp at the left.

McCrae and Samuel stretched out on their stomachs and strained their eyes as dusk began to emerge. They saw six makeshift tents positioned around a fire. Samuel handed the binoculars to McCrae and he got a better look. Two men appeared to be preparing food at the fire. Another pair reclined in hammocks stretched between trees. One man stood with a rifle casually pointed in the direction of a tall well-built man who pulled items that looked like tin cups from a pack. McCrae's heart raced as he saw the color of his hair. He wanted to shout out, "Randy, Randy, son we've come for you."

A clank of metal sounded—chains, McCrae thought—as Randy gave each rebel a cup; he pulled a package from the rucksack. Someone yelled out to the redhead who unwrapped the package, then moved quickly toward the fire. Each man filled his cup from a pot at the fire and took something from Randy's package. Some type of flatbread the rebels got from the campesinos, McCrae surmised. There appeared to be much camaraderie and laughter as they ate. At last the rebels motioned Randy to get his food. *Turn around son, so I can see your face.* But Randy squatted, his back toward McCrae.

Once darkness descended and the meal was finished, the binoculars were of little use. McCrae put on his night goggles and watched the rebels carry bedrolls into the tents. McCrae no longer saw Randy. The dim glow from lighted lanterns snuck through holes and from beneath the canvasses giving an eeriness to the jungle setting. Finally, one by one the lights went out, and quiet descended on the camp. McCrae and Samuel maintained their silent vigil. Where was Randy, McCrae wondered? In the darkness he could not tell. Did Samuel see something he didn't? He hoped so. Perhaps Santo and Pablo with a different vantage point had seen where Randy was.

McCrae had grown accustomed to many of the tropical forest sounds their first few days out. Yet tonight, in the silence of the watch McCrae felt surrounded by them. The night birds called out their shrill whistles and rattle-type chatters. He estimated at least a dozen different varieties. Tree frogs blasted their intermittent croaks. He thought of an early morning a few days ago. He had been mesmerized by far off cries calling back and forth, spine-chilling noises he could only describe as bellowing bulls with a bad case of laryngitis. Santo explained they were howling monkeys.

Time passed and McCrae's body stiffened. He pushed up on all fours, hoping to relax his limbs. As he did so, a small flame flared near one of the tents and he saw the glow of a rebel's face when the man lit a cigarette. One of the rebels is posted as a guard, he thought. Was he near the tent where Randy slept? McCrae lowered himself to his stomach, aware of Samuel's breathing beside him, and watched the glow of each inhalation until the cigarette was finished. A muggy coolness caused McCrae to shudder and he pulled the tarp they had brought over him.

McCrae's next awareness was Samuel's nudge. Embarrassed that he had fallen asleep, McCrae shook himself awake and noticed the beginning dawn sneak between the trees hovering above them. Samuel searched the camp with the binoculars and handed them to McCrae, pointing to the smallest and most dilapidated tent pitched closest to their lookout position. Randy crawled from it and called out to the guard who held an AK-47. The guard swung his weapon to the left. Randy nodded, and then dragged his chains into the forest. The guard followed. Soon Randy returned and McCrae saw the barrel of the rifle prod Randy's back, sending him stumbling over a loose stump. Randy righted it and sat down. There he remained motionless, his head cradled in his hands. McCrae could not bear the scene in front of him. He blinked again and again to keep his eyes from flooding.

Samuel and McCrae watched as the men vacated their tents and began the morning activities. McCrae was relieved to see that Randy slept alone. Samuel indicated it was time to leave. The pair did their best to remove any evidence of the night watch and crawled to a place where it was safe to stand upright and head back to their own camp.

The day, humid and hot, crawled at the pace of a leaf cutter ant carrying its unwieldy burden from the tree to its home. McCrae batted away the buzzing winged insects darting at him.

A rescue plan emerged as the foursome plotted. Leaves, rocks, and fungi became landmarks in their miniature layout of the rebel camp. They dragged pointed sticks from one landmark to another and finalized the sequences for movement. Santo translated as the men talked back and forth.

McCrae repositioned the rock representing Randy's tent. "I need to be the one to rescue my son. He'll recognize my face. I'll come from behind at the right to cut the tent." They had decided entering in the front opening was too risky.

Samuel waved the bolt cutters.

"Yes, you go with McCrae and cut the chains," said Santo. "Pablo will hide here, up the hill." Pablo could sound out a perfect imitation of the tree frogs and would make this call from time to time when sound cover was needed. Especially during the slashing of the tent and during the cutting of the chains.

"I'll watch from here." Santo pointed to a pile of fungi representing the ridge of bushes to the left opposite the tents. Santo was to be the diversion in case anything went wrong. He had a parcel of shooting flares that he could ignite. They would fly in erratic directions as all made their escape. At least that was the plan.

After lunching on arepas, a type of flat corn bread similar to a pancake, some fruits McCrae couldn't pronounce the names of, and hearty cheese, the men stretched out to rest beneath a makeshift net canopy. McCrae slept fitfully until the hour came to gather supplies for the night rescue.

They timed their arrival to the lookout point above the camp to coincide with the emerging darkness. The men took their places and watched as the camp closed down for the night. McCrae squinted into the blackness and decided it was time to put on his night goggles. Anxious for the success of this mission, every sense highly tuned, he heard his heartbeat quicken. Each sound, rush of air, pungent smell and image converged on him so magnified that he felt compelled to yell out to stop the over stimulation. *I must calm myself. Breathe slowly and deeply. Heart, slow down. I can do this. We will succeed. Randy, you will soon be free.* Then it was time for the rescue.

CHAPTER 19

Mel

Mel felt obligated to invite Conchita to ride with her to Colorado Springs yet was silently relieved by the refusal. With their reintegration at Brooke Medical Center in San Antonio completed, Gavin, Ben and Miguel would arrive in Colorado at 2:00 p.m. on Saturday. Depending upon traffic, the trip could take up to three hours. Mel and Charlotte expected to give themselves plenty of time. Though Mel was apprehensive about her parents' reunion, her mother seemed to approach the meeting with an eagerness Mel had not expected. Maybe the 'thing' with Arthur had little importance. Charlotte insisted on taking her car, a sporty silver BMW convertible with a good amount of get-up-and-go. She also insisted that Mel drive.

Speeding out of Greeley, they lucked out hitting all of the green lights. Reaching the interstate, Mel accelerated and zipped around a couple of cars and into the fast lane. *I'd never buy such a car, but it does bring out the tiger in a person.* Charlotte glanced at her daughter, her lips pursed perceptively. Mel heard a hint of southern as her mother said, "Think your father'll like the car? It's a fun little buggy, isn't it?"

"It is," Mel responded, and relaxed her judgmental attitude about her mother. *Yeah, Mom deserves some pleasure in her life.*

"You said Monica's not going to the Air Force base, right?" Mel nodded in the affirmative and her mother went on. "I imagine after their time at the medical center they said all they wanted to say."

"Especially since Gavin is at peace with Monica's marriage," said Mel.

"Lives change, don't they? What all did Conchita say after she got back? What about the kids?"

"As you can imagine the kids are pretty excited. Jack barely remembers his father, and of course Miguel didn't even know about the twins—that is until Conchita told him at the medical center. I guess that was a sticky wicket that Conchita hadn't anticipated."

"How's that?"

"Miguel accused her of sleeping around. Conchita would be last person to take a lover." Mel engaged the turn signal to switch lanes and continued, "I only saw him a few times before the expedition, but I thought he was arrogant and controlling. He seemed the same in San Antonio. I hope things go all right for them, but I'm not sure Miguel can handle the new Conchita."

"I know you said she was brow-beaten before, but much different now."

"Yes, confident, capable, a good mother, and quite accomplished in her career."

"Didn't some man help with the Habitat house?"

"Yeah, that 's Greg. Conchita says the kids really like him. They may all have to give up on that relationship," Mel said, thinking she'd like to ask her mother what she planned to do about Arthur. Somehow, she couldn't.

"Marilyn, somehow, things seem to work out," Charlotte said in a friendly tone. She inhaled and exhaled a sizable breath, and then continued, "As far as I'm concerned one can't get too worked up when life gives you lemons."

Mel hated the saying and waited for her mother to continue the phrase that "you just have to make lemonade", and when she didn't, Mel let out a lungful of relief.

"About Monica," Mel said, "she sounds almost like a new person. I've always sensed that she couldn't warm up to life, that nothing quite suited her, nothing quite satisfied her."

Charlotte turned toward her daughter. "Sounds like someone I know. Someone who's prone to holding back, not letting people get close to her, not enjoying life."

Mel shot a contemptuous glare at her mother. She wanted to shout out some cutting retort, but swallowed hard instead, certain her mother with her la-de-da attitude of life wouldn't get it anyway.

Driving through Denver, Mel sped into the left lane whipping around the lagging traffic in the slower lanes. "Hate, the exhaust fumes in all this traffic," Mel said. "Hope you don't mind if I hurry."

"I can handle the speed. You concentrate on negotiating the traffic. I'll focus on the downtown skyline and the Broncos and Rockies stadiums.

AT PETERSON AIR FORCE BASE, Mel and her mother stood on the outside of a chain link fence waiting for clearance to greet her father. The Air Force plane had landed and taxied to the de-boarding spot. Military personnel rolled portable stairs to its door. Mel hadn't spotted Conchita and her kids, but she had spotted three vans with Denver television station markings. Apparently, her mother had seen them as well.

"It looks like we'll be on the evening news." Charlotte formed a camera frame with her hands as if to capture the cameraman's view. "Let's see how you look." Nodding, she added, "Look good to me. Just don't forget to smile."

"Yeah, Mom," Mel said with disdain.

Behind them Mel heard excited chatter of children and turned to see Pamela, Jenny, and Jack race toward the fence. Conchita walked quickly after them. "Are we late?" Conchita yelled out.

In unison, Mel and Charlotte responded that they were in time. To their left an older woman leaned on a cane and eyed the exuberant children. A young man in jeans and a sweatshirt stood at her side. Mel decided they must be Gavin's mother and another family member. Mel introduced Conchita and her children to Charlotte. The children's excitement quieted to shyness, and the group stood shoulder to shoulder waiting and watching.

Soon a man dressed in military fatigues stepped from the plane followed by Ben, Miguel and Gavin. Two airmen stood ready to greet the released hostages at the bottom of the mobile steps. Before the men could descend, bedlam ensued as TV personnel rushed onto the tarmac with cameras and microphones. Mel grabbed her mother's hand and led her to the open gate. "Let's rescue Dad from the media," she said.

The interviewers waited patiently until the airmen had acknowledged each man. Mel's father shook hand after hand and looked out over the gathering crowd.

In an unusually giddy mood, Mel said, "I'm not waiting. Let's make a little drama for the viewers." Mel and Charlotte ran toward Ben. Mel yelled, "Hey, Dad. Over here. Over here." One cameraman ran alongside them catching the touching scene. Mel yelled toward the camera. "You can't catch us. Just try."

Reaching the plane, the pair pulled up short. "Pretty good run Mom."

"Well, can't let my daughter get ahead of me," said Charlotte, tossing her head.

Mel heard her father speak into the microphone thrust toward him, "There's nothing more glorious than stepping on Colorado soil. I'm home. And there are my two favorite ladies."

Ben stepped forward, opened his arms wide, and pulled both Mel and Charlotte to him. "Now give this ole man some space," he bellowed. Amazingly, the media stepped back in silence.

Tears streamed as Mel walked off of the tarmac. She had not felt anything more exciting than this moment, with the strong arm of her father around her shoulder, and his other arm around her mother. Mel wondered what rolled through her mother's head. Then she heard Charlotte laugh. *Yeah, she's happy.*

Racine

HOPE IS DECEPTIVE. HOPE KEEPS one dangling with no answers. Having hope is more painful than not having it. The thoughts left Racine's emotions paralyzed. Had she given up on hope? Would it hurt less if she did just that? Bleakness inhabited her home as she let the dark and sunless day cast shadows of dreariness. She refused to turn the switch to light a lamp. There'd been no news from McCrae since the broken message that a man with red hair might be in a guerrilla camp.

After the call Racine put on her lively face, a lie. She told no one, not even Chad about the newest hope. And out of respect for her feelings, no one asked anymore, "Have you heard anything about Randy?" There had been too much disappointment with each new possibility ending in total letdown. Telling might jinx the thinnest of hope, now hanging by a thread she envisioned as a single spider strand.

The others are back. It's not fair.

She had heard from each of the women a few days after the men landed in Colorado. Racine sensed their uneasiness as they conveyed their sympathy. Racine remembered the conversations. More somber than she expected. Were they trying to protect her? If Randy had returned, she'd be out dancing in the streets, yelling to the rooftops about his homecoming.

Maybe Mel's reserve came from disappointment. Mel's flight schedule had cut short the visit with her dad. Real talk-time would be postponed. She also worried about her parent's marriage. Though the reunion had gone well, Charlotte and Ben hadn't had much in common before the expedition. "Will there be enough glue to hold them together now?" Mel had asked.

Racine wasn't too surprised about Monica. Monica and Gavin talked by phone after he arrived in Greeley. Monica said to Racine, "I'm grateful Gavin and Nicola are good friends. Maybe that's why he accepted Peter and my marriage so readily. He'll stay with his mom, for now."

Recalling the conversation with Conchita brought a chill over Racine. She heard hesitation in Conchita's voice. "You can imagine what it must be like to find out you have five-year-old twins. The girls ask lots of questions and Jack's bent on having the party I promised before Miguel returned." Racine heard a sigh when Conchita said, "Miguel's not a patient man. I'm hoping he doesn't disappoint the children too much."

"I'm sure he'll be eating out of their hands before you know it. They are such precious children."

"I don't know. He's been with them the last few days while I'm at work and he seems to expect a lot from them. It's hard for him to let them be children."

Everyone, except her would be making new lives. *Face it. Randy is never coming home. Stop hoping.*

She heard a soft tap at the door. Chad, she thought. *I'm not up for company.* Chad had been to her place on several occasions—for a candlelight dinner, bringing her flowers or a bottle of wine, to take her for a Sunday drive. He didn't like doorbells. "They make you jump, don't you think?" he remarked. Thus, this light tap-tap became his trademark.

Racine's chest heaved. *Can't let Chad see this gloomy heart.* She ambled to the door and eased it open. There stood the handsome Aussie, a look of tenderness on his face, gripping the handle of a picnic basket lined with a blue checkered cloth. "Hello, charming one, I'm here to bring you cheer."

He put the basket down and wrapped his arms around a startled Racine and held her close. "It pains me to see you suffer," Chad said, his voice near a whisper. "If I could, I'd do anything to make everything right."

The caring in his voice, the warmth of his breath against her cheek, and the gentleness of his embrace waged against the emptiness she felt inside. A tingly glow danced through her, yet her mouth twisted in anguish and her eyes overflowed with their salty liquid. Racine returned his gentle hug and did not let go until her composure returned.

Finally, Racine pulled away. "Thank you, Chad. Thank you for coming to me. Sorry I'm such a mess."

"Racine Rabinowitz, I've never seen you a mess." He touched a wayward curl escaping over her forehead. "Why someone hasn't snatched you up, I'll never know. Not many can measure up to you, your good looks, and your way with people. And your good sense about business."

Racine pushed his words away with a wave of her hand. A bit of gloomy weight dissolved. "And you can talk? A fascinating foreigner with charm. You'd have many young things falling over you if you let them," Racine spouted, giving him a flirtatious look. "And what have you brought in your basket, you little red riding hood imposter?"

With a grin spread wide and his eyes sparkling with laughter, he made a deep bow. "Now Madame, won't you sit over here?" he said gesturing toward the couch. Once she sat, Chad made a ceremony out of placing the blue checkered cloth on the coffee table in front of her, and setting out chunky candles, two wine glasses, and a bottle of wine. He arranged generous portions of smoked salmon, Swiss cheese cubes, thinly sliced cucumber, and slivered carrot strips on a glass plate. He added a small pot of liver pâté and a basket of assorted crackers. Once he lit the candles, he joined Racine on the couch. Dancing flickers of light offered a gentle glow to warm the dreariness.

"Ever had a couch picnic before?" he asked. "I know this is a first for me."

"Same here," admitted Racine. "I didn't think I was hungry, but my salivary glands are changing their mind. Looks fantastic. I'm too Scotch to buy smoked salmon, myself. This will be a treat."

The wine went down smoothly between bites of salmon and cucumber sandwiches decorated with carrot straws. Racine spread the pâté generously on the sesame crackers and topped it with the Swiss cheese. The contrasting flavors with the wine satisfied a hunger that surprised her. Rarely, Racine had more than one glass of wine. Finishing her third one, she slapped a palm against her forehead, laughing at the tipsiness she felt.

"Oooh lordy. There's a little spinning in this room," Racine said, blinking her eyes.

"I'll get you some water." Chad headed for the kitchen. Returning, he handed her the tumbler and she took a few swallows and set it down on the table, containing only remnants of food. Chad rejoined her on the couch.

The pair watched candlelight shimmer against the surrounding shadows, saving them from the darkness of night. Racine leaned against Chad and said, "You've been a Godsend for me and the business. After Carlotta's heart attack, I wouldn't have made it." She turned to look into his face and touched her finger to his smiling lips. I haven't properly thanked you for your support, your good ideas…for being such a good listener…for being my sounding board."

"I think you've thanked me. You're welcome, a thousand times over. You know how much I admire you. I enjoy every moment working with you." He cozied her toward him and kissed her forehead.

A flush surged through Racine. Wispy breath whooshed between her parted lips. She turned to look into Chad's half-closed eyes—eyes heavily adorned with long, gently curved lashes. She closed her own eyes and felt their lips touch, first tenderly, then hungrily. Racine heard Chad murmur, "How amazing you are." They kissed again, and again.

Since the night with McCrae when Randy was conceived, except for a quick fling ten years ago, Racine had been celibate. She'd forgotten the trembling hunger, the ecstasy of feeling desired, the pleasure of exploring the corners of a man's body. Afterwards she lay snuggled against Chad's firm chest, his arm cradling her. Neither spoke for quite some time. Then Chad lifted the downy lap robe that had fallen to the floor and eased it over Racine's nakedness.

"You're very desirable, Racine. I didn't come to make love to you, but I hope tonight was a good thing for you. I want nothing but good for you."

Racine's chest heaved and released. "Tonight, I felt desired. It was… unbelievable. But I'm sorry. I didn't expect this of myself. I don't know what happened to my self-control."

"Let there be no regret…from either of us," Chad said, shaking his head side to side. "Don't ever feel sorry. I don't."

⚓

When Racine awoke, she couldn't exactly recall the turmoil of dreams she had experienced, but for the first time in months they didn't seem dark. She tried to push aside the memories of Chad and her on the couch the night before. She tried to deny the fondness she felt for this man, eight years younger than she. Not entirely successful, she got out of her bed. Racine needed to get to the restaurant and busy herself in her work. Focusing on something else helped to ease the lingering pain, even for a short time.

Racine grabbed the brightest, swishiest skirt she had in her closet. The swirls of green, turquoise, and gold were almost psychedelic as was the companion blouse in turquoise. After buttoning the blouse and zipping up her skirt, she whirled, and headed to the closet for her shoes. Her reflection flashed before her in the full-length mirror. Her crimson curls had not lost any depth of color. There was no gray peeking through. If there was, would she use the color from the bottle to remedy the situation, she wondered? Probably. Looking good was part of her trademark, helped the business, and gave her a punch of pizzazz that complimented her spunk and enthusiasm.

No more feeling sorry for yourself. You are the only one who can make this a good day. You can decide to bring some cheer to someone else, or you can drag the whole world down a hole.

With those thoughts hanging around her, she slipped her feet into gold high-heeled sandals and walked to the bathroom to put finishing touches on her face. Racine worked hard to conceal the dark circles below her eyes, applied some color to her cheeks and deftly filled her lips with crimson, a shade lighter than her hair. Her attempt to smile at her reflection resulted in a crooked one. "Oh Racine," she scolded herself. "You are a crazy dame. No matter. It's time to smile at the world. Get yourself goin'."

When she entered her office, Racine saw Chad seated at her desk scribbling frantically on a legal yellow pad with the receiver pressed against his ear. He motioned for her to come quickly to the desk. Racine heard the pitch of his voice increase with excitement as he said, "She's here now. You can tell her. I'm so glad you didn't miss her."

Chad stood and with a swooping gesture, indicated that Racine should sit down. Into the mouthpiece Chad said, "Now you take care and be safe. Here she is now."

Racine gave Chad a suspicious look and covered the mouthpiece with her hand. "Who is it?" He pointed to the phone and mouthed the words "talk, now".

She spoke cautiously, "Hello, this is Racine Rabinowitz. What can I do for you?"

The voice was clear and strong—as though it came from the next room. "Mom, Mom, it's me, Randy…I love you Mom. McCrae's bringing me home."

CHAPTER 20

Conchita

Before Miguel was rescued Conchita promised the children a party. She intended to keep that promise. Conchita sat at the kitchen table observing her children designing their invitations. Each child was permitted to invite three friends and the cards needed to be delivered the next day. Pamela and Jenny decorated blank cards with colored stickers of balloons and stars, while Jack penned the invitations in careful block letters.

"I like your work kids." Conchita beamed. "What do you think Miguel?"

Miguel leaned against the kitchen sink, picking at his fingernails with the point of a knife. "Yeah. Yeah, fine. Think I'll head over to my cousin, Johnny's. Ran into him. Said to come over for a beer."

"Papá," Jenny begged, "you promised you'd help me put the names on the envelopes. Don't go."

"Little one, you have to learn to do things by yourself. Be a big girl. You can do it. And remember I said no whining." Miguel thumped Jenny on the head and walked toward the door to the garage.

"But I wasn't whining, was I Mamá?" Jenny asked.

Conchita looked at her daughter with an empathetic smile. "Excuse me kids, I'll be right back." She followed Miguel into the garage and closed the door. "Miguel, if you are going to be drinking, Johnny should pick you up. The police have roadside checkpoints set up all week because of the Fourth of July holiday. I don't want you driving the car and drinking, period."

"Boy have things changed while I was gone. The assholes. A few beers never hurt anybody. Surely this is the U. S. of A., and we still have our freedoms." Miguel shot her a stabbing look. "I'll just have two. Will that satisfy you?"

Conchita heard the resentment in his voice and attempted to put a damper on her own rising steam. "Only *two*," she said with emphasis.

"That's what I said. Don't think my word is worth anything?" Miguel asked in a surly tone. Then he added more amiably, "Chita, let's not fight. Been home less than a week. I need a night out. Need to see some of the old gang."

Conchita glared at the man in front of her. Dressed in a new yellow polo shirt, clean shaven, and wavy hair combed back, he'd not lost any of his good looks. She tried to put herself in his shoes, tried to appreciate the husband who had swooped back into her life, and taken over her house, her car, and her children. *Can I do it? Do it for the kids?* He knew how to charm her and in offhand ways he'd spread it on thick during the week—grabbing her in a hug as she washed dishes at the sink, massaging her neck as she sat on the couch after supper.

"Ah, Chita, the kids are waiting for your help. Better go in. When I get back, we can…" Miguel rolled his eyes and raised his eyebrows, but left the sentence hanging. He crawled into the car and blew her a kiss. *Hold on, don't let the kids see your frustration. Just keep things smooth.* Conchita turned on her heel and went back inside.

The kids chattered on, avoiding any mention of their father as they decorated and completed the invitations, which Conchita would deliver tomorrow for the upcoming weekend event. Jack's organization impressed Conchita and she had approved his plans for food with few changes. She vowed to make sure the party went off without any disappointments. By 8:30 when everything was finished, the children helped with cleanup and got ready for bed.

In a grown-up voice Jenny said, "Don't forget tomorrow's a big day. We're playing baseball and we need our sleep, don't we Mamá?"

"Yup, that's right. Night niños."

The kids had begged to stay home tomorrow with their father rather than stay with their grandmother. Conchita hoped this was a good sign and signaled a positive father and kids' relationship. Miguel said he would play ball with them and they couldn't wait.

Exhausted from work, tension and all the activities of the night, Conchita slept so soundly that she had no idea when Miguel came home. All she knew was that he was there beside her when her alarm went off at 6:00 in the morning. She barely looked at him and moved quietly so as not to awaken anyone. She had an early schedule and needed to get a move on.

Before she left, she tip-toed back to the bedroom and taped a note on the mirror.

> *Miguel, don't forget—*
> *You promised to play ball*
> *Then you can fix a picnic and walk*
> *to the park—The kids*
> *would love it*
> *Lunch in the frig*
> *Don't forget!!*

MIGUEL SURPRISED CONCHITA AND INDEED did play ball with the children. He rolled grounders to the girls so they could hit the ball and run the bases. Jack hit pitch after pitch which Miguel bragged about. "That Jack has a good eye. Course being my son, what would you expect?" They even had the picnic at the park.

The rest of the week passed quickly. Jack, Jenny and Pamela stayed with their grandmother since Miguel needed to get his picture taken at the license bureau, given that the camera was down when he got his temporary. He also needed to complete paperwork with Social Security. Johnny volunteered to run Miguel around the town. Miguel also wanted to work on his speech for the upcoming welcome home celebration for the hostages to be held at the arena in Greeley the following week.

Conchita agreed that the kids could fill the water balloons on Saturday, the day before the party. Even Miguel helped and everyone got a little wet in the process.

Jack held a water-filled balloon, trying to tie a knot in the neck. It slipped from his hand and water shot toward Pamela's face. She stood sopping and dripping. "You did that on purpose," yelled Pamela.

"Honestly, I didn't."

Jenny laughed at her sister. "I wanta get wet, too."

At that, Pamela's accusation turned to laughter as well. "It's OK. It'll dry won't it Papá?"

"Hey kids wait for your papá," Conchita said. "Jack, you fill the balloons and he'll tie them. Girls, you put them in the basket."

Even Miguel had trouble holding the slippery water-filled globes. Water spewed from the first two and splattered across the front of his t-shirt. "I hope I get the hang of this soon. Never thought I had clumsy fingers. Hey Conchita, pull this end through this loop while I hold it."

Through much cooperation and do-overs, they finished the water-filling balloon project. Conchita looked at the large basket full of the 60 water-filled globes, four throws for each child, plus extras—just in case. *This is what family life should be like. It feels good. I hope it lasts.*

On the day of the party Conchita surveyed the backyard, colorful and bright in orange, purple and green. Each of her children chose a color and Conchita had to admit it looked great. Across the back-property line Jack had pounded ten stakes—about three feet high— into the ground. He looped streamers in a variety of colors between the stakes. Conchita helped attach a cluster of balloons to each stake. A neighbor lent his table with a mammoth umbrella attached. It held its own share of streamers and balloons as well and would serve as the food table.

"OK kids, we have enough balloons. Time to get cleaned up. The guests will be here pretty soon. Go change your clothes. Hustle along."

The lawn Greg had planted and helped nurture had filled in lush and velvety. Conchita smiled to herself remembering Greg's careful attention to pulling out the unwanted weeds. *Stop thinking of Greg. Your husband's back.*

The noisy sound of a revving engine coming from the front of the house jolted Conchita. She hurried inside. Could kids be arriving already? If so, some parent had a thunderous engine and liked to show it off.

Conchita rushed to Jack's room to hurry the kids along. She saw him slip on his second shoe and pull the laces tight. "I'm almost ready, Mamá. Just have to wet down my hair a little."

Conchita smiled at the spikes sticking every which way and said, "Yup, I can see that the hair could use a little taming. Otherwise, this Mamá sees a mighty handsome son." He'd look much like his father as he matured, she thought, but with a sweet-tempered personality. She knew that already.

Poking her head into the girls' room was a different story. Pamela and Jenny haggled over three pairs of shorts and a pile of tops laid out on Pamela's bed. Conchita insisted that each twin have her own individual clothes. The twins were not identical and had never dressed alike. Early on, Conchita recognized the different tastes her five-year-olds possessed. Today however, the girls were bargaining about exchanging clothes and neither was ready for company by any stretch of the imagination.

"What's going on here?" Conchita admonished. "You should be ready by now. Your brother is. It sounds like we have guests already."

"It's all right," Pamela cut in. "Jenny wants to wear my purple shorts and as a trade, I get to have her bug collection. We'll be ready in a minute."

What bug collection? Conchita wondered. Oh well, whatever it was they seemed to have made an agreeable deal. "Please get a move on."

Conchita stepped out the front door as the driver of a black low-slung car gunned the engine one more time. He shut off the motor and stepped from the car. *Good gosh, what's Miguel's cousin doing here on the day of the kid's party?*

Johnny yelled across the yard, "Hey, good lookin'. What ya been doing? You haven't come around to Ma's for ages."

Feeling shanghaied by the sudden intrusion, she headed for the car parked in the driveway. "Hi Johnny, we're just getting ready for a party for the kids…"

Before she could say another word, a very dark-skinned woman in tight shorts and a top knotted in the middle, exposing a well-pierced navel, stepped from the car. "Hi, I'm Charly, Johnny's woman. Kids you can get out now."

The kids did just what she suggested. The boy, his mouth full of permanent front teeth except for open space where the eye teeth would emerge, held out a friendly hand. "Hey, I'm Deke. Glad to make yer acquaintance."

Conchita guessed he was about Jack's age, not yet ten. Stunned, she took Deke's grimy hand. His mighty shake surprised her. The girl, nearly as tall as Deke, stood shyly on spindly legs and sported pigtails that poked out a few inches from each side of her head.

"This here's my sister, Shanae," Deke said.

Johnny cut in, "He's quite the little man, that Deke. Miguel said there's a party this afternoon. Bein' I'm family he said I should come and bring Charly and the kids. We thought we'd surprise ya. Where's your man anyway?"

At that moment, the garage door rumbled open and Miguel stepped out carrying a trash can lined with a black bag. "Hey, man you made it. And Charly, too. I hope you brought some beer." Addressing Conchita, he said, "I'll take this 'round back for all the trash." He added to the others, "Come on guys and see the decorations we got. Looks pretty snazzy."

Conchita stood cemented in place, speechless as the entourage tromped to the backyard. Johnny carried a twelve pack of beer. All enthusiasm for the kid's party drained to her toes while tears filled her eyes. Then a great knot of frustration and fury gathered in her gut and began to fester. The gall of this man to interfere with all the children's plans. Long before Miguel returned, she had promised the party. It had been postponed because of Miguel and now everything had changed. She had dared to dream of watching proudly as twelve children giggled and hopped around playing their children's games, and then gobbled down hotdogs and chips with all the trimmings, decorated their own cupcakes and made their own sundaes.

What could she say? What could she do?

You can do it. You can do it. We're having a kid's party.

Soon the backyard filled with noisy children, running and chasing after each other. The first game was tag. Jack was the first one to be *it* and galloped toward scattering kids. He caught Jason, the neighborhood boy with the mother who lived in her tattered blue robe. Even through Jason's shyness, he appeared excited to be *it*. The game continued with much squealing and laughing. Pamela and Jenny had turns at being *it* and ran nearly as fast as the older boys.

When Shanae was tagged, Deke taunted, "nana, nana, na, na— you're just a slow poke."

She ducked her head and bit her lip before she took off on a run. Once, she tagged a player, Conchita announced it was time for the second game.

"Come on kids. Over here. Sit on the grass in front of me. Jack's father will help us get started."

Conchita turned to call to Miguel who sat with Johnny and Charly near the back door. Charly flicked a finished cigarette to the grass. *Damn her anyway.* Johnny flipped open a lighter to light his own. *Don't make a scene.* "Miguel, we're ready to do the relay. Will you bring out the eggs and spoons?"

Miguel, set his beer bottle on the grass. It tipped and he righted it, and grumbled something she couldn't hear. He rose from the lawn chair, taking his time. He spoke to Charly and Johnny, "Sorry, gotta help the wife." Then he yelled, "Be right there Chita."

Conchita heaved a sigh, and then organized the teams. She counted one, two, one, two...until all the kids had a number. She stabbed two stakes into the ground—one with a blue balloon and the other with a yellow balloon.

"All the ones line up here beside the yellow balloon and the twos line up with blue," instructed Conchita.

Once they were in place, she explained the relay. The first team player on each team would carry a hard-cooked egg on a spoon to the other side of the yard and back, and then give the egg and spoon to the second player. If someone dropped the egg, he or she had to stop, pick it up and continue the relay. The team that finished the course first would receive a prize.

"What if the egg cracks?" asked a short, stocky kid.

"It's OK if it cracks, but if it breaks apart, you have to go back and get another egg and start the course again. So, you need to be careful," said Conchita.

Deke yelled out to the yellow team, "You guys don't have a chance. My sister always loses."

"Shush," said Conchita.

"Well, she does."

Miguel sauntered up with a box in his hand and handed it to Conchita. "Here's your stuff. Looks like they're ready."

"Can you hand out the spoons and eggs."

"Naw, I'll watch. You know what you're doin'." Miguel patted her cheek and walked back to his lawn chair and then picked up his beer.

Yes, I know what I'm doing, and I'll do it.

Conchita grinned as she watched each child balance the egg in the spoon, take careful steps and follow the rules, trying to do their best. That is, except for Deke, who decided to run, and when his egg smashed to the ground, it broke open. Muttering that it wasn't fair, he nevertheless went back to the line for a new egg. The yellow team jumped and squealed as the last teammate crossed the finish line. Conchita handed out a prize for each teammate—a small American flag on a stick.

The rest of the afternoon was a blur of activities and eating. Miguel helped bring out the food and clear away the paper plates, but most of the time he sat with Johnny and Charly laughing and telling stories.

Conchita felt sorry for Shanae. Her brother sent putdowns her way time after time, and Shanae said nothing. The knobby-kneed girl looked down as she listened and followed each instruction.

Deke surely had a good time, Conchita thought bitterly. He ate more than his share, and as the consummate know-it-all took over each activity, shouting out instructions—according to Deke—and explanations on the right way to do everything. He knew how to the blow the biggest soap-bubble, how to swirl the sparkler in the air, what decoration one should put on a cupcake, how to make a perfect sundae.

Conchita had to step in when Deke, for the third time, made fun of Jason. "Deke, come over here please," she said signaling with her come-here finger. When he cocked his head to the side and gave her a smart-aleck smile, she turned on her stern stare. He shrugged and came to her.

"What d'ya want?" he asked unabashed.

"I don't want to hear one more sarcastic remark about anyone. You are being very rude to our guests and to your sister." Conchita enunciated every word with precision. "Once more and you will sit in the car the rest of the time. Do you hear me?"

Deke shrugged again and smiled sweetly at Conchita. "Whatever you say, ma'm." He walked back to the water balloon game and took his turn. The throw was a dreadful miss, as was his last toss. Jenny and Jason scored three points apiece and tied as the winners.

Oblivious to the threesome who sat drinking, and apparently oblivious and to the intrusion of Deke and Shanae, the rest of the kids had a glorious time. When their parents arrived, Conchita witnessed their exuberance in telling of all the fun.

Conchita watched the taillights of the last car turn the corner and wondered what to do with Deke and Shanae. Johnny had made a beer run and Conchita thought it best to avoid the drinkers and keep the kids away. She pushed aside the children's request to dismantle the decorations. "We can do that tomorrow when it's bright and sunny. How about a game of Uno?"

Conchita's children explained the rules to Charly's kids and were surprised the game was new to them. The game served to keep them occupied for twenty minutes until Deke, who was losing, threw his cards on the table and grumbled, "This is a stupid game. I'm not playing anymore." After he walked out the front door, Conchita heard the door of the black car slam. *I'm glad to see Deke go to the car. I hope he stays there.*

Exhausted, Conchita talked the children into watching a Disney video in the living room. She offered each a pillow to each child. The girls chose to lay on the floor, while Jack curled up in the easy chair. In no time, the twins and Shanae were asleep, and she shut off the video. Conchita carried her girls to their bedroom and tucked them in bed, leaving them in their play clothes. Then she lifted Shanae to the couch and covered her with a light blanket. Conchita patted her and whispered, "Sleep tight little gal, till your Mom's ready to take you home."

Jack looked at her with sleepy eyes and said, "It was a really good party, wasn't it?"

"Yes, my son. It was a really good party. Think you'd like to snuggle in your own bed before you nod off, too?"

Jack shook his head yes and kissed his mother before going to his room. Conchita turned the lamp in the living room on low, left Shanae asleep on the couch and walked to her own bedroom. She changed into her nightgown and crawled into her bed. She stared at the ceiling. Why was she so irritated with Miguel? He didn't really cause a scene. Then she imagined how it might have been with Greg in Miguel's place—no intrusion with Johnny, Charley and her kids, no beer drinking and flicking cigarettes over the backyard, but plenty of support, help and involvement with the children. *Stop it Conchita. Can't think about that. Monday comes soon. Get your sleep.*

Mel

MEL PULLED UP IN FRONT of her mother's condo and jumped out of her car. Today would be the day for a real father and daughter outing. Though she had had dinner with her parents one night, her schedule kept her unavailable for several days following her father's return. Charlotte assured her daughter she had several errands to run and a meeting for the Symphony Guild and would not feel left out if she wasn't included in the outing.

Ben Jameson met his daughter at the door with a wrap-around bear hug. He stepped back to see her whole being. "Each time I see you, it's like an unbelievable dream. Five months ago, I couldn't imagine being back on Colorado soil, let alone seeing my daughter, the one who has earned her Captain's wings." He smiled.

The low rumble of his melodic voice washed over Mel and she was once again awed to stand in her father's presence after these many years. Her eyes misted. "You can't imagine how I missed you Dad. It killed me to think you might never know that I followed in your footsteps as a pilot."

"I never once doubted you. I knew you would achieve your dream. My mind made up wonderful pictures of you and your life. At times it kept me going."

Mel's cheeks flushed at her father's admiration for her. "I had a great teacher and a great model." She looked away from his face and continued, "Well, are we ready to go?"

"Sure enough," he said, and then turning toward the hallway he yelled out, "Charlotte, Mel and I are taking off."

Charlotte entered the living room carrying a notebook and a stack of papers. "Oh, Marilyn. I didn't hear you come in, dear. I hope you're doing fine." Without waiting for a reply, Charlotte continued, "Well you two run along and have and great day. I have a million things to do before I go to the Symphony Guild's meeting. Oh, don't forget the lunch I fixed."

In the car, Mel started the engine, swung the car around and headed out of the cul-de-sac. Ben said, "I thought we'd stop at that rustic inn in Estes Park for lunch, but your mother insisted on sending a lunch. Sorry."

"The one that had those mounds of fried onions sticks?" Mel asked.

"Yeah. You liked their chili dogs as I remember."

"I did Dad, but that place closed up last year. So maybe the packed lunch is good. We can find a picnic table somewhere."

"Closed huh?" Ben said as he clucked his tongue and shook his head. "Lot's changed. Like that building," he remarked as he pointed to his right. "It's a new one. I wasn't prepared for all the new construction and housing developments. Your Mom's condo wasn't even built when I left. I guess she thought the house was more than she needed. I liked that old house."

"I tried to talk her out of it. When it sold, I lost my childhood home. But Mother…"

Ben gestured with a flick of his wrist. "Oh, Mel, she needed to sell the place. I don't begrudge her that at all."

As they drove through the little berg of Windsor, then Loveland and toward Big Thompson canyon, Mel explained about finishing her pilot training and getting on with the airline. She said she was in the right place at the right time and perhaps being a woman gave her an edge as there was pressure to hire minorities.

When Mel was at Brooke Army Center, Ben told her a short version of his five years in Colombia. Now riding along, he filled in more details about their plane being shot down over Colombian jungles, being taken captive by guerrillas, moving from camp to camp and waiting the last few months for the final hostage trade negotiation.

Mel glanced at the handsome face of her father, the same one she remembered some five years ago, before the Cessna taxied to the runway and lifted into the deep blue sky. Yet now his skin had loosened over his cheeks and jaws and had formed creases where there had been none. Her heart warmed with gratefulness. *He's really here.*

"Dad, how did you keep going each day? You must have felt hopeless. How could this happen to you? You were robbed of a big piece of the prime of your life."

"Yes, daughter of mine. Life happens." Ben tapped on the armrest between them. "Remember, you were always in my thoughts. I couldn't give up. Couldn't let you down. Had to believe I would see you and your mother again. I had to."

They rode in silence for a while. Mel focused on navigating the curves as they drew closer to the mountain town that would be bustling with tourists the day after Independence Day. The Big Thompson River along side the highway alternated between a widened lazy looking stream where fly fishermen worked their lines, and a rushing gush of foam that furiously surged over boulders the size of Volkswagen Bugs and Mack Trucks. The river's sudden transformations spurred Mel to reflect.

"You know Dad, the flow of a river is much like the flow of life. Sometimes it's calm, peaceful and safe, then it's full of danger, uncertainty and difficult to negotiate."

Ben smiled and rubbed his freshly shaven chin. "Guess so. Tell me what your river's like now? And tell me about this pilot you have your sights on. And why hasn't anyone met him, little Miss Tight Lip?"

"Mother. She exaggerates. Erik and I see each other from time to time. He's a good man. But I certainly don't have my sights on him. Mom was trying to fix me up with some guy, so I stretched the truth a little about Erik to get her off that kick.

And about my river…It seems to be at a new peace and calm, now that you're here."

"Me too—about peace and calm as you call it. It'll take a while to get my feet planted and know which direction I'm going, but I'm content to take one step at a time." "One step, yeah—and pretty soon you're there, wherever there is…You'll find it, I know that."

"I will. Well tell me about this Erik anyway, even if it's a pretty insignificant relationship." Ben glanced sideways at his daughter and grinned.

"I can do that," Mel said as she turned off the highway at a little roadside picnic area. "I know it's a little early for lunch, but let's snag that empty table before someone else does."

Mel realized why it was the only table left. It had no shade and she surmised they would soon be sweating in the blazing high-altitude sun. Yet the sunny spot echoed the feeling in her heart, and she welcomed it. She unwrapped whole wheat sandwiches filled with layers of turkey, sprouts and cucumbers with a chipotle sauce, and then pulled a container of sliced strawberries, blueberries and grapes tossed with yogurt from the insulated lunch box.

Ben straightened the tablecloth Charlotte had tucked into a bag and set out brightly colored plastic plates and utensils. "Your mother seems to be on some health kick these days. Quite a change from jungle food," he said with a laugh.

"You've noticed, huh?" Mel resisted adding—ever since she met Arthur, the doctor. "And look, we have pomegranate juice to drink. Oh, oh, she slipped up. She made your favorite. Butterscotch brownies."

During lunch Mel told of her first dealings with Erik and how put off she was at his attempts to engage her in conversation, how she had taken it as sexual harassment, how she was dismayed when she was scheduled to fly with him during her maiden flight as Captain.

"I misjudged him Dad. He's not so bad. Been through some tough times. His dad was a helicopter pilot. Was shot down in Laos when Erik was pretty young. He adored his mom."

"Something happened to her?"

"She struggled with breast cancer for several years. Erik cared for her, especially when things got bad before she died."

Ben looked into his daughter's eyes. "He must have a good heart."

Mel shrugged. "Well, yes. Oh, and he's a runner. And he's heard about you. Can you believe? And wants to meet you."

Ben put his hand on his daughter's arm. "Sounds like more than a passing fancy to me".

Mel sighed and worked her mouth to a pucker before she spoke, "I've never done well with men. Other than you, that is. I pretty much had it in the back of my mind I'd be satisfied with a great career…never thought of something permanent."

"Sounds like you've tried to shut him out, yet he's still being persistent. Still hanging in there."

"I don't know why. He'll probably end up dumping me," Mel said.

Ben appeared to be deep in thought as he looked off toward a jagged mountain peak. He scratched the back of his head. "What happened to the daughter who never backed away from a challenge, who took every risk in the book to achieve her goals, whether it was in sports, academics or learning to fly?"

"This is different. It involves someone else. I know I can trust myself, but when it comes to someone else, I have no control."

"Ah, my little control monster. Nothing ever goes exactly as we expect. That is the wonder of this wild river of life we are on. So…if it isn't perfect, so…if it doesn't work out. You'll never know if you don't open your arms and heart to this fellow you say is 'not so bad.' No one knows where this river will end up ten years from now. And it's a darned good thing we don't."

The rest of the afternoon, Mel and her father wound through the crowds of people tromping the sidewalks of Estes Park. They went in and out of the shops selling everything from Western clothing, to Native American jewelry and Saltwater Taffy. They passed on the taffy but splurged on a double dipper ice cream cone. A cloud mass passed over and splattered a few minutes worth of oversized raindrops. Otherwise, the day filled with sun, bright blue sky and "white puffies" as Mel and her father had called the cottony clouds when she was young.

The ride home was quiet. Mel felt as peaceful as the wide spots in the river, and her father seemed to feel the same. They both enjoyed smelling the pristine air of the mountains and seeing the variations in rock formations. They laughed at the birds who flitted here and there and the ground squirrels that raced across the road, escaping the wheels of passing cars.

"You said you're not sure about the direction you're heading. But do you want to fly again?" Mel asked.

"It's in my blood. Think there's a chance to get on at the Loveland Airport. Need to attend to some licensing issues. Don't think there's a problem there."

Mel grinned. "You're healthy as a young moose. Passing the medical should be a snap, too. I know if you want it, you'll be in the skies again."

"One thing I know, I'm sticking close to home. Hey, I might even be a grandfather some day."

Mel shot her father a stunned glare. "I...I can't believe you said that." *You'd be a good one. I'm sure of that.*

As Mel pulled up in front of her mother's condo, Ben said, "Want to come in? I see your Mom's car is still gone. But maybe I can rustle up something."

"No thank you. Need to get home myself. I'm flying the next few days. But if you want to meet Erik, how about Thursday? We're both in town. See what Mother thinks and let me know." Mel hesitated, then asked. "How're things going with Mother? Are you going to make it?"

Her father's voice was quiet as he responded with a shrug, "Time will tell, Mel, time will tell."

CHAPTER 21

Racine

After Racine heard Randy's voice on the phone, she sat stunned and mute. Then she jumped up squealing and pounding the air with her fists. "Did you hear? He's alive. He's coming home." She grabbed Chad in a bear-hug and just missed his toes with her excited stomping. At that moment concern about the couch rendezvous of the previous night faded into the background.

Chad insisted she go home, relax, and get some rest. "We can handle things here and you need a couple days to be ready for your son's return."

"No. I'll go crazy two days at home. I need to be here doing something productive." At that she spun on her heel and floated from her office. She lent a hand here and there and greeted everyone with tinkling laughter and joyous banter. *I'll show them I'm back to myself, with renewed vigor.*

⚈

AT HOME THE NEXT DAY, a thousand images played through Racine's mind. Randy with a full red beard, wearing a T-shirt and faded jeans.

Randy, with his head shaved bald, wearing a camouflage jumpsuit. Randy with shoulder-length crimson hair, not unlike her own, wearing a flowered Hawaiian-type shirt with white shorts. She needed to be able to see him in her mind's eye as she waited for tomorrow. Racine studied his college graduation picture, varying the angle and tried to imagine the rounded jaw, squared by the passing of more than five years. Tomorrow Randy would land at DIA with McCrae. Tomorrow she would look into the eyes of her beloved son.

She gazed around his room, freshly aired and dusted, his bed lain with clean bedding and wondered what she had missed. She nodded approval of what she saw and hurried to the kitchen. She stirred up a batch of his favorite brownies and scurried in circles the rest of the afternoon, cleaning, dusting, and decimating spider webs.

Since he was not part of the hostage exchange, Randy was not required to go directly to San Antonio for debriefing and reintegration. For that Racine was immensely grateful. She could barely imagine the strings McCrae pulled, how he arranged for Randy to board a commercial flight. The whole thing took place in secret. Only Racine and Chad knew about the rescue and his return. Racine was adamant about meeting them at the airport and wondered how she could survive the wait.

But she did. Randy's welcome home day ended up being at night. She knew she was early, but she'd decided to wait at the airport rather than run the risk of being late with a flat tire or some other delay. Thus, at 9:00 p.m. she found herself roaming around DIA's mezzanine. The fifteen-hour flight from Bogota included layovers at Panama City and Houston, where they would go through customs. Racine hoped this should make disembarking quicker at DIA.

As restaurants closed, leftover trace odors of hamburgers and French fries lingered. This brought queasiness to an already nervous stomach. Night-time cleaning crews ran their scrubbing and polishing machines. The sounds hummed through her body.

Racine spotted a magazine someone left on a bench and sat to look through it. Almost deserted, the expansive hallway echoed as the shoes of an occasional passerby clicked against the marble floor. Forty minutes later Racine made her third attempt to read an article in the magazine she had picked up. The words danced around the page, she found herself staring in a stupor, or her eyes glazed over giving everything a fuzzy blur. She gave up, slapping the magazine against the bench. In her jitteriness, she needed to use the bathroom. Afterwards she took the escalator to the next level and checked the arrival and departure information. It appeared the flight was on time and would land at the scheduled 10:17. She sat again. *Patience, Racine, patience.*

Fifteen minutes after the scheduled arrival time, she took the elevator to the baggage claim floor. Since there were no chairs close by, she leaned against the railing which separated the hallway and baggage carousel. *You'd think they'd know some people have to wait awhile to meet the travelers. Can't they have benches or something to sit on?*

She stood alone until a fellow, possibly in his twenties, arrived looking as if he just came off the mountain trail with his hiking boots, shorts and backpack. An aging couple joined her at the railing. The man, somewhat frail, listened to his wife explain in a loud voice that this was the right place to meet, that Marcy, their granddaughter would come here to get their luggage.

Racine moved away from the couple, to give them some privacy. A few others joined the waiting group. Racine heard the carousel mechanism clunk and begin its rotation. Little by little travelers arrived and hovered around the baggage carousel. No luggage yet. She saw that the passengers came from the left. Should she walk down that hall and watch for Randy and McCrae? *Just wait where you are.*

A few cases and bags slid down the face of the carousel and rode around and around, until a traveler claimed one and then another. Her head swiveled from side to side taking in the expanse of the area, looking for McCrae's familiar graying mass of hair. The crowd gained in numbers. She caught a glimpse of McCrae weaving between some of passengers. She froze. *Where's Randy? Surely right behind him.*

But he wasn't. Where could he be?

She heard a voice beside her. It was mellow, yet strong, "Mom. I'm here. Can you believe it?"

She turned to look up at the most welcome smile she'd ever seen. Yes, Randy's jaw had squared as she imagined, but his face had thinned.

His blue-green eyes, flecked with hazel, looked tired. She grabbed the tall man in front of her. They rocked as they hugged each other. The firmness of his frame stretched taller than she remembered.

He pushed back. "Let me look at you. Yup, sassy as ever." Randy nodded. "I love you Mom."

Tears flowed from her eyes and refused to stop. "You're the best. I have so much to make up to you."

Randy put his arm around her shoulder and tugged her to him. "Hey. I'm home. This is the first day of the rest of my life. Remember? You always said so."

Racine bobbed her head a few times. She pulled a tissue from her pocket to dab at her eyes and nose. She sniffed and composed herself, just as McCrae rolled his luggage up beside them.

She smiled. "Oh McCrae, you brought him back. You never gave up. I don't know how to thank you."

"How about a hug for starters?" McCrae reached toward Racine. "That's easy."

As Racine pulled away from the hug, McCrae said to Randy, "We made your mom happy, didn't we? Well, let's get you home."

Once they reached Racine's car in the parking garage and tossed their bags in the trunk, McCrae insisted on driving. "You two sit in the back. You need time together."

As the car exited the garage, Randy took hold of his mother's hand. He whooshed out a deep breath. "Just wondered if this day would ever come."

"Don't know if you want to talk much about…all that happened. Maybe you need some down time, first," said Racine.

"We have a lot to catch up on, don't we? Maybe some time I can tell you the whole story."

"There's no rush." Racine squeezed her son's hand and released it.

Silence floated around them. Racine heard the muffled rumble of the car engine. She listened to Randy's deep breaths. Traffic was light as McCrae kept a steady pace on the toll road between the airport and I-25. They came upon a police car at the roadside, its brilliant red, blue, and clear lights flashing in syncopation. McCrae slowed and swung out around the officer standing beside a sports car.

"Racine, it's easy to speed on this road, but I'm under the speed limit. Don't worry about me getting a ticket."

"I'm not worried. I trust you. But aren't you tired? I could drive, you know."

"Doing fine. Probably slept better than Randy on the plane."

Randy laughed. "Guess so. I heard him snore."

"You could've poked me."

"No, I couldn't… Hey Mom, McCrae told me a bit about Nicola. Only saw her a few times after the plane got shot down. Must be some tough woman."

"I think so. She went through a lot. Her escape helped to bring about the hostage exchange. Oh, how I wanted you to be in that exchange."

"It's OK. Instead, I got rescued. My hero's sitting in the front seat." Randy thumped McCrae on the shoulder.

Randy clasped his hands together behind his head and leaned back. He stared into the night for a time. Then he spoke, allowing each word to hang in the air before the next. "It was pitch black outside. I was in and out of sleep. Don't know why I was restless. Then I heard it…this familiar voice whispering 'Randy, it's McCrae. We're here to take you out of this nightmare.' I know my eyes popped open. I saw his shadow."

Racine's eyes closed fleetingly, then sprang open. She gazed trance-like at the son she loved more than life itself. In the passing of lights flickering by in the darkness, she saw the tears flood his eyes.

With a catch in his throat, his words tumbled forth. "It was unbelievable. There was my very own father, come to rescue me."

Mel

THURSDAY, THE MEET-ERIK-DAY ARRIVED ALL too quickly and Mel had no clue what the food menu would be. She rarely cooked on her little patio. It held a small charcoal unit that looked like new because of its non-use. Erik made some suggestions and promised he would do the barbequing if Mel helped him with the shopping. Thus, at exactly 8:00 in the morning Mel's doorbell rang.

"You're certainly a man of your word. If you say eight, you mean eight," she said to the athletic-looking man standing in the open doorway. Mel buttoned the last button on her yellow and blue striped shirt and tucked the tail under the band of her shorts.

"If we want to get that brisket bought, marinated and slow cooked over coals and ready to impress your parents we can't dally, now can we?" Erik said as he entered the condo. "First let me look at you. It's been too long since I looked into those haunting eyes." He stretched his hands out and gripped her arms just below the shoulders, holding her in front of him. "Yup, sure good to see you."

"Don't know what you mean by haunting eyes," she said staring at his grinning mouth.

"They're almost smoldering this morning." He laughed, pulled her to him and held her close for a moment.

It felt good, her cheek nestled against his neck that smelled of spice, a fragrance she liked, his body gently against hers. She did not pull away. She did not resist.

"Well, Captain, are we off to the market?" Erik asked releasing her.

"If you say so. You're the head honcho for this venture."

At the grocery store, Erik removed a paper from his pocket and unfolded it. "What do you think?" he asked, spreading it out in front of her. "Is there anything else we need?"

Mel studied the list. "What's the fresh ginger and grape jelly for?" Mel wanted to know.

"The ginger goes in the marinade and the grape jelly is part of the barbeque sauce."

"Really? Hmm. Hey, I have brown sugar. So you can cross that off."

"All right. You push. Let's head off this way," Erik said motioning to his right.

Mel grabbed the cart and the couple strode up and down isles searching for the items on the list. She felt lightheaded and a little giddy with this confident and pleasant man beside her. Erik had offered her some gum and even chomping on the gum made her feel like a schoolgirl.

"This is my idea about the appetizers before the meal," Erik explained. "Mangos are on sale this week, so I thought we'd make a mango salsa to go on these crackers." He held the box in front of her. "What do you think? And they'll go well with that cheese you said you liked."

Mel shook her head in wonder. "Where'd you learn all this? Get all these ideas about food?"

"It was Mom. Dad was gone so long ago. She and I did a lot of cooking together. She let me experiment. Sometimes it was a fiasco, but usually a pretty tasty result."

Erik's eyes clouded and Mel heard the mood of a mournful dove in his voice. "When Mom was so sick, many of my concoctions kept her going, even when she thought she couldn't eat a bite. She raved about anything I fixed."

Mel wanted to say something tender, something comforting, but she couldn't find the right words. All she knew was this man had a gentleness somewhat like her father's. Yet, like her father, he was a man's man as well. Could she trust him as she trusted every ounce of her father? Somehow, little by little the knots in her heart began to loosen. Perhaps she could let him in. Didn't her father say something about not letting a good one get away? *I think he's one of the good ones.*

The day of cooking, interspersed with stimulating conversation, went well. Mel told about the trip she and her father made to the mountains. Their conversation jumped from one topic to another. Mel opened up concerning much of her past leading her to the present. Somehow the topic her father's attitude toward alcohol came up. "In the years he flew for various powerful CEO's there were many cocktail parties and lots of heavy drinking. Dad liked the taste of a well-blended drink and fell easily into the scene. At least that's the way he told it."

"I understand that. Even for us, layovers can be boring and it's easy to spend the evening in the bar," Erik said. "If one has a tendency toward alcoholism it can be deadly."

"I don't know if Dad thought he had a problem or if he believed he might end up an alcoholic, but one time he'd been pretty high on booze. Then there was some business emergency and he had to fly out immediately. He said he felt woozy at the controls and it was a miracle he got back safely. He decided alcohol could be a demon, change how you felt. *He* wanted to be in total control, not the alcohol. He hasn't had another drink since. Once I took the controls of a plane, he warned me about it."

"You and I had a few beers together. But I can take it or leave it. If you'd rather not, I'll follow your lead."

"A glass of wine or a beer hits the spot at times and I'm not against alcohol but drinking and driving or drinking and flying are unacceptable. Dad wouldn't care, but I won't drink around him."

"Sounds good to me."

Throughout the rest of the afternoon the pair worked cooperatively together as Erik sought Mel's know-how and suggestions with preparing the various foods. She enjoyed the connection, the feeling of teamwork. He definitely had the upper hand in the food prep arena and might have come across with an I-know-what-to-do and I'll-show-you attitude, yet he didn't.

By 6:00, the lingering smoky aroma of nicely seasoned beef brisket with its final slathering of homemade barbeque sauce had permeated each corner of Mel's condo. Everything awaited the guests. Appetizers, sparkling cranberry juice, crusty rolls, jicama, red pepper and cabbage salad, scalloped corn casserole and for dessert, fresh strawberry parfaits, colorfully layered.

"I think my mother will approve of our menu. Decent color, variety of flavors and texture. Maybe a little high on the calories." Mel said removing the towel she had tied at her waist for an apron.

Erik took the towel from her and tossed in on the counter. "It doesn't matter if you're in the cockpit, or in the kitchen, you make me catch my breath. Come here."

She snuggled into his embrace, then wound her arms around his neck, smiling from lips *and* her heart.

Their kisses left her hungering for more, yet she resisted, determined to save some for later. There would be many laters. Of that she was sure. The eyes she saw sparkled at her with affection and she couldn't change her gaze. "I can't believe how amazing it is cooking with you. I'm a bit of a dud in the kitchen."

"We did well, didn't we? But it can be dangerous. I wanted to kiss you all afternoon."

"Now you have," Mel said in a teasing voice. "Time to refocus. Never did a brisket before. Hope your specialty will impress Mom."

"Hey, it's *our* specialty and I'm certain your mom will be impressed."

Charlotte was impressed. She barely got through the doorway before she asserted, "My land Marilyn, I smelled something delicious wafting through the neighborhood the moment I stepped from the car. Wow, what have you laid before us?" Turning to Erik she offered her hand, "And you must be Erik King. If you brought about this transformation in my daughter who detests cooking, you must be a magician."

As Mel introduced Erik to her father, Charlotte made her way to the patio.

"Great to meet you, young man," Ben said as the two shook hands. "Charlotte is right. Whatever you have on the grill makes my stomach growl." Ben winked at Mel and looked directly into Erik's face. "Mel tells me you're quite an outdoorsman, but your trip up Pennock pass was a little harrowing with the horrendous lightening, thunder and downpour."

"Now we can laugh about it, but we could've been hit, not just scraped up slipping and sliding down the mountain." Erik responded.

The conversation easily turned to flying as the four gathered for appetizers and punch at a small table decked out in a checkered cloth, beside the charcoal cooker, puffing little whirls of fragrant smoke.

Charlotte sat sipping her beverage, offering little to the conversation. Mel tried to read her mother's far off expression. Not exactly bored, just in her own pleasant world, Mel thought.

During the main part of the meal all agreed that the food could not have been better, and they ate heartily. Mel watched her parents, their politeness with each other. She couldn't see a spark. Had it always been that way? Polite respect, but no spark. She'd had difficulty letting herself feel a flicker of fire with men. Yet, she wanted to touch the man seated beside her. Recognizing that simple desire caused a flush to rush through her.

As if Erik read her yearning, he placed his hand over hers and gave it a squeeze. His knee pressed against hers. Their eyes connected and held momentarily in some secret awareness. Erik's eyes lowered, then he turned toward Charlotte. "Your daughter is quite a gal and a good cook. I know you said it's not her favorite thing to do, but she does it well, thanks to you, I'm sure."

Addressing Ben, he said, "Mel's a top-notch pilot, a real professional. I know you're proud of her."

Mel scrunched her nose at him, protesting, "Erik. You'll embarrass me. I do my job. I'm nothing special, just plain old me."

"Marilyn has a way of deprecating herself," Charlotte said, "even though she's beautiful and talented. You seem to be an exceptional man yourself. I'm sorry you lost your dear mother to cancer. No brothers and sisters either. Just like Marilyn."

Charlotte sighed. "There was a time I thought we'd have more children, but the years went by and it seemed too late. What about you Erik? Do you want children?"

Mel glared at her mother. How could she be so brazen? This was something they hadn't spoken of, though Mel knew children gravitated to Erik.

"Oh, yes," Erik answered without pause. "I never minded being an only child, but Mother seemed to have great joy being a parent. I assumed I would be the same and I'd like a couple at least. I'd be proud to raise a child, guide her, or him." His smile broadened.

Charlotte nodded. "And Marilyn, dear. We've not broached that subject. How about you?"

Mel's eyes snapped and she breathed in deeply before she spoke. "Mother, you've caught me off guard. I guess…I like children," she said, almost defensively, "However, I've not given it much thought. That possibility always seemed so far in the future." As an afterthought Mel added, "For sure, they'd have to have a terrific father."

Ben smiled at his daughter, "If you have children, I'm sure they'll have a terrific father."

CHAPTER 22

Racine

Racine tip-toed down the hallway and lingered at the open doorway of Randy's bedroom. A ray of early sunlight drifted through the window and settled on her son's bare chest and muscular arm. It caused the hairiness of his chest to glow in a deep amber shade that was not evident when Randy left Colorado for Colombia. Life could be no better than this moment of pride, and gratefulness for his safe return. She decided to stay home today—just to be there for whatever Randy needed. Yet she felt at loose ends. What should she do?

She made a pot of coffee, watered the flowerpots on the front porch, pulled out the dead blooms and leaves. Now what? She picked up a novel she started months ago and found the bookmark at chapter 4. She'd have to skim the first chapters to recall the whole idea of the book. Forget that. *What will Randy say when he wakes up? Will he hate me for the rest of his life?* She sat gazing into nothingness and sipped on one and then another cup of coffee.

Randy's voice startled her to alertness. "I see you're up and around,

Mom. You don't have to stay home for me." He bent down and kissed the top of her head.

Racine jumped to her feet. "Good morning, kid. I'm so glad you're here. What sounds good for breakfast?"

"Haven't had a good cup of coffee since college." He sniffed the air. "Smells good. And it sounds crazy, but I'd like some of your tasty brownies with a mug of your brew—if you haven't already drained the pot. What do think?"

"Whoever said you couldn't eat brownies for breakfast? Well, maybe it's more like brunch," Racine said, as she looked at the clock on the wall. "I'll make a fresh pot while you serve up as many brownies as you want. How'd you sleep?'

"Like a log or maybe three logs. Forgot how comfortable my old bed is." Randy pulled a luncheon plate from the cupboard and lifted the foil from the pan of brownies, frosted with creamy chocolate frosting. He cut two monster sized pieces and put them on the plate. He pinched a corner of one brownie and dropped it in his mouth. "The best brownies in the world Mom. Just like I remember. Nuts and all. Maybe they'll make talking about Colombia sweeter."

"You don't have to talk about it. Maybe it's best to put it behind you and just move forward."

Randy sat at the kitchen table, rubbed his nose, tapped the table with his fingers, and waited for Racine to pour his coffee. "I want to get some of this off my chest. Maybe then I can put it behind me."

"If only I hadn't allowed you to go on that horrible…expedition."

"Don't call it horrible. I wanted to go. You couldn't stop me. How could anyone know that we'd get shot down by rebels? It's not your fault, not McCrae's either."

"But you missed a chunk of your life."

"Didn't miss it Mom. I was there the whole time." Randy sipped on the coffee. "I've thought about it—wouldn't be enough money to pay for all that experience. Learned more about the world and people in it, some good and some bad. Learned a lot about myself—what I can tolerate, my weaknesses, how tough I can be."

Racine wanted to say something encouraging, comforting, or venerating. But anything that came to her mind seemed trite and unmeaningful. Instead of words she chewed on her lip and nodded.

"The first several months were the worst. They treated us like animals, prodded, hit, and nearly starved us. The weather was miserable—hot in the day, cold in the night. Between rains, mud, bugs, slippery trails, and carrying all the supplies for the rebels like slaves, there were times I wanted to smash the face of those men. Miguel fought the rebels all the way those first days and they took it out on the rest of us."

"How about Ben? How'd he do?"

"Mom, he amazed me. He has a good head. We finally stopped to make a permanent camp and things got a bit easier. Ben figured out ways to build protection from the elements. He had better ideas. It helped the rebels and us. He'd probably win some survival show if he was on one."

"Nicola thought you'd go to some big fancy camp. You didn't?"

"Nope. We had to set up the whole camp. We spent weeks putting up pole structures."

"Did you ever figure why they took you there?"

"I guess. It was to be a big hostage camp. They brought in new rebel recruits. That brought the total to eleven, plus us hostages. We learned some guy named Uribe broke away from FARC and hoped to get more hostages moved into our camp. He thought he could get lots of ammunition and power using hostages."

"But nothing happened, right?"

"Right. A few more rebels trickled in with news that Uribe was dead. They said bringing in new leadership would take time."

"What about food? Can't imagine you had markets close by…That was a joke."

Racine laughed.

"You're right about that. Usually when food became scarce, a few rebels took off to raid villages down the valley. The campesinos couldn't defend against rifles. We didn't starve. With no real leadership though, we went on day to day. Thus, the guerrillas fell into limbo, and we did all the dirty work."

"Sounds like what happened to the group with Nicola and Gavin. Not so much danger during the limbo time, huh?"

"No. Sometimes when the guards hiked to villages to get food, they brought back jugs of home brew. Then there'd be a few days of drunkenness, target practice, maybe fights. Who knew what might happen during those times? I observed how people act when they don't have a goal for the day, some direction, some purpose. Pretty degrading, lazy and worthless way to live. For me that's worse than physical hardship and pain."

Racine mused over Randy's observations. "Hmm. What an interesting thing to learn in the jungle. Reminds me of Faulkner's quote, something like, 'Given the choice of the experience between nothing and pain I would choose pain.'" What pride she felt for this son. She didn't deserve him.

"What happened next?"

"Into the third year of captivity, new FARC leaders arrived. We were moved quite often after that. We ended up at a well-organized camp, complete with computers and high-tech equipment. Security was tight. Surveillance increased. Those last seven months we felt like real hostages, not just slaves. They brought in other hostages. Ben, Miguel and I were separated from each other. I learned Gavin was one of the new hostages, but I didn't get to talk to him."

"That must have been tough, being on your own without Ben or Miguel."

"Yes and no. When I was with Ben and Miguel, I didn't want to do anything that would jeopardize their safety, but at the new camp I didn't worry about that. And quite honestly Mom, I was guarded by some real, pardon me, assholes. I'd had enough."

Racine placed her hand over Randy's. She fought gathering tears.

"Guess I wasn't so smart with my escape plan. Got caught, and they worked me over a bit before they took me away."

"So that's why you weren't part of the hostage exchange?"

"My punishment for trying to escape. But I was alive. Ordered to work for this rough group heading further into the jungle. Thought I might be a slave forever...But here I sit with my lovely mother."

"More coffee? Brownies?"

"I suppose you think I need some fattening up. I'll take another brownie. And coffee, too. Makes me feel the reality of *home*. I need that."

Racine pushed the chair away from the table and stood. She poured coffee for Randy and ice water for herself and handed over the brownie pan. "Have all you want. This *is* home."

Randy scooped another brownie to his plate and speared a bite into his mouth. He dropped the fork to his plate, thumped his fist to the table and then said, "Now Mom, we talk about my father. Why didn't you tell me?"

Racine eased onto the chair across the table from Randy. She fingered a napkin and then sighed. "Son, I'm so sorry. If I live to be a hundred, I can never make it up to you. I should have told you, but I didn't want you to think you were a mistake. In the back of my mind I thought if you knew about McCrae, you'd feel less a person, like a mistake. It wasn't that I thought McCrae wasn't good enough to be a father." She fought the shame crawling up the back of her throat and paused to stifle the sob that lingered there. "Oh, a thousand times after you were missing, I regretted not telling you. It was a disservice to you, *and* McCrae."

Racine grabbed a tissue and blew her nose. "But you knew? How did you know?"

Racine was astounded to hear that Randy had guessed about his paternal parentage years ago. He had noticed things she had not. McCrae in a truck to the left of third base where Randy played in his Little League days, McCrae's head among the throngs of spectators at his junior high school basketball games. However, what had clinched it for him, when the pieces fell into place, was the day Racine discovered a shiny silver bicycle at the front door with Randy's name on it. The accompanying note read:

> The Greeley Good Citizen Committee wishes to award
> Randy Rabinowitz with this year's Young Good Citizen
> Award. Teachers and coaches who nominated Randy
> listed these qualities: a gentleman, conscientious,

hardworking, thoughtful to others, displays excellence
in the classroom and on the playing field, a young man
of character.
Congratulations Randy. Enjoy the prize of this new bicycle.
The Greeley Good Citizen Committee

Racine had not known about such a committee, but believed there
must be one, and certainly her son had the qualities to earn such an
award. She also did not know Randy had awakened very early that
morning and watched McCrae wheel the bike to the front door before
hot-footing it to his truck parked a few houses away.

How could he be so perceptive, so wise? "I vividly remember the time
we packed up your granpop's house in Akron and you asked me about
my mother," said Racine. "Afterwards you said you thought it was
good to know about one's roots. You already knew then, didn't you?"

"I knew. Yet, in the back of my mind there was a little uncertainty.
I didn't want to be wrong. I kind of liked the idea that McCrae was
my father. He was pretty well known in the community. It felt good
to be his son."

His gaze scanned the floor before he turned to fix his eyes on hers
once again. "Besides, I didn't want to embarrass you."

"My son didn't want to embarrass me. Oh, no. How wrong I was.
But you never said anything."

"I guess I decided if you wanted me to know my roots, you'd tell
me. I just wanted to make him proud, show him what I was made of.
It's one of the reasons I talked so hard about going to Colombia. Then
I let him down in Colombia. I failed him and didn't come home with
the hostages."

Racine's mind whirled. Her heart felt as though it had been cut
from her chest. She was a heartless, selfish woman. She had caused all
this grief, a loss of so many years, a loss that could never be made up.

"That wasn't your failure. If I had allowed you to have a relationship
with your father, you wouldn't have gone to Colombia to prove yourself.
You wouldn't have suffered all these years in captivity. I'm to blame.
Will you ever forgive me?"

"Oh, Mom I would have gone regardless." He looked away and held his gaze toward the window. The kitchen darkened from a passing cloud. Randy spoke in a hushed, but harsh tone. "But I wouldn't have been angry and bitter. Alone in the jungle it hit me. It wasn't fair. You were wrong."

Mother and son sat breathing heavily. Neither spoke. Minutes passed. Randy reached to cover the remaining brownies in the pan. He pushed away from the table to stand. "I think we both said all we want to say. No more talk about your decision. I forgive you, Mom. Today's the first day of the rest my life. Remember?"

"Thank you," was all she could say as the tears flowed freely.

Conchita

THE MORNING SUN WASHED INTO the corner of the bedroom. Conchita looked over at Miguel sprawled sound asleep on his side of the bed. She eased from the bed, grabbed her clothes, peeked into her children's rooms to see each child well asleep. She tiptoed into the living room. Nothing out of place from the party the night before. *That's good. Don't know if it's worth it to confront Miguel about the intrusion of his cousin and the others. Oh well, can't think of it now. Have to get to work.* She taped a note on the bathroom mirror.

> *Miguel,*
> *Please help the kids take down the stakes and balloons*
> *Remind them to get ready*
> *for tonight. I should be home by 4:15.*
> *Conchita*

He'd done OK when she left the note last week. She hoped he did as well today. She dressed, grabbed a banana, and drove off to work.

Nothing went well at Quail Creek Care Center. Bianca Muños had another spell, ended up on the floor in the TV room kicking and sputtering, then wailing that some hideous men were coming for her.

Three orderlies had to subdue her, and it took Conchita an hour to calm and soothe her in Spanish, the woman's childhood language.

Mr. Jenkins remained on death watch since his body could no longer tolerate dialysis. At least twenty-five family members shuffled in and out saying their goodbyes as Hospice monitored his care to keep pain at a minimum. His body was holding on longer than usual in such a situation. Different family members sought out Conchita for their own comfort and to answer questions about the dying process. Mr. Jenkins had been the delight of the north wing. He made everyone laugh. Conchita had said her own goodbye and would miss him terribly.

Conchita rushed through her leftover before it was time to head home. *Tonight's the big deal for the hostages. Better get a move on.*

Parking her car in the garage, she thought about the busy night ahead of them.

They were to be at Island Grove Park by 5:00. She surmised there would be all kinds of big-wigs, and plenty of media as the events of the evening unfolded. The schedule included music, introductions, speeches, and finally a chuck wagon dinner at 7:00.

Conchita stepped into the kitchen and rushed to change her clothes. Passing the bathroom, she noticed Miguel at the sink shaving the last bit of hair from his face. "Are the kids ready?" she asked.

"They better be."

Jenny stepped into the hall. "How do I look?" She twirled in an ankle length blue print skirt and powder blue t-shirt.

Conchita smiled at Jenny's choice and gave an approving nod. "I like it. How about Pamela? Is she ready?"

"She doesn't want to wear her long skirt. I told her she should dress fancy, but…"

Pamela peeked from the bedroom. Papa said I could wear whatever I want and I'm wearing my purple sundress."

"Yes, yes Pamela. That's fine, but hurry."

Miguel entered their bedroom just as Conchita stepped out of her work uniform. He walked to her and gripped her arms. "Let me get a good look at you. We haven't had much time, have we?"

"Let go. You said we have to hurry. I'm trying to hurry."

Miguel shrugged. "Yeah." Then he yelled. "Get in the car, kids. We're leaving."

Conchita moved in rapid motion pulling on black capris and a print tunic of white, black and gray. She coiled her long braid at the back of her head, securing it firmly with long pins, and then grabbed the gold ear rings Greg had given her to celebrate the completion of her Habitat house and hooked them in place. *I wouldn't have these, except for Greg. Hope Miguel doesn't ask where these came from.* She dashed a bit of color on her lips. *Guess this will have to do. Wish we didn't have to sit in front of everybody on the stage.* Conchita raced to the car and jumped in. "I'm ready."

Miguel pulled the car into a parking space at the park. "Well, look at that. Looks like the whole town came out to celebrate," he said. "Let's go join 'em."

The family climbed from the car and joined the crowd funneling toward the gate to the multipurpose arena. A school band played a rousing march inside.

Jack yelled out, "They play real loud don't they? I think I'd like to be in a band." Conchita smiled. "It would be great to play an instrument. I hope you can. What instrument do you like?"

Jack thought for a moment before he spoke. "Maybe drums or a trumpet."

Pamela interjected, "Can I be in a band, too?"

Miguel stepped to his son's side and tugged on his shirt sleeve. "Hey, don't let your mamá get you all soft. You won't have time for music. You're going to be an athlete. Ain't that right buddy?"

Jack looked up at his father and said, "I can catch and hit better'n anybody in my grade. Greg taught me. He gave me my own bat and glove." Jack turned to his mother and added, "I'm already an athlete. Aren't I Mamá?"

Conchita nodded. "You bet. And I bet you could be a musician, too."

"Well, we'll get you on the field this week," Miguel said, "and we'll see if this Greg taught you anything about handling a baseball."

Relieved to reach the gate, Conchita showed the gate keeper their guest passes and the family was ushered beneath the grandstand where dignitaries mingled with the hostages and their families. Conchita spotted Mel, Charlotte and Ben and went over to greet them. Miguel gave Ben a wave then walked to the punch table. He grabbed a tumbler for himself and one for each of the children.

A tall woman stood to the left with her back to Conchita. Her long silver-gray hair was clasped at the back of her head with what Conchita judged to be an heirloom clip. It's Nicola, she thought. The woman wore a long skirt in blues and grays. Conchita had not seen her so strikingly dressed. The sinewy built man, at her side held Nicola's attention with conversation. He placed the palm of his hand against the middle of her back. She turned toward him and laughed. He removed his hand and stepped to the side to draw a short round woman into the circle.

Conchita smiled. She saw a warm connection between Gavin and Nicola, and fully expected the pair to work together in the mission field once things settled down. His sweet little mother turned an adoring smile to her son and stretched on tip toes to kiss the cheek that he bent down to offer. Conchita wanted to greet them, as well, but resisted, not wanting to intrude. Just then, the sea of bodies pushed toward the arena. It was time to be seated on the guest platform.

Conchita had heard Miguel's story about his role in the hostage release when the family gathered at her mother's home. She wasn't sure how she felt about it. The welcome back get-together included both Miguel's and Conchita's sides of the family. The Señora ordered pizza for everyone. Knowing it used a huge chunk of her monthly food budget, Conchita tucked forty dollars into the pocket of her mother's apron before she left.

Despite the noisiness of the party, all in all the evening went well, partly due to the fact that Conchita's mother would not allow alcohol in her home. Everyone was excited to see Miguel and praised his bravery. Even Conchita's mother heaped admiration on him, though the Señora never had much respect for him. In fact, the day Miguel and Conchita married her mother said, "He's too smooth. I don't trust him. He'll only bring you heartache."

Tonight, at Island Grove, was Miguel's night to shine. She hoped his speech would go well and wondered if she would have a different gut reaction when she heard his story again.

All the hostages and their immediate family members sat on the platform. She nearly cried seeing Racine, Randy and McCrae join the group. There was a time when she wondered if Randy was lost forever.

The introductions and speeches went on entirely too long for Conchita. She hated to be in the spotlight on the front row but beamed at her children beside her. They were well-behaved and required reminders only a few times, as Conchita placed her hand on the knee of one twin and the other to quiet the kicking of their dangling legs. Jack sat proudly beside his father.

Finally, it was time for Miguel to speak. As he stepped toward the speaker's stand an eruption of cowbells and whoops exploded. Johnny, Deke and Charly's catcalls were unmistakable. Miguel had jotted some notes, and at the podium he unfolded the piece of paper torn from a yellow legal pad.

"OK my friends," he said as he reached his arms out, palms down in front of him with a silencing motion. "I'm happy to be here, happy to see family and friends and some Rockies fans too. What about those Colorado Rockies?"

"This here's the first time I've spoken publicly about our five-year ordeal in Guerrilla camps in Colombia. Sorry we didn't get to work those emerald mines, McCrae." Miguel turned to salute the man behind him. And what about Randy? Say man I'm so glad you finally made it back and can sit on this heroes' platform with us.

"Yeah, there were times when it was damned tough, and I wondered if there'd be a tomorrow. Jungle livin' with all the rain, muck, and blood sucking insects ain't my first choice for a five-star vacation, especially when we had to do all the grunt work when we changed camps, which we did fairly regular.

"But once we got into a routine, some of the rebels were like any normal guys, doing their job." Miguel scratched his head and breathed in heavily. "Don't think we didn't dream about escape. We did. But them guys didn't trust us much and kept us separated most the time. At different times, there were maybe ten to fifteen hostages in one place. Some of hostages were Colombians. Course we were in chains and under guard. If ya want to hear something really ear-splitting just listen to the firing of several rounds of ammunition from an AK-47, under the umbrella of trees in the rain forest ya can hardly see the top of.

"We were told that the FARC guerrillas wanted to extort money for their cause using us hostages. That meant we were herded together for the taking of pictures from time to time. Some of those pictures were finally released and our family members looked them over, hoping to identify us. With beards, those ugly uniforms we wore and poor detail, I guess not many faces were identified. That is all except me. I refused to wear a beard, so my wife tells me she saw my face in the 'hostage line-up', as we called it.

"Anyway, I'm here to tell ya about the release. And we're home. Yeah," Miguel yelled out as he raised a clench fist into the air. Several listeners in the stands did the same, raising a clenched fist and yelling 'yeah'.

"Let me tell ya. The only way to have a voice is to con those devils into thinking yur on their side. The last year I started doing just that. Since I spoke the language, I talked to the guards a lot. They told me all that ideological stuff, how the Colombian government isn't for the people, how the rebels are foot soldiers for the people. I learned a lot and learned how to be on their side. I learned how they took over the coke farms and trafficked in cocaine to pay for weapons and ammunition. They also used the cocaine money to get fancy equipment and computers. The head guys used them to communicate, organize maneuvers and keep ahead of the Colombian government."

Miguel took a gulp of water from the glass on the podium and raised it to the crowd. "So ya might say I went undercover. When I joined their side they took me to a different camp. I sure hated to leave my brother hostages. I had to keep cool about my plans. They didn't know I crossed over and became a rebel myself. Proving my loyalty cost my fellow hostages. That's another regret. I had to put in the order to reduce their food rations from time to time. Another time I had to order a flogging. Randy got that one. Sorry brother," Miguel said and turned around to face Randy. "They tested me, and I had to prove my loyalty, so I could be considered a FARC guerrilla.

"Colombian officials sent messages about working out a hostage trade. You see, 'we', and I'm talking as one of the rebels now since they thought I was one, had FARC members in Colombian jails and some were in U.S. prisons. If we could make a trade, everybody wins. Right?

"FARC members didn't trust the Colombian government one bit. FARC wanted an area designated as demilitarized to meet at for negotiations. What the Colombian government suggested didn't fit with FARC's ideas. Well, I can be mighty persuasive, and I got to meet with some of the high ups in FARC. Little by little we worked out an agreement for a place for the talks of a hostage exchange."

Miguel explained that FARC allowed him to sit in on talks with the Congressmen from the U.S. who were in Colombia to assist in the negotiations. He said that he looked the part of a FARC guerrilla, thus the Congressmen had no idea that he was one of the hostages.

Miguel went on to talk of the dedication of the FARC members and how they sacrificed for their cause. Miguel said he met a few cutthroats who hungered for blood and wouldn't hesitate to shoot the enemy in the eye if they had a chance. However, for most, it was the cause, not blood they were after. Often, he could relate to their ideology and at times he felt almost like he belonged as a rebel.

Finishing up his story, Miguel concluded, "Of course I was frustrated with the setbacks and delays. I had to be patient. Then when the agreements were made and a date set for the exchange, things became sticky for me. I knew I had to be part of the group to march the hostages to the rendezvous. Otherwise I couldn't walk away with the hostages. At first, they said I couldn't go since they said I hadn't had enough experience with their rifles. I finally convinced them I didn't need to carry one, a prod stick would do.

"Imagine this. Two guards with guns, myself, and the hostages marching out of the camp. I sidled up beside Ben and gave him a heads up about my plan. We walked about 3 hours to the demilitarized area for the exchange, a clearing about the size of a football field. We were all hot and sweaty and waited in the shade at the side of the clearing. Two military copters loaded with prisoners from Colombian jails landed in front of us. When the prisoners left the copters, one of the guards ran to welcome them. The other guard and I ordered the hostages to move out.

"Let me tell you. My legs were like jelly. When the last hostage boarded Ben and Gavin's copter, I made a big scene and pushed my way on board—saying that my buddies and I needed water and I was going to get it. There was a lot of confusion, but once I was inside Ben convinced them to close the door. I never felt so good as I did when the ground grew farther and farther away as we gained altitude."

The crowd sat in silence. A shiver tingled through Conchita. Her husband had captured the audience.

"They say I'm a hero." Miguel shrugged. "You be the judge on that one." He spread his arms wide to the crowd. "I've done a lot in my life, even got to be a star Rockies pitcher. I don't know what's ahead. For the time being my wife has a good job. I can watch over my niños," he said as he turned to shake a finger at each of his children. "Maybe I'll be a policeman. We need tough guys there, don't you think?"

The crowd stood and cheered. Conchita thought the thunderous clapping and stomping would never end. Perhaps he was a hero. Yet a piece of her wondered if he really joined the rebels to negotiate a hostage exchange. If the government had not initiated the idea of an exchange, would he still be in Colombia as a rebel?

Miguel turned to Conchita who smiled at her husband, yet inside uncertainty lingered. When he spoke of the future Conchita had been stunned. A policeman? He wanted to be a policeman? She'd tried to broach the subject about getting a job, but he'd shushed her with, "Oh, Chita, give me a break. Don't you think a hero deserves a vacation and some good times?"

At the time she couldn't argue with his statement…Now what?

CHAPTER 23

Monica

Monica moved quicker than she had since the accident and it was invigorating. During her last physical therapy session, the therapist maintained that her leg was almost like new. It had good strength, mobility, and flexibility. She was finally out of the walking boot and leg brace and was able put on a pair of shoes with a short heel. Her skirt, a print of many colors, swished against her calves as she orbited around the dining room table, setting out her fine china, flatware, and her best linens, including the monogrammed napkins. It had been months since she and Peter had entertained. She was good at it, the enviable hostess, yet she had never delighted in it. Most often the guests were business associates of Peter's and though she maintained a polite interchange with the women associates or the wives of the men associates, she had not become close to any of them.

Tonight's event would not be business related at all, and she skittered around giddy with anticipation. It had been Peter's idea. When he first broached the subject, Monica thought he had fallen off the loony truck.

He finally convinced her it was the right thing to do. Gavin, his mother, and Nicola were coming to dinner.

Stepping from the shower he had looked directly into her eyes. "Monica love, Gavin is not an enemy. There is no reason to live like he is. We all have a common focal point and that focal point is you. In other words, we are interconnected through you." He tossed his towel toward her to emphasize the point. She grabbed it from the air, glaring at her husband before he went on.

"I'd like to meet Gavin, and perhaps he'd like to meet me. Nicola, too. She sounds like an exceptional woman. And we can't leave out Gavin's mother, since he's staying with her."

Monica balked at the idea with her protests, "I don't relish being a focal point, as you call me, and I'm not sure I like the interconnected part. Besides don't you think the whole thing is a little bizarre? Won't you be uncomfortable sitting across from your wife's ex? It won't be like we ran in to him at the supermarket. This meeting would be on purpose."

"Of course, it would be on purpose. That's the point. It's not like you resent or detest Gavin. It's not like either one of you chose to be the other's ex. I don't know how you can call him your ex, anyway. He didn't run off with another woman, you weren't divorced. He was declared dead." Peter paused and with a wave of his hand rushed on, "It was one of the flukes of life. You, you were caught…," Peter stumbled over the words as they tumbled out, "in the jaws of providence."

Laughing, Monica threw her head back, "In the jaws of providence? You are so dramatic." She shook her head grinning widely, "Peter, I love you."

Taken aback by her reaction to his choice of words, Peter retorted, "Well, it's true, things happened that you had no control over, and you each had to go on, couldn't stop living. The things that happened ended your marriage, not you."

Monica thought for a moment. She rather liked the phrase. It held truth and had a ring to it, which she wasn't ready to admit to Peter. She snapped her lips and said, "And here I am, no longer caught in the jaws of providence, married to a man that can't wait to be a father. And now he wants to meet my first husband. Not my ex. Is that better?"

Rolling his tongue against his lips, he shrugged. Monica stabbed a finger toward her husband and acquiesced, "You're on. A dinner party it is."

Both Monica and Peter met their guests at the door. Gavin stepped aside allowing his mother and then Nicola to enter. Cora Humphreys looked wide-eyed as she crossed the threshold. Monica thought she had shrunk a little since she saw her several years back. But she appeared trim and fit with the usual topsy-turvy white mass of fluff on her head. Monica leaned over and grasped both of her hands in hers and greeted her warmly.

Introductions ended up being a round robin type of thing with Monica and Gavin alternating until everyone had met Peter and Peter had met everyone. The group then moved to the family room beside the adjoining kitchen. Peter served a pineapple/banana slush punch that Monica was famous for, while she uncovered the smoked oyster cheese ball and passed it with whole wheat crackers.

Cora Humphreys remarked, "How nice to have your delicious punch. I've written the recipe for many friends and family over the years. Takes me back, you know."

Peter said, "So she was famous before I knew her, Mrs. Humphreys. I might have known. Don't you think we should offer a toast?"

They all agreed. And as they raised their glasses, Peter said, "Here is to health, happiness and a productive future." There was tenderness in his voice as he resumed the toast, "Friends, miracles happen. What a miracle that Gavin and Nicola are no longer bound by chains. What a miracle we can join together."

Monica pondered Peter's toast. It had a poetic sense, something she hadn't expected. She knew part of his reference to miracles was about their baby. His thoughtfulness regarding Gavin and Nicola and all they had experienced touched her. The moment hung suspended as each seemed to hold fast to Peter's words, then they reached forward and clinked glass to glass.

Following a time of nibbling, sipping and small talk, Monica excused herself to the adjoining kitchen. Nicola followed, asking if she could help. "You may put the ice and water in the glasses and set them on the table in the dining room," Monica said.

She lifted the glazed pork loin from the oven and placed it on the counter so it could absorb the meat juices before carving, then checked the rice pilaf in the rice steamer. Removing the plastic wrap from the salad, she drizzled the spinach leaves, mushrooms and onions with a tarragon vinaigrette dressing and sprinkled toasted almonds on top. Monica removed the Angel biscuits from the warming oven, piled them in a breadbasket and covered them with a fine linen cloth. This will be a good dinner, she thought.

Nicola returned from the dining room following her assignment with the ice and water glasses. "What a gorgeous table you set for us." Nicola cleared her throat, then went on in her rasping voice. "I love all your miniature lights. It looks like an elegant fairyland." She eyed the spread Monica laid out and remarked, "It's been a long, long time since I sat down to such a meal. It is such a blessing to be here with you and Peter."

"Oh, thank you. And thank you for coming," Monica said, feeling a twinge of stirring in her chest. "We haven't used the dining room for several months. We'll have to rechristen it tonight…Talk about elegant, it's hard to imagine you living in military fatigues in the jungle. You look particularly stunning."

"Thank you."

"Peter, I'm ready for the carver," Monica called out.

The evening carried on with enjoyable banter. Monica had forgotten the quick wit of Cora Humphreys. As she told one story and then another on herself, everyone laughed.

"There I was young man," Cora said addressing Peter, "hanging on for dear life clambering up the steep roof of my home, dragging a milk crate at the end of my yellow and blue nylon rope. No way was I gonna have another litter of raccoons in my chimney. So, at the peak of the roof, you know, I teetered a little before I got my balance and pulled that blue milk crate up, lifted it over my head and scrunched it right over the chimney." Cora's voice grew more animated, "I yelled out to the heavens. No more coons in my house."

Gavin laughed, "Yup, Mom's pretty brave about heights, about most things. I wasn't there, but I can see her now, determined as a stallion breaking out of the barn. She meant to solve the problem of raccoons." Gavin smiled at his mother and continued, "We have a lot of raccoon stories. I raised one. He'd climb the drapes and crawl across the heavy rods at the top. Then he got too big to come into the house."

Cora added, "Rocky liked his wieners, didn't he? Grabbed like any kid and nibbled away. Remember when he got in the cupboard and dragged the syrup to the floor. What a sticky mess."

Monica watched with interest as Nicola seemed to take in every story Gavin or his mother related, her eyes glistening with appreciation. Gavin turned toward Nicola, apologetically, "Nicola, you've heard most of these stories. Sorry you have to put up with them again."

She patted his arm and said, "I guess our stories kept us going those years in the jungle, didn't they? I'm happy to hear them in the company of friends, rather than in the company of Ferocious Franco."

"Who's Ferocious Franco?" Monica asked.

Nicola's hoarse voice became fiercely gruff as she imitated Ferocious Franco, "Ustedes son extranjeros estúpido. Son ignorante. Sea silencioso. No hablando. Nada es gracioso."

"You do a good impression of Franco, Nicola," Gavin said laughing, then he turned to the others and explained, "Most of the guards let us talk at the end of the day before we went in to our bunks. In fact, they didn't pay much attention to us, since we were in chains. Franco did everything he could to degrade us. He never smiled either, did he?"

Nicola shook her head, "Never smiled at anybody, surely not us. He just yelled. 'You foreigners are stupid, you are ignorant, keep quiet, no talking. Those were his favorite. There were other insults and if we laughed about anything, he'd tell us to be quiet and that nothing is funny."

Gavin became serious. "It was a struggle living in the jungle. It was uncomfortable, primitive. If we did what we were told, some rebels treated us OK. Others were like Franco, surly and abusive. Nicola helped to find humor in things. She was a miracle worker in my book." Nicola only smiled. Monica was glad to see the affectionate glances between the two. It lifted her heart.

During dessert Monica broached the subject of Nicola's plans. "You said something about going back to school, maybe attending Regis in Denver. Have you thought more about it?"

Nicola glanced at Gavin as she said, "Gavin and I are in the process of applying for the Peace Corps. We were told that with my nursing and missionary background and his mechanical knowledge we have a good chance of being selected. We hope to be placed as a couple."

"Wow. What a great thing to do," Peter said. "I bet your experience as hostages is a plus, also. Don't know if I could live isolated in some third world country. I admire you guys."

Cora piped in, "Yes, just when I get him home, he's wanting to take off again, to some far-off land. And remember you said you'd get some things done around my place. Lot's of fixing to do."

"I know Mother. Don't worry," Gavin said, "It takes a while to get everything approved and set up. If we get to go, by that time I'll have all the repairs and remodeling done, and you'll be tired of having me around."

After the guests had given their appreciations and accolades for the fine food and hospitality, they said their good-byes. Peter helped in the cleanup and setting everything in order. Monica turned to her husband and said, "What do you think? Was it a successful party?"

"Absolutely. We make a good team, I'd say. It was a nice evening. You seemed quite relaxed."

She looked around to stare at Peter. Had they become a team? Often in the past she felt at odds with Peter, whether it was his ill-planned yard project, his haphazard cleanup in the kitchen or his lack of picking up after himself. For the first time, she had undeniably enjoyed the planning, preparation, and the whole evening. "You're getting to be quite handy." Monica scrunched her nose at Peter. "Carving the meat, helping serve, keeping the conversation stimulating and all this cleanup," she said, splaying her arms wide. "Now I wonder how you'll team up with changing diapers."

He grimaced slightly, "I guess we'll find out. I wondered if you would say something about the baby coming. How might Gavin react if he knew?"

"I don't know. He wanted to be father at one time. He seems excited about the Peace Corps now. I want to keep the news to ourselves for a while. What do you think?"

"I think you're wise," he said. Then he came to her and placed his hand on her belly. "Someday this little guy will make his own announcement."

"Or *her* own announcement," said a grinning Monica.

Racine

*LEAVE THAT SOMBERNESS BEHIND YOU. **Randy forgives you. You have to move forward, make it up to your son.***

"Randy, I'm heading to the pub? Need to get some work done. Want to go?"

"I can't wait to see what's changed. Absolutely I want to go."

Racine introduced Chad and Randy and noticed they hit it off immediately. While Racine worked on orders and paperwork, Chad showed Randy around the business pointing out the recent changes.

Assured that Randy had someone to talk to, Racine concentrated on the sheaves of paper spread across her desk. So deeply focused, Racine was unaware of the figure that entered the office. Minutes passed until Racine, feeling a presence in the room, looked up. She saw a beaming smile spread across the face that greeted her, a face embellished with dark eyes flickering with the brilliance of dancing miniature lights at Christmas.

"Carlotta. My dear friend. How wonderful to see you. How delicious you look."

The two women rushed to each other, embracing as though nothing could pry them apart. They rocked in unison, Carlotta murmuring how ecstatic she was to see Randy wandering around the restaurant with Chad, what a beautiful man he is, how thrilling it must be to have him safe at home. Racine pleading forgiveness for being so wrapped in her own anguish, for neglecting her best friend as she recovered from her heart attack.

Racine drew away from their embrace, taking in the full view of the Italian beauty. "You look ten years younger. Chad told me you're doing well. I know you've been coming in a few evenings every week after I go home. I'm sorry I missed you. I'm sorry I didn't call. Particularly this past month. It was…" Racine searched for a word. "Difficult," she finally said. "I was down a lot."

"I guess we both hit our low, but it looks like we're back on top." Carlotta said with exuberance.

"You said it!"

"I'm ready to come back to the business full time, if you agree. I need to be here with all our friends. I'm strong as a mother moose. I assure you. I've changed my diet. I'm working out."

"You're sure you're ready?"

Carlotta nodded, "And you need to take some time away to spend with Randy. Maybe a little trip. We can handle things here just fine while you regroup. I'd like to begin tomorrow. The old schedule alright with you?"

"Of course. It'll be like old times." Almost, she thought. So much had happened in the last several months.

Following Carlotta's departure, Racine vowed to finish every task represented by the stack on her desk. Chad had payroll in order, but it needed her signature before it was finished. By 6:00, Racine had her desk cleared and everything on her checklist had been crossed off.

She leaned back in her chair, thinking again about the miracle of Randy's return. What would he want to do, job-wise? His business degree should open many fields. Things change over five years, however. Perhaps he'd need a brush-up course or two. She wouldn't push him. There was no hurry. Maybe a little trip would be good for both of them.

Just then the door opened, and Randy stepped into the room. "Ready for dinner? The crew has a table set up for Chad, you and me."

Seeing her precious son sent tingles through her body, once again. Every cell expressed gratefulness it seemed. "I'm ready. I'll dine with two handsome men any day, especially if one is my own flesh and blood."

Unhurried, the threesome ate leisurely and allowed one of the waiters to hover over their every need. Various patrons having their own evening dinners, conspicuously strolled by to get a look at the hostage they knew had returned. Several paused to offer their expression of relief, praise or congratulations. Puffed with pride, Racine wanted to yell to the rooftop about her son's bravery and resourcefulness. Instead, she held her head high and grinned endlessly.

No one ordered dessert, but once the table was cleared, a commotion began in the bar area. The clang of spoons striking pots and raucous singing grew closer to their table. In the lead was the chef, sporting a dome of chocolate cake and ice cream topped with a sparkler sputtering its brilliance. A snake of waiters and waitresses followed as the paraders wound through the restaurant singing For He's a Jolly Good Fellow.

Gathered around their table, the entourage finished their somewhat off-key singing and the Chef deposited the giant dessert on the table. Someone started, "Randy, Randy, Randy," and most of the patrons joined in. Two familiar faces emerged from the crowd and stood beside the table. A tall, chunky man yelled above the noise, "Boy are you a sight for these ole eyes."

Randy stood and clapped his hand on the shoulder of his high school friend, Curt, "Hey man. We have lots of catching up to do." Turning to a shorter, yet equally broad guy, Randy added, "Tank. How'd you know I'd be here tonight? Let me get some extra chairs. You two gotta help me with this dessert."

As the excitement around the table subsided, Curt and Tank hugged Racine, and Randy made introductions between his friends and Chad. After some small talk Racine said, "You boys," then she corrected herself, "you men sit here, enjoy the dessert and have a good visit. Chad, what do you think? Shall we head to the office?"

"Sure. I need to show you something I received yesterday. I've been waiting for the right time."

In the office each sat in one of the leather companion chairs. Racine kicked off her high heeled shoes, the ones of many bright colors that went with half of her wardrobe and propped her feet on the footrest. She reclined her head against the cushioned hide and squeezed her eyes shut, still unable to grasp the reality of recent days.

Chad traced the edges of the armrest with his fingers, then looked toward Racine and spoke, "I'm glad you can, for the moment anyway, relax with complete…" He paused searching for a word. "Abandonment," he finally said. "I can't imagine how intense these last several days have been. Randy's a mighty good bloke."

"Thank you."

"He has your heart and charisma you know. So much like you, but a quieter version."

"So, in a few hours you have him pegged?"

"I believe I'm a good judge of character. Just like the first time I saw you and the way you make every patron feel important and worthy, the way you run a tight ship, but with love. I knew all that in the first few moments. I've not changed my first impression all these months."

"You forgot about my quick temper," Racine added.

"Lassie, your fuse burns out before the explosion. I'm not sure I'd call it temper, more of an annoyance."

Racine opened her lazy eyes and shrugged one shoulder, "If you say so. Now tell me my matie," she said mockingly, "what is this thing you want to show me?"

Chad pulled a folded envelope from his pocket and retrieved the pages it held. "This letter came yesterday from Australia. It's from my Auntie Cardinia, my father's sister. She lost her husband in a hunting accident years ago. I'm the only family she has. It's been six years since I saw her, but since Uncle Neil died, every other month I send her some money. So, she keeps tabs on me."

"You never told me about this Auntie. It seems you have been a good nephew. Is she doing all right?"

"Yes and no. She's pushing eighty and has lived in the same house since she and Neil married more than a half a century ago. She has a little yard and raises a garden. But you might say it's nearly in the Outback. A few weeks ago, she had a bad spill and broke her pelvis. It's mighty painful and there isn't much to do but lie around and let it heal. Auntie Cardinia has been staying with a friend 'bout sixty kilometers away. But she doesn't like being a burden and feels like she's wearing out her welcome."

"Oh, Chad. What can you do?"

"Once she's recovered, she wants to sell the place, set up some type of trust and move to town. She needs my help with the move and all the legal and financial stuff."

"Of course, she does." Taken aback Racine stared at the winsome man whose eyes looked beseechingly into hers.

"I'm sorry to be leaving you so suddenly. I can't tell you how much working with you has meant to me."

Racine blinked. "Boy, there'll be an empty hole in this place with you gone. Guess, I thought you'd be here forever. Probably, I didn't even think."

"You'll be fine," said Chad.

"You surely arrived at the right time. You were here the minute I needed you. You held everything together remarkably. Helped me to hold together, too. I'll miss you."

Chad stood and grasped Racine's hands in his, pulling her out of her chair, then said, "Seems like fate struck again. Guess it's time for the Racine and Carlotta team to be pulling the wagon once more. What timing, I'd say."

Racine nodded. "Glad to have Carlotta back to her old self, after the heart attack and by-pass." Standing in bare feet Racine snuggled her face against the Aussie's chest and let a tear squeeze out against his pocket. "I wish you well. Your Auntie is lucky to have you."

Chad hugged her for a long moment and released her. "It'll be apples for all of us."

"Yeah, everything will be all right."

They said their goodbyes then and there. Racine tried to give Chad the blue Billy, the tea pot that had survived the fire in which Chad's father died. He refused, saying, "You need to have it when I come for a visit someday. You'll have to put the Billy on so we can have our tea."

After Chad left, she stared at the blue Billy, remembering so many special moments. Chad had been an interlude in her life at a time she needed him. Now he was gone.

THE NEXT MORNING RANDY JOINED Racine in her kitchen at 7:30. "Thought you might sleep in," said Racine.

"Nope. Lot's to do. Sorry to hear Chad's returning to Australia. He told me about that. I'm sure you need go in today."

"You're right. This is Carlotta's first full day back. She'll be taking the evening crowd like before, but we need to get everything pinned down."

"Is there anything I can do for you, Mom?"

"Thanks, but no, hon. I'm sure you have a lot to take care of as well. Why don't you drop me at the restaurant and go get your driver's license? Then you'll be legal with the car. I can use the restaurant van if I need anything. Also, McCrae called. He wants to take us to some fancy place in Denver for dinner tonight. Are you up for it?"

He said he was.

By 6:00 the three were off to Denver in McCrae's luxury SUV. Racine remembered the last time she sat in the vehicle after the meeting with Nicola at Monica's home, when McCrae confronted her about being Randy's father. Shortly after, McCrae received the call about his wife. So much had happened since that moment.

And here they were, her son, his father and her, chatting away as they whizzed down the highway. Racine had never pictured this scene in her mind. At first, she felt awkward, and said very little. She knew that a certain topic, one which McCrae had asked her permission about, would be broached at dinner and wondered how Randy would react. She had mixed feelings about it herself and needed a little time to chew on it before… Oh, well, she thought, stop your worrying, and enjoy the evening. And with that she jumped into the conversation, adding bits and pieces concerning whatever topic came up.

An hour later as they arrived at the restaurant, the valet took the car and they were escorted through a plush lobby, past a trickling waterfall festooned with ornamental grasses and spiky green plants. Racine's heels clicked on the marbled floor designed in swirled patterns the color of ebony, coffee, and raw linen. The expansive walkway made a wide curve as it descended deeper and deeper into the building. At last it opened into a huge room bearing numerous cubby holes of private tables splendidly set with white linens, hurricane lamps encasing a group of flickering candles, and sparkling stemware waiting to be filled with wine or other beverages. The lush burgundy carpet muffled all sound except for light tinkling music echoing throughout the dining room.

"Not quite the same atmosphere as my pub," Racine said, once she stepped into the room. "This is lovely McCrae. How did you ever find it?"

"Nothing wrong with Racines. But this is a special celebration. A business acquaintance brought me here a while back." Turning to Randy, he said, "What do you think son?"

Randy's eyes glistened in the room's subtlety of light. "For a Jungle Joe, it's out of this world. Yeah, this is a night for celebration, particularly since I can be with both of you."

The meal matched the elegance of the atmosphere but could not compare with the pleasure of being with Randy and McCrae. Racine found herself floating in a dream world of incredible ecstasy, one she feared she might awaken from.

McCrae leaned onto the table and said, "Randy, I've talked to your mother about an opportunity I'm proud to offer you. I'm happy to say your mother agrees with it. We both want what is best for you and hope you don't feel any pressure from either of us. You know I own a conglomerate that consists of several companies that deal with a variety of commercial ventures, properties, and different businesses. I need a right-hand man to manage my organization. With your college background, your..." McCrae raised his hand and closed his fist decisively, punching the air. "Strength to survive the jungles and do so with such optimism, without an iota of feeling sorry for yourself, I know you are the man I want by my side."

Randy lowered his head, visibly overcome with emotion. His shoulders heaved gently as he drew in and exhaled an ample breath. Racine placed her hand on his forearm, stroking the silkiness of his shirt. He smiled at his parents. No one uttered a sound in the tenderness of the moment.

"Excuse me a minute," Randy said as he rose from his chair, "I'll be right back."

"Do you think he feels cornered?" McCrae asked, once Randy was away from the table. "I'm sure my offer came as a surprise. You said he was thinking of getting something part time while he took a few classes."

"I think he's overwhelmed about working with you, maybe he doesn't know if he's ready for such a responsibility."

"I like to think of myself as a good teacher. With me he doesn't need more schooling. He has all the traits I want in a right-hand man."

Racine fingered the napkin in her lap before she responded. "I don't know. Perhaps he'd like to be independent from both of us."

"Certainly, if that's what he wants he won't get any guff from me. However, a part of me wants to make up, even if it's just a tiny bit, for the years he's lost. I don't want to have him start at the bottom as if he's a fresh-out-of-college guy."

Randy's return to the table cut short any further speculation concerning his future. He sat, took hold of his mother's hand and squeezed it gently. "Mom, so much of my life was spent hovering in the background, watching others step out and take risks. I watched you jump in with both feet, taking a risk on owning a business, trying out new menus, taking a chance on an employee who wanted to turn her life around. Each time you landed upright, standing tall." With emphasis he continued, "I jumped in whole hog on the trip to Colombia and I'm standing tall."

He released his mother's hand and turned toward McCrae. "Sir, I'd be proud to be your right-hand man. I promise I'll work my tail off for the business, learn everything I can and do you proud. I saw Mom jump in with both feet. Surely I can do the same."

The two men stood and after a firm handshake, affectionately slapped each other on the back, then smacked their hands together in a high-five. McCrae exclaimed, "I'd say this is an awesome day. Welcome aboard."

"Thanks McCrae. This is a night of surprises. I believe you have another one," Randy said speaking to his father.

Racine felt the electricity of the moment and it was several seconds before the tingles resonating through her body subsided. What did Randy know that she didn't? A second surprise?

McCrae reached under the chair and withdrew a chunky box gilded in shiny gold paper. Your son's right. I do have a surprise for you, a memento from Colombia, a place that's not all bad." Handing the gilded gift to Racine, he said. "I'd be honored if you'd open it now."

As she carefully pulled the wrapping from the box and lifted the lid, her sight blurred. She had difficulty focusing on the items nestled in folds of green velvet. Catching the light in flickers of brilliance were three exquisite gold pieces, a ring, a necklace and a bracelet, each set with an exceptionally cut emerald.

"I do believe, Racy," McCrae said, "you were born to wear emeralds."

She pulled her hands away from the box as if it was on fire. "They are the most beautiful pieces I've ever seen." Shaking her head, she uttered, "I can't accept them. Thank for the generous thought, but I can't accept them."

McCrae's voice filled with exasperation. "You can't reject them. They were designed for you, and you only. We want you to have them. Don't we Randy?"

"Hey Mom, when the man speaks, don't argue. They do look as though they were meant for you. And don't make a liar out of me. I told him you'd be thrilled with them."

McCrae lifted the ring from its velvet compartment and slid it on Racine's finger. "It's a perfect fit. You're destined to wear it and the others, too." With great tenderness he said, "I just wanted you to have something from the mine. There are no strings attached."

CHAPTER 24

Conchita

If most Friday nights were like this one Conchita believed she would be satisfied. Miguel and Jack watched the Rockies' baseball game while Conchita kept her hands busy with some embroidery. She smiled at the voices coming from the kitchen, as Jenny and Pamela played school. Once the ballgame was over, she instructed the twins to put everything away. Afterwards the pair bounded into the room. They had a request they said.

"Pamela has a good idea. Why don't we invite Greg for a cookout? Papá, you can meet him and tell him about the guerrillas."

Despite the TV announcer's banter, a cloud of silence fell across the room. Jack watched warily for his father's response. Conchita wondered if her son knew honoring the request was an impossibility. Probably. Whether he sensed the complexity of the situation or not, Conchita didn't know, however she felt Jack's desire to protect her as he stepped to her side and sat on the arm of her chair.

Stretched out on the couch, Miguel flicked the television off with the remote and tossed it on the coffee table. "Who's this guy anyway? No need for us to know each other."

Before his mother could speak, Jack declared in a clear and confident voice, "He's our friend, Papá. He helped build our house. We wouldn't be living here if it wasn't for him."

Jenny chimed in, "You'll like him. He's nice. Brings us food and surprises sometimes."

Miguel pulled himself up and sat on the front edge of the couch. Ignoring Jenny's comment, he shook a finger toward his son. "Well, mi hijito, you might have needed help when I was gone. But nobody in this family needs him anymore. I will take care of things. I'm your father."

Eyeing the twins seated on the floor, Miguel spoke directly to them. "Hijitas, this guy is in your past and that is where he will stay. No more friends and no more surprises. Do you understand?"

The subject was closed. Almost. When Conchita tucked her son in bed the same evening, Jack appealed to her. "Mamá, we have to see Greg. We have to tell him he will always be our friend, even if we don't see him anymore. Please. We can't let him down."

Alone in her own bed, she heard the news coming from the living room. Miguel would come to bed when the sports were over. She forced extra breath from her nostrils and squeezed her eyes tight hoping to stifle the tears attempting to gather. She couldn't turn her own husband away after all he had gone through. He was the father of her children. Yes, there would be adjustments for everyone, and they would get through them.

Greg was her special friend. He had warmed her heart with his kindness, and she believed there had been more than a friendship growing, but once the hostages were identified, the connection between Greg and her had become more polite than familiar. Even if she and Miguel separated and she wanted to continue a relationship with Greg, she didn't know if it could happen. She had no idea if Greg wanted to marry again, if he wanted to be a stepfather. They had never talked about it, ever. There was a great affection between the children and him, but the children had not thought of him as a father figure. Everything seemed too complicated to face.

Conchita examined her feelings toward Miguel. Would she ever feel more than a respectful compassion for what he had endured, an honorable acceptance of him as her children's father or the responsibility of being a loyal wife? At this point love was not a part of the picture, but duty was, and she accepted it.

Miguel treated her with more respect these days, especially since she stood up to him about having people at the house on weekends drinking and carrying on. He agreed to a cookout with the family on Fridays and to hang out with his cousin no more than twice a month. He asked for the car when he needed it and took her to work. The notoriety he received since arriving back in Greeley brought him some job possibilities. That was good. How long it would last, she did not know. She did know if he fell into his old ways, she would not tolerate it. She emphatically told him so.

It was a day when the children were at the neighbors when she said, "You will not grab me, push me, force me in any way…And if you ever touch the children, you will not stay in this house." His response to her warning had been quite mild and it surprised her.

"Ah Chita, you know I wouldn't hurt you for anything. The children either."

Her chin lifted slightly. "I don't trust that temper of yours. We will see. Just know I mean it. No anger, no violence in this house. Ever."

"I know. I know," he said.

⚓

The day for good-byes arrived. The endless blue, blue of the August sky, and the warmth of the sun glowing over her did nothing to transform the gloom lingering inside. Conchita pushed it deeper, willing it to be indistinguishable in her face, her eyes and in her smile. Could she and the children say goodbye to their dear friend Greg? She guessed they would have to. There was no other way.

She had called Greg, saying the children wanted to see him. Then she bravely told Miguel, "When you were gone so long it was important for the children to have a friendship with an adult male. That person was Greg. It's unfair to not allow them to see their friend. They need to know he did not reject them just because you are home."

She saw the tight jaw and smoldering eyes, but he didn't say a word. "Miguel?"

"Do what you have to do."

Miguel went off with Johnny to work on some car early Saturday morning. Conchita told him she and the children were going to the park for the afternoon.

When Conchita and the children arrived, Greg was already seated on a shaded bench near the playground equipment. A good-sized package stood on the grass beside him. Bounding from the car, the children ran toward their friend yelling exuberant greetings.

Greg beamed at all of them. "My goodness. I can't believe how fine you children look. Jack, you must have grown an inch in the last month. And Pamela and Jenny, I bet you're excited about school starting next week. What shall we do first?"

The girls wanted to use the swings, the slide, and climb on the jungle gym. Jack brought the ball equipment Greg had given him. He hoped they could play catch. Greg gave each of the girls a good start on the swings and then Jack and he found a spot to play catch. Jack did well catching high flies and hot grounders while Conchita supervised the jungle gym and slide activities.

Once the girls had tired of the equipment and Jack had shown off his skills at fielding balls, the group gathered at a shaded picnic table. Greg carried the large package to the table and invited the children to open it. Each scrambled to rip a piece of brown wrapping away to reveal the contents.

"Now remember," Greg said, "This is a family gift. You will need to share every part of it and take turns, even with your mother and father. Jack, you can help your sisters since you are the older brother. I bet you can share with your neighbor Jason, too."

For the next minutes, the children pulled the items from the box and laid them on the picnic table for inspection. "Look," Jenny said to her brother, "We have our own bats, and T's until we learn to hit better."

Conchita watched the happy faces of her children. "Why how nice. They're just your size. And of course girls can play ball, too." She wanted to picture her children with Miguel and her running bases in a family ball game and cheering the children as they made one hit and another. Could they be that kind of family? She had to put her focus in that direction for her children.

The children pulled the other gifts from the box—Frisbees, beanbags, and a children's version of Croquet.

Jenny hugged Greg and said, "Thank you, thank you."

"Can we try them Greg, please," squealed Pamela.

Greg grinned. "You bet. Have fun."

Leaving Greg and Conchita at the table they took the items to a nearby grassy spot where they tried out each game. Conchita looked across the table as her friend. The words she wanted to say had played through her head into the morning hours as she lay in bed and now the time had come for her to say them.

"You know how much you mean to me and to the children. Jack told his father the other night that we wouldn't have our house if it wasn't for you. And it's true."

"Conchita, I was only one of the volunteers. There were many hands, including your own that built your home. I cannot take any more credit than anyone else."

Conchita looked away from the warmth of his eyes, fearing her own might belie the tenderness she felt for her steadfast friend. "You know it was not only the skill of your hands that brought us our home. It was a multitude of things, your advice, your support through worry and uncertainty, your care and encouragement of the children."

"Conchita, you were an inspiration—for all of us. We followed in your wake—the brave woman. Alone forging forward—going to school, providing for your children, loving and guiding them, wanting a home for them. And now you are no longer alone. Your children's father has returned from his…" Greg searched for a word. "His unasked-for ordeal. Now you must build…rebuild a family for all of you."

A chill crawled through her body. He had said some of the words for her. She needn't say them. He understood. "This is true. And to make it work, we must step away from you. Miguel sees you as a threat, taking away his role as a father." She left unsaid, *and also a threat to our marriage.*

Greg nodded his head in understanding. "We men can be funny that way. There was a beautiful time when we touched each other's lives, when you and your children brought joy to mine and I brought something to yours. That time is past, but the wonderful memories live on. In life we move on. It is always that way."

This time she let her eyes cloud, her lips tremble as she grasped his hand across the table and looked directly into his face. "I can truthfully say that knowing you is one of the best things that ever happened to me and my children. We will always remember. We will always be grateful. You've taught us many lessons. Life doesn't always happen the way we expect and when it catches us in unexpected ways we go on and do our very best."

Greg pulled his hand away as if to ease the moment of letting go. "Yes, we do our best. I wish you the very best. Who knows what's ahead? Just know, my fondness for you and your children will not fade. And please, if ever you need me, for anything, please call."

Driving home from the park, Conchita zoned out and did not register the children's happy chatter about seeing Greg and playing with their new games. The lump in her heart numbed her. She tried to think, but each thought fractured before she could complete it. *We had to say goodbye or else…Miguel cannot be denied his…How can I stop remembering…*

"Mamá!" yelled Jack.

Conchita heard the simultaneous squeal of brakes, and the blare of a horn. With lightening reflex, she stomped the brake pedal. The seat belt caught her as she lurched forward, forcing every ounce of air from her lungs.

"Oh, my children, are you alright? I'm so sorry."

"You scared me," Jenny forced out the words in jerks, "I thought we were going to die."

"I'm bleeding. I bit my tongue," said Pamela.

Conchita released the seat belt and grabbed a tissue from her purse and handed it back to Pamela. "Here, hold this to your mouth."

A rap on the driver's window caused Conchita to jump. There stood a blond, broad-shouldered man in cut-off jeans and a t-shirt. Conchita lowered the window.

"What's wrong with you lady? Are you blind? Didn't you see that stop sign? You might have got us all killed."

Conchita stepped from the car. "I'm so very sorry. Are you hurt? You're right. I could have killed us all."

The blond grabbed Conchita's arm and pulled her forward. "Let me show you something, lady. I lost a lot of rubber keeping you from smashing into the side of my car. What if I hadn't stopped in time?"

Conchita shuddered. Yes, she saw the ugly black stripes angling away from her car, smelled the rubber, saw that no more than 10 inches separated the cars from being mangled together.

"There is no excuse for my…my reckless lack of concentration. I've had a lot on my mind, and I let it threaten the safety of my children and… and you. I can assure you I will not let distractions affect my driving again. Ever. Forgive me for my actions. I need to attend to my children."

"You need to attend to more than your children, lady." The blond waved a hand of dismissal, climbed into his car, and squealed off.

Conchita returned to her car. She hugged each of her children and attended to Pamela's bleeding tongue. "Children, I learned a very important lesson today. Whenever we drive a car, we must not let anything distract us—not music, not phones, not children, not thinking about other things. We need to think about driving, reading road signs, following driving rules and…"

"And watch for kids crossing the road," said Jenny.

"Yes, and watching for kids crossing the road is one of the most important things to do," said Conchita.

"Did we make too much noise, Mamá? Is that why you weren't watching?" asked Jack.

"Sometimes, you kids are pretty noisy. But this time you didn't distract me. I was thinking about other things. I wasn't paying attention to my driving."

Everyone remained quiet the rest of the trip home. Once Conchita parked in the garage, she said, "Please bring your gifts inside. We'll store them in the hallway closet. They'll be close to your bedrooms."

Conchita stepped into the kitchen and was surprised to see Miguel standing at the counter slicing onions. He turned and watched the children bring in their games. "Hey, guys. Looks like you got some fantastic loot. You better clean up. I'll have lunch ready in a jiff."

"Can we play till it's ready? Please," asked Jack.

Miguel rubbed his forearm against his nose and turned toward Conchita. "Guess it's up to your ma."

"Guess what," said Jenny, "Mom got distracted and we almost got killed."

"We did not. She stopped before we hit that guy," said Pamela.

Miguel straightened and placed the knife on the counter. "So, she got distracted, huh? What's this all about Conchita?"

Conchita looked into Miguel's eyes waiting for them to fire in anger. But she saw a hint of amusement instead. "Yes, children, go play with your new games, while your papá and I get your lunch."

Once the children were gone, Conchita began, "I ran a stop sign and nearly hit another car in the intersection. I wasn't paying attention. It could have horrible." Conchita shook her head and stared at the floor.

Miguel stepped closer to his wife. His face took on a seriousness. "I know what can happen when you aren't thinking right and you're behind the wheel." He paused. "Your whole life can change in a snap." Miguel snapped his fingers. "My…temper changed our lives. Don't think I haven't wondered where we'd be if I hadn't wrecked my baseball career. You have to know I learned something in those Colombian jungles."

Conchita stared into Miguel's clouded eyes. She couldn't believe her ears. Miguel admitting to some mistake?

"You wouldn't have had to go it alone, and this Greg guy wouldn't have had to step in to help you. I get that." Miguel breathed in heavily and exhaled. "I get that quitting that friendship for both you and the kids is tough. But I can't be a father and a husband with him in the picture. Understand?"

Tears rolled over Conchita's cheeks. She stood paralyzed. Was she crying over losing Greg or finding a new piece of this husband in front of her?

Miguel pulled her to him. His arms wrapped around her and he held her close. Her tears blotted against his shirt. Then Miguel held Conchita away from him at arm's length. "Aw Chita, I only want to see smiles. Believe it or not, we finished up early with the car and I came home to surprise you. But I need some help with the fajitas."

Through smiles and tears Conchita said, "Let's cook up some fajitas."

CHAPTER 25

The women

The weekend excursion was McCrae's idea. In fact, once he made the arrangements, and set the late August date, no one could refuse his generous offer. In the years since they met, the women had never shared a joyful time all together. One called another to check in, but their friendships had been disjointed, and revolved around loss and going on with life. This weekend would provide the opportunity to bind their friendships.

The Château wasn't visible from the main highway between Estes Park and Allenspark. No doubt many missed the turnoff as it was unmarked. However, following careful instructions, the four women found the right road, then winding through the mountain pines, arrived at the elegant archway marking the entrance to the well-manicured grounds surrounding the alpine-style Château.

"If that doesn't look like a storybook castle for a prince charming and his princess, I don't know what does," Conchita cried out.

"I agree," said Monica, "What a setting. Looks peaceful."

"We can pretend we're four princesses on this two-day slumber party." Racine said, her eyes flashing with mischief. Since Randy was home, the old, crazy Racine was back.

Mel pulled the car into the covered garage and turned off the engine. "I don't think I can play the princess part Racine, but I'm eager to see what a suite with four bedrooms is like. Usually I'm not too keen on the hotel scene."

Racine giggled. "Did you hear that clever rhyme ladies? Well listen here." With the rhythm of a rapper she clipped, "We'll see what you got—this can't compare, to the places where, you spend the night, for a turn-around flight. I'm not being mean, but you'll soon be keen, on *this* Château scene—princess or not."

"Criminey willikers," Mel yelled. "We have our own rapper whose rockin' the car. Literally. How can I top that?"

"I got one," Conchita blurted. "P's are fine to talk about. Proper, Pious, Private, we shout. No Princess for Mel. That she'd quell."

"Am I getting picked on or what? You all think you're cute, don't you?"

"Hey, I'm innocent. For now, anyway," exclaimed Monica. "I have no skill, in the rapping mill."

Laughter reverberated throughout the car. Mel got the hiccups. Every hic brought more giddiness.

"What's going on? I never get the hiccups. Sugar, I need sugar," Mel roared between giggles and hics.

Inside the suite, Racine rummaged through the full kitchen. "I found it." She pulled a crystal bowl from the cupboard. "You need real sugar, or the fake stuff?"

"Real, of course. Surely you know, *hic*, letting a spoonful of sugar dissolve on your tongue, *hic*, cures these dadnabbed irritations."

Racine tore the corner from a sugar packet. "Open up." She poured the white crystals onto Mel's tongue. Mel closed her mouth, her eyes, and let the sugar do its work.

Silence—as three pairs of mirthful eyes watched.

"See, I told you." Mel opened her mouth and shook her head side to side. "No more hic-ing. Now let's explore this *princess* hide-away."

Mel led the women through the dining room, appointed with white painted furniture trimmed in gold. "I guess we won't be cooking, but if we wanted to, everything's here."

They moved to a sitting room complete with several groupings of puffy couches and chairs covered in soft-colored floral prints.

Conchita plopped on a couch. "Well, it passes the bounce test. I could nap on this baby."

"Don't get too comfortable. We need to choose our bedrooms," said Monica.

"Look at this one," Mel said, "It has to be Racine's. She's the colorful lady."

"Well, if you insist. The color scheme kind of fits me, particularly the tropical design of the spread."

Once the bedrooms—each decorated in a different color scheme and theme—were divvied up, the women unpacked. They expected the weekend to be a relaxing one, enjoying the special entrées prepared by Chef Adrienne, taking walks on the well-planned labyrinth of hiking trails, sitting among the several gardens. There would be moments to be alone, as well as sharing time for the group.

Being the first one to have her space organized, Racine returned to the sitting room, and stretched her body into the comfort of a couch. *Conchita was right. This feels good. A great place to clear the cobwebs.* When the others joined her, Racine sat up. "What do you think gals? Shall we get outside and explore the place?"

"I'm up for that," Mel responded. "I never get enough of the mountains."

Conchita picked up the information flyer and thumbed through it, "Dinner is from 6:00 to 8:00. That gives three or more hours before then. Let's not waste a minute." Turning to Monica she asked, "How's your leg? Are you up to hiking?"

"Should be fine. The doctor says it's stronger than ever now. Still have a little stiffness. The problem is, I feel out of shape. Hiking the hills may leave me puffing. I'm warning you all."

The women explored several interlocking trails before returning to the main grounds of the resort where they sat in one of the gardens.

Deep red geraniums flanked by purple and yellow pansies displayed their last triumph of color before the coolness of fall arrived in the mountains. A breeze carried a wafting of pine scent around them.

Conchita drew a big sigh and wiped moisture from her brow. "Nice to sit in this lovely spot. Guess I need to do more of that walking business. You'd think chasing kids and the residents at work I'd be in better shape. Monica, I don't think you huffed a bit on that steep spot. No sweat either. You're a powerhouse."

"Well, I know I slowed you all down, but I did better than I expected. It was invigorating for me. And all that beauty. Whew."

Racine raised a hand toward the sky. "The world seems so…so immense up here. I've not spent much time in the mountains, being raised out on the plains and nose to the grindstone at the pub. It's kind of a healing place, isn't it?"

"It is," said Conchita.

Mel pulled her knees up in front of her and leaned back in the garden lounge chair. "Hey Monica. Any news about Gavin and Nicola? I hear they applied for the Peace Corps."

"Just received a note yesterday. Nicola sounded quite excited. They've been approved and are scheduled to start training next month. They're going to Africa."

"Good for them," Conchita said. "I can't believe you worked things out so there's no awkwardness between the four of you."

"Well, you know, the credit goes to Peter. He insisted on a dinner party with Nicola, Gavin, and his mom. Then Nicola caught me in the kitchen, and we talked."

"How'd that go?" Mel asked.

"Weird. Yet, Nicola has a way of putting one at ease and making a crazy situation seem almost ordinary. Mostly she wanted me to know how much Gavin loved me and how loyal he was. And how over the years, their relationship grew in admiration and respect. They became quite close. She also wanted to free me from any guilt about marrying Peter." Monica smiled and looked off in a far-away gaze. "We both agreed things worked out in a good way."

Racine nodded. "That cloud hanging over you with—kind of two husbands—seems to be gone. Now you can really go forward, you and Peter."

Monica fell silent, rolled her eyes to the sky, made an off-hand grimacing look, before she spoke again. "There's some news I haven't told you about."

Racine burst out, "You're pregnant!"

"How'd you guess?"

"It just had to be. There's quite a radiance about you. You must be thrilled."

"For someone who never thought she was 'mother material,' it's a bit mind boggling, but wonderful." Monica pressed her fist to her heart. "I feel complete peace inside."

Each offered her congratulations. They wanted to know how she'd been feeling, when the baby was due, how Peter reacted. Thus, for a while the talk revolved around babies and pregnancies.

When the conversation lulled, Mel said, "Things have taken a little twist for Dad and Mom. It looks like they're going to split up."

"What happened?" asked Monica.

"Nothing really. The whole thing is quite amicable. Dad's staying with me until he finds a place for himself. He arrived on my doorstep with a dozen roses. He was afraid I'd be devastated and was reluctant to tell me. From what he says, they both respect each other and want the best for the other, but there doesn't seem to be a feeling of partnership and union."

"You were afraid of something like that when Arthur came on the scene. What *do* you think about it?" Monica asked.

"I'm still working at letting go of the idea that Mom's cheated on Dad. Logic says, 'Hey she didn't know Dad was alive and would be coming home. She waited years before becoming involved with another man, yet in my heart I'm still ticked. There's that fairy tale that parents belong together." Mel gazed off for several seconds before she continued. "Actually, even if there wasn't an Arthur, I'm sure they would have separated. They'll be better off going their own ways."

"I'm sorry," said Racine. "Is it going to be a treat having your Dad with you, or a burden?"

"Maybe I'm kidding myself, but I can't wait to have Dad all to myself for a little while. You know how these guys are. They don't talk a lot about their ordeal. Maybe Dad'll feel comfortable about getting it out. Seems like a lot is buried there."

"I'm sure you'll be good for him," Conchita said, "You've always been close. But will he interfere with you and your pilot friend? How's that going?"

Mel's grin said, 'do I have to answer that question?' "Well, if you have to know. Things are quite good. He's a great guy. In fact, he's helped me trust someone other than my father."

Racine smacked the arm of her chair. "Mel, it's about time you stopped pushing men away."

Mel's head whipped around. "Well, you've run your life so perfectly. Right? When have you had a man in your life?"

"I was teasing, but I guess it wasn't funny. You're right, I haven't been open to having a man in my life all these years."

Monica cut in attempting to smooth the feathers. "Talking about pushing men away, I hear Chad's gone. What happened?"

Racine explained about Chad's ailing Auntie in Australia and how Carlotta's return to the restaurant filled the void created by his leaving. "Chad was my lifesaver, not only with the business, but also when I was depressed and a mess. He's a dear friend. I miss him." *Can't tell them about the night he brought the basket to cheer me up. They wouldn't understand.* "He's leaving a big hole at the pub, even with Carlotta back."

Conchita twirled a lock of hair, and then looked up. "You're sure about the Auntie? You don't think he decided he'd better move on since there wasn't much left for him here with Carlotta recovered and back working?"

Racine looked surprised. "I would have kept him on as long as he wanted. You think he wasn't telling the truth?"

"I don't know. The timing could be a coincidence. I shouldn't have said anything. I don't even know the man. Just wondered if he might be a wanderer."

"I believe him, Conchita. I have no reason not to. He sent a note after he got to Australia. He plans to start clearing out the Auntie's property this week. He did say it was nice to be back on home ground."

"I'm sure you're right. Sorry I said anything."

As the air cooled with the lowering sun, the women left the garden to dress for dinner. Arriving at the dining room they chose the perfect private and quiet spot, away from other groups dining at the Château.

Perusing the menu, the four raved over the variety of selections, including trout, shrimp, duck, Cornish hen, various beef and pork dishes, plus a variety of pasta entrees. Each chose a different dish. During dinner, they focused on the attractive presentations, guessed at the ingredients in each sauce, and sampled each other's entrees.

Afterwards, the waiters displayed elegant platters of sumptuous desserts. "We'll probably have to go on a starvation diet next week," Mel declared, "but I intend to try something new at every meal. For some reason, cooking sounds appealing to me these days and I want all the ideas I can get."

Monica quipped, "We know. Since Erik's a good cook, you might as well join him, since he's going to be around awhile."

After dessert they sipped on coffee and Racine told them about Randy joining McCrae's business team.

"I bet you're pleased to have Randy working for his father," said Monica.

"Actually, I'm a little concerned. I think he should be on his own and be independent. He's never had that."

"You aren't a bit jealous, thinking McCrae's taking your son away from you?" said Mel.

"It's not that. At least I don't think so. I just want the best for him. I hate to see him jump right into something. McCrae's taking Randy on some business venture next week in Santa Fe, and he wants me to go with them. I don't think that's a good idea."

Conchita remarked, "I don't know why not. And about Randy working for McCrae—well McCrae has a solid reputation in the community, and it'll be a bonus for both of them. I don't mean to be bossy. You have to work it out in your head." Conchita sipped her coffee and looked up. "Not to change the subject, but I'm still pinching myself about our weekend here at the Chateau. McCrae is a jewel to make this happen for all of us."

"He sure is," said Mel. "By the way, talking about jewels, I've been eyeing the emeralds you're wearing, Racine. It can't be a coincidence that the men went down for emeralds and now you're wearing some."

Racine stammered, "Well…You're right. They came from the mine. McCrae wanted me to have a memento from Colombia. He had the stones cut and set for me. The pieces are beautiful, aren't they?"

Monica caught Racine's hand in hers. "OK Racine what's going on with McCrae and you?"

"Nothing, honestly. He just wanted me to have some jewelry."

Monica continued, "The man goes down to Colombia, rescues your son, spends a chunk on you and you don't think that means something?"

"Of course, it means something. It means he has a few dollars in his pocket, he's a generous man, and he wants to make up for all the time I thought Randy was dead." Racine moved her hand from Monica's grip. "But that's all. He even said, 'Racy, there are no strings attached'."

"Ah, ha. No strings, huh? You can't tell me there's no chemistry between you two," Mel said, "I could see you together in a minute. And Randy. He'd be ecstatic. Don't push McCrae away. Weren't you on me about pushing men away this afternoon? Let him court you. You have nothing to lose."

"Yes, you deserve a good man. I'm rooting for you," Conchita added.

"Root all you want, but nothing's going to happen. Yes, McCrae's in my son's life and I'm sorry I kept it from happening long ago. He's a handsome and appealing man, but that's all." Racine thrust her hands into a halting position in front of her. "That's all there is to it, period."

The women sat quietly for a few minutes as if letting the dust settle. Then Monica spoke in a tentative voice. "Conchita, how are things for you, the kids and Miguel? How's Miguel handling all his recent publicity?"

Conchita pulled herself up displaying a bit of defiance. "Everything's fine. The kids are getting used to having their father around. He expects a lot of them and can be a little bossy, but like many mothers, I'm the buffer." Conchita relaxed her stiffness and continued, "The kids miss Greg a lot. I hadn't realized what a big part of our lives he had become."

"You think having Miguel in your lives is the best?" Monica asked.

"Who knows what's best? He's their father. He's my husband. It's not his fault he was away from us for so long."

"He's not rough with you, is he?" Mel asked.

Conchita took several seconds to respond. "He was before. I won't tolerate it again. Never. That's one thing he knows. And if he lays a hand on the kids…he's out."

Racine sighed, "We just want you and your precious children to be happy."

Conchita saw concern and somberness in the three caring faces looking at her. "Hey, don't look so sad. This is a wonderful weekend. Cut the gloom. You know I'm strong, I have wonderful children and I'm an optimist. I've seen some of Miguel's rough edges soften. And Miguel has a chance for a job in construction. I'm praying it works out."

"You're one amazing gal, Conchita," said Racine. "You're right, we've all weathered a great deal these past years. There's nothing we can't accomplish, nothing we can't work through. Just know we're pulling for you all the way."

The solemnness of the moment evaporated, and Racine spouted, "Let's plan tomorrow's adventures. I've been reading about the Spa Treatment and Styling Salon. Let's have a luxurious make over. What do you think?"

"I'm in," Monica said, "I need all the help I can get before I'm fat and ugly."

"Pregnant women are never ugly, Monica," Racine retorted.

Mel interjected, "OK, I know this will blow you away. But I'd love to wallow in luxury, just this once. I'll even be a princess for a day." Her voice turned sing-song. "What was that thing you said, Racine? I'll soon be keen, on the Château scene."

People turned to stare as their unbridled laughter filled the dining room.

"Careful Mel," said Racine. "Oh well we have packets of sugar at the table."

When the laughter quieted Monica raised her goblet into the air. "I think we need a toast."

The four friends stood. Through the tinkling of glassware, and with great dignity Monica offered her words.

"Here's to four women of worth. May tomorrow be full of frivolity and fun. May our futures be grand. Few escape the bonds of providence, where lives twist, transform and are amended. In fact, complete control eludes us all. My friends we've lived through rough times. Now hail to us. We survive and thrive."

www.ingramcontent.com/pod-product-compliance
Lightning Source LLC
Chambersburg PA
CBHW061339310726
48974CB00001B/113